"REGGIE, I NEED A DRINK . . ."

"What? You mean blood?"

"Yeah."

"Well, partner, don't look at me."

"No, I meant her." Chris pointed to the unconscious fat woman, the butcher knife still in her hand.

Reggie gulped. "You're not going to drain her?"

"Of course not. I'm just going to take enough to satisfy my hunger."

"Well, I guess a vampire's got to do what a vampire's got to do."

Chris nodded. Then he bent down and exposed her throat. He opened his jaws and bit deep, slaking the great thirst that gnawed at him. When he finished drinking, he got up. "Okay, let's take her down and book her."

"Jeez," Reggie said, wincing as he rubbed his neck, "remind me never to have *you* over for dinner."

VAMPIRE BEAT

Vincent Courtney

PINNACLE BOOKS
WINDSOR PUBLISHING CORP.

To my wife, Beth
Thank you for your faith, your love,
and your inspiration. I could not have
written this book without all three.

PINNACLE BOOKS

are published by

Windsor Publishing Corp.
475 Park Avenue South
New York, NY 10016

First printing: June, 1991

Printed in the United States of America

PART I

Prologue

The knife was poised above her heart. Her screams cut through the dead, rotten air of the warehouse. Batiste Legendre smiled. He bent down and soul-kissed the terrified eighteen-year-old who was to remain that age forever.

"Oh mighty Cannus!" Legendre's voice was as cold as death as he addressed the hooded members of his congregation. "The night is short, and soon the hour of darkness will be upon us. The time of Walpurgis will begin."

The fifty or so cultists hummed in an oscillating drone that cascaded up and down, creating a wave of powerful sound. They swayed back and forth in unison with the eerie humming like the head of a giant cobra ready to strike.

Every member was dressed in a black robe, a red slash emboldened across the left side of his chest symbolizing the figurative tearing out of the heart, the loss of his compassion, a necessary step in his journey toward purity. Hadifes, the god of hate, had decreed it in the third book of Cannus.

The weakness of compassion must be completely destroyed in order to achieve purity. A pure mind can act without sympathy or pity. It is not concerned with the means of how something is accomplished: only the fact that it is accomplished is important. Any trace of the blight of compassion will cause indecision at a critical moment and obstruct the way to one's destiny.

So it is written in the third book.

The other symbol on each robe was a silver knife above the

7

slash. It represented Hadifes, the dark underlord, whose teachings were the blade that would cut away compassion like a cancerous tumor and cleanse the mind to accept total power through the purity of evil.

Tonight Legendre would rip the heart out of the girl who lay nude before him and by doing so complete the ritual of Hadifes. He would be one step further in his quest for total evil and the power that it brings.

"Dark lord, hear us," Legendre cried as the cobra swayed back and forth. "Give us the strength to destroy this thing in us that blocks our path to power. Fill us with hatred for this girl who has done nothing to us . . . who, for the very fact of her innocence, must have her heart torn out and crushed to represent the death of the compassion we hold in our hearts."

Christopher Blaze peered up from his hood at the leader of the largest demonic cult in the city. He was ready.

Legendre continued the ritual. The gleaming blade in his hand moved upward imperceptibly. With a jagged finger-nail he drew the crude shape of an X across the girl's breast. Her terrified screams echoed against the sides of the warehouse. A slow trickle of blood began to make its way down the curve of her breast.

She was doomed.

"Your thirst for blood must be satisfied. We ask you to accept this meager sacrifice in your honor. We release her soul to you."

The group began to chant: "Release her, release her, release her."

The sound of their voices increased in fervor as the moment of the girl's death grew nearer.

The cobra was ready.

The raised knife would soon be rushing downward in a sickening thrust through flesh and bone. The chant had reached a maddening crescendo: "Release her, release her, release her!"

The voices rose and fell like a black tide of death.

Chapter 1

1

Blaze knew he had to move and move fast. In one motion he threw back his hood, pulled out his .45, and flashed his Miami PD badge. As their voices ebbed, Chris shouted, "Release her!"

The chanting stopped. The transition from a cacophony of sound to total silence was as if someone had dropped a ten-ton weight on a crying baby. The swaying stopped. The cobra turned its head toward the infidel that had defiled the ritual and prepared to strike.

Chris Blaze aimed his gun between the cold eyes of the leader of the Cannus cult.

"Freeze, Legendre, or I'll blow your fucking head off," Chris screamed. Blaze knew the line sounded like something out of a B movie, but it never failed to scare the shit out of a perpetrator. Yet Legendre didn't appear at all frightened. As a matter of fact, a wide grin spread across his face like a slow, creeping fungus. "Ah, Christopher, a policeman? You disappoint me. You disappoint me greatly."

"Sorry to dash your expectations, Batiste," Chris replied.

"But, I thought you were one of us."

"No, I'm afraid I'm not a very good devil worshipper," Chris said as he pointed the gun at Legendre. "But I *am* a helluva shot. Now, put down the knife, or . . ."

"Or *what?*" Batiste hissed through a grin straight from

hell. "You'll shoot me? But what of the others? Do you propose to shoot all of us?"

A few of the congregation moved menacingly toward Chris. The hatred in their eyes burned into him.

Suddenly the big gun in his hand shrank to the size of a peashooter, but still it was Chris's turn to smile.

"No," Chris said, "but they will." He pointed to the catwalk that ran along the inner sanctum of the warehouse. Twenty big cops with twenty big guns had their weapons trained on the startled cult members. Captain Tom Draper, Chris's superior, grinned and pulled the hammer back on his .357 Magnum.

Legendre's cocky smile decayed and crumbled from his face.

"Now," Chris continued, "put the knife down and back away from the girl."

Sensing defeat, Legendre lowered the knife and dropped it to the floor. The young girl burst into tears of relief as policemen poured into the warehouse and started to arrest the cult members.

Chris walked slowly toward Legendre, his gun pointed at the leader's heart. He was glad that the undercover operation to bust the Cannus cult was finished. It had been a frightening three months.

Chris Blaze was a handsome man with delicate features. His piercing blue eyes rivaled Paul Newman's. He was about six feet tall and worked out regularly at the gym. His good looks only served to accentuate just how repulsive Batiste Legendre could be.

He was the high priest of Cannus, a former member of the Tonton Macute, the elite secret police of the Duvalier regime in Haiti who dabbled in the black arts. He eventually broke away from the police group to form the strange Cannus cult and for a time was a powerful force in Haiti. Legendre and his minions would use their dark powers to enforce the laws of the Duvalier government. The Cannus cult in Haiti finally met its downfall along with the exile of Baby Doc Duvalier in 1982. The cult leader and some of his more ardent followers made their way to Miami and started over, building their membership from the poor people of Miami. The group was involved in a series of bizarre incidents, but the police could never prove that the cult was responsible—until now.

"Now," Chris said, "get down from there. You and I are going down to the station."

Suddenly Legendre's looks seemed to change. His coal-black eyes rolled back in his head, exposing the whites.

Strangely, the first thing that came to Blaze's mind was that Legendre looked exactly like the old Chinese master Po in the TV series "Kung Fu." He half expected to hear the whispered proverb of a Shaolin priest come out of the mouth of the cult leader. But what emerged instead was a sound that seemed to corrode the air with its evil.

Legendre's voice burned through the night and straight into Christopher Blaze, whose testicles made a beeline to the safety of his stomach.

"Hear me, oh mighty Cannus," Legendre's eerie hiss scorched the air. "Hear me! I curse this blasphemer to the life that is death, the death that is life!"

The big man's face was black with rage as he continued the curse that was to change Chris Blaze's life. Legendre began to speak in a tongue from another world, a world so foul that you could feel its corruption as the words were spit from his mouth.

"Hadifes, becten karalas kilen. Cannus secten Hadifes, Cannus nosferen terrae sectemen Hadifes."

Electricity seemed to crackle from his hands as he raised them toward the ceiling. Blue flashes of light crawled across his white eyes. Blaze thought they looked like neon worms bursting from the sockets of a corpse.

Macabre, incandescent worms.

Winding in and out.

Worms of death.

Without warning, Legendre thrust his hands at Blaze. The stunned cop felt a force hit him squarely in the chest. He dropped his gun. The strange force spread like the icy hand of death across his body.

"You will live on after death, my friend." Legendre spat out the word *friend* as if it were an obscenity. "You will

11

become one of the undead and walk the earth at night."

Then, quick as a cat, Legendre bent down and grabbed the sacrificial knife. *"Hadifes nosfere secteme."*

As he intoned the words, the knife glowed with the same curious blue fire that had come to Legendre's eyes moments before.

Chris stood mesmerized by the hypnotic flame as the cult leader drew the knife back and prepared to stab it into the heart of the detective.

"Now," he chortled as the phlegm in his throat rattled like death, "I will end your old life so that you can begin again."

Legendre hurled the blade just as the slug from the .357 Magnum tore into his chest and spiraled its way through his vital organs. The next thing that came out of his mouth was a gout of blood and perhaps a bit of lung. He crumpled to the floor.

The errant knife sliced across Blaze's throat, narrowly missing his jugular vein, and clattered noisily across the cement floor.

Captain Tom Draper lowered his weapon. He was about six-foot-four in his stocking feet, with a build that earned him the nickname "Skyscraper Draper" down at the station. No one called him that to his face. The only out-of-place feature on his ruggedly handsome face were the coke-bottle-lens glasses his kids occasionally snuck away from him while he was sleeping. They liked to go out in the sun and fry ants with them.

The big cop holstered his gun and ambled over to Chris. He looked at him through the thick glasses. His magnified brown eyes only served to heighten his look of concern. "You okay, buddy?"

Chris Blaze had worked for the good captain for the past five years in homicide and had come to trust him with his life. Tonight he had proved that that trust was well placed.

"Yeah," Chris replied hesitantly as he touched his neck and looked at the thin trail of blood across his palm. "I'm fine, I guess—the knife just grazed me. Thanks." The pain, not really pain, more a strange sensation, seemed to spread down from the wound and across his body like a malignant virus, a chilling impression of disease and death.

"Here." The captain handed him his handkerchief, which Blaze pressed against the cut.

"Call the morgue to come pick him up!" Draper barked to a passing patrolman. He turned back to Blaze. "Now, what the hell was that all about?"

"It seems I've just been cursed."

"Cursed?" the captain asked, incredulous.

"Yep. It seems, according to our late host, that when I die I'll come back as some kind of zombie or something." He dabbed at the wound, checking to see if the blood had stopped flowing.

"Jesus Christ, that guy was some nut case. I'm glad we finally put him out of business."

"I think you permanently revoked his occupational license, Captain."

"Yeah, I guess I did." The captain smiled weakly, then added, "You know, Blaze, that was the first time I ever killed a man."

The aftershock of taking a life, no matter how tainted a life it was, hit the captain like a kick in the gut. He turned and threw up the remains of his Moo Goo Gai Pan from Lo He's Chinese Emporium.

Chris felt a surge of pity for the big guy who always acted so tough around his men. He put a hand on Draper's shoulder. "It's okay, Cap. Everybody feels the same way."

The captain nodded and felt for his handkerchief. Realizing that he had given it to Blaze, he wiped the cold sweat from his brow on the sleeve of his shirt. "Listen, Chris, let's call it a night. You've been on this case for a long time, and at the moment I'm not feeling so hot myself."

Chris was unaccustomed to this generosity. Usually Draper would have him down at the station, filing a report.

"You sure you don't want me to go in and write up a report?" Chris asked, hoping the captain wouldn't take his sense of duty too seriously.

He didn't, and Chris Blaze was on his way home.

The weary detective climbed into his '67 Mustang and started the engine. He instinctively cranked up the radio as

13

he headed for his apartment. It had been a long and tiring case, and he was glad the whole thing was over.

The Cannus cult had been a thorn in the side of the Miami Police Department for a long time. Mysterious disappearances, animal mutilations, desecration of churches. They had always suspected Legendre and his minions, but could never gather enough evidence to mount a case. So Draper and Blaze had the idea to infiltrate the cult and bust it wide open. Through some shady connections, Blaze got into the cult and became a member. It took some time before they fully trusted him, but slowly they began to feel secure enough to let him participate in a few rituals. In the beginning, most of them had been harmless: weird chants. Midnight black masses. Staying awake for days until they hallucinated. As the leader's trust in him grew, he began to become a part of the more dangerous rituals. Chris had watched them slaughter chickens and drink the blood. He had witnessed the desecration of the Catholic Church as the cult members placed phalluses on the statue of the Virgin Mary and urinated into the holy water. The desecration had made Blaze turn white with rage. He wanted these assholes bad. But according to the law, it was only trespassing and vandalism. It wasn't even worth the trouble of busting them, and Blaze wanted these sick bastards to spend a long, long time in jail. Then the break he was waiting for happened, the ritual of Hadifes on the night of Walpurgis. Translation: a human sacrifice. They could get them for attempted first-degree murder and assault with a deadly weapon, the kind of charges that could stick them behind bars for a good long time. After he found out all the gory details, Chris called Draper and set up the bust. He had no idea that it would be the end of the cult and its vile founder.

2

Captain Tom Draper couldn't get the killing out of his mind. He'd always thought it wouldn't bother him if he had to use deadly force. But it did, damn it! He'd wanted every-

14

thing to go smoothly, but when that lunatic went for the knife, he had to pop him. "Pop him"—it made it sound like a tap on the wrist instead of a lead projectile traveling at 1700 feet per second. The sheer force of it could make a man's insides look like they'd been through a blender. But didn't Legendre deserve it? He was a scum who had probably committed every heinous crime in the book. After all, he was going to sacrifice the girl and rip her heart out, according to Blaze's description of the ritual. And wasn't she about the same age as his own daughter? The picture of his daughter lying naked on a concrete slab, her chest ripped open in a welter of gore, with Legendre smiling and holding her bloody, beating heart above his head flashed in his mind. He squeezed his eyes shut to drive the image away.

When he opened them, he saw that Chris Blaze's Mustang was right in front of him and that something was wrong. The car was swerving all over the road.

3

Chris was thinking about how he was almost glad that Draper had taken Legendre out. The cult leader probably would have gotten off on some plea bargain or legal loophole and been out on the streets in no time, able to start all over again—recruiting the misfits and maltreated of the world into his cult and transforming them into remorseless killing machines that could mutilate an eighteen-year-old girl as easily as they would carve up a turkey on Thanksgiving. Yes, Legendre was much better off burning in hell.

As Chris rounded a sharp curve, the strange, cold force he'd felt when Legendre had cursed him returned to the wound in his neck and spread across his body. He shivered and recalled the glowing worms that crawled in the white-hot eyes of the macabre cultist. A chill began to creep slowly along his spine, taking its time, making sure to touch every nerve along the way.

Chris rolled up the window and turned on the heater. He cranked up the radio even louder, hoping the spiritual wailings of Mick Jagger would somehow ward off the fear that was quickly spreading like a cancer within him.

"The life that is death! The death that is life!"

Legendre's words slapped Chris in the face.

The curse!

Did that come from the radio?

Chris's mind whirled.

The radio blasted "Sympathy for the Devil."

Blaze was confused. Was his mind just playing tricks on him? He couldn't possibly have heard what he was certain he had.

"You will live forever!" the voice from the pit cried.

Blaze was sure it had come from the radio. Legendre was broadcasting to him straight from h . . . e . . . double fucking toothpicks. Chris looked at the Philco in disbelief. He expected to see the evil face of Legendre staring back at him, but it was only a radio playing a rock song from the Sixties.

Please allow me to introduce myself, I'm a man of wealth and taste. . . .

"God damn it, you're tired, Blaze, you are imagining this shit." Chris spoke aloud, hoping that hearing his own voice would wake him up from the dream he was in.

"You will die and walk the earth forever!" Batiste Legendre, the DeeJay of Death, croaked.

The radio seemed to smile at Chris and wink.

Pleased to meet you, hope you guess my name. . . .

Blaze grabbed the knob and turned it off. The only sound in the car was the heater. It was blowing air that smelled like the inside of a tomb.

4

Captain Draper immediately wondered what was wrong when he saw Chris's car swerve into the gravel at the side of the road. He thought Chris must have dozed off at the wheel and then snapped awake when he felt the car hit the bumpy shoulder. Draper tried to pull up and signal Chris by

16

blowing his horn, but the Mustang suddenly began to pick up speed.

"What the hell has gotten into him?" the big cop asked himself.

He stepped on the gas and sped after the Mustang. He hoped Chris would have a reasonable explanation for his actions, but at that moment there was no reasonable explanation. Christopher Blaze was trapped in the unreasonable world of a nightmare.

5

Legendre blasted through the big Pioneer speakers in the back of the Mustang.

The life that is death, the death that is life.

Blaze ripped the knob off the radio.

"This is bullshit," he screamed. "You're dead, you fucking bastard! Do you hear me, you are stone fucking dead!"

The terror he experienced made him feel as though his head would explode. If his bowels didn't beat him to it.

"Dead . . ."

The voice he heard was his own. The radio was intact and playing "This One's for You," an old love song by Barry Manilow. The warm air of the heater had that same old familiar odor that burned at your nostrils. In less than two minutes Chris had lost his mind and found it. He smiled, then laughed out loud. "Jesus, this devil shit is really getting to me," he chuckled. "My imagination is going nutzoid."

This one'll never sell, they'll never understand. . . .

"Sing it, Barry, sing it," Chris said. He glanced down at the speedometer and just happened to be cruising at about eighty miles an hour. "Cripes, I'd better slow d. . . ."

The words froze in his throat as he looked up from the speedometer to see Batiste Legendre standing in the middle of the road.

In the brief instance before impact, Chris could see the bloody hole where the bullet had entered and ripped

17

Legendre apart. A slimy snakelike creature fell out of the mouth of the cult leader, whose hair had turned white. It wasn't until Legendre's head slammed against the windshield that Chris realized that it wasn't hair at all, but maggots. Chris had tried to avoid hitting the gruesome zombie, but couldn't. He struck him at about seventy miles per hour. Legendre flew over the hood, bounced off the windshield, and flipped fifteen feet in the air. The impact of the collision caused Chris's car to veer out of control. His Mustang flew off the road and slammed into a tree.

Then darkness overwhelmed him.

6

Tom Draper was on his radio almost immediately. The ambulance would be there in ten or fifteen minutes. He pulled to the side of the road and hurtled out of the car toward the mangled Mustang.

"God, let him be all right," Tom whispered.

But it didn't look as if he would. The car looked like a contracted accordian. There was no movement or sound coming from it.

As Tom ran up to the crushed vehicle, the sweet smell of gas hit his nostrils and the word *fire* leapt into his brain. He had to get Chris out of there. The door to the driver's side was crushed and useless. He ran to the passenger side and tried that one. It was stuck. He pulled as hard as he could, but still the door wouldn't budge. The smell of gas was getting stronger.

"Come on, you fucker, open up!" Tom yelled as he thought about what would happen if the gas ignited. *Got to get him out.* He put his foot on the side of the car to get some leverage, grabbed the handle, and yanked with everything he had. It simply wouldn't open. At that moment he lost his cool. He banged his fists on the door and kicked it in frustration and anger, then smiled.

"You dirty bastard!"

The damn fool thing was locked. In his panic, he didn't

bother to check. Quickly he pulled out the big gun that had ended one life and slammed it into the window of the door in hopes of saving another. The safety glass shattered into a heap of little cubes. Popping the lock open, he gave the door a mighty heave, and it lurched open. He grabbed Blaze and pulled him out, carrying the limp body of his best undercover man away from the car. He set him down gently, took his arm, and held the wrist between his two fingers and thumb.

There was no pulse.

"Shit!"

The paramedics wouldn't be there for another ten minutes. Draper's mind raced: he had to get his heart started. He would have to give him CPR. The police captain tilted Chris's head back and started the resuscitation. He blew five quick breaths, put his hands on Chris's chest, and pushed.

Behind him, the Mustang exploded in a ball of flame. Then everything was quiet.

Chapter 2

1

The door to the emergency room burst open as the paramedics brought the victim in. Timmy Marks and his five-year-old little brother Joey had just seen *Dr. Jekyll and Mr. Hyde* on the creature feature and had decided to concoct a formula to turn themselves into monsters. In an old, empty bottle of Hawaiian Punch; they had mixed together everything they could find: orange juice, a little Alka Seltzer for fizz, some pixie sticks filled with grape powder, and a bottle of neat-colored water that just happened to be rat poison laced with arsenic. The boys mixed it all together. Then one of them would pretend to be Dr. Jekyll and act like he was drinking the concoction while the other pretended to be a policeman. The brother playing the doctor would curl into a ball, like he was in real pain, the way Doctor Jekyll did in the show; and when he unwound, he would be the horrible monster Mr. Hyde, covered with hair and with big fangs like Dracula or the Wolfman. Then Hyde would attack the policeman and they would wrestle. One time the cop would shoot the monster man and win. The next time, Mr. Hyde would beat the cop up and kill him with his cane, in this case, a cardboard tube that used to hold wrapping paper. At first the game had been a lot of fun, but after Timmy had killed Joey for the umpteenth time, he got tired of make-believe and wanted to do something different.

"I wonder what it would be like to be a real monster," Timmy said, more to himself than to his baby brother. "I bet it would be real cool."

He picked up the bottle that held their magic elixir and looked at it for a long time. Then he drank down a big gulp of it just like that. It tasted terrible.

"You're gonna get in trouble, Timmy," Joey chided him.

Timmy turned to him and said, "I'm gonna really turn into a monster, and then we'll see who gets in trouble."

Joey got scared and ran off into the living room. *Let him turn into a monster,* the little boy thought, *see if I care.* He would just watch Tom and Jerry and forget about his dumb old brother. He watched TV for a little while, but soon curiosity brought him back into the kitchen. As he entered he saw his brother on the floor, writhing in pain, acting just like the doctor in the movie. Just like him. Joey stared in terror, thinking that at any moment Timmy would sprout fangs and a hairy face. He didn't know what he would do. He thought Timmy would probably try to eat him. Little Joey ran away in terror, calling for his mommy.

Carol Marks was upstairs ironing when she heard the terrified wailing of her younger boy. She wished her husband was still around to see what was wrong, but he had left her months ago to go and "find himself" in Colorado. Now she had to take care of their two rambunctious boys all by herself. It wasn't an easy task. As she hurried downstairs, she wondered what they were into now. Joey ran up to her and screamed in an excited voice that Timmy was turning into a monster and was going to eat him.

"Timmy, stop scaring your brother," she called out angrily. The boy should have known better than to scare a three-year-old. "Timmy! you get out here!"

There was no answer.

"Joey, where's your brother?" she asked the frightened boy.

"In the kitchen," Joey cried.

Carol started to walk toward it.

"Don't go in there Mommy, he'll eat you."

Her tiny son clutched her dress, trying to hold her back.

Carol looked down at him. Timmy had gone too far. She picked the terrified Joey up and hugged him.

"Don't you worry, JoJo," she said, kissing him on the cheek. "Your brother isn't going to turn into a monster." Just a seven-year-old boy with a tanned fanny after she found him, she thought to herself.

As Carol entered the kitchen, she saw the body of her son lying in a grotesquely twisted position. His eyes were glazed, and he was moaning softly. The bottle of Rat Snak poison sat open on the counter, along with the other ingredients. The sight of it tore her brain apart, and white stars exploded in front of her eyes. It seemed as if it and her son were the only things in the room; the rest of the kitchen was just a white blur. Her whole body felt weak as if the energy had been drained out of her. Her knees were shaky. She tried to move but couldn't, as if she was in a dream in which a monster was chasing her and she couldn't move her legs. *Don't panic,* her mind screamed. *If you lose it, you'll lose your boy, too.*

Lose my boy?

Lose Tim. . . .

No way!

With the sheer force of her will, she pulled herself together. The distressed mother whispered a short prayer and then rushed to her son. As she drew close, she could see that the boy was in real trouble.

"Oh my God. *Timmy!*" she cried, the panic rising up in her again, threatening to overwhelm her and send her son to his death. She fought it back and ran to the phone. Carol dialed Poison Control and hurriedly explained what had happened. They told her what to do in the event of arsenic poisoning and said they'd have an ambulance there as soon as they could. She ran to the medicine cabinet and gave him a tablespoon of syrup of Ipecac and eight ounces of water to induce vomiting. How long had it been since he'd taken the Rat Snak? The Poison Control people had said that after an hour there was a very real danger it could be fatal. She prayed it hadn't been that long.

22

Fifteen excruciating minutes later, the ambulance had arrived and taken him away.

2

Dr. Sue Catledge was just beginning a cup of well-deserved coffee when she heard herself being paged.

"Dr. Catledge, please report to the emergency room," the disembodied voice said. *"Dr. Catledge, please report to the emergency room."*

"Damn, don't even have time for a cup of coffee," Sue said to herself.

She had gotten out of surgery ten minutes before, having removed a bullet from a wino who had inadvertently stumbled into a drug deal gone sour. The surgery had been a tricky affair. The bullet had entered one Chester C. Meers, or "Toothless," as he was known on the street, in the right side of his chest and stopped an inch from his heart. The surgery took three hours but was a success, and Toothless was resting comfortably in his room. Now she had another case. She took a couple of quick gulps of coffee in the hopes that the caffeine would give her a needed jolt. She wondered what was in store for her as she headed for the E.R.

As Sue entered the room she saw three things that added up to a tragedy in the making. The paramedics were holding back a hysterical woman, who was attempting to follow them into the emergency room. A little boy was holding her hand as she gestured wildly for them to let her go with her baby, his face a mask of confusion and guilt. The lifeless form of another little boy lay on a stretcher.

"What happened to him?" Sue asked Rick Church, the paramedic who had picked him up.

"Swallowed some rat poison, arsenic base."

She checked his pulse. It was very weak.

"Take him to X-ray and let's see how much he has taken," she said in an even voice.

An unusual aspect of arsenic is that it will show up on the

23

abdominal wall of a patient when he is X-rayed.

"Start him on an IV of sodium bicarbonate and give him shots of BAL to start kelation."

The BAL would bind to the arsenic so that it could be eliminated from the body.

"I want a urine sample sent to the lab, *stat*."

"Right, Doctor Catledge."

"Will my boy be all right, Doctor?" Carol Marks cried shakily. "Will he be okay?"

"We'll do everything we can, he should be fine," she said, hoping she was right. In an hour she'd find out.

She walked into the waiting area. She had news to tell the young mother about her boy. As she approached the dazed-looking woman and her sleeping son, she thought of how many other times she'd had to make the same trip.

"Mrs. Marks?" she said softly.

The woman awakened from her stupor, disoriented for a moment, then quickly realizing where she was. "My boy, is he all right?"

"There were complications and we . . ."

Carol Marks broke down. The worst had happened.

"Oh my God, no! Timmy, no!" she sobbed.

Her boy was dead.

Sue hated to see people cry, especially when there was no need. "Your boy is going to be just fine, Mrs. Marks. There were some problems, but we took care of them. He's going to be just fine."

Carol Marks looked up, blinking back her tears. She couldn't believe her ears. She had been expecting the worst all night and now she knew that all her worrying was for nothing. Her son was going to be all right. She got up and hugged the doctor. "Thank you so much, Doctor Catledge. God bless you."

Sue returned the hug. "You're welcome. Now, Tim just needs a couple of days' rest and to take his medication, and he should be up and around in a week or so."

"When can he come home?"

"I'd like to keep him here another day for observation—I just want to be sure."

"That's fine. I'm just so happy he's okay."

She wiped away a tear.

She handed her a tissue as her youngest son, Joey, woke up. He rubbed his eyes with his little fists.

"Is Timmy a monster yet?" he asked.

His mother smiled through tear stained eyes, then laughed. "No, Joey, Timmy is not a monster, yet."

"Good, cause I don't like monsters," he said, "they're bad and they kill people."

"Nobody likes monsters, Joey," Sue said. "But you don't have to worry about them, the police will protect you from all monsters."

"All kinds of monsters?" the little boy asked.

"Yes, all kinds."

3

The coffee tasted wonderful. She had just saved a little boy's life, saved his family from the horror of losing a loved one at so young an age and having his memory haunt them for the rest of their lives. She hated to have to make that long walk down the corridor to tell a family that their little child wouldn't be going home with them. She could feel their shock as if it were a living thing that struck out without warning and left its scars forever. She was glad this time there would be no scars. The little boy would be sick for a few days, but he'd be up and around in no time. Sue sipped on her coffee and contemplated her chosen profession. It was both a joy and a sorrow: one moment you were the hero who had just saved a child's life and rescued his whole family from an eternal living hell. The next moment you had an identical case in which the child died. Same symptoms. Same medication. Same procedures, only this time the child succumbed and you had to tell the family the horrible news. Sometimes they'd scream at you through a mask of rage and intense sorrow, saying they hated you for not being able to do more. Sometimes they just stared at you, then turned away and walked out. You never saw them again. But their pain stayed with you for a long time afterward. You tried to tell yourself you did everything possible, but still there were nagging doubts. *If I had only . . . or maybe I should have. . . .* The second-guessing bombarded your brain. You could try and tell yourself that it was all part of the job, but still the incongruity of it struck at your mind like a hammer. Same exact case. Same exact procedures. Same treatment . . . but one lives and one dies. Was God playing a game with her? One for you and one for me. Or did He already have it all laid out? Who lives and dies. Who will be rich and who will be poor. Who will grow up to be president and who will grow up to murder twenty people in a McDonald's parking lot. She took a drink of coffee. If God did have a master plan, she wondered what He had in store for her. In the next twenty-four hours she would find out.

Chapter 3

1

The casket was slowly lowered into the grave. His former comrades fired a twenty-one-gun salute. The gunshots were muffled. Captain Tom Draper had delivered the eulogy. It had touched everyone deeply, but no one moreso than Chris Blaze.

He had heard every word.

The late Chris Blaze was alive and well and living in a three-foot-by-seven-foot box. The sound of the earth thumping against the outside of the coffin as they began to bury him sounded like an explosion each time it hit the sides of the casket.

Thump!

He couldn't scream. He thought it might have been an aftereffect of the embalming fluid. God, did that burn when they replaced his blood with the sickly sweet smelling liquid. Perhaps his throat had been torn out in the accident. He couldn't be sure what had happened. He understood only that he was mute and that they were burying him alive. If he could only scream, they would hear him and set him free so he could try to make sense out of the nightmare in which he was trapped.

Thump!

Suddenly, as an afterthought, he realized he couldn't move his arms or legs. There was no room in the coffin. *Can't move,* his mind screamed. He felt as though he was bound as tight as a mummy. His muscles tensed and pressed against the sides of the box that held him, but he couldn't budge it. The feeling of claustrophobia overwhelmed him. He remembered the times when he was a kid and his father would play a game called "The Spider and the Moth." Chris would be watching television and his dad would simply say that the spider was hungry and wanted to eat a nice little moth. Then he would come at him at a slow, deliberate pace, hooking his arms into giant spider jaws, a wide-eyed grin on his face.

Hyung . . . yung . . . yung . . . the spider would say as he stalked the moth, its great mandibles opening and closing. The moth would try to run out of the living room, but the giant arachnid would block his path.

Hyung . . . yung . . . yung . . .

Sometimes the moth would get by and run into his room, but the spider was relentless in its pursuit. Chris would try to hide. He could hear the spider approaching.

Hyung . . . yung . . . yung . . .

The sound got louder as it approached. The moth would hide in his closet and wait, hoping the spider would tire of the game. All would be quiet until the closet door burst open and there would be the spider, opening and closing his jaws, his eyes wide.

Hyung . . . yung . . . yung . . .

The spider would pull him out of the closet to the ground and trap his arms and legs so he couldn't move. Then it would pretend to eat the moth. Chris would push and kick, trying to get away, but his dad was much too strong. A horrible panic would sweep over him. For some reason he thought his dad wasn't going to let him up, that he would hold him down forever. He would scream for his dad to get off him. Sometimes his father would keep on playing, thinking his son was just being a baby. He didn't know Chris was really terrified that his dad would stay on top of him forever and that he would never be able to move again. Finally, often after Chris's mother yelled at her husband for picking on the boy, his dad would let him up. Chris would breathe deeply in a hitching sob and run to his room crying. How he had hated that fucking game. His father had no idea how it had tormented him. . . .

Then a thought struck him: now he really wouldn't be able to move! He would be trapped forever! He struggled against the sides of the casket, hoping somehow the sides would burst open so he could climb out. A sense of panic threatened to overwhelm him and he was afraid he'd lose what little sanity he had left.

Thump!

Then his nightmare increased in terror as his body began to itch all over and he couldn't move to scratch it. His skin was alive with activity. It felt as though a thousand beetles were crawling all over him, their little legs digging in as they marched across him, looking for a good spot to lay their eggs. He would be excellent nutrition for them to grow up healthy. He cackled hysterically as a television commercial popped up on the screen in his mind. A mother beetle was telling another mother that if she wanted her maggot to grow up big and strong, she should feed him Wonder Chris. Wonder Chris had all the vitamins and nutrition a growing maggot needed. Chris laughed even louder until his raucous laughter turned into racking sobs.

God damn you, Legendre. God damn you to hell. And Chris knew, of course, that He had.

Thump!

The sound of the dirt hitting the casket was getting softer as the earth gradually began to fill in the final resting place of Christopher Blaze and trap him for eternity.

Thump!

He had to tell them he was alive or he would have to spend the rest of his life . . . he couldn't even finish the thought.

Thump.

My God . . . let me speak . . . just for one second, that's all I need. . . . The tears were rolling down his face.

Just for one second.

Then it came.

All his frustration, all his pent-up fear was released in one bone-chilling scream. Blaze closed his eyes and screamed and screamed. "I'm not dead! Let me out! I'm not dead! Not dead! Not dead!"

"No, you're not dead."

The voice was soft and sweet. It sounded as though it had come straight from heaven. Then he realized what was happening. He knew it with a clarity so sharp that it cut into his very soul. An angel had come to save him from eternal damnation. Blaze opened his eyes to see her, but his vision was blurred. His angel was nothing but a haze of color. He concentrated, squinting his eyes, focusing his thoughts on one thing, seeing the face behind that lovely voice. Slowly his vision started to clear and he knew he'd been right. As she came into focus, Chris knew he was looking into the face of an angel. Her eyes were green, with specks of yellow that looked like daffodils in a green field. She was beautiful, this angel. She had flowing brown hair that cascaded down over her shoulders, a cute little nose, a tender smile that warmed his heart, a stethoscope.

Stethoscope?

"You had quite a bad accident, Mr. Blaze," the angel said. "It was a miracle you weren't killed."

Stethoscope? It didn't make sense. He was in heaven, wasn't he? His eyes focused on the room around him. A television set blared as Pat Sajak spun the wheel. An old man in white was shuffling along. A bedpan. A bottle with a tube that ran . . . into his arm? "I'm in the hospital," he said with such wonder that it made the angel smile.

"Yes, you are, and you're going to be just fine, Mr. Blaze."

But surely this was the voice of an angel, Blaze thought. He said, "I was in an accident?"

"Yes, you fell asleep at the wheel of your car and ran into a tree."

Suddenly the ghastly visage of Batiste Legendre and his maggot hairdo burst into Chris's mind. "What about the man I hit? Did you find the body?"

The urgency in his voice filled her with pity. "There was no one else involved. Now, please take it easy. You need your rest."

"No one else? But that . . . that can't be!"

Chris could still hear the splat of Legendre's head as it exploded like a melon onto his windshield. It had been real.

"I hit him with my car!" he cried. "I tried to swerve out of the way, but I was going too fast."

"But I can assure you that there was no one else involved," she said as she placed a soft hand on his cheek. "Your captain was right behind you. He saw you veer off the road and crash. It was a good thing, too. He pulled you out of the car just before it caught fire and gave you CPR."

That son of a gun . . . twice in one night. He saved my life two times in one night, Chris thought.

"You must have been dreaming," she continued. "Your captain said you had just come off a very stressful case."

Was it all his imagination? Did he imagine the whole thing? He was stressed out to the max from the creepy case. Maybe his mind did deal him a bad hand. Maybe he had just dreamed up the nightmare.

Suddenly he felt silly, so silly he had to laugh.

And he did. He laughed as though he had heard all the funniest jokes in the world rolled into one megajoke. He laughed and laughed and laughed, until the tears streamed down his face. It had been a dream, the whole thing had been a horrible dream. He had fallen asleep at the wheel and crashed his cherry Mustang against a tree. A poem burst into his mind: *Tra la la twiddle de dee. Crashed my car into a tree.* His little poem made him laugh even harder.

"Are you all right?" the angel asked.

"Oh my God, yes," he cried out between giggles. "I'm fine, wonderful, great. Thank you, Nurse."

"Uh, I'm not a nurse. I'm your doctor."

"I'm sorry, Doctor," he said as he wiped away tears of joy. "Uh, I don't think we've formally met. I'm Christopher Blaze, and you are?" The absurdity of his introduction made Chris break out into more hysterical laughter.

The doctor couldn't help it. She started to laugh, too. The man's hysterical joy was contagious.

After a few moments, Blaze settled into a broad grin and the doctor decided to introduce herself.

31

"I'm Dr. Sue Catledge, and I know who you are."

She pulled the clipboard off the end of the bed and started reading from it. "Christopher Blaze, Detective Sergeant Third Class. Awarded Medal of Valor for bravery in the line of duty."

She was beautiful. That part of the dream had been real. He could see that she had a shapely body under her doctor's coat. Here was a woman he wanted to get to know better.

She continued reading. "Awarded numerous commendations. Single, six feet, blond hair . . ."

"Okay, okay, enough of 'this is your life, Chris Blaze.' What about the Sue Catledge story?"

"I'm afraid it will have to be some other time. I've got other patients to check up on."

"How about dinner?" he asked.

"The nurse's aide will bring something at above five," she replied.

"No, I mean how about dinner, you and me, cozy restaurant, you can tell me your life story then."

"Only if my fiancé can come, too."

Blaze felt like someone had just sucked the air out of his lungs with a heavy-duty Hoover.

"I should have known," he said dejectedly. "Good-looking, rich doctor. You *would* have to be some lucky devil's girl."

"I'm a second-year resident at a county hospital. I'm hardly rich."

"But you are beautiful."

The doctor blushed. "Thank you very much."

She put back his chart.

"Now I really do have to go," she said.

Chris shrugged. "Oh, well, maybe you and your man will have a big fight before the marriage and break up. You'll look me up at the station and we'll go out and fall madly in love."

She smiled that angel smile again.

"Keep a good thought," she said as she turned and left.

Chris grinned and closed his eyes. As he drifted off to

32

sleep, his last thought was of the doctor's fiancé telling her that he was gay and that he was in love with a mime from the park.

2

He was good looking, there was no doubt about it, Sue thought to herself as she went to check on Mr. Johnson, the patient in 212. And he seemed to be very charming as well. Maybe dinner wouldn't be a bad idea. It would only be conversation, then maybe a little dancing. . . . No! What's wrong with you, Susan Marie? You're engaged—to be married in six months to Jonathan Wadsworth the third. The man you've dated for the past six years, remember? After all, he did pay the way through your last two years of medical school. And wasn't it Jonathan who got you your internship at Mercy General? You owed him a lot. So he was a bit of an arrogant snob, he always treated you fairly. He wasn't a bad lover—a little selfish, perhaps. Then a little voice popped up in her head. *A lot selfish.* . . .

She dismissed it as another voice came into her head. She recognized this voice immediately. *He's a good catch. You're not getting any younger, you know. Having one of the city's most prominent financiers in the family wouldn't be all that bad.*

It was her mother's voice. Mom had always liked Jonathan. He was rich and handsome, and that was good enough for her.

The other voice, her voice, returned. *But was it good enough for you, Sue?*

That was the question.

3

Tom Draper glanced out the big bay windows of the hospital lobby. The sun had gone down an hour ago. It was an unusually dark night for so early in the evening. He glanced at his watch. 8:00. Perfect. The sign said visiting hours were 7 to 9. He walked over to the visitors' registration desk.

"Hi, I'd like to see the patient in room 210, please." Draper said to the little old lady dressed in pink.

"What's that room number again?" she asked, cupping her hand to her ear.

"210, ma'am."

"Number ten, let's see," she said as she looked down the registry. "That would be Mr. Orlock."

"No, ma'am. I want to see Chris Blaze in 210."

"Sorry, there's no Miss Graves in room 10. Only Mr. Orlock."

Draper sighed. "He's in room 210."

"No, 210 is a Mr. Christopher Blaze, not Orlock."

"Right," he said trying to hold his temper, "that's who I want to see."

She peered at him suspiciously through her horn-rimmed glasses. "Then why did you tell me you wanted to see Mr. Orlock?"

"I told you I wanted to see the patient in room 210," he said, emphasizing the 2. Draper felt as if he was trapped in an Abbott and Costello sketch. Then, to make matters worse, a delivery boy came in with some flowers.

"Pardon me," she said to the captain while she turned to the boy.

"What's the patient's name?"

"Jackson," the boy replied.

"Just a minute, I was here first," Tom cried.

"Sorry," she said, looking at the registry. "There is no Japston listed as a patient."

"I said Jackson," the delivery boy repeated.

"This is where I came in," Draper said to himself. He bent over the desk and picked up a visitor's pass.

"Just a minute, sir . . ."

"Lady, I've got to deliver these flowers."

"Now you hold on . . ."

Tom Draper kept walking and never looked back.

Marie Espinosa was working the corner of Jackson and Barney, but there wasn't much action. She was jonesing bad for a hit of the rock, but she needed to turn a couple tricks first to get some money. A likely candidate in navy whites walked by.

"Hey, wanna date?" she asked, trying to look sexy as she trembled from the craving in her body.

"No thanks," he said and walked on.

Maria forked him a bird. *This place is beat. Better start walking toward Fox Street,* she thought to herself. The action was always better there.

Maria was seventeen going on forever. She first started in the business at the ripe old age of fourteen and began her slide into hell from there. Drugs . . . kinky sex . . . violence . . . a stint in a skin flick. In three years she had gone from ponytails to cat-o'-nine-tails.

Maria glanced at herself in a shop window as she passed. She was still a pretty girl with the dark hair and eyes of her Latin heritage, but she had the jaded look of someone who had seen too much in too short a time. Maria had the hardened eyes of a hundred-year-old woman. The heavy makeup she wore to make her look older covered her face like a death mask. She thought how it made her look like a doll. But wasn't that what she was, a great big love doll? *Maria, your sexual playmate. See instructions. You don't even have to blow her up. You just stick it in her mouth or her pussy and get your rocks off, no strings attached.*

But "love doll" wasn't quite the right phrase. In her whole life no one had ever loved Maria. Her mother had run away from their home when Maria was only nine. Her father had come home one day from his job as a dishwasher to find the note. It had said that his wife couldn't live the lie anymore and had to leave. She was in love with another woman and had to be with her. She was sorry, but she couldn't fight her true feelings any longer. The father had screamed with anger and begun destroying everything that reminded him of his wife. Pictures shattered. Their wedding china crashed to the floor. That fucking *puta!* She'd left him not for another man, but for a woman! His mind reeled. He could have handled her jilting him for another hombre . . . maybe. But his wife and another señorita? His machismo simply couldn't handle that.

From that moment on he had begun to change. He grew sullen and remote, staying home for long stretches of time. He lost his job and they started on welfare. Her father started to hit the booze heavy . . . and he started to hit Maria. It all began when he made a set of rules for the house. He posted them on the wall and enforced them if they were violated. He would beat her for the slightest infraction.

Coming in late.

Turning on the television too loud.

Not wiping her feet.

She couldn't do anything right. To make her life more unbearable, her father added more and increasingly bizarre rules each week.

Brush your teeth six times a day.

No television from 9:00 PM to 9:20 PM.

Sleep on the floor from 1:06 AM til 6:00 AM.

Each time she broke a rule, which was often, she received a beating. Once he hit her so hard that he cracked a couple of her ribs. She had forgotten to put the salt and pepper on the table. Finally, after he whipped her with his razor strap for not putting a box of cereal back in the cabinet, she had left him and hit the streets. Not long thereafter, her father went crazy. He had gone to bed with his white girlfriend and not been able to get an erection. She laughed at him and called him *muy impotante,* so he slashed her throat and hacked out her vagina with a switchblade. His neighbors had heard the unearthly screaming of the woman and called the police. A uniformed patrolman who had answered the call was charged by a naked madman waving a knife and screaming that all women were lesbians and that they should all have their filthy cunts cut out. The cop shot her father dead bang between the eyes. She had cried when she'd read about it in the papers.

No, in her whole life Maria Espinosa had never known love, and the tragedy was that she never would.

5

Chris Blaze was reading the latest edition of *Playboy*. Tom Draper tapped lightly on the doorjamb of room 210. "Hey, pard. How they hangin'?"

Chris looked up from the magazine he was reading. "Hey, Captain Draper—thanks for the magazine," he said as he held up the centerfold for the captain to see. "Not bad reading, either."

"Are they taking good care of you?"

"Great. I should be checking out of here tomorrow. By the way, I haven't had a chance to thank you for saving my ass, not once, but twice in one night."

Draper had never been any good at taking praise. "Hey, I just did it because I need you for our next big case."

Chris smiled. "Right. Anyhow, if there's any way I can repay you for risking your neck to pull me out of that car, just ask."

"Okay, I will," Tom said. "I want you to go undercover and set up Tony Mancetti for drug trafficking."

"The king of crack? I dunno—he's a pretty dangerous dude."

"Come on, Blaze. He can't be any worse than that whacko Batiste Legendre."

The hellish vision of Batiste Legendre and the slug creature falling out of his mouth flashed in his mind. No fucking way it could be any worse than that.

"Okay, Captain. I'm in. When do we start?"

6

Maria turned down the alley that she used as a shortcut to get to Fox Street from Barney. She was about a third of the

37

way in when she realized the street light that usually lit the way was broken. Fucking *hijos* with their rocks, she thought. No matter—she could make it. She had been down the dank shortcut enough times to go through it with her eyes shut. The smell of garbage, urine, and turned wine accosted her nostrils. She could almost feel the bacteria and disease crawling on her. Garbage was strewn all about. In the dim light, she could make out overturned trashcans and stacks of old papers. The broken glass from a shattered bottle of Mad Dog 20/20 crunched under her feet. She hurriedly walked along, but not too fast, for fear of tripping and being swallowed up in a pile of rotten meat and dirty books. A gust of cold air brushed past her, raising the gooseflesh on her arms. Suddenly Maria felt very nervous about the dark alley. It was as silent as a graveyard. The only sound was the crunch, crunch of the glass under her high-heeled shoes. Suddenly she felt the high-heeled spike of her right shoe sink into something soft and mushy. Maria looked down, hoping that she had not stepped in a brown surprise left by some drunken wino who couldn't find a gas station. She hadn't. The spiked heel was stuck directly in the glazed eye of a dead cat. As the stench from the decayed animal assaulted her senses, she felt her stomach turn and hot bile rise up in her throat. With a great effort, Maria willed her stomach to settle down. She pulled her foot up to extricate the spike from the eye socket of the carcass. The cat's head rose with her shoe, the heel still embedded in the gooey aqueous humor of the *gato's* eye. She put her foot back down and took the sole of her other shoe and placed it on the cat's neck. She held it down as she jerked her foot up to try and pull the spike from its disgusting trap. With a great effort the heel popped out and the cat's skull thudded to the ground, but the force of her momentum sent her shoe flying across the dark alley.

"Son-of-a-bitch."

Maria hopped on one foot to where her shoe had landed. As she bent over to pick it up, a rat scurried up her arm, jumped off at the elbow, and ran away. Goddamn filthy thing. She picked up a bottle and hurled it at the rodent. It crashed against a trashcan. Two red, beady eyes peered out at her from behind a pair of filthy old BVDs. The rat squealed and was gone. While she was balancing to put her shoe back on, she teetered on her remaining high heel, lost her balance, and fell with a crash onto a pile of old boxes.

"Fuck! I can't believe this shit!" she said.

After a moment, she laughed as she thought of what she must look like, sitting like a queen on her throne of trash. "This has not been a good night!" she said.

Maria put on her shoe and brushed herself off. As she struggled to get up, a hand as cold as death seized her by throat.

No, this definitely was not a good night for Maria Espinosa.

Chapter 4

1

At first glance Tony Mancetti was a very handsome man. If he had lived in the twenties, he might have been mistaken for Rudolph Valentino. His jet black hair, combed straight back, and his smoldering good looks were reminiscent of the great Latin lover. Tony was a sharp dresser and liked to spend big bucks on custom-designed suits and flashy jewelry. He was known to drop a couple grand on an outfit if he thought it made him look good. There was only one flaw that marred the almost perfect looks of Anthony Louis Mancetti: his left eye. It was covered with a thin white film that gave it the glazed-over look of a corpse. He had been born with it, and at the time the doctors could do nothing about it. In his first year of school he had been chided by his classmates, who called him "Creepy Eye" and "Monster Boy." They teased him unmercifully. Rusty Brown was the main troublemaker. A classic bully, he was bigger than the other kids and was always letting them know it. He had red hair, a turned-up nose, and big freckles that almost covered his face. He looked a lot like the tough guy Butch on the *Little Rascals*, and he wanted to make Tony Mancetti his Alfalfa. The big redhead was always trying to pick a fight with him, but Tony would always do nothing and walk away. All Rusty's pals would tease Mancetti and call him "chicken" or "fraidy-cat." The little Italian acted as though he never heard the taunts or didn't care if they called him a yellow-belly. Then one day at lunch, Rusty Brown opened his Daniel Boone lunchpail and there, staring at him from inside old Dan'l's box, was his dog, Sparky. His head had been hacked off. Rusty screamed and pissed in his pants. Then he freaked out and started crying uncontrollably. Mrs. Peterson, the school nurse, had to take him home. By the time he got to his house, he had settled down—that is, until he found the headless remains of Sparky hanging on the fence that surrounded the Brown's white A-frame house. Rusty Brown had to stay out of school for a long time after that.

Tony Mancetti was never caught, and Rusty Brown didn't tell anyone he thought it was Tony who'd done it. In fact, he hid the dead dog from his mom and dad and buried him in Turner's Woods. Old "Creepy Eye" was definitely not someone you messed with.

As Tony grew older, he wore sunglasses as much as possible to conceal the hated defect. The young tough began to get involved in illegal activities, and by the eighth grade he was dealing pot to his classmates. As the years passed, he found that there was more profit in hard drugs and started dealing cocaine, LSD, and bennies. By his senior year he was driving a better car than most of his teachers and had gotten himself in tight with the Luccesi family. They had heard about the mean young shark who'd cut the nuts off a black pimp who'd tried to move in on his turf. They respected a young man with initiative and gave him a piece of their action. He would be in charge of all the cocaine on the East Side. Tony took to his assignment like Jaws to a surf filled with porkers from an Overeaters Anonymous beach party. He devoured anyone who stood in his way.

As Mancetti's reputation grew, he took over more territory and controlled more drugs than anyone else in the Luccesi organization. The man with the white eye had quickly become a powerful figure in the underworld. Mancetti could have gotten one of those new colored contact lenses to mask his affliction, but he knew that the eye struck fear into the hearts of his enemies, and fear was a powerful weapon. Besides, he had enough money to get most any woman he wanted, and he wanted all of them. Still, he did have some leftover resentment of the cruel trick God had played on him, and on more than one occasion that resentment reared its ugly head. Once, after a night of drinking and womanizing, one of Mancetti's men kiddingly had called him "Dead Eye," thinking his boss would appreciate a nickname like all the bigshot wiseguys had. Charles "Lucky" Luciano. Alfonse "Scarface" Capone. Anthony "Dead Eye" Mancetti. The bodyguard knew he had made an error in judgment when the switchblade Mancetti always carried, clicked open, flashed and lopped off two of his fingers. "Dead Eye" was never heard again in the presence of Tony Mancetti, although Luigi "Three Fingers" Favata would take his nickname to his grave.

Tony Mancetti. Drug kingpin. Enforcer. Murderer. This was the man who Christopher Blaze was going to put away.

Blaze started the undercover operation by putting the squeeze on a junkie named Frank Middleton, who was trying to get out of a possession rap, to get him into the Mancetti organization. The junkie crumbled under the pressure and arranged a meeting. He had told one of Mancetti's men that Chris was a buyer from out of state named Don Wiley who wanted to make a big score. After they checked Chris out, a meeting was arranged.

At first, Chris and the drug kingpin's meetings were casual affairs, with the chat ranging from the Yankees to the stock market. Never once was the word "drug" ever mentioned. Mancetti hadn't gotten as far as he had by playing the fool. Many times the various precincts where he plied his trade had tried to put together a sting operation, and none of them had ever met with success. But Chris was good: he knew how to talk the talk and walk the walk. He and Tony became good buddies. They would go to the fights together and afterward hit the nightclub scene to check out the action. Mancetti offered Chris coke on a number of occasions, always through a friend, but Chris refused on the grounds that a good supplier never dealt to himself. This impressed the drug czar. He, too, never indulged in the addictive white powder, a fact Blaze had picked up from Mancetti's files.

Everywhere they went they were followed by a cadre of bodyguards led by the ominous Drago Stikowski. Stikowski was a paid assassin who just loved to gouge out an eye or grind a victim's teeth on the pavement before icing him with the custom-made .44-caliber Smith and Wesson he carried. He was about five-five and tipped the scales at about 250 pounds. Drago could bench-press well over 600 pounds. His strength was legendary among the wiseguys, who loved to tell their favorite Drago story about how Stikowski had ripped the junkie Johnny Terry's arm completely out of its socket and swatted him over the head with it. Drago had a face only a mother could love, and even then she would have to be blind. His bulging eyes were ringed with dark purple circles. His cheeks were pocked, and he had a long scar running from the corner of his left eye to the corner of his mouth—the result of a young lady who had taken exception to his advances slashing him with a nail file. He had enjoyed killing her. It was truly amazing how easily that nail file had gone through her eye and into her brain. Just one push and bingo, a dead hooker. He had enjoyed that one immensely.

Chris had been on the case for about a month when one day out of the blue, Mancetti offered him the opportunity to make a big buy. The drug czar was going to give his new buddy a chance to make some real money. It was the break they had been waiting for, the chance to put Tony Mancetti behind bars for a long time.

2

In the same period of time as Chris's infiltration of the Mancetti organization, Sue Catledge had been torn between her impending betrothal to Jonathan and the constant thought that she was making a huge mistake by marrying the rich playboy. Did she love him, or was it just a marriage of inevitability? They had been going together for so long that it seemed like destiny that they would take the next step in their relationship. All their friends thought the marriage was a good idea. All her colleagues at work thought she was making the right move. Everyone was so sure that she was doing the best thing for her. The only one who wasn't sure was the bride-to-be.

And then there was the cop. She couldn't get that damned handsome detective off her mind. Why did he attract her so much? He was a good-looking guy, but so were lots of other men she'd met. But somehow she knew he was the kind of man she wanted. When he was lying in the hospital bed, he looked so vulnerable. His firmly muscled body shook violently with chills as the horrible nightmare tormented him. She had wanted to hold him to her breast and stroke his blond hair and comfort him until the shaking stopped and the nightmare ended. But she was his doctor, and if someone had come in. . . .

Well, she didn't want to think about that.

A few times she had gone to the phone and dialed the number to the precinct. But she had hung up each time after someone picked up. Her conscience told her it was wrong to go out with another man when she was soon to become Mrs. Jonathan Wadsworth the third. But she just wanted to get to know him better, she told herself—to become his friend. He'd seemed so nice when they had had their brief conversation at the hospital, and she wanted to know more about this Christopher Blaze . . . strictly in a friendly sort of way, she reminded herself.

But of course, she knew that was a lie.

Sue Catledge had her finger in the dial and was all set to call the Fifth Precinct when the phone rang. Startled, she pulled her hand back, as if the phone had suddenly come to life and snarled at her. She recovered before the second ring and answered it.

"Hello?"

"That certainly was fast," the voice at the other end of the line said.

She immediately recognized the voice of her betrothed. "Hi, Jonathan. What's up?"

"I was calling in regard to our dinner date this evening."

God, he sounded so pompous when he talked like that. It

was as if he were making a business appointment instead of a date for a romantic evening with his lover and wife-to-be.

"What about it?" she asked, her irritation barely concealed.

"My, aren't we testy?"

"Jonathan, I'm very busy. We *are* still on for dinner. Pick me up at seven. Now, if there isn't anything else . . ."

"No, nothing else. I just wanted to be sure that our evening plans are still intact," Jonathan said, then added in a sarcastic tone, "I mean, you may have to take care of a wino who drank too much formaldehyde, or some other pressing medical emergency of one of your wonderful patients."

"Are you going to start this again?"

"Well, really," Jonathan huffed. "When I got you the position at Mercy General, I didn't expect you to volunteer to work on all the paupers in the city. I thought you'd stay awhile at Mercy, then go into private practice. I have lots of friends who need a good G.P. I mean, you were groomed for better things."

Groomed? Now he was really pissing her off. "You listen and listen good: I am not your little project, Jonathan. I got into medical school to help people who needed me. Those patients need my help more than any of your rich friends do."

"I could have sworn we'd talked about private practice when I was helping you through school."

Now he was throwing *that* in her face again.

"You know I appreciate you putting me through school. But I really don't think we talked about that."

"Perhaps not, perhaps it was just wishful thinking on my part," he said.

"Look, Jonathan, how many times are we going to have this conversation?" she asked him. "I've told you I enjoy what I'm doing. Why can't you just accept that?"

"I only want what's best."

What's best for your image, she thought but didn't say.

"Okay, then let me stay at Mercy without you always hammering on me about it."

"I'll try, but I can't promise it won't slip out every once in a

45

while," he answered.

"Once in a while I can deal with," she said. "Now I really do have to get back to work."

She wanted the conversation to end before round two began.

"Very well, I shall be by to pick you up at seven. Please see that you are ready."

Before Sue had a chance to comment on his ultimatum, Wadsworth hung up.

Round two didn't even have a chance to get started.

As she hung up the phone, Sue remembered how Jonathan's sophisticated manner that so irritated her now had swept her off her feet when she was a second-year med student from Indiana. Up until then she'd been with only one guy, her high school sweetheart, Jimmy McGinnis. Jimmy and Sue had grown up together in Gary and had started dating in the ninth grade. They stayed together all through high school. They had planned to get married after graduation, but never set a date. Then he got a basketball scholarship to the University of Oklahoma and she went off to the University of Miami, where she'd been offered a scholarship. The first two years they saw each other on holidays and special occasions, but gradually they drifted apart. Eventually their relationship settled into the good friendship that it had started out as those many years ago. She dated on and off in college—never steadily, though. Between her chemistry classes and analytic calculus, she barely had time to go out and get a quart of milk at the grocery store, let alone go out on a date. And she really wasn't interested in starting another long-term relationship. That is, until she met Jonathan.

It was a Saturday the day after finals ended when her friend Tammy Myers asked her to go with her to a tennis tournament her dad was sponsoring down at the Briarwood Country Club. They had driven to the club in Tammy's Porsche, a graduation gift from her father. As they drove through the heavily wooded entrance to the clubhouse, Tammy pulled up to the valet parking section. A good-looking college student opened the door for them, took the keys, and hopped in. As he was parking, they entered the clubhouse. The first thing that came to Sue's mind as she stepped into the huge foyer of the Trophy Room was that she didn't belong there. The place looked like the large, opulent den of a wealthy adventurer. Fine polished oak bookshelves lined the walls with first edition copies of books that ranged from Kipling's *Jungle Book* to Hemingway's *The Old Man and the Sea*. At each table was a pipe rack and a fine brass lamp. On the matching oak walls were trophies of the big game the club members had shot on expedition. Lions and tigers roared in silence. A polar bear stood eight feet tall in the corner of the room. A lone water buffalo stared at her. They all looked like they wanted to be someplace else, and Sue felt a kindred spirit. There was a huge fireplace in the middle of the room that looked as though it could heat her entire dorm back at school. The room oozed wealth, and at any moment she expected money to come tumbling out of the mouths of the stuffed animals. Sue had never been to such a fancy place. So this was what rich people were up to, she thought. Tammy smiled at the awed expression on her friend's face, then took her by the arm to lead her to the terrace where they could watch the matches. Sue had enjoyed the tennis immensely. The competition was fierce, as most of the players were just a notch below professionals. Afterward, she went with Tammy to the lounge to have a drink. As Sue was sipping at the last of her Tom Collins, she felt a tap on her shoulder.

"Pardon me," the handsome man said, "I believe I'd like to buy you a drink."

Ordinarily, Sue would have told the guy to take a hike, but she didn't want to offend Tammy. Besides, maybe this was the way they bought a girl a drink in Camelot. She remembered looking up and seeing this good-looking blond standing in front of her. He had been slimmer in those days and had the tan of a man who could afford to spend his days playing tennis in the sun. His perfect white teeth were even brighter in contrast with his dark skin. He looked like a rich playboy, and by God, he was. She accepted his offer, and the man joined them at the table.

He introduced himself as Jonathan Wadsworth the third and they started to chat. They talked the rest of that day and into the night about a variety of different topics ranging from the works of Jung to the politics of Richard Nixon. Tammy had gone home after Jonathan said he would give Sue a ride back to her dorm in his Jag. After a cup of espresso at a charming little bistro, Jonathan took her back to her dormitory. He was a gentleman and gave her a light kiss goodnight. This was her knight in shining armor, and he had come to take her to his castle.

They dated for three years and went all over the world while she was on break from school. She was happy and enjoyed his company. He knew all the right wines to order and what dishes were the specialty of the house at all of the fine restaurants where they went. Jonathan knew about art and culture. He was handsome and charming, every girl's "dream date." When she got into financial trouble, he bailed her out. After she graduated, he helped her get her job at Mercy. With all the good things he did, it was easy to overlook certain things she didn't like: his arrogance towards the "lower class," as he called them. Jonathan had been born into wealth and parlayed his inheritance into an even greater fortune. He simply had never been around people who weren't rich and had little time for them. Another thing she didn't like was his selfishness in bed. The first time they made love, he satisfied her and made her head spin. But gradually he began just to take pleasure from the oral sex she gave him or from making love until he was satisfied, not caring about her.

As their relationship wore on, she began to stop overlooking the things that bothered her. She started to confront Jonathan when he did something that upset her. They had some bitter quarrels, but things started to get a little better between them. Then he surprised her by asking her to marry him. She didn't accept immediately and voiced her concerns about the problems in their relationship. The weeks that followed were nearly blissful, as though they had gone back into the past. Jonathan took her out to dinner, sent her flowers, made love to her the way he used to do, all the things

48

that had been missing from their lives. Because of his willingness to try, Sue decided to accept Jonathan's proposal.

For several months their relationship was really good, but as the wedding date drew near, the old arrogant and selfish Jonathan began to surface from time to time. For the most part, Sue ignored it, choosing to believe that it was only a momentary lapse. It was a mistake she would later regret.

The phone rang, interrupting Sue's thoughts.

"Sue, this is Frank Claber. Could you come in tonight and work a shift? Dr. Kaye has come down with the flu, and we're really shorthanded."

"Sure, Frank," she said, forgetting about her date with Jonathan.

"Great, see you then."

"Okay."

As the phone clicked, she remembered the dinner with her fiancé.

Oh, well, she thought to herself. Round two was on again.

3

As Chris punched the numbers on the pay phone to call Draper and tell him the good news, a premonition of foreboding swept over him, a feeling that something bad was going to happen to him if he went through with this deal. He pushed it out of his mind as Draper answered the phone.

"Hey, Cap, we're in," Chris said. "My *paisan* Mancetti is going to sell me a hundred grand of cocaine at 8:30 on Thursday night of next week."

"Son-of-a-bitch, that's fucking fantastic!" the captain said, excited about the prospect of busting one of the city's biggest pushers.

"Can we get that much cash in so short a time?" Chris asked.

"Leave it to me. I can get it released to you. Now, where is this going to go down?"

"Room 192 of the Antares Hotel."

"Is it easy to access?"

"Yeah, I've been there. It's on the first floor, last door in the hallway. Mancetti will have men inside and in the hall."

"Shit, that's gonna make it tough."

"Mancetti is one cautious dude. He isn't going to make it easy for anybody trying to bust him."

"Well, I'm going to have men stationed in the lobby and in the surveillance van."

"I snuck a gun behind the toilet in the bathroom when I was there the other day checking it out. After they frisk me I'll tell them I've got to take a leak and then I'll sneak back in with the gun."

"Who are you, Michael Corleone?"

"Hey, you got a better place? If I hide it outside the room, they'll send somebody with me, and besides, the bathroom is the one place where I can have some privacy."

Draper broke into an impromptu Brando impression as the Godfather. "Michael, I respect your judgment. You make a case I cannot refuse."

"Don't quit your day job," Chris said, commenting on Draper's impersonation.

Draper laughed. "Okay, then it's all set. Thursday night, next week, Tony Mancetti is going down."

Chapter 5

1

The sun was shining brightly as detective Reggie Carver sauntered toward the precinct house. He was in a particularly good mood this day as he headed in to work. He had just made a righteous bust of two big-time crack dealers who were selling their particular form of death in his old neighborhood. It was a shame that the barrel of his gun had accidentally cracked one of the dealers upside the head and given him a fractured skull. Yeah, that was a real shame. Reggie smiled as he pushed open the door to the station. The Fifth Precinct station was constructed in the early 1920s and had not advanced very far from there. The station was originally designed for a hundred policemen. At last count, there were two hundred cops on duty at the Fifth. They jammed together like so many sardines. The desks were old, but you really couldn't tell under all the paperwork and dust. Reggie had been with the force for five years and had never seen the squadroom look any different. It was as though there was a special detail of janitors who came in at night and arranged everything so that it would look exactly the same way every morning.

Reggie Carver was a flashy dresser, with a quick wit and a wicked sense of humor, especially for a well-executed practical joke. When he was up to something, Reggie would get the mischievous grin of a twelve-year-old and everyone would be on the alert. They knew the grin meant that someone was about to get zinged, and usually that someone was Lieutenant Charles "Assface" Burnson.

Burnson, Reggie's immediate superior, had taken an immediate dislike to the young black man. He always tried to make life difficult for Carver by giving him the crummy details or making him do his paperwork over for minor errors. Carver took it all in stride, biding his time until the right moment when he could play a joke on the lieutenant, a joke that could not be linked to him. He got back at his ill-tempered boss with a series of these jokes that he had engineered to drive the man crazy.

As Reggie walked past the desk of Lieutenant Burnson, he thought about his latest installment in that series and laughed. Oh, this one had been a dilly, a real slam-banger. Burnson would learn not to give him the shitwork details he always assigned him. Yes sir, no more crap after this one. This one was an A-number-one Reggie Carver joke extraordinaire worthy of a Dick Clark and Ed McMahon special.

2

Lieutenant Charlie Burnson was waiting in the office of his family doctor. He nervously played with his keys as he watched the door to the office, hoping Dr. Tobin would come in and tell him the news about his condition. It had better not be what he thought it was.

Charles Edward Burnson was a sour man who always looked as though he had just finished sucking a lemon. "Handsome" was not a word you would use to describe him. In fact, "ugly" would be a compliment. He had a big nose with wide nostrils that actually flared like a horse's when he was angry. Under this monstrous proboscus was a scrawny mustache that looked like a caterpillar with mange. As if that wasn't bad enough, he had a wad of scraggly hairs under his bottom lip that he referred to as a goatee. When he smiled, he looked like an asshole with teeth. Hence the nickname "Assface." No one at the station liked Burnson because he was such a tyrant, which was fine with him, because he didn't give a shit about what they thought of him, especially that little black bastard. He was the boss, and if they didn't like it, tough shit.

The door to the office finally opened, and Dr. Tobin came in with a chart in his hand. The doctor was a kindly old man who looked as if he had just stepped out of the pages of Reader's Digest. He sat down on the examining table.

"Well, Mr. Burnson, it looks as though you have a case of gonorrhea," the doctor said in the matter-of-fact tone doctors use when they tell a patient the bad news.

"Shit, you've got to be fucking kidding me!" Charlie gasped.

Inwardly, the doctor cringed at the foul language of this vulgar man. Outwardly, his face was as stoic as a bust of Hippocrates.

"It's not permanent. If you take the medication I prescribe it will go away," Tobin said. "But you should tell anyone you've had contact with that they may be in danger of catching it."

Burnson thought of the sweet young girl Carver had set him up with. The little fucker had said he had wanted to bury the hatchet and fix things up. Burnson cringed as he thought of Reggie saying how he had this friend who had seen Charlie down at the station and wanted to get to know him better. Burnson was suspicious, but he let his little head dictate to his big head. The date he had with May Ling had gone smoothly, too smoothly. Charlie thought how easy it had been to get the foxy May into bed. Charlie Burnson was by no means a ladies' man. Most of the girls he had cheated on his wife with were "coyote women." If they were asleep on your arm in the morning, you would have to chew it off so that you wouldn't wake them up. But May Ling was a good-looking oriental woman with a tight ass and surprisingly large tits. She was by far the best-looking woman to whom he had ever slipped the salami. The day after their date, he had bragged to the guys at the station about taking her out and giving her the old boneroonie. He had gone on and on about how she said he was the biggest stud she'd ever laid and how he had the biggest cock she'd ever seen. He felt like the biggest chump in the world when they all cracked up and laughed for what seemed like hours. They were led by Reggie Carver. After they had explained to him what she did for a living and how Reggie had paid her to go out with him, he had attacked the black detective. The other cops pulled him off before any blows were exchanged. *Lucky thing, too,* he thought, *I'd have kicked his black ass all over the building.* Burnson hated Carver from the word go. His cocky attitude. His stylish dress. His way with the women. God, how he loved to assign Carver the shittiest assignments. It always pissed him off that Carver was such a good cop and made the most of the dog cases that Burnson gave him. The little dildo was even awarded a medal of valor, something Burnson himself had never gotten in his ten years on the force. He would get that fuck if it was the last thing . . .

"Are you still living with your wife?" The doctor interrupted Charlie's thoughts.

The policeman's stomach caved in when he thought of his wife. She was a hundred and eighty pounds of mean. He remembered the time he told her that he had wanted her to go on a diet and lose some weight. It had been a week before the lump went down on his head where she had hit him with a shoe. Now he had to tell her that he had a venereal disease and in all probability had given it to her. How would he explain it? He could already picture himself dodging the frying pan or plate that she would toss unerringly at his head. He had to tell her and then run like hell. That would be his plan.

Then he thought of what he would do to one Reggie Carver, the man who had put him in this predicament.

He would make his wife look like an angel.

3

"Are you sure?" Tony Mancetti asked the informant.

His milky eye narrowed when he heard the news. His hand instinctively tightened around the phone.

"Okay, I'll have Jackie drop the money off to you. I'm giving you an extra fifty as a bonus. Right. Later."

Tony slammed the receiver down and turned to Drago. "Boy, are you gonna have a good time tonight."

4

The wire was always a pain in the butt, but he had to wear it. The tape tugged at the hair on his chest, and he was always afraid that they would find it. The problems of undercover work were many. The fear of discovery. Having to make sure to follow every procedure to the letter, so that the bust would stand up in court. The possibility of gunplay. But still the night of a sting operation was always exciting. The adrenaline starts to pump. The senses become keener. The element of danger is always present. You fight with the specter of death that looms over you. If you win, you kick death in the teeth. If you lose, it's a one-way ticket to the morgue. Chris had been on many such operations, and tonight was no different. But somehow it felt different.

Something was wrong.

He shuddered.

The vision of Legendre with blue neon worms flashing across his eyes flashed in his mind.

Maggots for hair.

Creatures falling out of his body.

Slimy creatures from hell.

Death.

Then Chris felt that familiar cold touch in the place where Legendre's cursed knife had hit him.

The cold touch of evil.

He told himself it was just the microphone. It always felt like they kept those suckers in the freezer before they taped them on. That's all it was, the microphone. Chris checked the tape one more time and then buttoned up the silk shirt. He tucked it into the dark pinstriped pants that matched the

$450 coat he had selected. It was a lot of money, but he had to look the part, and besides that, it was the taxpayers' money, not his. He finished the ensemble with a $50 silk tie. As he admired himself in the mirror, Captain Draper entered the room.

"Well, don't we look snazzy," Draper chided him. "The big wheeler-dealer going out to make the big buy."

"Hey, if you got it, flaunt it."

"Well, I've got it, and you'd better not lose it."

The captain put the briefcase he had in his hand onto the bed. He popped the latch and there before them, sitting in the case, was a hundred thousand dollars.

Chris whistled. "God, look at that money."

"I know, ain't it beautiful?" Draper said, smiling.

They both stared at the fortune, each of them thinking about what he would do if he had that kind of money. They stood in silent awe, eyes fixed on all that cash, contemplating how to spend it. Both of them looked up at the same time. Their eyes met. They both had the silliest grins on their faces.

Draper asked the question that was on both their minds: "So what would you do if you had that kind of cash, Chris?"

"Oh, I don't know—I guess I'd quit the department and head for Tahiti."

"Bullshit, you'd never quit the department. You're too good a cop, and you know it. You've got it in your blood. You'd take that money and get yourself a new car to cruise around in and give the rest to me so I could retire and send my kids off to college."

"I might help the kids go to college, but help you retire? Then who'd give me all these great cases where I risk my neck to put some criminal in jail and have the judge let him get off on a legal technicality?"

"Cynicism doesn't become you."

"Well, optimism doesn't suit me either."

"So we'll settle for pessimism and leave it at that."

They both smiled.

Chris put the finishing touch on his outfit, a red silk handkerchief in his coat pocket. "All right, let's do it."

Reggie was laughing and joking around in the locker room. He had just gotten off duty and was sitting on one of the benches, talking to some of the guys about a particularly fine fox he had given his ebony love lizard to the night before. "Man, this girl was so hot," Reggie said with all the enthusiasm he could muster.

All the cops in the room said in unison, "How hot was she?"

"Man, this bitch was so hot, she would char you white boys' dicks black if you were to put it in her box."

"Shit, Reggie," Ed Jones said sarcastically. "She wouldn't even want our scrawny little white weenies after she had a stud like you."

"Damned straight," Reggie boasted, "one taste of the black pole of Calcutta, and a girl don't want nothing else."

"Carver," Rob Jackson, a black officer, joined in. "I've seen you in the shower. And I think you are one of the worst-hung brothers I know."

"Yeah, Reggie," Jones said, changing his tune. "I've noticed the other black dudes make it look like you got an earthworm hangin' from your crotch."

"Well, my man, a poorly hung black dude is still bigger than a well-hung white dude."

"Tell it to Johnny Wadd," one of the cops said from the back.

"What, has he got a phone in his coffin?" another one said.

They all laughed.

This was the way it always was in the locker room. The guys talking about getting pussy, making comments about the size of another guy's manhood, death jokes. Typical cop humor. Immature, junior high humor.

Reggie loved it. He was laughing and having a great old time. He didn't even see Burnson until it was too late.

The Antares Hotel was swanky enough to charge $500 a night for a room. Marble was everywhere. Huge silk flower arrangements burst colorfully out of large porcelain vases. Bellmen in fancy jackets with gold braid and epaulets waited on guests of the hotel. The marble dolphins swimming in the fountain playfully squirted water out of their blowholes. It was not exactly the type of place you would expect a major drug deal to go down.

As Chris entered the plush lobby, Chris was approached by one of the bellmen.

"Get your bags, sir?"

Chris recognized him as Carl Spoon, a vice cop from downtown.

"No, thanks. I'm just visiting a friend," he said.

He looked over the lobby and saw another cop, Jack Turley, sitting in a plush chair, sipping a drink. Chris went by him and headed down the hall toward room 192.

As Chris approached the room, he was greeted by a man he didn't recognize.

Something was wrong.

"There's been a change of plans," the man said. "We're going up to the seventh floor."

Mancetti is one cautious dude, Chris thought as he walked with the stranger to the elevator.

7

The first punch was a glancing blow off of Reggie's chin. Carver instinctively lashed out and caught Burnson with a right to the cheek. Burnson didn't even move. He was so enraged that he didn't even feel the blow. He fired a hard punch that nailed Reggie squarely in the sternum, and the pain shot through the black man like a knife. As Burnson prepared to strike again, Reggie let go with a kick that crashed into Charlie's ribs. He grabbed Burnson by the hair and slammed his head into the locker. Burnson's forehead split open, and blood splattered Reggie's shirt. Carver grabbed the front of the lieutenant's shirt.

"All right, motherfucker, you want some of me?" Reggie shouted, drawing back his fist.

Burnson spun out of his grasp and threw a haymaker that caught Reggie flush in the nose, busting it open. Now the black man's blood would mingle with his own. As Burnson tried to punch Reggie again, Ed Jones grabbed his arm and put it behind his back while Rob Jackson held his other arm. A couple of other cops grabbed Carver and held him back. They tried to calm him down.

Burnson raged, "You fucking shit cocksucker, I'm gonna get you one day!"

His eyes blood red. They were the eyes of a man who would commit murder.

"What the fuck is wrong with you, Burnson?" Reggie roared back. "What'd I do?"

"I got the clap from that cunt you set me up with, you motherfucker."

Reggie looked at the other cops and then bursted out laughing. "What? You got the clap? From May Ling? That's impossible."

"Go ahead and laugh, you little bastard. I'm gonna make sure you pay for this."

"Sure, I'll pay. How much is a bottle of penicillin?"

Reggie cracked up, and so did the other cops.

Burnson's eyes were death. "I'm gonna get you, Carver. You got that? One of these days I'm gonna hurt you real bad."

Reggie wiped the blood from his nose. "Anytime you want to try, Burnson. Anytime."

"Let me go," Burnson hissed, and shook his arms loose.

"You gonna be cool, Lieutenant?" Jackson said.

"I'm not gonna start again."

As he was about to leave, he turned to Reggie and stared at him with those death eyes.

Something was different about Burnson, Reggie thought.

He didn't know that Charlie "Assface" Burnson's sanity had just gone on a permanent vacation.

8

The stranger cleaned his fingernails with a toothpick as the elevator carried them up. He was a short, thin man, about five-six, with a weasel face and little weasel teeth that protruded from huge gums. His head was balding, and what little hair he did have was stuck to his forehead in three greasy rows. Chris could see a bulge under the man's black suit. He knew it was a gun.

"You got a name?" Chris said.

"Ralphie," the man replied coldly.

Chris extended his hand. "Pleased to meet you, Ralphie. I'm Don Wiley."

The man looked at him. "A pleasure."

He didn't shake Chris's hand.

The elevator stopped at the seventh floor. Chris stepped out in front of Ralphie. "What number?"

"727," the little man replied.

Chris hoped the cops downstairs had heard where they were now going to conclude the deal so they could come up at the appropriate time. He didn't see that Ralphie had pulled the "emergency stop" button on the elevator.

9

"Room 727. Did you get that, Spoon?"

The detective in the fancy jacket talked into the lapel. "Roger, got it. We're making our way up there now."

Spoon motioned to his partner, Turley, to join him at the elevator. The detective got up from the plush chair and made his way over to the shiny gold doors of the lift.

"They moved upstairs," Spoon said to his partner as he pushed the "up" button and waited for the elevator to come down.

10

There was only one bodyguard outside of room 727. It was Three Fingers Favata. He was sitting in a chair reading a dirty magazine, or at least looking at the pictures. He stood up as the two men approached.

"Hey, Ralphie. I see you found our man."

Ralphie nodded. The same dull expression remained on his face.

"What's up, Three?" Chris said nonchalantly.

Favata smiled, exposing a gold tooth with a diamond embedded in it. "Nothing but the sky, dude."

Favata opened the door with his malformed hand and let Chris and the weasel Ralphie in.

Tony Mancetti was sitting in a black leather chair with his feet up on a glass coffee table. The bodyguard, Drago Stikowsky, was at the bar, mixing a drink.

"Hey, Tony, what's going on?" Chris asked.

"Nothing, man," Mancetti answered. "Nothing at all."

"Drago, my man. Break anybody's legs lately?"

"Not yet," the ugly killer said ominously.

Chris felt a cold chill run up his spine.

"You got the stuff?" he said, trying to remain cool.

"And what stuff would that be?" Tony replied with a smirk on his face.

"Hey, what the fuck's wrong with you guys, you're acting funky."

"Nothing, we just get a little edgy when we're gonna make a deal."

"Yeah, well, lighten up. I've got the money right here. Now where's the stuff?"

"Stuff? I'm not sure what you mean."

Warning bells were sounding in Chris's head. He knew something was wrong. Still he tried to play it off. "Look, Tony, I hope you're not backing out on this deal. I mean, we both would lose a lot of money."

"Right, now what is it you want again?"

"You know what the fuck I want. Now let's cut the shit. I ain't got the time."

"That's right," Tony said. The grin fell off his face. "You ain't got the time . . . *cop!*"

Chris's heart froze. It was the worst nightmare of every undercover cop. He had been discovered.

Drago pulled out his custom .44 pistol and aimed it at Chris. His face was as cold as a tombstone.

11

"They made Blaze," Detective Brian Waters said to his van partner, Mike Melvin, as he monitored the conversation in room 727.

He grabbed the microphone that linked him with the two cops in the lobby and shouted. "Spoon! Blaze's cover is blown. You got that? They made Blaze!"

"Oh, shit," was the reply back at the van.

"You guys get the hell up there and hope they're not stupid enough to waste him in the hotel."

Waters got on the police radio and called in to alert Draper that the bust had gone sour. As Dispatch put him through to the captain, Waters hoped that Spoon and Turley would get to the seventh floor on time.

12

"Come on. Come on."

Turley impatiently tapped his leg with his fist. "What the hell's wrong with it?"

"I don't know," his partner Spoon said. "But it sure the fuck ain't coming down."

"Jesus, they must have pulled out the emergency stop."

"The stairs," Spoon said, pointing to the door.

The two detectives rushed through the door and started up the long flight of stairs. Their legs churned like pistons as they wound their way up to the seventh floor.

"Shit."

"Damn."

"Son-of-a-bitch."

The two cops cursed under their breath as the frustration of knowing that a fellow officer was in trouble and that they weren't there to help him racked their brains. And they had to haul-ass up seven flights to get to him.

Spoon took a quick glance at the numbers on the doors they passed on their way up.

Three.

The third floor.

They kept churning up the stairs.

Four.

Legs like pistons.

Five.

Running up the steps.

Six.

Almost there.

Seven.

Bingo.

They paused for just a second to catch their breath after the long, fast-paced climb. Just a second.

After they got their wind, the detectives pulled their pistols and stepped out through the stairwell door, and the shooting started.

13

Chris stared in disbelief as Drago's gun went off and the slug ripped into his chest. An expanding red spot marked where the bullet had entered. Another flash, and a bullet from Ralphie's pistol opened a red hole in his stomach.

His first thought was that they had ruined the expensive suit he was wearing and that he would have to pay for it. He turned and saw Tony Mancetti with the P38 Walther trained on him. The gun fired three times.

Blam! A lung exploded.

Blam! A shot to the gut tore open a kidney.

Blam! A bullet went in and out of his throat.

Chris slumped and fell to the floor, his eyes still open wide in disbelief. Drago pumped two more shots into him, just for kicks. The detective gasped once, and then Detective Sergeant Christopher A. Blaze, Miami PD, died.

14

As detectives Spoon and Turley turned the corner of the seventh-floor hall, Three Fingers Favata popped off a couple of shots at them. The bullets struck the wall next to them and splattered the cops with plaster.

"Get back!" Spoon shouted, pulling Turley back behind the corner.

Turley cried out to the gunman, "Police officers! Drop your weapon!"

Favata answered with a couple more shots.

Detective Spoon pointed to his partner, then to the floor.

Turley got down low as Spoon readied to fire his gun around the corner. They were going to take this guy out. Spoon breathed heavily and then held his breath.

"Ready?" he whispered.

Turley nodded.

On the count of three, Spoon fired as Turley rolled out into the hallway. Favata hit the wall by Spoon's head twice.

Turley pumped two shots into him, one striking him in the hand, the other hitting him in the jaw, shattering it.

"Nyu muga fuckas," Favata screamed, his lower jaw hanging.

The injured bodyguard fired another three rounds that hit plaster and wood, but nothing else.

Spoon dropped him with a perfect bulls-eye to the head.

Favata fell back and slammed into the door.

They were looking around for another man when they realized that the shooting in room 727 had stopped and the screaming had begun.

64

15

Tony Mancetti holstered his pistol and motioned to Drago and Ralphie. "Throw that piece of shit out the window," he said, his voice thick with disgust.

"A pleasure," Ralphie replied in the same toneless manner he'd used with Blaze.

Drago smiled.

As the big bodyguard bent over to pick Blaze up, the dead man's eyes suddenly burst open and he grabbed the stunned Drago by the throat.

The late policeman's eyes were blood red.

Blaze was on fire, as if he had suddenly been tossed into a furnace. His body prickled with what felt like tiny dancing matchheads. He remembered the guns firing and the impact of their deadly rounds and the sudden darkness. The visions of his life, his father, his mother, his childhood friends passed before him, and he watched as they slowly perverted into vile creatures with blazing blue eyes. Things with hooked claws and slavering mouths. Beasts so awful as to defy description. All manner of hellspawn flashed through his brain in those moments.

Then he had been cold, so cold. Ice.

He was dead.

Suddenly.

Heat.

Hot lips pressed against his own sent a surge of scorching air that filled his lungs, igniting a burst of energy. Blaze could picture its blue light crackling through his veins like electric blood as it coursed through his body. He could see the image clearly in his mind, although he knew it was impossible. There was nothing after death. The bullets inside him felt alive, crawling through him like maggots in dead flesh. It was as though they were trying to escape him. But that was not possible.

He was dead.

He had seen them shoot him. He'd felt the bullets, so many bullets, rip into him. He knew he could never have survived such an onslaught, yet he must have. He could see. He could hear, smell, move. He had seen Drago reaching down for him. He'd heard Mancetti order the big man to get rid of him. He could smell the burnt gunpowder in the air and the blood, his blood. It had been so easy to reach up and grab the man who had killed him by the throat.

He was alive.

Blaze growled as he lifted the 250-pound bodyguard up as though he was made of paper and then delivered him across the room. Drago landed with a crash on top of an oak dresser.

A piece of lead fell out of Chris's chest onto the floor.

Ralphie stood with his mouth open, paralyzed with fear, as he watched another bullet work its way out of Blaze's side. It fell harmlessly to the floor.

Chris smiled, exposing pearl white fangs. He reached out and lifted the little man by the arm and tossed him ten feet into the glass coffee table. He turned and started toward Tony Mancetti.

The drug kingpin pulled his gun again and aimed it at Blaze's heart. "Eat this, you smiling son-of-a-bitch." He fired two shots right into Chris's heart.

The force of the blows drove Chris back but did not harm him. Quickly he grabbed Mancetti by the arm and spun him across the room. The criminal kept firing wildly. A slug caught Ralphie in the side of the head as he tried to rise, killing him instantly. Chris let go of the druglord, whose momentum carried him crashing through the big bay window. He plummeted seven floors to his death.

Suddenly the big man, Drago, had Chris around the throat with his forearm—a chokehold from which no man had ever escaped alive. Chris pried the bodyguard's arm off as though he was removing a scarf. He whipped Drago around to face him. He hissed and exposed his fangs.

Drago's eyes grew wide and then he screamed as his sanity left him. He stood slackjawed, his spirit broken.

There was a banging on the hotel door.

Muffled voices shouted.

"C'mon," Chris said as he pulled the big guard with him toward the door. "Let's go see who's come calling."

16

Detective Spoon had heard the glass shatter and then the screaming that faded as quickly as a watercolor painting dropped in a pool. Turley dragged the stiffening body of Three Fingers Favata out of the way. He and Spoon simultaneously kicked the door to the apartment. Both of them felt their shins vibrate from the force. Both of their knees were jolted with pain, and both saw that the door was still firmly shut.

"God damn it! Open this door! Police!"

"Let's break it down." Turley said.

They both backed off and hurled their bodies toward the door. At the point of impact, Turley thought he heard someone at the door. In his mind he pictured the door opening and him and Spoon flying through it like they were in a Bugs Bunny cartoon. Turley even relaxed his body a little, as if preparing to run through the opening instead of slamming into three inches of solid oak. They hit the door full tilt and it gave.

It gave them both a shoulder ache.

Then the door opened . . . from the inside.

A ghoulish apparition stared at them.

Drago Stikowski stumbled out the door. "That guy ain't real. Eight shots. Got up like it was nothing. *Eight shots.*"

Turley and Spoon looked at each other and shrugged. They didn't anticipate the sudden catlike quickness of Drago as he grabbed Spoon's .38.

Turley reached for his gun, but it was too late.

The .38 fired.

Blood splattered the wall.

A body fell.

Turley didn't even have time to clear his holster.

Spoon stared in horror.

Drago Stikowski's brains oozed out of the back of his head, his eyes frozen in terror. The .38 was lodged in his mouth, his finger still on the trigger.

Chris Blaze walked out into the hallway. His appearance startled the two detectives. He was covered in blood. His white shirt was a deep red. The expensive suit coat had several holes in it. His mind raced as he tried to gather his thoughts about what had just happened to him. He remembered the guns blazing, the pain, the total darkness, and then grabbing Drago by the throat and the ensuing fight with the criminals. He tried to put his thoughts together to come up with a believable story until he could figure out what exactly had occurred.

"Holy Christ, what happened to you?"

"Uh, well, they, uh, blew open my cover and Drago pulled a gun."

"That part we figured."

The words just flowed out of Chris as he made up a version of the story that the others might believe. "Anyway, uh, I tossed my briefcase and caught Drago in the face. Mancetti tried to fire, but I grabbed his arm and started to swing him. He started firing wildly around the room, and one of his shots popped that Ralphie guy in the head. He fell back on the glass table."

"Did Mancetti hit you?" Spoon asked.

"No," Chris lied.

"Then how the fuck did you get so bloody?"

"I'm getting to that," Chris said, making it up as he went along. "I was, uh, swinging him around when we slammed into the window. It shattered, and I guess it must have cut an artery. Mancetti started bleeding like a stuck pig."

"So that's his blood?" Turley said, still skeptical.

"Where is Mancetti?" the other cop asked.

Chris ran his fingers through the hair and sighed. "I floored him. Seven floors, to be exact."

He pointed to the broken window where Mancetti had fallen out. Tony's silk scarf still hung there on a jagged shard of glass.

68

Spoon whistled softly.

Turley rubbed the back of his neck.

"So, what the hell made Drago go crazy enough to shoot himself?"

Before Chris had a chance to answer, a cadre of uniformed officers, led by Captain Draper, flew out of the stairwell door. Draper stopped in his tracks as he absorbed the scene in front of him. Three Fingers Favata lay in a pool of gore. Drago Stikowski stared at him through lifeless eyes. Two of his detectives were white as sheets, the other a crimson mess.

"What the hell happened here?" Draper asked as he took in the gory scene.

Blaze smiled sheepishly and prepared for a long night of explanations.

17

The night air was cool, and a blanket of fog had settled in over the city. The streetlamps had halos of diffused light. The neon signs flashed on and off in a blurred rainbow of color. The streets were dead quiet, as though someone had turned down the volume on the world. The whole effect was surrealistic.

Chris had spent the last part of the evening explaining his story to Captain Draper, the commissioner and members of Internal Affairs. Finally they had let him go.

As he walked down the deserted street, the strangeness of the evening was just sinking into Chris's weary brain. Once again he must have imagined his own death. It had all happened so quickly. The bullets tearing into his body. The feeling of sudden and total darkness. The awesome surge of power coursing through him. The one-sided battle. He could see Tony Mancetti flying through the window and plummeting to his death. The terror-stricken face of the big bodyguard, Drago, his gun in his mouth, dead. The images floated to the surface of his mind and burst like horrible bubbles. Had Drago taken his life because of what he'd seen, a man blown away from point-blank range who came back to life? No! The thought was too incredible. Chris had imagined the whole thing . . . a mental flash that had spanned microseconds but seemed as real as the concrete on which he walked. The human mind was capable of playing tricks that would turn Blackstone the Magician green with envy. Chris remembered how vivid the cult leader Batiste Legendre had been, standing in the middle of the road, and how real the coffin that entombed him had seemed, but none of that had not been real. Chris had not been killed then, and he was alive now. It was all his imagination.

Chris's apartment house stood on the corner of Dade and Orange. Carfax Apartments' architecture was that of an old English castle. The walls looked like they were built of great blocks of stone but were in reality concrete block coated with plaster that had been sculpted to look like the walls of the castle. Tall spires stood on either side of the building. Inside, the units were nice enough, if you were a jockey. They were small and cramped, but Mrs. Williams, the landlord, gave Chris a police discount to stay there because she thought having a cop in the building would help protect her tenants from the crime that plagued the city. It was a good price, and on his pay, he couldn't exactly afford a room at the Fountainbleau.

Chris opened the door to his place and flicked on the lights. His apartment was neatly kept and sparcely furnished, with one chair and a loveseat, non-matching, of course. A television set sat on a beat-up cabinet. A lone picture of a wave crashing on the rocks decorated the wall. It was a typical bachelor's pad, designed for sleep, sex, and entertainment.

Chris trudged wearily into the kitchen, opened the fridge, and pulled out a cold one. Popping the cap, he drank down a swallow of the icy beer. As he took the can from his lips, the taste of what he had just swallowed gagged him. The beer had an awful taste, as if it were mixed with spoiled milk and Windex. He coughed and threw up into the sink. He smelled the beer. It had that familiar aroma of brewed hops and barley. He took a small taste. It was as horrible a flavor as before. Shaking his head, a bewildered Chris poured the foul brew down the sink. He needed to get some sleep.

Chris entered the small bathroom. The medicine cabinet was open. An array of old prescriptions, razors, aspirin, and condoms cluttered its shelves. Chris bent over and splashed water in his face, hoping to rinse away some of the strangeness of the night.

He grabbed his toothbrush and plopped a gob of toothpaste onto it. He began to brush his teeth, moving the toothbrush side to side and up and down, trying to scrub away the horrible taste of the bad beer. Finished, he spit and rinsed. The water had a different taste, too. But Chris figured it was just the aftertaste of the bad Bud.

The exhausted detective rubbed the sides of his cheeks.

"Jeez, I must look like hell," Chris said. "Let's see what police work has been doing to you, Blaze."

He closed the door to the cabinet and stared into the mirror. There was no one looking back!

Panic.

Disbelief!

Pure terror!

All of these emotions slammed into Chris like a load of buckshot. He gaped at the mirror, touching his face to make sure that it was still there. It was. It just wasn't reflected back. As his hand brushed against his mouth, he felt his teeth and was racked again by the sheer force of his horror. His canines were long and sharp. He could feel them.

The mirror revealed nothing.

A chuckle escaped from Chris's mouth. It was an odd little laugh, the kind that people sometimes broke into at a funeral to relieve the tension.

For Blaze, it was either laugh or scream, and he knew that if he screamed, he might never stop.

Legendre! The image of the cult leader came into his mind. "That son-of-a-bitch did it!" he said aloud. "He really did it! I think I'm a vampire!"

71

Chapter 6

1

Reggie went to Mercy Hospital to have his nose checked. He didn't think it was broken, but he wanted to be sure. His ribs also hurt like hell from the fight. He would have the doctor check them to see if they were cracked or broken.

He walked into the emergency room. It wasn't too crowded. A young boy was crying as his mother stroked his hair. A fat man was reading a magazine. A young couple was holding hands as a doctor told them the news about their daughter. Carver walked over to the registration table.

"Hey, babe," he said to the cute redhead behind the counter, "Reggie Carver, Miami Police Department. I need to see a doctor."

"What seems to be the problem, Mr. Carver?" she asked.

"Oh, I just got into a little scrape. Nothing serious. Just need to have my ribs and my nose checked."

"Who'd you get into a fight with? Some menace to society?"

"Yeah, you could say that."

"How badly are you hurt?"

"Not too bad," he said, "I just got clipped a couple times."

"Okay, just have a seat and fill this out. Someone will be with you in a little bit."

Reggie sat down and started filling out the medical forms.

"Damn, I hate paperwork," he said to no one in particular.

A man wearing a strange turban tapped him on the shoulder. The stranger smelled like the north end of a southbound mule. "Do you like trees?" he asked, sounding like a bad imitation of Mahatma Gandhi.

"Excuse me?" Reggie said, trying to be polite while at the same time trying not to breathe through his nose.

"Do you like trees?" the stranger asked again.

"Yeah, I guess. Why?"

"Paper comes from trees, you know, and if you like trees, it is only logical that you like paper."

"Right." Reggie hoped that by agreeing with the loony bat he would get him to fly back to his belfry.

"Do you like to do your laundry?"

"No," he answered, then couldn't help asking why.

"Because laundry is work. You see now what I am saying?"

Reggie's head was beginning to throb, and his sternum was one dull ache. His body wished this guy would just leave. But his mind couldn't resist trying to find out what the hell the guy was talking about. "What do you mean, man?"

"Don't you see? You said you hate paperwork, but by loving paper and hating work, you have set up opposing forces in your mind. This leads to constipation, and one knows a healthy stool is a wonderful thing. To defecate freely is to express oneself freely."

Reggie just looked at him and shook his head. This guy was definitely exercising his freedom of expression, because he was clearly spouting shit.

Before Mahatma Gandhi got going again, the cute redhead interrupted their conversation. "Detective Carver, Dr. Catledge will see you now," she said.

As Reggie got up to go, the man in the turban farted.

"Express yourself," he said, smiling.

The examination room was typical. The antiseptic smell of alcohol smothered the air. Old magazines sat in a wicker basket, none of them less than five years old. Bottle of Q-tips and tongue depressors were neatly arranged on a small table.

A picture of a smiling face with the motto "Health—Happiness! See Your Doctor for Checkups" hung on the wall.

The white tissue paper crinkled as Reggie sat down cautiously on the examining table. Whenever he visited the doctor's office he always felt a little worse than when he'd come in. A kind of a mental trigger. You went to the doctor's office when you felt sick, so your mind associates sickness with the smells of the doctor's office. Reggie thought that it was sort of like when you were out in the woods or at a certain bookstore or video rental house and you always had to take a crap. Same thing. He pondered the complexities of the human mind for a moment and then got up and went over to the little table. He picked up the stethoscope and put it on.

"Yes, Doctor Zorba," he said, "I understand."

Reggie had always liked Ben Casey when he was a kid, and at one time he had wanted to be a doctor . . . that was, until he saw an episode of NYPD. Then he *really* knew what he wanted to be when he grew up, or as some of his friends would say, when he got older. Reggie Carver would never grow up.

Reggie had the stethoscope to the wall and was trying to hear what was going on in the room next door when Dr. Sue Catledge came in.

"Hear anything interesting?" she asked.

"Nah, they were just talking about . . ." Reggie stopped, embarrassed. "Oh, I was just, oh, you know . . ."

"May I?" Sue stuck out her hand for the stethoscope like a mother asking her little boy for the slingshot he'd just used to break a window.

"Oh, sure," he said as he handed her the stethoscope, which she put around her neck.

"I'm Dr. Catledge," she said.

"A pleasure. I'm Reggie Carver."

"Have a seat on the examining table."

Carver sat down.

"Now what seems to be the problem, Mr. Carver?"

"I got hit in the nose and in the ribs and I want to get them checked out."

"Very well, then. I need you to take off your shirt."

Reggie unbuttoned his shirt and laid it on the examining table.

Sue began probing his ribs, feeling for any breaks.

"Does that hurt?"

"Yeah." Reggie winced.

"How about there?"

"No."

She continued to check his ribs.

"I believe your ribs are okay. They're probably just bruised. If you wait two weeks or so and they still hurt, come back in."

"Right."

"Now let's see about that nose."

Reggie nodded.

"Okay," she said as she gently touched Reggie's nose and examined it.

"So?" Reggie asked.

The doctor took a long Q-tip and dipped it into a bottle of disinfectant. She inserted it into his nose and swabbed the medication on the damaged tissue. Reggie felt like a bee had flown up his nose and was stinging him.

"Yeow! Take it easy, Doc," he cried.

"Just cleaning it out and disinfecting it. It's not broken. Your nose is just fine. You've just had some capillaries broken inside. It should be good as new in a couple of days."

"Good." Reggie adjusted himself. The tissue crinkled and tore. "Sorry."

"That's quite all right, Mr. Carver," Sue said. "We do have more."

Reggie felt a little silly apologizing about the tissue paper, but he hated to waste things. He had come from a poor family who had saved and used everything. His father, Will, was a good, honest man who worked hard for his living as a maintenance man in their apartment and knew everything there was to know about plumbing, electricity, and fixing things. He just never learned much about contraception, as attested by Reggie's six brothers and two sisters. When he was a little boy, Reggie had always thought his mother was magic, because she would change shape every nine months and then he would have another brother or sister to play with. He called her the expanding woman and even drew a comic book about her. Reggie spent most of his time drawing or watching television shows and old movies. His all-time favorite show was Johny Quest, one of the prime-time cartoons that had tried and failed to make it in that prestigious time slot.

Every week, Reggie would follow the adventures of Johny and his Indian pal Hadji, Race Bannon, Dr. Benton Quest, and of course, Bandit, their little bulldog buddy, as they battled the evil Dr. Zin, monster lizards, and all sorts of villains and creatures. To this day Reggie still heard the pounding theme song of Johny Quest when he was in the middle of a particularly harrowing moment of police work.

Dun duh da da da da da da dumpah.

The song infused him with the courage of Johny Quest and his gang. He still occasionally saw it some Saturday mornings on cable television, but not enough for his taste.

"Now," Dr. Catledge said. "I'm going to tape up your ribs and . . ."

"So," a man's voice interrupted her. *"This* is why you stood me up."

Jonathan Wadsworth was standing in the doorway of Sue's office. He was wearing a Lacoste shirt, Ralph Lauren pleated khakis, and Timberland boat shoes, a walking advertisement from the pages of Esquire. Impatiently, Jonathan tapped his fingers on the doorjamb.

"I thought we had a dinner date."

"I'm with a patient, Jonathan. It can wait."

"I'm not a man accustomed to waiting," he said curtly. "I want an explanation. Now!"

"Who is this turkey, Doc?" an irritated Reggie said as he stood up.

"You didn't have the courtesy to call," Jonathan said.

"I didn't have time."

"I will not play second violin to the likes of him," Wadsworth said, his voice dripping with contempt.

Reggie clenched his fists. "Look here, dude—I don't know who you are, but you'd better get out of here before the likes of me kicks your ass."

Jonathan ignored him as if he were a homely girl at one of his parties. He continued his tirade against Sue. "I *demand* an explanation."

"I was called to an emergency, all right. And then Mr. Carver came in, so I had to treat him. I was just about to call you."

"I am sick and tired of having to take a back seat to paupers and Negroes who don't have the money to pay for your services."

"You motherfucker," Reggie said as he tossed a punch at Jonathan's head. Reggie missed and his fist cracked against the door.

"Stop! This is a hospital!" Sue shouted.

A backfist crashed against a cheek.

A knee exploded into a gut.

A man fell to the ground, quickly defeated.

Sue bent over to help the fallen warrior. "Get out, Jonathan, you've done enough," she said.

Jonathan adjusted his shirt collar, turned on his heel, and left.

The doctor helped Reggie over to the examining table. He sat down, shaking his head.

"Damn," he said, "this just ain't been my night."

"I'm very sorry, Reggie," Sue apologized. "My fiancé is not too keen on my working here at the hospital."

"Hey, I shouldn't have let my temper get the better of me, but I don't like that kind of talk."

"Jonathan had no right to say those things."

"I shouldn't have tried to hit him," Reggie said, then added, "especially since he kicked my butt. Damn, I thought all those high-society boys were supposed to be pushovers."

"Jonathan is a black belt in karate. He's been doing it for fifteen years."

"Well, you should get him a button that says, 'Karate man

in yuppie's clothing.'"

"Are you okay?" she asked.

"Yeah, I'm fine, just fine."

"Well, I still have to tape your ribs."

"Okay."

"I'm very sorry this happened," Sue apologized as she started to tape him up. "I'm not going to charge you for the examination."

"Now, hold on—I've got money and I'm going to pay," Reggie said in a voice that ended any chance of argument. He wasn't going to be one of those "deadbeat Negroes" Mr. Karate had spoken of.

Sue could tell that Carver's pride had been upset by Jonathan's comments. "Very well," she said, finishing the taping, "the girl out front will take your payment."

"Damn straight. Reggie Carver don't take no charity."

He stood up and put his shirt on. "What do I need to do?"

"Your nose and your ribs should be fine. If the pain bothers you tonight, just take two aspirin."

"And call you in the morning?" Reggie said jokingly.

"No, just take the aspirin. I work until 4:30 A.M. and I like to sleep in the morning."

Reggie smiled, got up from the table, and shook her hand.

"Thanks, Dr. Catledge. I appreciate your help," he said, then bent over and whispered in her ear. "Just between you and me, lose Mr. High-and-Mighty. I'd hate to see you end up with a chump like that."

Sue smiled and thought about another cop who had wanted the same thing a few weeks before.

2

Her shift was over, and Sue was on her way home. She was still upset about the incident with Jonathan and the black policeman. There had been no cause for Jonathan to make the comments he had. She realized he'd been upset, but still he had no right. Sue had half a mind to call him and bitch him out, but she decided to chill out. Besides, it was 5:30 in

78

the morning. She wanted to get home.

The young doctor lived in a house on the outskirts of the city. She had wanted to stay in a place where she could have peace and quiet after a long night in the chaotic world of the emergency room. Her nearest neighbors were about a quarter of a mile away on either side. A patch of woods was across the street from her home. Occasionally she would take a walk in them to relax and enjoy nature.

As she pulled into the driveway, she sensed that something was wrong. There was nothing unusual or out of the ordinary, but she felt as though someone had been there . . . or still was. She parked the car and cautiously got out, pulling the stun gun out of her purse. She crept slowly toward the front door. At any moment someone could come rushing out of the darkness and attack her.

As she looked into the dark shadows of the doorway, she made out a shape in front of the door. She thought she could see it moving, but it could have been her eyes playing tricks on her. Then she saw it and knew someone had been there.

Jonathan.

He had left something for her: a huge bouquet of roses, so many in number that they looked more like a rosebush than a flower arrangement. Sue could barely get around the arrangement to open the door. She slipped past and got the key in the door. She opened it and picked up the bouquet. Sue carried the flowers over to the dining room table and set them down. She plucked the card from the elegant silk bow and opened it.

It read:

My dearest Sue,

I am so sorry for the dreadful way I acted tonight. I had no right to intrude on you at your job. It's just that I haven't seen you enough recently and I had planned a special evening for us. Please accept these roses as a token of my great love for you and as an offering of forgiveness for my boorish actions at the hospital.

I love you.
Jonathan.

Sue's anger melted. Jonathan had apologized, a first for him. Usually after they had an argument, he would act as though it had never happened, especially when he was the one who'd been wrong. He must have realized that tonight's little incident was a big mistake and was trying to make amends. Although Jonathan didn't mention the fight, it was still definitely a step in the right direction. After all, the policeman did throw the first punch, even if he did have every right to do so after the comments Jonathan had made. The important thing was that Jonathan realized that he was wrong and was trying to make things right. The least Sue could do would be to forgive him and see if he was truly trying to change his ways. She would call him in the morning, but for now she needed to get some sleep. The sun would be coming up very soon.

3

The alarm bell rang. Its sudden disruption of the solitude of Reggie's bedroom caused Carver's heart to jump.

It was 5:30 in the morning.

As he reached out from under the covers to hit the snooze button, he thought about how more people died of heart attacks in the morning than at any other time of the day. His pounding heart told him why. Reggie slammed down the snooze button. Five more minutes . . . that was all he needed. As he laid his head back down, he felt the pain in his jaw where the doctor's dickheaded boyfriend had nailed him. The pain did a beeline over to his nose, which throbbed in alternating rhythm to his jaw. As the twin bongos of pain played a marimba across his face, he turned over on his back and closed his eyes. The pain drained away like something was sucking it out of the back of his head. Maybe he could get some shuteye.

As he drifted off, the room began to get louder, as it does sometimes just before you fall asleep. The refrigerator sounded like a generator in a factory. The faucet was a waterfall cascading down a mountainside. Gradually the noise faded and Reggie slept . . . for a moment.

The alarm went off, sounding like a church bell that was being kicked by Quasimodo. Carver lurched up from the bed and slammed his hand down on the clock. The ringing clock stopped, but its loud ticking reminded Reggie that it would be back to haunt him again another day.

Wiping the sleep from his eyes, he got out of bed and shuffled off toward the shower. Reaching in, he turned the hot water on. As the water heated up, he added a touch of cold. The shower in his apartment was about as predictable as a schizophrenic impressionist. One day it would take even amounts of hot and cold water to get the right temperature, other days all hot and a half turn of cold. He touched the water spraying out of the faucet. It was incredible. The temperature was just right. Reggie took off his red briefs and stepped into the shower. He pushed the shower button in and a blast of cold water hit him, shriveling his balls into wrinkled walnuts. As the water warmed up, they went back to normal. He picked up the bar of soap and lathered up, letting the hot water hammer against the sore muscles of his neck and back. Reggie could feel the tension melt away. He started to sing an old Al Hibler tune called "After the Lights Go Down." Reggie had been a Hibler fan ever since his old friend Howard Goldberg had played an album by the big band singer for him. As Reggie sang, he had a feeling that today was going to be a great day.

4

Chris sat on the edge of his bed and wondered what he was going to do. He glanced at the clock.

6:00.

Chris walked to the window of his apartment and stared outside. The sun was coming up. He felt a strange tingle all over his body. His head felt light. What was wrong? The sun peeked out from behind the old McDuffy building. A beam struck Chris's hand. It felt as though someone had slammed a red-hot poker onto it. Chris recoiled and slammed the

81

shutters closed. The room turned black as pitch.

All policemen had some type of shutters, curtains, or blinds to keep out the sun in case they pulled night duty and had to sleep during the day. In this instance, the shutters saved Christopher Blaze from incineration. He didn't know it, but if the sun's rays had hit him full force, he wouldn't have been able to pull the shutters closed and would've been burnt to a crisp.

All of a sudden the urge to sleep overwhelmed Chris. He barely made it to his bed before he collapsed into a deep sleep.

As he lay there, there wasn't a sound in the room. No faucets dripping, no radio playing and . . . no breathing.

It was the sleep of the dead.

5

Reggie finished shaving and gingerly slapped on some cologne. His jaw was still tender from his battles of the night before. Quickly getting dressed, he slammed down a couple of Pop-Tarts, a glass of milk, and a banana and left for work. He passed Mrs. Kowalski in the hallway.

"Hello, Reginald. How are you?" the little old lady said as she swept a cloud of dust onto Reggie's polished shoes.

"Just fine, Mrs. Kowalski. How about you?" he brushed the dust off his shoes.

"Oh, I can't complain," she said, "even though my back feels like a piano is resting on it and my arthritis is acting up, I'm just fine. Except that the old knee has been giving out."

Everyday she couldn't complain, Reggie mused, and everyday she did. Mrs. Kowalski continued her litany of ailments as Reggie walked toward the exit. He waved to her. "Hope you feel better soon, Mrs. K."

"Oh, I feel fine, except for the headaches I get."

Her voice trailed off as the door slammed behind him.

The sun was shining brightly and the sky was as blue as a robin's egg. Yes, Reggie thought, this was going to be a great day.

Sue woke up just at about the same time Reggie had received the worst news of his career. A strip of yellow sun dotted with dust cut a path directly into Sue's eyes and awakened her. She walked over to the Levelor blinds and pulled them shut. She glanced over at the clock.

12:30.

She had better get up.

There was a loud knock on her door.

"Damn! I must look a mess," she said as she grabbed a brush and started trying to style her hair.

"Just a minute!"

"Sue, it's me," a muffled voice said through the door.

Jonathan, she said to herself as she went to the door and opened it.

A box of her favorite chocolates from Givenios greeted her.

"Forgive me?" Jonathan said, smiling.

She returned the smile and invited him in. He stepped through the door and they kissed.

Then, for the first time in two weeks, they made love and it was good.

7

It was bad, Reggie knew as soon as he stepped into Captain Draper's office. Lieutenant Burnson was standing behind the captain. A pair of aviator sunglasses barely covered the nasty black eye that Reggie had given him. Burnson greeted him with a big smile that expressed joy and hatred at the same time. He looked like the cat that had just swallowed the canary . . . and the goldfish . . . and a can of Nine Lives' tuna deluxe.

"Sit down, Reggie," Draper said without looking up from his paperwork.

"What's this all about, Captain?" Reggie asked, trying to remain cool.

"It seems as if you and Lieutenant Burnson are unable to get along," the big cop said.

"No, we just have a slight difference in personalities. I have one and he doesn't."

Burnson actually laughed at the joke.

Something was definitely wrong.

"Reggie," Draper continued, "time after time I have told you to stop playing jokes on Charlie, and time after time you've continued."

"Ah, Captain—I was just having a little fun." Reggie sensed he was up shit creek without a paddle or even a boat. "I promise I won't do anything again."

"That's what you said the last time, right after you nailed his shoes to the floor."

"But, Cap . . ."

"Or there was the 'I'll never do it again' joke where you put a bag of dogshit in Charlie's desk."

"Yeah." Reggie couldn't help himself. "Took him a week to find out where the smell was coming from."

The black detective chuckled in spite of his predicament. "Ah, come on, Captain," he said, "they were just little jokes."

"Well, this isn't."

Draper looked at him with his huge, magnified eyes. "I'm assigning you to graveyard shift as of tomorrow night."

"Graveyard shift!" Reggie protested. "But you can't—I've worked hard to get where I am."

"You're a damn good cop, Reggie, but you have to learn to respect your superior officers."

"Burnson may be an officer, but he damned sure ain't superior."

Burnson laughed out loud, but didn't say a word.

Draper looked down again. "You'll report for duty to Watch Commander Brown at 10 P.M. tomorrow night. Dismissed."

As the stunned detective left the office and wandered to his desk, he said to himself, "Damn! Graveyard shift! Who the hell wants to work graveyard shift?"

"Graveyard shift? You want to work graveyard shift?" Draper said.

He couldn't believe his ears. Earlier that day at 12:30, he had sent one of his best detectives to work graveyard shift as a punishment. Now, at 6:30, another one of his best men was volunteering for the late-night stint. "May I ask why?" he said to Chris.

Blaze shifted in his seat. "It's really private, Tom. I just need to work nights for a while."

"What is it?" the captain asked, concerned about his friend. "Can I help?"

God, I wish you could, Chris thought, but said, "No—It's just something I have to deal with."

"C'mon, Chris, we've been through a lot together," Draper said, then added, "Besides, you still owe me another favor for the second time I saved your life."

"Okay," Chris weakened, then lied. "I've developed an allergic reaction to the sun."

"What?"

"I've developed a reaction to sunlight due to the stress of my job. It's called 'PMLE.'"

"Which means?"

"Polymorphous light eruption, and I'm afraid I've got it."

Chris had gone to the library prior to coming in to work to see if there was such a thing as someone being allergic to the sun. He had looked it up in several medical dictionaries and found that there was such an allergy. He knew it sounded absurd that all of a sudden this allergy had just come over him, but the truth would have sounded a whole helluva lot stranger. Besides, because of its absurdity, it was just weird enough to be true.

"Son-of-a-bitch. When did you find this out?"

"This morning. I went out in the sun to get some things at the store and I felt really strange. A couple of hours later I broke out in a rash and felt sick to my stomach. So I went back home and called a doctor. He came over and took a look at me."

"A doctor made a housecall?"

Draper sounded as though he found this harder to believe than Chris's story about the allergy.

"Yes, I explained what happened. He told me a bunch of mumbo-jumbo about PMLE, photoallergic reactions, eczematous lesions. The bottom line is that I have to stay out of the sun."

Draper scratched his head. "Well, I'll be dipped in dogshit."

"So, how about it, Captain?"

"Sure, Chris, you got it, no problem. Just report to watch Commander Brown at 10:00 tomorrow night.

"Thanks, Captain," Chris said as he got up to leave. "I'd appreciate it if you would keep this under your hat."

"Sure," Draper said, then added, "Can't they give you any medication?"

"No, it just has to run its course. See you later."

As he watched Chris disappear into the crowded chaos of the squad room, he shook his head.

"Allergic to the sun. I'll be a son-of-a-bitch."

Chapter 7

1

A storm had come up suddenly that night and it was a real
burner. Lightning sizzled. Thunder crashed. Rain poured.
And Millie Carpenter died.

Millie was a waitress at Sardino's Italiano Emporium. She
had just gotten off work and was heading toward the bus
station. A looker, as her boyfriend called her, Millie was a
tall woman with a slinky walk that no doubt added greatly to
her tip coffers. She had large breasts that swayed in perfect
rhythm to her particular sexy style of walking. Blue eyes,
blond hair, a real looker. Millie had been born and raised in
Miami and knew well of its treacheries. The small .22-caliber
pistol she carried assured her that she was well equipped to
deal with anyone who attempted to deal on her.

As the rain came down, she walked with confidence
toward the bus station. The rain had kept most everyone off
the streets, but Millie was in a hurry to get home. The rain
didn't bother her; she had a man waiting for her at home with
hot food and a hot body.

Lightning flashed.

Thunder roared.

Millie rounded the corner of 22nd Street as another bolt of
lightning lit the streets for a brief moment. Did she just see
someone behind her during the flash? The thunder roared
again. Another huge bolt of lightning crashed so close she

felt her hair tingle from the sudden dispersal of ions. The lights on the block went out. Total darkness engulfed Millie. The street was a black abyss into which Millie plunged deeper.

As the rain drummed down on the sidewalk, she thought she heard someone walking behind her. Millie whipped around. She peered into the pitch black, squinting hard, as if to draw the image in through sheer force of her will.

Lighting lit the area for a brief second.

No one was there.

She continued to walk. There really was no reason to be afraid, she thought as she pulled the gun from her purse. Millie practiced at the gun range twice a week and could hit in the black five out of six shots. Still, fear gnawed at her like a giant rat, digging into her bit by bit, chunk by chunk, scurrying and digging its claws into her trying to get inside.

Then she heard the footsteps again. Someone was definitely behind her. She could hear their footsteps breaking in every so often over the sound of the pouring rain. She picked up her pace.

Why doesn't someone fix the power, her mind cried out. Millie had the gun in front of her and walked as quickly as she dared in the pitch black. The hairs on her neck stood up and tingled. The sense of doom and the oncoming burst of lightning worked together to elevate her fear ever higher.

The rat was almost inside her.

The lightning flashed and the terrified waitress thought she had seen someone. As she closed her eyes, her mind revealed a negative of what the lightning had briefly burned into her retina. There had been something.

2

Chris Blaze walked the streets, his mind a jumbled mess of electron snafus and synapses that didn't seem to connect. He was a real vampire, or so it seemed. Batiste Legendre had been strong enough and the god Cannus real enough to make it so.

Blaze felt a deep urge in him that he couldn't quite understand. It was as if he had not eaten for days and his appetite was huge. He had tried to choke down a couple of hot dogs, but nothing would stay with him. He couldn't eat or drink. His stomach growled as if it were furious with him for not knowing how to relieve the pain.

Then the answer came with such a hideous clarity Chris almost turned and ran. But you couldn't run from your destiny. He knew what his body needed, and he knew what he had to do to get it.

3

The gun in her hand was shaking from a mixture of fear and cold, heavy on the fear. The change in temperature signaled that the cold front was pushing its way through. The rain was coming down heavier than before, obscuring everything else. Where the hell were the cars? Millie wondered. This was Miami, for Christ's sake. She didn't know that the street she had chosen as her path was under repair. No cars would be coming through.

A trashcan tumbled behind her.

She whirled around. Her finger almost squeezed the trigger.

The blackness concealed everything.

She waved her hand in front of her as if she could part the black pitch and see what was there. Her heart hammered in her chest as if it were trying to escape, knowing that soon it would beat no more. She turned.

Lightning flashed.

He was there.

His red eyes gleamed into hers.

She fired just as there was a huge crash of thunder.

Her shots were obscured. His powerful hand seized the gun from her grasp, crushing her hand like it was a brittle twig. The bones stuck out of her skin like pins in a pincushion.

She tried to scream, but a hand clasped her mouth shut.

She gagged as she felt stiff, bristly hairs on the palms. The creature pushed her head back to expose her throat, snapping her spine.

Then he drank.

4

He had not found the taste as unpleasant as he'd thought it would be. It had not been bad, and it had quenched the awful thirst that had burned his stomach. And it had been so easy. Still, it had all seemed like a dream. The break-in, the burglary, taking what he needed. The only strange thing was the two jolts he had felt in his chest, two strange thumps that had force, but no pain, as if he had been shot in the chest with an air gun. Had he imagined that? And what about the strange face of the woman that had flashed in his mind? His thoughts seemed to run together and then separate like oil and vinegar. Had he gone to the hospital and taken the blood, or was that just something his mind had dreamed up to cover a more horrible reality?

He was a vampire, and vampires needed blood.

He shut his eyes tightly, as if to drive his thoughts out in some coherent pattern. Who was the girl? What was the strange double thump to his chest? Had he kil . . .

He couldn't finish that thought. He chose to believe that a vampire hadn't committed any murders that night.

He was wrong.

5

Charlie Burnson was zipping up his pants. He had just given the old boneroonie to one of the little groupies who liked to hang out at the sports bar. *Yes siree,* he thought to himself, *this has been a great day. Got drunk, got laid, and got the little nigger. A three-for-one special.*

"Do you have to go, Looey?" A thin nasily voice cracked the stale air of the sleazy hotel room.

90

"Yep, police business, honey. You understand."

"Oh, sure I do. I used to work in receiving, you know," she said, hoping to impress the policeman.

"Did you? That's great."

He smiled to himself as he thought, *Yeah and you still do. You just received the Burnson sausage and a special surprise to go with it.* He knew he still had the clap, but he didn't care. The little slut deserved to get it. Charlie decided that he would wait until he had infected all the little sluts of the world before he cleared up the disease.

Charlie was insane.

The girl purred, running a wet finger between the lips of her labia. "Are you sure you can't stay? I'm still horny."

Burnson felt a twinge in his old boneroonie and began to unzip his pants. He knew he would be able to get it up again.

Yessiree, he thought. *This was one special day.*

6

While Charlie Burnson was giving the little groupie a double whammy, Sue Catledge was looking through wedding books, trying to find a pattern for her china. Things had gotten much better between her and Jonathan after his fight with that black detective. He had apologized. They had made love like they'd used to make love. And tonight he had taken her to a play and treated her like a queen. He even mentioned helping her raise funds for the hospital. Perhaps he realized how angry she'd been and didn't want to lose her because he loved her so much.

Then another thought crept out, just long enough to throw a monkey wrench into her bliss. Maybe he just didn't like to lose.

Damn, must you always be so cynical, Sue Marie? The guy is crazy about you, and he's a good friend. You're picking out patterns, aren't you? And besides that, he's rich, the little voice in her head said. Her mother's voice.

Sue continued thumbing through the magazine, but she wasn't concentrating on flatware. She was thinking that no matter what she said, thought, or did, she could never love Jonathan the way she knew she would have to love someone in order for her to spend the rest of her life with him.

She closed the magazine, picked up the phone, and dialed Jonathan's number. As it rang, she hoped she would have the courage to go through with what she knew she had to do.

Her fiancé answered his phone. "Hello."

"Hello, it's me. We have to talk."

7

It was almost sunup. Chris got the strange tingling, as before. He knew that soon the sun would be creeping over the horizon with its killing rays that could reduce him to a pile of ash. *That wouldn't be so bad,* Chris thought. *What if I did kill someone?* No! He wouldn't allow himself to believe that. He was still the same man he'd been before the curse changed him. Only now he had a disease, and diseases could be cured. If he just gave up and let the sun do its dirty work, Legendre would win even from the grave. At that moment Chris decided to fight the curse.

He headed for his cramped apartment and safety from the sun. As he approached the Carfax Apartments, he smiled ironically as he thought of what he used to call the "tiny efficiency" where he lived. The nickname he had chosen was "Christopher Blaze's coffin." It was a most appropriate choice, now that he was one of the undead.

8

Jonathan could not believe his ears. She was calling the wedding off. The bitch was on the phone at 5:30 in the morning, telling him she didn't love him like a husband, but like a good friend, and that she couldn't marry him. All the arrangements had been set, all the plans made, all the invitations sent. But this woman was calling it off. He would look like a jilted fool in front of society. Oh, poor Jonathan, he could hear them say, poor rejected Jonathan. The thought made him cringe. He had to get her back, if only to marry her and divorce the ungrateful slut within a few months. He had to save face. Jonathan turned on his considerable charm.

"Sue, please listen to me. I love you more than anyone I have ever known. It doesn't matter to me if you love me as a friend right now. To me that's enough. I know you loved me before, and I can make you have those feelings again. I want you for my wife so that you'll be with me for eternity."

"But Jonathan, I can't . . ." Her voice was weakening.

Jonathan smiled, returned to his role of lovelorn suitor, and zeroed in for the kill. "Just have dinner with me tomorrow night. I'll pick you up at 7:30. Please, you owe me that much."

She hesitated, then relented. "Okay, but I don't think it's going to work."

Jonathan narrowed his eyes and grinned. He looked like a snake in a bird's nest. *Oh yes, it will, my darling,* he thought. *It will work like a charm.*

Chapter 8

1

The air hissed as it filled his inert lungs. His eyes opened suddenly. He got up. There was no need to check the time. Chris knew night had fallen. He ran his hand through his hair and walked to the bathroom. He didn't feel the need to pee . . . it was just habit. Realizing he didn't have to go, Chris decided to take a shower. He bent over and turned the knobs on the shower. The pipes shuddered, and the water burst out. Chris got in. The water was scalding hot, but he didn't notice. He quickly soaped up and rinsed off. The hot water was a force against his body, but it did no damage. Chris poured a dab of shampoo into his hand and placed it on top of his hair. He scrubbed it into a rich lather and let the water rinse it out.

Stepping out of the shower, he grabbed a fresh towel and dried off. He picked up his comb and closed the mirrored medicine cabinet. No one stared back. *Shit!* Chris thought, *how the hell am I going to comb my hair if I can't see what it looks like?*

Chris decided the easiest thing to do would be to put gel in his hair and comb it straight back. His new styling requirement reminded him of Tony Mancetti and the night they'd both died. The only thing was, Chris had come back. Squeezing a glob of gel into his hands, he rubbed them together, coating his palms. Chris ran his gel-coated hands through his hair, smoothing it in. He pulled the comb through straight back and gingerly touched it to see if it was staying in place. It was.

He slipped on a black t-shirt, a pair of faded jeans, his tennis shoes, and his shoulder holster with the .38 packed in it.

Tonight was his first night on the graveyard shift. He wondered how he would fare as the first vampire cop in the history of the Miami Police Department.

2

Reggie Carver didn't get out of bed as easily as Christopher Blaze. He had had trouble trying to get to sleep in the middle of the day. He tossed and turned, trying to convince himself it was time to get some shuteye. But his clock knew it was 3:30 P.M. and it wasn't fooled by the dark curtains or the hissing snow-filled television screen that Reggie had purposely turned on in the hopes that the monotony would lull him to sleep. It was no use. It was about 7:30 that evening when he finally drifted off to sleep. But not for very long.

The alarm went off with a thunderous clanging. Reggie lurched awake. It was 9:30 and he suddenly realized that he had to be at work in thirty minutes. For some strange reason he had thought the graveyard shift was at midnight, the witching hour. He had set his alarm for 9:30 to give himself time to get dressed, get a bite to eat, and maybe even a little coochie from the new girl he was dating. Now he barely had time to get a shower and a burger from Mickie D's, let alone have a little fun with Tracy.

He hurriedly showered, dressed, and headed out the door, grabbing his windbreaker as he left for his first night on graveyard duty.

The dress Sue had chosen was a deep scarlet affair that matched her shoes perfectly. She draped the white scarf over her shoulder, as was the fashion. Her hair was perfectly coiffed. She looked in the mirror and had to admit that she did look good. Gorgeous was what she would have thought, if not for her Midwestern modesty. Jonathan would be by soon to take her to "Chez," the trendy French restaurant downtown. She tightened her belt and her resolve. She was going to end her engagement to him tonight.

The doorbell rang at exactly 7:30. He was prompt, as usual. Sue opened the door and was greeted by a beautiful orchid corsage. Jonathan smiled and pinned it to her dress. It matched her outfit perfectly. Jonathan kissed her lightly. "You look absolutely beautiful tonight, Sue."

"Thank you." She smiled.

Jonathan was dressed to the nines, in an expensive tailored suit, alligator shoes from Italy, a silk tie with the little tietack she had given him after their first year together. It was a tennis racket, in honor of the first time they met. The handsome playboy gallantly gestured toward the door. "Shall we go?"

"Let me get my purse," Sue said. She scooped her handbag off the couch and tucked it under her arm. "I'm ready."

Jonathan opened the door for her. As she passed him, he smiled to himself. This would be like taking candy from a baby.

4

Reggie flagged down a cab. Normally he would take his car, but it was in the shop. He hoped he could make it to the shift briefing on time, because he'd heard that Watch Commander Brown was not a man who put up with tardiness. The scoop around the station was that if you were late to a Brown briefing he would change assignments and give you the worst detail, usually wino detail. God, that was terrible.

The bums usually were docile enough, but they had that smell to them, the sickly combination of fermented wine, aged body odor, filthy clothes, and the intangible smell of hopelessness that clung to street people like a leech. Many years ago, Reggie had worked at a liquor store when he was in college studying for his law enforcement degree. He remembered that smell and how it lingered on long after the alcohol soaked derelicts left with their bottle of MD 2020 or Thunderbird. It hung in the air with a life all its own, waiting to land on another of the numerous alcoholics who entered and infested them with the disease of futility.

A cab pulled up to the curb. Reggie jumped into the back.

"Fifth Precinct station, buddy, and step on it."

The cabbie nodded, tripped the meter, and gunned the gas.

Reggie arrived at the station at 9:55 and hustled out of the cab.

"That'll be four bucks, pal," the cabbie said through teeth that clenched a cigar.

"Here you go," Carver said as he tossed the cabby a ten by mistake. "Keep the change."

"Thanks," the cabbie grinned.

As the cabbie was about to drive off, Reggie realized his error. "Hey, wait a minute," he said, then thought for a second and waved the cabbie to go. Getting change from a cabbie was a three-minute procedure at best, five minutes if you were asking the driver to give you back the six dollars he thought you'd given him as a tip. He didn't have time.

"Thanks again, mister." The cabbie pointed his finger at Reggie and pulled the trigger. He drove away.

Carver smiled halfheartedly and started to run toward the precinct door. When he got inside, he moved like a halfback through a wave of defenders on his way to a touchdown, cutting in and out of the cops and perpetrators that cluttered the precinct. As Reggie entered the briefing room, his special watch played "Dixie" as it struck ten. He clicked off the alarm and sat down. He looked around the room and saw a sea of unfamiliar faces. Next to him was a blond guy with slicked-back hair and strange blue eyes. He had a haunted look about him, as though he had a horrible secret he was trying to conceal. Reggie hoped he didn't get assigned to work with this chump. He looked like he had big problems, and Reggie had already had a partner with big problems once. He didn't need that mess again.

"All right, gentlemen," Commander Brown boomed. "Here are the assignments for the night."

Brown was a former basketball star for the University of Florida who had once been destined for the NBA, until his destiny exploded along with his knee in a pickup game at the YMCA. The injury was bad enough to prevent him from being drafted into the pros. In time the injury healed, but not soon enough for him to play pro basketball. He was too old to start over, and besides, the scouts were wary of a player with an injury as extensive as his. So he joined the police department. The years had added a couple of pounds to his stomach, but he was still an imposing figure. At six-five and 275 pounds, and as black as the night, Brown commanded attention. He read the duty roster in a clear, deep baritone that rumbled through the squad room. "Cohn, you and Harrelman are gonna be on the Grigsby thing. Hacker, you and Piler will stay on the murder of that Haitian down in Freedomtown." He went down the list of detectives, reading assignments. When he had finished, he added, "One more thing, we have two more fellow officers joining us on our happy shift. Detective Reggie Carver."

Carver stood up. "Thank you, thank you. I'd like to thank everyone involved in allowing me to work at this ungodly hour."

The other cops cheered. Brown froze the smile on Carver's face with his steely glare. Reggie sat down.

Brown continued. "And Sergeant Chris Blaze."

Chris nodded to the crowd.

Brown tapped his forehead with his index finger. "Oh, yeah, a couple more things . . ." As Brown continued with a lecture on procedure in a car search, Chris's stomach began to ache with the need for blood. He grabbed his midsection, bent over, and hammered his fist on the desk.

Reggie noticed him and thought to himself that Blaze was

98

hurting for something, just like his old . . .

The thought was cut off by Brown's deep-throated voice. "By the way, Carver, you and Blaze are going to be partners."

Shit! Reggie thought, *I knew I'd get stuck with that guy.* He looked over at his new partner warily. Blaze glanced up and forced a smile. Reggie just knew this guy was trouble, but he would make the best of it. He extended his hand.

"How do, partner," Reggie said.

Chris grasped his new partner's hand and the smile fell away from the black man's face as he felt the cold grasp of Christopher Blaze.

This guy was definitely jonesing for something, Reggie thought to himself.

"Good working with you," Chris said, then grunted vaguely.

"All right, you guys," Brown boomed. "Let's do it. And remember . . ."

The men finished his Hill Street Blues line for him.

"Be careful out there," they said in unison.

Brown looked down at his pad, embarrassed. "Uh, right."

The cops filed out and the graveyard shift began.

5

Reggie got into the driver's side of the 1987 model Ford LTD that was one of the many that the station house assigned to its plainclothes detectives. Chris got in on the other side. He was concentrating with all his might to stem the tide of the hunger that gnawed at his guts. Reggie looked over at his partner, who was visibly in pain.

"Hey, you okay, man?" he said.

"Fine," Chris replied, "Can we just get going?"

Carver shrugged. "Whatever rings your bell."

Reggie cranked the engine and backed out of the precinct parking lot. Yeah, Reggie knew this dude was jonesing, just like Rizzo used to do. He didn't want to mess with that shit again.

When Reggie had first joined the force, he had been assigned with a lifer, a twenty-year man by the name of Alphonse "Big Al" Rizzo. Rizzo was a semi-legend around the precinct. He had been a head knocker who had kept his beat clean for many years, but as Carver was to find out, the years of stress had taken their toll on the big cop, and he'd started to nip the bottle. As they patrolled the streets in their black-and-white, Carver noticed that Big Al was subject to mood swings and stopped frequently. He always claimed that he had to go the pisser or take care of a little business. At first Reggie hadn't thought much about it. But the stops became more frequent, and Rizzo grew sullen and morose. After each stop he would come back sucking on a breath mint or smoking a big, smelly cigar. Reggie had wanted to tell someone about his suspicions, but he had no real evidence. To go against a police legend like Big Al Rizzo without proof was like taking on Godzilla with a cap pistol. He would most definitely lose. Then one night when their patrol car was stopped in front of a little bar where Big Al had stopped "to make a personal phone call," they got a call to break up a fight in progress. Carver had gone into the bar to retrieve his wayward partner, but found him passed out in front of a half-empty bottle of Scotch. Unable to rouse the big guy, Reggie left him there and went to the scene of the altercation. When he got there, he saw three guys beating the living shit out of one unfortunate dude. Reggie called for a backup and then intervened. The trio decided they had had enough fun with the one guy and attacked Carver. Reggie had spent the next week in the hospital for treatment of the terrible beating he'd received from the hands, feet, and elbows of the three thugs. When he got out, he was determined to have it out with Rizzo and see that he got help, but it wasn't necessary. Two days earlier, Sergeant Alfonse Rizzo, supercop, had swallowed his police special and blown his brains out against the bathroom stall of a sleazy bar. Reggie had cried when he heard the news. He should have said something earlier and tried to help Rizzo. But he hadn't, and Rizzo had ended up dead.

Reggie Carver didn't want to deal with another cop with a

monkey on his back. Little did he know that his new partner, Chris Blaze, was giving a piggyback ride to King Kong.

6

Wadsworth's sleek XJ5 pulled up to valet parking at Chez, the chic French restaurant where all the "haves" ate and the "have-nots" wanted to eat. The valet opened the door for Sue and she got out. The attendant, a spry young high school senior, Ben Lewis, hurried to the driver's side. Jonathan got out and Ben hopped in. As the valet drove away, Jonathan offered Sue his arm. She took it and they went into the restaurant.

The owner of Chez was Battello Marucci, an Italian who thought his people could cook better food than the French, even French cuisine. He had opened Chez three years ago to prove it, and fortunately for him, it had become the place to go. Marucci had decorated the restaurant like an old Italian courtyard, which was part of the reason why it had hit the charts on the trendometer. The yuppies thought the combination of Italian decor and French food was so strange, so hip, that they flocked in droves to be able to tell their pals at work that they had been to Chez. One thing was true: Battello had served some of the best French cuisine in the entire state and had won the Golden Spoon Award every year since he'd opened the restaurant.

The maître'd showed Jonathan and Sue to their table. They sat down and immediately a waiter was at tableside.

"What may I get you from the bar?" he lisped in a voice better suited to a waitress.

"We'll have a bottle of Mouton Rothschild '63."

"Very good, sir," the waiter said, then swished away.

"Jonathan, I don't think I'm going to change my mind about . . ."

He cut her off. "Sue, let's not talk about it now. Please, let's just try to enjoy the evening. At least for a little while."

He was right, she thought. He deserved at least that.

The wine came and the waiter popped the cork, giving it to

Jonathan for his approval. He sniffed it, nodded, and handed it back. The waiter smiled and poured them each a glass. The red wine matched the color of Sue's dress perfectly: from Jonathan's vantage point, it looked as though she had an empty glass in front of her. She picked up her glass and sipped the wine.

"No, Sue, please allow the wine to breathe," Jonathan said so instinctively that he could have kicked himself. He knew she hated it when he reprimanded her for not having the knowledge that was second nature to him. Here he was, trying to get her back, however temporarily, and he was reminding her of one of their major bones of contention, the differences in their cultural upbringing.

Sue set down the wineglass.

"Thanks for reminding me. It does taste much better when it breathes."

Good, he thought . . . she wasn't angry. He would still be able to win her back, and he intended to do just that.

7

"Pull over!" Chris commanded Reggie Carver.

"What is it?" Reggie's eyes combed the street for the source of his partner's alarm. There was nothing there.

"Pull over! Now!"

"All right, hold your horses."

The black cop whipped the car over to the curb. Before it stopped, Chris was out of the vehicle and running.

"Hey, Blaze, hold on," Reggie shouted. "Damn."

Reggie picked up the radio and called in to dispatch and told them that they were on break.

Chris Blaze passed a girl on his way into the alley. She smiled and offered her services. Blaze refused as politely as a starving vampire could, then ducked into the alley.

The vampire detective was nowhere to be seen as Carver drummed on the dashboard. "Man, I am definitely not going through this bullshit again."

After a few minutes, Reggie saw Chris come out of an alley

wiping his mouth. Blaze walked toward the Ford. Reggie got out and stood arms on the door. "Man, where the fuck did you go?" Reggie's irritated tone demanded an instant answer.

"I'm sorry," Chris replied, "I just felt sick to my stomach. I had to get out."

"Look man, if you've got a problem, you'd better tell me about it now."

"Okay, but you're not going to believe it."

8

The meal had been superb. The duck was done to perfection, and the asparagus with hollandaise melted in her mouth. For dessert, Jonathan ordered Crêpes Suzette. They were just as heavenly as the rest of the dinner. Jonathan knew the way to romance better than most, and he really poured it on. A trio of violinists played tableside. A dozen roses were delivered. It was a grand show, and he knew she would be his again by the end of the night.

"More wine?" he asked.

"Thank you."

She held out her glass. "Jonathan, can we talk now?"

The trio struck up "As Time Goes By," and Jonathan topped off her third glass of wine.

"In a little while, please, let's just enjoy the music."

"Okay, but I want to talk soon," she said, and took another sip of wine.

9

"Allergic to the sun from stress?" Reggie cried. "Man, what do you take me for?"

"Reggie, I swear it's the truth."

As they cruised, Blaze explained his illness. "Sometimes," he said, "I get queasy from the medication I have to take. It makes me feel a little claustrophobic."

"Uh-huh."

Reggie looked at Chris through the skeptical eyes of a man who had heard every excuse in the book.

"You can believe me if you want to." Chris said.

Reggie stared out the window, then said, "Look, let's just forget about it, okay?"

"Fine. Let's roll."

They drove down Dade Boulevard, checking for illegal activity. Neither man spoke until they got the call from dispatch.

"2/25 Signal 5 at 1010 Flagler Place," the nasally voice of the dispatcher said. "All units be advised."

"Let's go!" Reggie said, pulling out the portable detective's light and sticking its magnetized bottom on the roof. Chris answered the call and switched on the siren. The Ford lurched as Reggie gunned the engine.

1010 Flagler Place. Chris's mind raced faster than the big 318 V8 under the hood of the LTD. That was where he'd just stopped to get blood from one of the bottles he'd stolen from the hospital, he was sure of it.

Or was he? Had he gotten his blood from the bottle? Perhaps the power of hunger had distorted his perception. Last night he had felt the strange air bullets and seen the face of the girl. Maybe they were the reality, and the clandestine trip to the hospital had been in his imagination. Perhaps he had killed the girl last night and then killed another one tonight. He didn't know.

"Up . . . Blaze." A voice bursted through his confusion, adding to it. "C'mon man, wake up!"

It was his partner. He shook Chris.

"Huh?" Chris awakened from his stupor.

"What's wrong with you, man? We're here."

How had the time gone by so quickly? Chris wondered. It was as if he had so much going on in his mind that it had become clogged, his thoughts mired in the sludge of madness. He couldn't focus.

"Blaze, are you coming?" Reggie asked, irritated.

Chris concentrated, and slowly his mind started to clear. He opened the passenger side and got out. The two cops walked to the alley where the police photographer was already snapping pictures.

"Hey Chris, isn't this the place we were just at?"

"Yeah, it sure is." He tried to sound cool, but his head throbbed.

"Damn," Reggie said, "if we'd been here an hour later we might have stopped this, or at least rounded up a couple of suspects."

Chris had one suspect in mind, but the thought skated away.

A crowd of onlookers had gathered, trying to get a glimpse of the dead girl who lay behind the dumpster. Chris waded through them and went over to where a patrolman was questioning an old man. The man was babbling to the policeman about a dark stranger. It seems he had stumbled upon the suspect in the act of jamming a wooden stick through the girl's chest. The old man had screamed. The suspect had gone for him, but then stopped short and was gone as quickly as a shadow in a floodlight. The old man hadn't gotten a good look at him, it had all happened so fast. Chris wanted to know more, particularly about the appearance of the killer.

As he advanced toward the old man, he was repelled by what was hanging down on a chain from the man's neck, a golden crucifix. The cross seemed to leap across the ten-foot span that separated it from Chris and slap him in the face. He reeled from the invisible blow. He looked again and the cross resumed the attack, crashing against him. Quickly Chris turned away and walked toward the alley.

He certainly couldn't approach the old man and his vampire repellent, so he turned his attention to the girl. The sight of her face hit him even harder than the cross. It was her—the girl he had seen in front of the alley. The hooker. She stared at him with dead eyes. Accusing eyes. Reggie Carver was examining the twin punctures on her throat. A piece of wood protruded from her chest.

"What the hell do you make out of this, Blaze?"

"Huh?" Chris was still stunned by the fact that he had killed an innocent human being. Maybe it would be better if he just let the sun swallow him up. He made up his mind that he would let the sun destroy him the next morning.

"What do you make of these marks?" Reggie said.

"Looks like a puncture of some kind."

"Brilliant deduction, Holmes. Man, they look like a bite or something."

"Could be."

"The weird thing is, there's no blood. No blood anywhere."

And Chris knew why.

But still it didn't make sense. He was sure he'd taken the blood from the bottle, and only enough to quench his thirst. Even now his stomach was protesting the lack of nourishment. If he had drained the girl he would be satiated. Then what could . . .

Suddenly an image burst into his mind, a pair of red eyes burning. A strange voice whispered into his brain. "Join me. Join me," the voice echoed in his mind.

"Another one!" he said aloud.

"What?" Reggie turned toward Blaze. "What's another one?"

"Huh?"

"You said 'another one.' Another what?"

Chris snapped his attention toward Carver. "Oh, I, uh, just meant another weird case."

"No kidding," Carver said, then turned his attention back to the crime scene.

In spite of the grisly corpse that lay in front of him, Chris's heart soared. He hadn't killed her. There was another vampire in the city who was somehow trying to communicate with him. He could feel its presence. It made sense: this other vampire was the one who had killed the girl. The old man had seen him, and luckily for him had been wearing the cross. It had stopped the vampire from killing him, just as it had stopped Chris from approaching the man to question him. Chris was sure he was right.

There was one other thing of which Christopher Blaze was sure. This other vampire was evil. Totally evil.

10

When she stood up, Sue knew she'd had too much to drink. She thought if she had a couple of glasses of wine it would bolster her courage to end it with Jonathan. But two soon turned to four and then five, and now she was bombed. She reached for her purse and knocked over a glass of water. Jonathan grabbed her arm and steadied her.

"C'mon, babe, let's get you home."

"Okay."

She held his arm and they walked out.

The valet pulled the Jaguar to the front and left the car running. He got out, took the five that Wadsworth held out, and started back to the lot to retrieve the Harrisons' Bentley. Jonathan gingerly put Sue in the car and got in. He put his foot down on the accelerator and the Jag headed for Jonathan's beachfront condo. Wadsworth pushed the Gato Barbieri cassette into the tape player. The sultry tones of the saxophone filled the car with their sensuality. Jonathan would take her to their romantic beach rendezvous where they had shared so many intimate moments. He hadn't counted on Sue getting bombed, but that could work to his advantage.

Sue's mind was confused by the alcohol. Maybe it was a mistake to end their relationship. He had been acting so nice recently. Maybe she should just move back the wedding date. It would give her more time to think. Jonathan was trying, and he hadn't tried for so long. She had loved him before . . . maybe she could find that love again. The alcohol was distorting her thoughts. She couldn't focus. Jonathan was talking to her, but she couldn't make out what he was saying. She leaned back in the chair to try and gather her thoughts and everything went black. She had passed out.

"So you got any theories?" Reggie asked as he stood next to the dumpster in the alley.

"Uh, no . . . not at the moment."

"It could be one of those cult groups getting blood for one of their weird rituals. You know anything about any cults around here, Blaze?"

"A little," Chris lied. He knew more about them than he cared to think about.

"But why the stabbing with the wood? And what made those two marks?"

Chris knew, but Carver would never believe him.

"I don't know, Reggie. It could be a psycho."

"Yeah, could be, or maybe we've got us a real life vampire running around the city." Reggie chuckled, then pretended to bring a cape to cover his face. *"Blah, Blah, I vant to suck your blood."*

Reggie's imitation of Bela Lugosi's vampire was distinctly lacking, but closer to the truth than he would ever know.

"What do you think, Chris? Maybe some guy out there thinks he's a vampire."

"It's possible, I guess."

The van from the morgue pulled up. Burke and Hare got out of the county "meat wagon," as it was called down at the station. The two attendants, actually Mark Thompson and Bill Harris, had been given the nicknames of the famous bodysnatchers by none other than Reggie Carver.

"Hey!" Carver shouted. "It's the Burke-and-Hare Show!"

"Howdy, Carver," Hare said in a dull voice, "where's the deceased?"

Reggie hiked a thumb toward the girl. "She's right over there."

"Thanks."

"Don't mention it." Reggie said, then turned to Chris. "So, how about my theory on the vampire?"

Chris didn't have time to answer. It was almost sunrise.

"I've got to go, Reggie." Chris said, walking toward the car.

"Why, man? We've still got reports to fill out."

"The sun will be coming up soon, and I can't afford to be out in it when it does."

"Oh, that's right," Reggie remembered, "that allergy thing."

Chris put his hand on Reggie's shoulder. "Could you do the report for me? I'll owe you one."

"Damned straight you will."

"You'll do it?"

"Yeah, I'll do it," Reggie said grudgingly.

Chris got into the car. "Do you think you can get a ride back to the station?"

"What? Why should I have to get a ride?"

"If I don't take the car, I'll never get back to my place before sunrise."

"Shit, man, that allergy is some funky shit." Reggie shook his head. "All right, go ahead. I can get a ride back with one of the lab boys."

Chris started the engine. "Thanks, Reg."

"You know, you are one strange dude, Blaze," the black detective said.

Chris pulled away from the curb and drove off.

Reggie said to himself, "Yep. One strange dude."

12

Yosekaat Rakz lay in his coffin thinking. He had made a mistake killing that girl and not disposing of the body where it would never be found, but he hadn't reckoned on the old man and his accursed cross. How he wished he could have twisted that old fool's head from his shoulders and crushed it like a grape, but the power of the crucifix was too much even for one who had lived as long as he had.

He was confused by the other, the one called Blaze. He was most surely a vampire, but when he had tried to communicate with him there had been no answer. He wondered if Blaze had understood the communication or if he had just chosen to ignore it. Perhaps it had been wrong for Rakz to try and exchange thoughts with the other so quickly. He didn't even know this vampire. The policeman might not have stepped over to the dark side and could try and harm him. It had just been so long since he'd felt the presence of one of his kind that he didn't even consider the consequences before he acted. He wouldn't make that mistake again.

Rakz wondered how the man had become one of the undead. He certainly hadn't bitten him, and even if he had, he always made sure his victims never rose again. He thought he was the last of his kind, but now there was someone else. Rakz couldn't figure it out. Perhaps someone had summoned a dark lord to do their bidding, but he knew of no one who possessed such powers.

The vampire policeman bothered him, but he let the matter rest. The sun was rising, and he had to sleep. He would deal with Christopher Blaze one way or the other. He closed the lid on his coffin. It slammed shut as the sun rose on another day.

13

Sue woke up disoriented at first, then gradually realized where she was. Jonathan Wadsworth the III was asleep next to her in the big waterbed. The surf crashed softly in the background. She was naked. Jonathan stirred next to her.

"Good morning, darling."

He brushed the hair from her eyes and kissed her cheek.

Sue rubbed her eyes. "Good morning. What am I doing here at the beach house?"

Jonathan smiled. "Why, I drove you here, don't you remember?"

Sue's memory was as thick as a bowl of lumpy pancake batter that had sat out all night. She could only remember small caches of the night. The delicious dinner. The musical trio at their table. The wine. Ouch, the wine. The last thought made her head hurt. There was absolutely nothing worse than a wine hangover. Your head felt like someone was sticking an air hose in your ear and trying to inflate your skull like a balloon.

"Ooooh," she moaned, "what a headache I've got."

Jonathan got up from the bed and went into the bathroom.

"You did have a little too much to drink last night, I'm afraid," he said loudly.

To Sue it sounded as if he was shouting into a megaphone inches from her ear. Her head exploded.

He emerged with a glassful of fizzing water.

She gulped down the salty, bubbly water and laid her head back down on the pillow.

"Did you really mean what you said last night about the wedding?" Jonathan asked hopefully, knowing damn well that she had said no such thing.

"What did I say? I don't remember."

"You don't remember? You said we would try and make it work."

Sue felt like a fool. She had remembered thinking something along those lines, but she wasn't sure . . .

Jonathan interrupted her thoughts. "Sue, I love you very much. All I ask is that you give me, give us, a chance. I admit I've been wrong about a lot of things, but I want to try and make it work. We've come so far together. I don't want to throw it all away."

The rich playboy was oozing with sincerity. He almost believed it himself.

Almost.

He knew that if he won her back, it would only be for the pleasure of giving her the ax later. Jonathan was a poor loser, and he was determined to win. He continued his plea. "I want us to be together, I can't imagine us apart. Don't you see, darling, I'm finally willing to accept you the way you are. I know I can't change you. I don't even know why I wanted to try. Please."

Now for the coup de grâce.

He cried.

111

Ever since he was a little boy, Jonathan had been able to cry at will. It helped him to get what he wanted when his overindulgent parents felt a twinge of guilt about spoiling their boy. Now it would come in handy once more to get him something that he wanted.

"Please," he cried, the tears streaming down his face. "Just one more chance."

It was a performance worthy of an Oscar.

She was moved. She had never seen Jonathan so touched, so vulnerable. She wiped away a tear from his cheek. "Okay, Jonathan." Her eyes were moist as well. "We'll try and make it work."

"Oh, darling, you've made me so happy."

He hugged her tight. Sue couldn't see the big smile that spread across his face. He had won.

Part 2

Chapter 1

1

The next month firmly established the team of Christopher Blaze and Reggie Carver as the star players on the graveyard shift. In that short time they made a number of busts that other divisions had been working on for months. They broke up a ring of car thieves that had been boosting expensive cars from their parking garages at night, dissolved a protection racket that had been shaking down small businesses, and nabbed a burglar-turned-rapist who had been prowling the Hallendale district.

Chris found Reggie to be a good partner but still thought the black man suspected him of taking a drink now and then. His partner's suspicions were well founded as Chris had secreted thermos bottles of plasma at various key locations on their beat. He had been forced to steal the blood from local hospitals and bloodbanks. He knew it was wrong, but the alternative was not even to be considered. Whenever the hunger threatened to overwhelm him, he would stop at the nearest location and drink enough blood to relinquish the agonizing grip of the hunger. *The hunger.* Chris had named his craving for blood after the Whitley Strieber book of the same name. The hunger was a feeling that was hard to describe. It felt like hunger pangs, but was much stronger. At first it burned into his stomach and spread throughout his body like an overdose of adrenaline, filling his mind with one thought: blood. When he was on call or couldn't get to one of his bottles for nourishment, the hunger would spread through him like a corrosive acid. Eating away at him. Tearing at his mind. At those times only the sheer force of his will kept him from ripping the throat out of the nearest human being and slaking his thirst with their blood. But those moments were rare. He usually kept the hunger under control and functioned as well as any other person. Of course, some things were different.

Chris had to avoid mirrors at all times. Someone would find it just a little suspicious that he cast no reflection. Also, he found that he couldn't go near a crucifix or garlic. Reggie had ordered a pizza once and Chris had nearly passed out from the garlic. He was weakened just being in the proximity of the pungent plant. Chris imagined that garlic was to him like kryptonite is to Superman in the comics, a force that could weaken or even kill if he was exposed to it long enough. The Superman comparison wasn't far from the truth as Chris discovered that he was almost as strong as the man of steel.

One evening while he was working out at the police gym, he found out that his "illness" had given him great strength. He had put 250 pounds on the bench press, his max, and had amazed himself by repping it ten times. Ten easy times. He could have kept going but thought it would be wise to quit, considering his workout partner Captain Draper had never seen him bench 250 pounds more than five times. Five very difficult times. Draper had commented on the strength increase but didn't find it unusual. He could rep 300 pounds ten times, no problem.

Curious to see just how strong he really was, Chris had gone into the gym late one morning when no one was there. He amazed himself by benching 800 pounds. Twice. He was definitely the man, or rather, the vampire of steel.

The police gym where Chris worked out was small and had only one mirror for the cops to check out their biceps and pecs. It was a shame when Chris had "accidentally" tripped and shattered it with a barbell. It would be weeks before they could requisition another one from the city. Chris didn't want one of his buddies to freak out when they looked in the mirror and saw a barbell loaded with weights moving up and down by itself in mid-air.

Chris was fairly happy, considering the circumstances. He was doing a good job at work. He had learned to deal with the curse by treating it as if it was a disease with which he had to live. The only thing that bothered him was the other vampire. True, there had been no other strange murders. At least, no one had found any more bodies and Chris hadn't felt the presence of the other vampire. Still, he knew that the other vampire had to have blood to exist, and that meant he would have to get it one way or another. Chris only hoped that the vampire would choose his way. But in his heart he knew the other vampire wouldn't.

2

During the same period of time, Sue Catledge had picked out the patterns for her china, her wedding dress, and the church where she would be wed, and she had called Chris Blaze. She couldn't believe she had done it. Calling a man out of the clear blue sky was definitely out of character for her, but she told herself that she just wanted to see how he was doing and talk a little while. No harm in that. It was a Thursday morning when she had gathered the courage to call. She had tried the precinct, but they'd informed her that Blaze was on night shift and told her to call him at the precinct after 9:30. Instead, she looked up his number in the phone book and called him at home. There had been no answer, so she had left a message on his machine.

Chris called her at 6:17 that evening, a little after the sun went down. He seemed excited that she'd called him. They asked each other how they were. Talked about how their respective jobs were going. The weather. Typical small talk. But as they conversed, they found out that they had a great deal in common. After an hour on the phone, Chris asked her to go to the movies with him the next night. Sue expected he would ask her out and prepared to tell him no. After all, she was soon to be Mrs. Wadsworth the third. The next night, she found herself sitting next to Chris Blaze in a theater watching the movie "Rain Man," the Academy Award winner starring Dustin Hoffman, and having a wonderful time. The young couple enjoyed each other's company immensely, so much so that Sue swore she would never go out with him again; she was to be married soon and couldn't possibly go out again. But that Saturday she and Chris had gone to a Miami Heat basketball game and then out to a late dinner. It was another wonderful date. They talked about so many different topics and every conversation was as interesting as the last one. Chris told her all about himself, his childhood growing up in a small Florida town, his job, his likes and dislikes. She was so easy for him to talk to that he opened up like a clam in a steambath. He even told her about his allergy to the sun so that she wouldn't wonder why they could never go out during the day.

In her years as a practicing MD, she had never treated a photoallergic person. She knew that such a condition existed but was not really familiar with its treatment. She decided she'd read up on it sometime, but at the moment she was having too much fun falling in love.

Sue also felt totally at ease with Chris and told him all about Indiana, her rough times at med school, the pain and the triumphs. She told him about how she met Jonathan and how he had helped her so much. And that he was a good man. When Chris asked her if she loved Jonathan, she said that she did . . . in a special way. Both of them knew what that meant, but Sue had promised Jonathan another chance and was trying to keep that promise. She told Chris that they could keep going out, but it would have to be on a "just-friends" basis.

They continued seeing each other regularly. They always had a great time except for when they talked about the future of their relationship. Chris would ask Sue about her impending marriage and she would always skirt the issue. He would press her, but she would never give him a straight answer. It got to be very frustrating for the police detective, and he thought he should probably just forget about Dr. Susan

Catledge. But he couldn't. She was the first woman he'd ever truly loved.

Chris wanted Sue very badly, but he knew it would never work. She was going to be married; he was married to his job. She was a doctor; he was a vampire. The usual incompatibility. And yet he still fell deeply in love with the beautiful angel who had once saved his soul from eternal damnation.

Sue suspected that she'd been in love with Christopher Blaze from the very first night he'd arrived at the hospital. He'd been so helpless, so vulnerable as the terrible dreams tormented him throughout the night. Even now, every so often, he would slip into a deep melancholy, as if he had some terrible burden or secret to bear. His crystal blue eyes would stare off into space searching for an answer to a question that seemed to have no answer. Sue knew that one day Chris would share his secret with her and that she would be able to help him overcome it.

It was three days before her marriage to Jonathan Wadsworth that Sue decided to call it off again. Only this time, nothing Jonathan said or did would change her mind. She was in love with Christopher Blaze, and it was the real thing.

3

Reggie Carver, in typical fashion, had made the best of a bad situation and had done well on the graveyard shift. He and his partner had made several good collars that would stick like glue in court. They were a good team, and they worked well together. Blaze still made the strange sudden stops for no apparent reason and would disappear for a short time. But he was always fine when he came back and never smelled of booze or chewed mints to cover up the smell if he had been drinking. After trying to follow Chris a few times, Reggie quit because he felt like he was spying. If his partner's stops didn't effect his work, then Reggie really had no reason to complain. Besides, if they kept up the good work, Reggie would soon be reassigned back to regular duty anyway, and he wouldn't have to worry about it. Still, he liked Chris. They got along well. If Blaze did have a drinking problem, maybe Reggie could help him get over it. He decided to play it cool and bring up the subject casually, just to test the waters. If Chris did have a problem, Reggie would do all he could to help him out. After all, they were a good team, and Chris was gonna help him get off the graveyard shift and back to regular duty.

4

The month had been a long one for the now quite mad Charlie Burnson. His wife had left him after learning of the gonorrhea. She didn't say a word, just packed and left. And it was all Reggie Carver's fault. Burnson's obsession for the hide of the black man had spread within him like a rotten fungus. Each time he heard of a righteous bust by the team of B and C, as Blaze and Carver were known around the station, his mind would swirl deeper and deeper into the whirlpool of insanity. His victory of Carver's assignment to graveyard shift was turning into a loss as Carver continued to show him up. During the day, Charlie was preoccupied with thoughts of the black detective. What was Carver doing? Had Carver made any good busts the night before? Why couldn't he be as lucky as Carver? Burnson pondered the questions over and over in his mind. His work began to slip, and he would receive constant reprimands from Captain Draper. Charlie couldn't accept the fact that no matter what he did he couldn't break the spirit of Reggie Carver.

And then there was the dream.

And each night it was the same.

Burnson would be making love to the beautiful Asian, May Ling. Kissing her. Licking her nipples. She would be wet with pleasure and would roll him over on his back and start giving him head until he was hard. Then she would mount him and slowly start to ride his firm member. She would slide up and down, increasing her speed as she bucked

120

furiously with pleasure. As the hooker rode him, Charlie would close his eyes with delight as he enjoyed the best sex of his life. When he opened them, May Ling was no longer a beautiful girl, but a horrible hag with sores bursting all over her face, her hair a stringy mess of thin snakes, her teeth the color of baby shit. She would keep riding him, all the time laughing in ecstasy. Then her joyous laughter would slowly pervert into the hideous cackling of contempt. As she bucked up and down, laughing at Charlie, her rotten teeth would fall out of her mouth onto his chest. The fetid brown chiclets would change into worms and bore into his body, chewing through his flesh. Then her entire face would blister and slough off. The gooey, bloody mess would land on his face, smothering him. Then they would all be there, laughing at him along with the hooker—Carver, Draper, Brown, and the others—the mouths growing and engulfing their bodies until they were just huge gums and teeth. Laughing. Screaming with laughter. Pounding against his eardrums. He would scrape away the mess from his face, and through the slimy haze he would see that May Ling had become a giant scab, caking off and crumbling onto his body. He would turn away and beside him he would see Reggie Carver, his face huge and distorted. He was laughing. Laughing at Charlie. Screaming, "Assface! Assface! Assface!"

Burnson would wake up screaming Carver's name and wouldn't stop until his throat was raw and ragged.

The dream of a madman.

It had been the night after B and C had busted Willie Tyler, the pimp/pusher, on possession charges that Charlie realized what he must do. He had been lying in bed when suddenly it had struck him. The thought crystalized in his mind and sparkled like a chandelier. He would have to murder the little nigger if he was to be free from him. He lay back on his pillow. The thought of jamming the barrel of his gun into the black bastard's eye and blowing the back of his head off sent a ripple of excitement through him. His cock was as hard as a diamond cutter when he freed it from his boxer shorts. He stroked it as he thought of bashing Carver on the head and tying him down. Then he would put on his cleated track shoes and run all over Carver's body as the cleats ripped away bloody chunks of flesh and muscle until Carver's insides were exposed. He continued to run in place, churning his feet into the guts of Reggie Carver, organs bursting open as he crushed them under foot. He climaxed as he jumped into the air and came crashing down on Carver's mouth, hard cleats snapping off teeth and driving them inward. The power of his orgasm almost caused him to pass out. That was the night Lieutenant Charlie Assface Burnson had started plotting the murder of Reggie Carver.

5

Burnson was not the only one who was interested in the team of Blaze and Carver. But it was for different reasons.

Things had gotten back to normal after the night Yosekaat Rakz had been discovered feasting in the alley by the old man with the cross. Since then he had been very careful to dispose of the women upon whom he had feasted, making sure to drive the ash stake cleanly through their hearts. Their untimely return would surely stir up trouble for him. As he thought about that night, he couldn't help but think about the vampire policeman Christopher Blaze. He wondered how long Blaze had been one of the undead. Rakz remembered how he had tried to communicate with him but had received no response. He didn't think Blaze understood the innate ability of vampires to communicate telepathically, to sense each other's presence. This was a sign that he was a relative newcomer to the world of the undead.

Rakz had been undecided if he should reveal himself to the vampire policeman and see if he would join forces with Rakz or if he should follow him and try and discover if the vampire could be trusted. He decided the latter would be more prudent and started to follow Blaze on his rounds at night. Rakz had discovered much about Christopher Blaze. The policeman drank from the bottle, a weakness. But perhaps he had yet to enjoy the feeling of draining a human being's life force. The sudden surge of overwhelming power. The feeling of rebirth each time you sucked every drop of warm blood from a living person. As he continued to watch Blaze, he discovered that the policeman was good at his job and seemed to enjoy it. This concerned him, because Blaze was still working in the human world instead of accepting his destiny and making the transition from mortal man into immortal being. The policeman had yet to embrace his power. Rakz knew that if he and Blaze joined forces, they could rule the city. Perhaps Rakz could show Blaze the way.

Rakz also discovered that Blaze had a girlfriend of sorts. He had never seen them kiss, but Rakz could sense the love the cop felt for this woman. It sickened him. Love was a weakness he could ill afford. Still, the girl fascinated him. She was most beautiful. And beauty was a thing he appreciated. He loved to own beautiful things. The first time he saw her he decided that he would want to own her, body and soul. Perhaps he would even share her with Blaze. It might be just the thing to draw out the dark side of the vampire cop's nature and allow him to shed the last vestiges of humanity and become reborn into the undead world of the vampire. Rakz decided that he would take this woman for his bride and share her with Blaze.

Chapter 2

1

Patrolman Dan McIrney was passing by the alley when he heard a muffled scream. He pulled out his nightstick and went down the darkened street. He saw the figure of a man bent over a young girl. He was kissing her on the neck. A rapist was the first thing that came to the burly patrolman's mind.

"Hey, you! In the black! Freeze!" McIrney shouted at the man, who looked up at him, smiled, and went back to the neck of the girl.

McIrney replaced the nightstick and pulled out his gun. Anticipating trouble, he radioed dispatch for backup.

"I said freeze, asshole, or I'll shoot!" he shouted.

The man looked up again and smiled. He stood up, staring at the big Irish cop. Eyes like fire burned into the dark. McIrney felt a cold sweat break out all over his body and a strange tingle in his mouth.

"Put your hands above your head and lock 'em."

Unearthly laughter spewed forth from Yosekaat Rakz, laughter so foul and rancorous that it chilled the marrow in Dan's bones. McIrney tried to assert his authority. "Look, fucker, if you don't put your hands up in five seconds I'm going . . ."

Before he could finish his sentence, Rakz was on him. McIrney fired a shot that ricocheted off the wall. Useless. He tried to fire again, but the man in black was powerful. He took the gun from his hand and threw it deep into the alley.

McIrney tossed a hard punch at the face of the vampire, who dodged it as easily as if it were a two-ton weight thrown by a 98-pound weakling. Rakz's first glancing blow tore half of McIrney's face off in its ferocity. The big cop spun and crashed into a trashcan. He tried to call for help on his radio. A hand seized him and lifted him into the air like he was a rag doll. Another slashing blow ripped off his ear. McIrney screamed.

That awful laughter erupted again.

With one hand, the man in black slammed the cop against the wall as though McIrney was a rug and he was trying to knock the dirt out of him.

Wham! A punctured lung.

Wham! A burst liver.

Wham! A fractured skull.

In the span of five seconds, McIrney had collided viciously with the brick wall ten times. His autopsy would later reveal twenty-two broken bones.

The vampire was about to feast on him when two police officers came barreling down the alley. People began to arrive, beckoned by the sirens and flashing lights. Rakz could have easily dispatched the police and it would have been most enjoyable to him to do so, but he decided that it would be better to avoid conflict and disappeared into the night.

The two cops saw their comrade-in-arms and hustled down the alley trying to find the perpetrator who had been there only seconds before. He was nowhere to be found. They went back to see if they could help their buddy, but after they saw the grotesque condition he was in they knew there was nothing they could do.

Chris and Reggie arrived moments after the double slaying had occurred. They hacked their way through the crowd and approached the patrol officers.

"What happened?" Reggie asked one of the policemen, a young cop named Mike Dickson.

"My sweet Jesus, will you look at him," Dickson said, his

voice breaking. He was only twenty years old.

"Settle down, man," Reggie said, "and tell us what happened."

Carver put his hand on the rookie's shoulder.

Dickson was unnerved by the distorted body of the battered cop. He tried to maintain, but his stomach couldn't hold in the churning liquids. He vomited hard.

Reggie had seen murder before. His stomach was queasy but he managed to calm it.

"Feel better, Dickson?" he asked.

The young cop wiped a sleeve across his sweaty brow. "Yeah, I guess."

"Tell us what happened."

Dickson breathed in a hitched sigh and steadied himself. "We got a call from HQ telling us that a cop was in trouble on Biscayne at this place. We were nearby and rushed over. Katie and I saw this guy in the alley slamming McIrney into the wall. Then he looked like he was about to . . . to . . ."

"About to what?" Carver asked.

"To bite him."

"Bite him?"

Chris's skin crawled.

"Yeah, or something. Hell, I dunno, it was dark."

"Hey, over here. There's another body," Dickson's female partner, Katie Breed, called out.

Chris didn't even need to look. He knew what lay in the alley.

Reggie walked back and flashed his light on the corpse. It was a young girl about seventeen. She was as pale as the full moon in the sky above their heads. There were twin punctures on her throat.

"Chris, looks like it's the same guy as last month. The lunatic is back!"

As Reggie spoke, a vivid image came into Chris' mind. Livid eyes, burning like fire.

Join me. Join me, the strange voice whispered sweetly in his mind. It was melodious and yet chilling. He knew it was the other vampire.

"Did you hear me, Chris?" Reggie asked, then added, "I

said our vampire man is back."

Chris rubbed his eyes. "I hear you."

The comment was not directed toward Carver. It was directed toward the voice inside Chris's head.

Carver scratched his chin. "This guy must be some kind of strongman to be able to do that to a big guy like McIrney. I mean, Dan was strong as an ox. Why are the crazies always so strong?"

Join me. Join me, the voice in Chris's head said again. Fear crept into his heart. The voice of the murderer was in his brain. He didn't know what to do. He concentrated and tried to send a message to the vampire. His concentration was broken as Reggie shouted. "Hey, Chris, I think I may have found something!"

Carver reached down and pulled out the piece of fabric that was clutched in the late Dan McIrney's hand.

2

The unemployed Charlie Burnson sat in his '79 Cutlass brooding over the loss of his job and loading his .45 revolver. Burnson had been let go from the department after he had brutally beaten up a lady cop who was posing as a hooker. When he had found out she was a police officer, he lost it and sent her to the hospital for three days. That incident, coupled with Charlie's increasingly bizarre behavior, led to his downfall. He, of course, blamed it all on Reginald Carver.

Now, as he sat in the car loading his .45, every insertion of a shell accompanied by a curse directed at Reggie Carver, Charlie knew that tonight he would blow the black bastard to hell and be set free. He clicked the last bullet into the chamber. He was ready. Burnson watched as Reggie and Chris continued their investigation of the murders. There were too many cops around for him to shoot Carver with the big gun, so he pointed his finger at Carver and pulled the trigger.

"Bang," Charlie giggled. "You're dead."

Burnson's stomach burned with butterflies at the thought

of really pulling the trigger and blowing a hole through Carver's head. But he would have to wait until the right moment. It would be too risky to shoot Carver with all the other cops around. Maybe when Carver went over to his car.

As he caressed the cold steel of his service revolver, he watched the proceedings across the street. His eyes riveted on Carver and his every move. Burnson had no idea that he himself was being watched.

3

The vampire could feel the evil emanating from the man in the green car. Rakz had been observing Blaze, trying to communicate with him again, when he had felt a sinister presence nearby. He searched until he saw Burnson sitting in his car. Rakz could sense the malevolence of this man. He thought that perhaps he could use that evil to his advantage. Now that the police had discovered another one of his victims and he had killed one of their own, he would need protection during the daylight hours. He wasn't sure if Blaze would risk his own secret in order to reveal what he knew about the murders. He hadn't before, but Rakz couldn't be sure. The vampire had killed one of Chris's fellow officers. He would need someone who could watch over him and make sure he was safe during the time of the death sleep. He hadn't needed a servant for many years as he was certain no one believed vampires existed. But now there was a need.

His last servant, Peter Kuerten, had been hanged in 1932 after he'd been found guilty of the murders of eleven women in Dusseldorf, Germany. Kuerten was named "the Vampire of Dusseldorf" by the press because of the way the girls had been killed. No one was aware that it had been Yosekaat Rakz and not his servant Peter Kuerten who had killed those women. Kuerten had helped by bringing them to Rakz, who killed them and drank their blood, but Kuerten was merely a pawn. Rakz was king. Peter Kuerten was far from innocent, though: he was an evil man before he joined forces with Rakz. All Rakz servants had been evil men. The man in the car had the same evil aura about him that Kuerten did. Yes, it was time to enlist a new servant, Rakz thought to himself, smiling.

But his smile faded when he saw the man get out of the car. In the man's hand was a gun.

4

Reggie looked at the handkerchief he'd pulled from the grasp of the dead Dan McIrney. He shouted to Chris, "Hey, check this out, Blaze. I think I may have found a clue."

Chris walked over to where Reggie was standing. "What have you got?"

"This," Reggie said as he held out the handkerchief. It was made of the finest silk and had the initials Y R embroidered on it.

"It looks like this dude might have some bread."

"Looks like it."

"So," Reggie said, "what we need to do is find some rich guy who can bench-press 500 pounds and likes to drink blood."

"We aren't sure the guy drinks the blood. He might just drain the bodies."

"Yeah, but what the hell for?"

"I don't know, but does it make any more sense if he drinks the blood?"

"I guess not."

Charlie Burnson had reached the curb and was starting to cross the street.

Chris wanted to tell Reggie and the others the truth and get if off his chest. He had been able to function pretty close to normal since the curse of Batiste Legendre had changed his life forever. Perhaps if he explained the whole situation to everyone they would understand. Maybe he could tell them about himself and the other vampire . . . *No!* his mind shouted. No one would understand. He could certainly prove it. He would show them that he cast no reflection. He could let them shoot him. He knew he wouldn't die. They would have to believe him. But once he proved it, his life would be ruined. He would lose his job, his friends. He would become a freak, an outcast of society. The government would probably send him to a research institute where scientists would test and probe him to see what powers he possessed and determine whether they could isolate the cause of them. The government would probably cover the whole thing up. If the military or the CIA got involved, they might even want to use him and his vampiric powers as a secret weapon. Chris Blaze, secret agent V1, the first vampire agent in the history of intelligence.

Chris knew he should tell them about the other vampire, but in order to do that he would have to be prepared to reveal himself as a vampire, otherwise they wouldn't believe him. If he told them he knew there was a real vampire doing the killing without telling them how he knew, he would probably get a long vacation, if they didn't send him straight to the booby hatch. He knew they wouldn't believe him and would proceed as though the other vampire was an ordinary man. A lot of cops would get hurt. As he pondered the alternatives, Chris realized he couldn't tell them the truth. He would have to find the vampire himself and take care of him in his own way.

Burnson was crouching behind the car next to Carver and Blaze's patrol car.

"So, partner, I think we're all done here." Reggie said as the boys from the morgue arrived. "Let's go back to the station and run a check on the files of offenders with the initials Y R. There can't be too many. Maybe we'll get a break."

"I hope so. This guy is very dangerous." Chris walked toward the car.

Reggie followed. "Y'know, I think this guy really *does* believe he's a real live vampire. After what he did to McIrney, I just hope we don't run into him without our guns pulled and ready to fire."

Burnson stepped out and took aim. Carver was dead in his sights when the powerful hand reached out and plucked the gun from his hand.

"What the fu . . ."

Another hand pressed hard across his mouth. He was picked up and carried into the stairwell of an old apartment. Burnson struggled to break free but was held tight as a coyote caught in a steel trap. A deep, resonant voice broke through the silence of the darkened corridor. "Relax, my friend, I'm not going to hurt you."

The voice was melodious, calming. Burnson relaxed. He stared into the eyes of the man with the soothing voice. They were dark and vast. He could see images in them—vague, unidentifiable images, the eyes of a thousand years. Charlie was transfixed. He felt his soul leave his body and sink into the black morass of those eyes. Deeper and deeper into the abyss he sank. Frightening images of death and destruction passed by him. He could see himself falling towards a huge pool of blood. He silently dived into the thick liquid. His breath sucked out of him. His lungs burned. He felt himself getting dizzy, lungs bursting, as he sank deeper into the sanguinary fluid. He couldn't breathe. His heart pounded hard against his rib cage. The pool of blood swallowed him up. As his lungs could stand the lack of oxygen no longer, he gulped in, hoping that somehow air would fill his lungs. The blood poured in, drowning him. But strangely he felt exhilarated. The blood filled him with life. It tasted like the finest wine in the world. He gulped some more, greedily sucking down gouts of it. Then suddenly he was thrust out of the pool and rocketed upward. He felt himself reenter his body. He saw the face of the man with the eyes. His mind cleared. Charlie willed himself to speak. "Who are you?"

The man ignored him and asked a question of his own. "Who were you going to shoot with that gun?"

Burnson was angry that he had no control of the situation. Still he felt compelled to answer. "The nigger."

"The black detective? But why?"

"He has to die."

"And what about the other detective, the black man's partner? What do you know about him?"

"I don't care about him. I want to kill Carver. Why did you stop me?"

131

"As I said," Rakz said. "I need your help."

Burnson regained his will for a moment. "Why should I help you? I don't even know you."

"Because I can help you eliminate the black man. All I ask from you is a small favor."

"What's that?"

Rakz smiled, exposing his fangs. "Why, I want you to be my new servant."

He grabbed Charlie and pulled him close. The vampire bit deep and Charlie Burnson was employed again.

5

Carver and Blaze were back at the station checking through the files for offenders with the initials YR, but were getting nowhere fast. Chris suspected it was a waste of time. The vampire probably had never been caught, but he went through the motions anyway.

Reggie kept digging. "Man, most of these dudes are either in jail or six feet under," Carver complained as he continued looking through the files. "How are we supposed to arrest a suspect if he's in the slammer or in the grave?"

Chris shrugged. He couldn't tell Reggie that the grave was precisely the place where they would probably find their killer.

They continued to search.

They would find nothing.

Chapter 3

1

The next night, Chris and Sue met at the park. She was going to tell Jonathan that the engagement was off, and she needed Chris's support.

"Are you sure you don't want me to go with you?" Chris asked earnestly.

"I want you to go more than anything," Sue clasped his hand in hers, "but this is something that I have to do myself. Jonathan deserves that much. Besides, I don't think he'll make a scene in a public place. He cares too much about his image."

"Where are you two meeting?"

"The 2001 Club. It's always crowded, and I want a lot of people around when I tell him. I just hope he doesn't get violent. Jonathan has a wicked temper."

"Are you sure you don't want me to tag along? I could hang out just to make sure nothing happens." Chris was concerned about her last remark about Jonathan's heated temper.

"Nothing will happen. I must make Jonathan out to be more of a monster than he really is."

"Well, I never met the guy."

"He was very sweet to me at one time in my life, and he always took care of me. I just don't love him."

"Do you love me?" Chris asked, knowing the answer, but

wanting to hear her say it anyway.

"I love you more than I thought I could ever love anyone."

"I feel the same way."

He kissed her warmly on the lips. No other words were spoken.

Sue got up and broke the silence. "I guess I'd better get going and get this over with."

"You sure you don't want me to go? Last chance," he said.

"No, I can handle it," she said as she bent over and kissed Chris on the forehead. "For luck."

He kissed her forehead in return. "For luck."

2

The Happy Christian giftshop was a quaint little place that catered to the born-again faction of the community. Religious artifacts and books cluttered the shelves. The store had a rosy cinnamon smell from the potpourri of cinnamon and rose petals in a wicker basket that hung from the ceiling. Miss Quigmire, the proprietor, was mildly surprised when she saw the sharp dressed black man come through the door, the tinkling of the little bell signaling his arrival.

"May I help you?" The little lady peered from over the counter.

"Yes, ma'am, I'd like to get one of those and a couple of those."

"Certainly," the old woman said as she got the items Reggie had pointed to on the shelf behind her. She smiled. Reggie smiled back. Her smile was there because she had just made a tidy profit. Carver's was because he'd come up with an idea that might just save his and his partner's lives.

3

Why did she want to go out to 2001 two days before the wedding, Jonathan wondered as he splashed on the expensive cologne. Sue had been acting very strangely of late. Maybe she was getting nervous about the marriage, having second thoughts about his change of attitude. He had tried hard to make it seem as though he was really trying to make it work, but he had slipped on a couple of occasions. Surely she wasn't thinking of backing out, he thought . . . not at this stage of the game. Then what was it? She had sounded so solemn on the phone that something had to be up. He couldn't imagine what it could be.

He put on his linen slacks and a pair of alligator shoes. He buttoned up the light blue shirt, then draped a sweater over his shoulders and tied it loosely. He stood in front of the full-length mirror and assumed a modeling pose. He was looking good. Jonathan figured a girl would have to be crazy to turn down a catch like him, and Sue was definitely not crazy. He had nothing to worry about. She was in his hip pocket. He grabbed his ostrich-hide wallet and tucked it into his pants as he headed for the garage. He would take the Ferrari out tonight. It had been a long time since he'd really cut loose on the highway, and he was feeling his oats. He knew Sue was frightened when he went 140 in the red speedster, but he figured the wedding was so close that he could scare her a little and it wouldn't jeopardize a thing. Everybody needed a little scare now and then.

4

"The woman's name is Sue Catledge. She's a doctor at Mercy General."

"Excellent. You've done well, Charles." Rakz smiled and handed Burnson a token of his appreciation.

Charlie grinned and hustled over into the corner of the darkened apartment. He sat down and looked at his little present.

Yosekaat Rakz had decided that tonight he would begin the ritual of the vampire wedding and take the girl for his bride. It had been a long time since he'd felt the pleasures of a woman. Most women were unworthy of his attention,

135

nothing more than a source of food. But Sue Catledge was different. She had that rare quality of beauty that reminded him of his beloved Tasha. Lovely, exotic Tasha. There was no physical resemblance between the two, it was just that they had the same spiritual quality of beauty and grace. Rakz wondered why Blaze had not taken Sue for his own. He had had plenty of opportunities, yet hadn't taken advantage. Rakz decided the young vampire was not to be trusted, as he was still denying his powers and trying to live like a normal man.

Rakz remembered when he was first bitten by the vampire and had tried to resist the dark powers. It was three centuries ago. He had been a nobleman of sorts and was vacationing in the Carpathian Mountains. One night as he went riding on horseback, he strayed from the road and was attacked by a tall man dressed in evening clothes. That man was not a man, but a vampire. He bit Rakz and drained him of all his blood. The next night Rakz had risen as one of the undead. The monster who had bitten him was the vampire Armand Dracul, the creature upon which the legend of Dracula was based. A year after infecting Yosekaat Rakz, Armand Dracul was killed by the vampirologist Dr. Abraham Van Helsing. Van Helsing had kept a diary of his pursuit and destruction of the vampire and had later tried to publish it as a work of nonfiction. Publishers laughed and sent him out on his ear. After a couple of years of fruitless attempts to sell the diaries, he gave himself the pen name of Bram Stoker and sold the chronicles as a work of fiction. It was a best-seller.

After he was bitten, Rakz had tried to resist his newfound power. It was two weeks before he succumbed to the allure of the powers that he now possessed, powers beyond his wildest dreams.

Those had been simpler times, but far more dangerous for the vampire, as superstition had not yet given way to science. Then people still believed in the undead, and they lived in fear of them. Therefore they took measures to protect themselves from the vampire, making it difficult for vampires to feast on humans. Only the fools and the enlightened fell prey to the undead, the fools because they didn't know any better,

136

and the enlightened because they thought they knew too much. They thought that belief in the creatures of the night was superstitious nonsense and that they had nothing to fear. But they were wrong.

At one time Rakz commanded an army of vampires and was responsible for the plague of the undead on the Island of Balta off the coast of Greece. Three hundred people had been infected. It wasn't until General Karlokia and his legion of vampire hunters were called in that the plague was put under control.

General Andreas Karlokia was a Cyprian general whose sister had been vampirized when she was eighteen. One night after she had died, he found her in their home, about to bite his little brother. He personally drove the stake through her heart. Ever since that incident he had had a pathological desire to rid the world of the vampire. The general led an army of cutthroats and mercenaries. Men who knew no fear . . . for a price. He paid them well, and they were ruthless. Karlokia and his men had killed many of Rakz's brethren, including Rakz's wife, Tasha. Their final battle took place on the island. Karlokia and his men kept the vampires engaged until the wee hours. As the vampires fled the rising sun, they found that the villagers had destroyed their resting places and killed all their lamias. Lamias were humans under the spell of the vampire who aided and protected them during the daylight hours. The villagers had tortured the unfortunate servants into divulging the secret lairs of the vampires. All the vampires perished—all except Yosekaat Rakz. He had escaped because he secured a secret resting place of which even his servant was unaware. Rakz swore vengeance on the Cyprian general who had killed his beautiful Tasha and finally caught up with Karlokia one night at a bar the old general frequented. Rakz tore his head off with one powerful blow. The general had looked up just before he was killed and seemed almost grateful. He had seen too much evil and destruction for one lifetime. Death was welcome.

It was after this battle that Rakz decided to stake all his victims and dispose of their bodies so that they would not rise from the dead and start another epidemic that would draw the wrath of the villagers on him and rouse them to action.

As time passed, superstition gradually gave way to science and the old beliefs faded. People no longer believed in the supernatural, so they no longer needed the charms and icons that had once protected them. Hunting for prey became easy for Rakz. No one believed in vampires; therefore they didn't exist. It was science and not superstition that led many a person to his death from the bite of the living dead.

A high-pitched squeal broke the vampire's train of thought. He turned toward the source of the sound and saw that Charlie had bitten the head of his reward, a rat, and was drinking its blood as one would drink a can of Pepsi.

Rakz smiled. The servants always amused him with their petty blood lust, so easily satisfied by the small creatures upon which they feasted.

As Charlie gleefully licked the sticky fluid from his fingertips, his master called.

"Come, Charles," Rakz said, "we have wedding plans to attend to."

5

Jonathan picked up Sue promptly at eight and they headed for 2001.

The nightclub that was decorated inside to look like the spaceship in the movie of the same name: intricate circuitboards and strange hallways, waitresses in spacesuits, windows that looked out into space. It was the place to be on a Saturday night.

"Why are we going out tonight?" Jonathan asked. His voice had an irritated tone to it.

"I just wanted to go out," Sue said, sensing his annoyance. She didn't want the conversation to start in the car. She wanted to be around people when she told Jonathan the news.

138

Jonathan wouldn't let it go. "Two days before the wedding?"

"I just felt like going someplace, okay?"

Jonathan started to continue his questioning, but decided to let the matter drop. "Sure," he said, not wanting to pursue it any further, just in case she was telling the truth. He wasn't sure what was wrong and didn't want to start a fight needlessly. Jonathan popped in a cassette of Mozart's "Figaro" and laid his head back on the headrest.

Sue relaxed. She could wait until they got to the club before she broke the news to him.

6

Reggie and Chris arrived at the station at the same time. They went down to the briefing room and listened as Lt. Brown read off the night's assignments. After he finished, they walked to their car. Reggie whistled a happy tune as he approached the passenger's side.

"What's got you in such a good mood?" Chris asked.

Reggie smiled. "I'll tell you when we get going, but I think I figured out a way to help us catch this guy."

"Can't wait to hear it. Let's go."

Chris got in. The motor roared and they were off on another night's patrol.

"So, tell me the plan," Chris said as he headed up the highway.

"First things first," Reggie replied. "Now, is Sue gonna tell that asshole to take a hike tonight, or what?"

"Yeah, she is," Chris said, then asked his partner a question he had been wondering about for a long time. "Tell me, why don't you like Jonathan? You never did say how you met him—or Sue, for that matter."

Reggie rubbed his jaw as he remembered that eventful night. "I met Sue in the hospital after I had a fight with Burnson."

"Assface Charlie Burnson?"

"Yeah," Reggie said contemptuously. "I'm glad that son-of-a-bitch finally got himself fired."

"I think everybody down at the station was happy about that."

"No lie. So anyway, Sue was fixing me up when this dickbag Jonathan came in and starts giving her a bunch of shit about her working with poor folks and coloreds like me."

"So you punched him out?" Chris asked laughing.

"Sort of. He punched and I went down." Reggie winced at the thought of the backfist that had laid him out. "That sucker is a black belt, y'know."

Reggie paused and looked suspiciously at Chris. "You mean to tell me Sue never told you this story?"

"To tell you the truth, she did," Chris laughed again. "But I just wanted to hear your version."

"Very funny. How come you never asked me about this before?"

"I just wanted to see if and when you would 'fess up."

"Yeah well, I don't like braggin' on myself, especially when I get my butt kicked."

Chris grinned. "Now that the truth is out, what's this big plan you've come up with?"

Reggie got excited. "Oh, yeah. Well, this whole vampire angle got me to thinking. Now, if this guy thinks he's a real vampire then he should act like a real vampire."

"Yeah, so?"

"So if he thinks he's a vampire, he should be afraid of this."

Reggie pulled out a crucifix he had purchased at the Happy Christian out of the bag in his lap. The sudden appearance of the cross caused Chris to lose control of the vehicle and swerve up onto the curb and into a trashcan. The car jumped back down, veering off into the other lane, narrowly avoiding an oncoming semi.

Reggie screamed, "Shit, man, what the hell are you doing?" He dropped the cross back down into the bag. "You trying to kill us?"

"Sorry, there was a, uh, dead dog in the road."

"Well, shit, run the mother over. He ain't gonna feel it. But we damn sure would have felt that semi."

Chris put his hand on Reggie's shoulder. "Sorry."

"Damn, man, put both hands on the wheel," Reggie said, then added under his breath, "You drive like you're drunk."

Reggie sat back in the seat, an angry look on his face. Chris glanced at the bag that contained the cross. He hoped his partner would keep it in there.

After a few moments of silence, Chris spoke. "That sounds like a good plan."

Reggie's ears perked up.

Chris looked out the front windshield as though he were talking to himself. "Yeah, not a bad plan at all."

Reggie's ego was tweaked. He responded. "You really think so?"

"Yeah, it makes sense."

Chris was glad Reggie had the cross in case they did run up against the other vampire. Carver would need it for protection. Suddenly he was hit by a jarring sensation. The hunger! It burned at his guts like a flaming torch. Occasionally it hit him harder than at other times, and this was a bad one. Where was his nearest bottle?

The answer came: 38th Street. They were four blocks away. Chris sped up. The hunger hit him again. The desire was so intense that in his mind he momentarily saw himself tearing into his partner's throat. He would have to hurry or something bad was going to happen. Something very bad.

7

Arby Finch was an inquisitive boy of eight. The dark-haired son of an Irish father and a Cuban mother was playing a game of treasure hunt when he had found it. The magic potion in the bottle was a really neat color. He poured it into an empty Gatorade bottle of clear glass so that he could see it better. He looked at it for a few minutes and then decided to take it home and show his mother.

Arby walked in with a mischievous grin on his face. Mirna

Finch recognized it immediately as his "I've got a secret" look. She wished her husband, George, was home. She knew he got a kick out of their son's elaborate secret stories.

"What have you got behind your back?" she said in a thickly accented voice.

Arby's grin widened. "It's a secret potion."

Mirna bent down to eye level with her adorable little boy. "Can your mama see it?"

"Yeah, but you have to say the magic word."

She had played this game many times before.

"Cabeza de la culebra," she said.

Mirna wondered why her son used *snake's head* as his secret word. She attributed it to his wild imagination. Someday that boy will be a writer, she thought.

Arby was so excited by his discovery that his palms were sweating. When he took the magic potion from behind his back, it slipped from his grasp and crashed to the floor, exploding its contents all over the kitchen.

Mirna Finch fainted when she saw all the blood splattered on her floor and cabinets.

"Oops," Arby shrugged. "I made a boo-boo."

8

The 2001 Club was packed tighter than John Holmes in a Chinese condom. The flashing lights gave everyone a reddish-blue tint. A large mirrored wall surrounded the dance floor. You could watch the more flamboyant dancers eyeing themselves as they gyrated across the floor. A goof in glasses with pants just a little too high asked a foxy blonde to dance. She smiled and confessed that she was totally worn out. As the song changed, the mutant saw the "exhausted" lady out on the floor dancing like she was on "Star Search" with a stud who could probably benchpress the state of Rhode Island. A snooty-looking bitch came out of the little girl's room with her nose up in the air. She looked good and knew it. Everyone she passed smiled at her. She could see them out of the corner of her eye. Too bad she couldn't also

142

see the trail of toilet paper she was dragging behind her. So it went at the 2001 Club.

The back room, HAL's Place, was named after the computer of the same name in the Kubrick classic. It was usually frequented by drunken couples who had met that night and wanted a quiet place to get to know each other and swap slobber. It was in HAL's Place that Sue told Jonathan the news.

"You can't!" he shouted.

"But I have to, Jonathan. I've thought about it for a long time, and I can't marry you."

Jonathan was beside himself. "The wedding is only two days away."

"I'm sorry, but, I . . . I just don't love you. I mean, I love you, but not the kind of love you marry for."

"So you just end it?"

Sue looked sadly at Jonathan. "It just wouldn't work. It's over."

Jonathan had had enough of this. He knew this time he had lost her for good, so he gave up on getting her back. He switched gears into the more rewarding revenge mode.

"You ungrateful little bitch," he roared. "After all I've done for you, you repay me like this!"

"There's no need to call each other names. It's better for both of us in the long run."

"But what will everyone think?"

Sue started to lose her cool. "Is that all you care about, what people will think?"

"I will not stand idly by and be humiliated. You will go on with this marriage!"

"You don't understand," Sue said, adamant. "I don't love you."

"And do you think I love you?" Jonathan shouted.

Sue was shocked by the ferocity in his voice.

The enraged playboy continued his tirade. "After the first time you broke it off, I swore I would make you pay for rejecting me. I am the best thing that's ever happened to you and you don't even know it. You could have prestige, power, money to buy anything you want, but you throw it all away because you want love. You are undoubtedly the most foolish girl I have ever met."

Sue started to get up from the table. Jonathan grabbed her roughly by the arm. *"You will hear me out,"* he hissed.

A shiver of fear ran up Sue's spine as she saw the wild look in Jonathan's eyes.

"I only got back with you so that after we were married I could humiliate you by getting a divorce in the first month."

Sue wanted badly to get away, but she was afraid.

Jonathan saw the fear in her eyes and like an animal went for the kill.

"You were always beneath my station," he spat contemptibly. "But I tried to nurture you, to make you more than you were. I put you through school, got you a job, showed you the finer things in life. Still you clung to those small-town ideals."

At that moment, Sue saw Jonathan as he truly was: a shallow, screaming brat of a man who all his life had gotten what he wanted. Right before her eyes he shrank from a thirty-seven-year old man into a seven-year-old boy who hadn't got his ice-cream cone. At any moment she expected him to fall to the floor kicking and screaming.

"You will never amount to more than a small-time doctor for dirty, filthy trash," he yelled.

Sue's fear began to change into anger. "That's enough, Jonathan."

"I haven't even started," he roared.

Sue's beeper rang. She looked at the LED message: she was needed at the hospital. She got up to leave. Jonathan grabbed her arm again, but she twisted free and hurried out of the room. She wound her way through the crowd with Jonathan in hot pursuit.

9

Chris sped quickly to the corner of 88th Street, where he kept one of his supplies of blood. Reggie recognized the corner and decided it was time to discuss Chris's problem.

"Chris, why are we slowing down?" He asked, knowing the answer.

"I have to stop."

"Hey, man, enough is enough. If you have a problem, let's talk about it."

"I can't. Gotta get out." The hunger was thundering inside his body. He parked the car and leapt out.

"Wait!" Reggie shouted as Chris disappeared into the night. He got on the radio and called in. After he got the roger on his break call, he got out and started to look for Chris. He was going to have this thing out right now.

Chris ran to the spot where he had hidden the thermos bottle of blood and lifted the old crate. His jaw dropped open in confusion and disbelief. It was gone! The blood was not there. He tossed the box aside and began searching the area, tossing trash everywhere in his frenzied search.

The hunger was almost out of control.

The bottle was nowhere to be found.

A sharp pain ripped through him. The hunger was beginning to overwhelm him. He had to slake his thirst or he would lose control, and then who knows what would happen. But he didn't have time to get to another location.

"Hey, mister," a raspy old voice croaked. "Wanna buy a dog cage?"

Chris whirled and saw the little old bag lady standing in front of him. She was dressed in an old navy peacoat, over-sized shoes, and a ridiculously feathered hat. In her hand was an ancient wooden dog cage. He had no choice. He grabbed her by the arms and pulled her to him.

"Just a minute, Sonny," she said indignantly, "I'm not that kind of a girl."

Chris bit into her neck.

"Oh, you are a fresh one!" the old lady crooned.

Chris drank deeply, but only enough to quell the pain. He set her down gently and whispered, "Forgive me."

As he stood up, Chris felt disoriented. When he took his first steps, he wobbled and careened into a trash can.

"Son-of-a-bitch," Chris said, but it came out as "Shun-off-a-bish."

145

The old lady was plastered, stone-drunk out of her mind, and now her alcohol-tainted blood flowed through his veins. Chris had taken a couple more unsteady steps when Reggie turned the corner and saw him stumbling toward him.

"God damn it, I knew it! It was just a matter of time!" Reggie shouted as he put his shoulder under Chris's arm and helped him walk to the car. "I knew you had a drinking problem, I should have said something, but no, I had to turn the other cheek."

"I'ne shorry, Reshee. I dint know she wash loaded."

"Who was loaded? What in the hell are you talking about?"

"Ze lady back zere." Chris tried to clear his mind. "Oh, nefer mine."

They stumbled to the car. Reggie opened the door and poured Chris into the passenger side.

"Sho shorry," the drunken cop said.

"Yeah, well, it's too late for that. I can't believe you wouldn't let me help you."

"Can't help. Nobody can help," Chris mumbled.

"Shit," Reggie said under his breath. He reached into the backseat and pulled out the thermos bottle full of hot coffee. "Man, we need to get you sobered up."

Reggie poured the coffee into the thermos top. It was too hot to drink. The black detective blew on it to cool it down. He looked over at Chris and a thought hit him: how could Chris have gotten so drunk so fast? He would have had to drink a fifth straight down to get that plowed. It didn't make any sense. All the other times they stopped, Chris came back and he was fine. Either he held his liquor well or maybe he hadn't been drinking. Maybe it was drugs. Whatever the problem, Reggie was going to find out.

The coffee was almost cool enough to drink.

"Here. Drink this. It'll help put you back together."

He put the coffee to Chris's lips and poured a little into his mouth.

Chris spat it out. "I never drink . . . coffee."

"Well, you will tonight." Reggie said and put the cup back up to his lips. Chris lashed out and knocked the thermos top out of Reggie's hand. Coffee spilled all over the seat.

"What's wrong with you?" Reggie shouted, reaching down to pick up the top. "You almost broke my . . ."

The detective stopped in mid sentence as he looked into the curved polished glass of the thermos top. It showed a distorted reflection of the front seat. Reggie's mouth went as dry as a bleached bone in the desert.

In the reflection, there was no one sitting on the passenger's side of the car.

10

"Hold on, Sue!" Jonathan caught up to her as she got to the pay phone outside the club. She was going to call a cab to take her to the hospital.

"There's nothing more to say," she said as she dialed the number for the cab company. "I know you're upset, but I want you to just leave me alone."

Jonathan clicked down the switch hook of the phone. "You will hear me out."

Sue stepped away and started walking towards the bus stop.

If there was one thing Jonathan hated, it was to be ignored. He grabbed Sue by the arm and spun her around. "Now you'll listen, you two-faced little slut!"

Without thinking, Sue slapped his face. The sharp sound of the blow ricocheted off the wall of a nearby building.

Jonathan drew back his fist and sent it flying at Sue's startled face. It slammed hard against flesh.

Jonathan winced as if his hand was caught in a vise.

"Is there a problem here?" the deep voice of the owner of the death grip said.

Sue looked over at the mysterious stranger who had just saved her from being hit. She was unaware that he was far from a savior.

Rakz released his grip on Jonathan. The enraged Wadsworth got down into his fighting stance and whistled a kick at the vampire's head. Rakz's arm was a blur as he easily deflected the blow. Jonathan jumped back and prepared to strike again.

"You motherfucker," Jonathan hissed. "I'm gonna kick the living shit out of you!"

Sue recoiled from the violence in her ex-fiancé's voice. She had never heard him use the F-word before. It sounded so alien coming from his mouth, so frightening. She felt sorry for her would-be knight in shining armor, as she had seen Jonathan in action before.

Her pity would be wasted.

Jonathan fired a hard right at Rakz, who moved out of range with uncanny speed.

"Please," Rakz smiled, a patronizing grin that suggested his sorrow at the mismatch between him and Jonathan. "Let's not have any more of this."

He reached out with the speed of a rattlesnake and grabbed his startled foe by the throat.

"Now," he said, "I asked you to leave her alone, so be a good fellow and be on your way."

Jonathan's face was turning blood red as Rakz squeezed. He kicked out and caught Rakz in the crotch. The vampire dropped him and Jonathan set up to kick again. He never had the chance, as Rakz's arm cut the air like a knife and crushed Jonathan's windpipe. He clutched at his shattered throat and gurgled, a thin spittle of blood trickled down his chin.

Sue stared in horror as Rakz picked up Jonathan by the crotch and tossed him fifteen feet into the side of the building. The stranger's eyes seemed to leap out of their sockets like fire.

As Jonathan struggled to get up, Rakz moved quickly to him and kicked him so hard in the face that it knocked his right eye out of its socket.

Sue screamed at the top of her lungs. Two bouncers heard her and came outside to investigate. Another was on the phone to the sheriff's department. Other people, sensing the excitement, went out to see what was happening.

Rakz saw that he would have to flee. He cursed himself for letting his temper get the better of him. Now he would have to find another way to get the girl. He ran off and was gone within seconds. No one would ever have known he'd been there except for the brutalized condition of Jonathan Wadsworth. He lay in a crumpled heap, the right side of his face already swelling to grotesque proportions.

Sue rushed to his side and checked his pulse. It was weak but steady. He was breathing with extreme difficulty. The upper part of his larynx had been crushed, and he didn't seem to be getting enough air. Sue knew what she had to do.

"Quick," she shouted at one of the bouncers. "I need a sharp knife or a razor blade, some straws, bandages, and some alcohol."

A smartly dressed Latino did his good deed for the day and produced the razor blade. He didn't need it anymore, as he had just cut up his last line.

Big Marty Salinas, a bouncer, went inside and came out with some straws, clean bar towels, and a bottle of 151-proof rum.

Sue was ready. She was going to perform an emergency tracheotomy on Jonathan to prevent him from suffocating. She poured the rum onto her palms, the razor blade, and Jonathan's throat. She had to concentrate to steady her trembling hands. The whole incident had shaken her up badly, but Jonathan needed her to be calm if she was to save him.

Sue put the blade against his throat and made the incision. The razor cut easily through the skin. She kept cutting until she hit the tough muscle of the trachea. She began to cut through it to open an air passage. After she had cut through, Sue placed the straw in the incision and the involuntary muscles of the lungs took over. He was breathing again, but Sue was worried. He had taken some very hard blows. There were probably internal injuries and possibly a fractured skull. He was far from out of the woods.

Marty, the bouncer, crouched beside her.

"The ambulance will be here in a few minutes," he said.

Marty felt sick when he saw the condition of Jonathan's face. His eye was completely shut and swollen to the size of a grapefruit. A gruesome reddish-blue tint had already begun to show up around it. Blood and saliva covered his chin. He was a mess.

Sue wiped away the blood and saliva. Marty put some ice in a towel and placed it on Jonathan's swollen eye, partially because it would reduce the swelling, but mostly so he wouldn't have to look at it. He glanced over at the lady doctor.

"Who the hell was that other guy? I only caught a quick look at him."

"I don't know," Sue said. "I've never seen him before and I hope I never see him again."

11

Reggie turned the thermos back and forth, trying to capture the image of his partner in its polished glass. He simply was not there. Shakily, Reggie reached up and slowly turned the rearview mirror toward Chris. He gulped down the lump in his throat when he saw that it too showed that Christopher Blaze cast no reflection. Carver simply could not believe what his eyes were telling him. His partner was sitting next to him in the car. He could see him as plain as he saw his own face in the mirror, yet when he tried to see his partner in the mirror, he was not there.

A rapid succession of pictures ran through Reggie's mind: Reggie pulling out the cross and Chris swerving, the wild look in Chris's eyes that he got sometimes, the hooker with the two bite marks on her throat. His next thought was out of a nightmare, but he knew it was true.

Chris awakened from his stupor. The blood had already been absorbed and the hunger was beginning again. The effects of the alcohol had dissipated as quickly as they had come. He looked over at his partner.

"Hey, Reggie, I'm sorry. I just lost my balance for a moment," he said, "I hope you didn't think I was, uh, drinking."

Reggie just stared at him.

"Reggie, what's wrong, man, you look like you've just seen a ghost!"

"No, not a ghost," Reggie gasped, "A goddamn shit-for-sure vampire!"

"Reggie, let me explain!" Chris said, trying to remain calm.

"Unh-uh! Get back," Carver shouted.

Reggie reached into the bag and brandished the cross. Chris turned away, repelled.

"I can explain!"

"No way, man," Reggie cried. "You don't cast no reflection!"

"I know. I'm a vampire."

"Shit, you admit it. What the hell am I saying? This whole thing is totally fucked up." Panic crept into Reggie's voice. "There really is a vampire in this city, and I'm sitting in a car with him."

"Reggie, listen to me. Do you remember the Cannus cult bust that I made a little while ago?"

"Yeah," Reggie said suspiciously.

"Well, it all started that night . . ."

As Chris went into the incredible story behind the curse, he hoped that Reggie would believe it. If not, Chris would have to decide what he needed to do to protect his secret.

12

The ambulance took Jonathan away. Sue had tried to call Chris at the precinct, but he had been out on patrol. She was afraid to go home alone, afraid the mysterious violent stranger would find her. He had been so odd—a tall, thin man with strange eyes. He had been attractive, yet at the same time repulsive. His fingers seemed long and pointed, like talons, but surely that had been her imagination. He had a cruel mouth and a thick Fu Manchu mustache. But his most distinguishing feature had been his eyes, those coal black eyes. When she had first seen him, his eyes had drawn her in as though they were a whirlpool that sucked in everything around them. They seemed to have a power that compelled her to look into them. As she stared into his eyes, she could almost see images from the past. Dark, vile images. When he had attacked Jonathan, the coal black eyes seemed to burn red hot. But surely that had just been the reflection of the bright red sign that flashed *2001*. Her imagination was getting the better of her.

Sue decided it would be best if she went to the hospital to check on Jonathan's condition. She had stabilized him, but she wanted to be sure he was okay. She decided to call a cab and headed for the pay phone outside the club. Her heart leapt into her throat as a hand reached out and grabbed her.

13

Reggie sat quietly, his face a mixture of disbelief and terror. The story Chris had just told him was unbelievable, yet it had all made sense. There was no denying that his partner didn't cast a reflection, that they did always make frequent stops, that he had never seen his partner during the day. It all made perfect sense. But one image gnawed at Reggie: the girl in the alley. Reggie knew that they had stopped there before on the night of the murder, that Chris had gotten out and bitten her. He admitted that. But this thing about another vampire, that was hard for him to swallow. It was too convenient. If this whole case had to go to trial based on what Chris had told him, Reggie thought Chris would most definitely be found guilty of being a vampire and murdering the girl. But this was not a court of law, this was a man and his partner sitting together in their patrol car, two friends in an unbelievable predicament. Now Reggie would have to decide.

He thrust out the cross. Chris recoiled.

"What about the girl in the alley?" Reggie said warily. "The first murder?"

"I told you there's another vampire in the city!"

152

Reggie kept the cross up. "But that was the same alley where we had stopped!" he said.

"I know. But I didn't kill her, and I know I didn't put a stake through her heart."

"How did this other vampire know to bite that girl?"

"I believe there is some kind of strange telepathy between us. I get feelings sometimes that he is trying to communicate with me. He must have been following me."

"Why?"

"I don't know. This is just as strange to me as it is to you, Reggie. I didn't ask to become what I am."

Reggie still held out the cross.

Chris sighed. "Would you please put that away? If I wanted to kill you, don't you think I would have by now?"

Reggie hesitated, then put away the cross. "So: say I believe I think you're a good vampire and that there's another vampire in the city, and say I believe that you can sense his evil presence. What are we gonna do about it?"

"The question is, what are *you* going to do?"

14

Sue froze as the hand grasped her shoulder. She turned, expecting to see the coal black eyes of the stranger. She just knew she was going to die. But she wasn't, as the hand belonged to the bouncer, Marty.

"That was really great what you did, saving that guy," the muscular man said.

Sue nodded, trying to maintain a brave front.

"Listen," she said, "I have a big favor to ask."

"Go ahead."

"Could you take me to the hospital? I know it's a big favor, but I really do need a ride."

"Let me see if I can get off. I'll be glad to take you if I can."

He came out moments later, putting on his light windbreaker.

"Let's go," he said.

They got into his Camaro and took off toward the hospital. Sue wanted to be sure Jonathan was all right.

When Sue arrived at the hospital's emergency room, she tried to find out which doctor was on duty when Jonathan had come in. She found out and asked the girl at the desk to page him.

Dr. Ted Randall saw Susan Catledge standing anxiously in the waiting room. He knew of her impending engagement to the man who had come in earlier. He didn't relish having to tell her the awful news. He pulled off his glasses and looked directly into her eyes.

"Sue, I am sorry, but . . ."

She didn't have to hear anymore. It was the same speech she had given before to others.

Jonathan was dead.

She stood stunned, unable to move. It had all happened so fast. The argument . . . the slap . . . Jonathan trying to punch her. And then the stranger. The murdering stranger with the morbidly fascinating eyes.

"Can I do anything?" the concerned Dr. Randall asked.

"No," Sue said, blinking back the tears. "Well, yes, there is something—could you please call me a cab? I need to go home."

"Certainly." The doctor put his hand on her shoulder. "Right away."

Sue sat down heavily on the couch in the emergency room lobby. *Oh, Chris, I need you,* she thought, *I need you so badly.* Then the floodgates opened. She cried and cried, releasing the pent-up fear of the murderer and the sorrow of Jonathan's death.

A small, wiry man sat down next to her. He kindly put his arm around her, one human being comforting another. Sue looked up. The ugly little man smiled and pulled her head to his shoulder. She accepted this needed human contact in her time of sorrow. She sobbed quietly as the friendly stranger patted her on the back.

"Go ahead and cry," he whispered, "it will be all right. Everything is going to be all right."

"Well?" Chris asked.

"Hey, man, if I told people my partner was a vampire, they'd put me away in the nuthouse."

The black man rubbed his hand over his thick curly hair. "Shit," Reggie laughed, "I thought you had a drinking problem—alcohol. But no, you've got an entirely different kind of drinking problem."

Chris laughed too. "I wish I *was* a drunk."

"This is crazy," Reggie said, then pretended to introduce Chris to his family. "Hey, Mom, Dad, I'd like you to meet my partner, Chris. Mom, Chris is one of the undead. Yes, ma'am, a vampire. Sure, he can stay for dinner. Just no stakes or garlic. Jeez, Blaze, you really are fucking up my evening."

"Does this mean we're still partners?" Chris asked hopefully.

"Yeah, we're still partners. Just one question. If you get thirsty enough, you're not going to want to take a drink of Chateau Carver, 1958?"

Chris shook his head. "Scout's honor."

The two sat in silence for several moments.

"Hey, Chris, I just had a thought," Reggie said. "Maybe we can track this other guy using that telepathy thing."

"I don't like to use my powers." The word sounded so funny. "Powers." As if he were some superhero about to do battle with an evil villain. "I'm afraid they'll make me lose my human side," Chris said.

"But you're not sure, right?"

"Well, I guess I don't know. But the other vampire hasn't tried to communicate with me for a long time. He may not even be in the city anymore."

"Look, Chris, this guy is probably killing someone every night. We've got to try and find him."

Chris was torn. He knew Reggie was right: the other vampire was evil and had to be stopped. But what if by using his powers to track the vampire he became as evil as the other?

It was a chance he would have to take.

"Okay, Reggie, I'll try."

"Right. Well then, Count Blaze, let's find us a vampire."

16

Sue wiped her eyes and sank back into the comfort of the couch.

"Thank you. I'm Sue Catledge," she said, dabbing the corners of her eyes with her hanky. She paused, waiting for the man to introduce himself. "I didn't get your name," she said.

"I know how hard it is to lose someone." He smiled sweetly, but it didn't touch his eyes. "Feel better?"

"Yes."

"I hope you don't mind, but I couldn't help overhearing that you needed a ride. I'd be glad to give you one."

"That's all right," Sue said, "the doctor called me a cab."

"I think I heard him get an emergency call right after he talked to you. He might not have had time."

It had been a long time since Randall was supposed to have called. Sue didn't know this man, but he had been kind to her, and she did want to get home. "Okay, I accept," she said.

He smiled again, that benign smile with an underlying current of evil that Sue was too distraught to notice. The man helped her up. "Come on, Sue," he said. "You need to get some sleep."

"Thanks," Sue said, standing. She thought about how in times of trouble the human race was sometimes quite amazing. People who had never met joined together to overcome the sorrow and hurt of the loss of a loved one. Just ordinary people bound together by the very human need of contact and friendship. A case for the family of man.

Chris concentrated with a fervor. He was trying to focus on the vibrations, the feelings that he got on the occasions when the other tried to communicate with him. Images flashed in his brain. Strange images. Violent images. Blazing eyes. Hundreds of blazing eyes. Whirling images. Images from times gone by. Decayed, rotten images of a thousand lives. A thousand deaths.

The thoughts assaulted him, his mind a cauldron of visions. Bubbling up. Exploding. Chris was probing too deeply into the other's mind, too far into the past. He lessened his concentration and the images began to change. The dead hooker. A young Spanish girl. A stormy night. A gunshot. The ghastly visage of Patrolman Dan McIrney.

The images were all of death.

Chris was rocked as the next image popped into his mind. Sue! The vampire was thinking about his lady, and the thought that Chris found in the vampire's mind sent an icy blade of fear slicing down his spine.

18

Sue got into the old '79 Cutlass and sat down in the passenger seat. The man went around the front of the car and got in the door to the driver's side.

"You know," Sue smiled, "I don't think you ever told me your name."

The wiry man with the scrawny goatee smiled and extended his hand. "Oh, I'm sorry. My name is Charlie. Charlie Burnson."

19

Yosekaat Rakz drummed his long, talonlike fingers on a crate that was stacked in the old warehouse. He had sent Charles to find the girl and bring her to him. Rakz would have gone himself, but she could have recognized him and caused a scene. He might have been able to put her under his spell, but he hadn't wanted to take the chance.

Rakz smiled to himself. He had made an excellent choice in his selection of Charles. The ex-policeman was crafty and had a knack for getting information, no doubt a habit picked up in his many years on the force. By using his police credentials, Charles had discovered where Sue lived and had gotten her beeper number from the hospital. He simply followed her and her boyfriend to the club and then, at the right moment, dialed her beeper number to get her to leave. When she went outside, Rakz was there waiting. The vampire hadn't anticipated her boyfriend's attack. It had been a pleasant diversion. It was just unfortunate that it had set him back. But it was only for a moment, as he would have the girl back very soon.

20

Sue had begun to wonder what was happening when Charlie had turned left on 23rd Street instead of right, as she'd told him. He'd assured her that he knew a shortcut. She was still disoriented from that evening's events and thought he might know a quicker way to get to her house—that is, until he turned on Dade Boulevard and headed west. Then she knew something was wrong.

"Hey," Sue cried, "you're going the wrong way!"

Her blood chilled as Charlie turned. His face was contorted into a leering, evil grin. He lashed out and slapped her face. The blow stung like a thousand scorpion stings. Tears welled up in her eyes.

"Shut up!" he hissed. "The Master is waiting."

Sue was stunned. The Master? What in God's name had she gotten herself into?

"Let me go! I haven't . . ."

Another slap crashed against the side of her face. The coppery taste of blood oozed from the inside of her cheek.

"I told you to shut up!" Charlie said through clenched

teeth. "You won't be hurt if you just stay calm!"

How could she stay calm? She was in a car with a madman barreling down the street at 65 mph in a 30-mph zone.

Sue figured she had a couple of options. She could attack Charlie with the hard spiked heel of her shoe and hope she could knock him out and take control of the wheel. It was a long shot. Even if she was able to knock him unconscious, the car would probably crash before she could gain control. The other option would be to wait until he stopped the car, then jump out quickly and run for her life, hoping someone would see her before he caught her. That was a much more prudent plan, and Sue decided it would be her course of action. But that plan suddenly changed course as a blue light flashed into their car. A patrol car was signaling for them to pull over. She was saved.

21

Chris was trying to control his telepathic powers, but the images careened wildly from past to present. He tried to focus on the present, but it was difficult.

Reggie sat next to him, feeling helpless as he saw his partner's face register everything from terror to happiness as it mirrored the thoughts in the evil vampire's mind.

"Come on, man," Carver whispered, "You can do it . . . c'mon."

Chris gradually began to eliminate the clutter of the past and focused on the present. He saw a building. An old building. There were boxes. Stacks of boxes. He could smell the musty odor of a building that hadn't been used. He could taste the dust.

"I see images of an old building. I can't make it out."

"Keep trying," Reggie urged his partner. "You can do it."

The image of an old store sign came up into full view and then disappeared quickly, as if it was a subliminal flash. Blaze couldn't read it. It was almost as if someone was teasing him. Someone who had the power to control his thoughts. Someone like Yosekaat Rakz.

22

Charlie Burnson coolly drove the car over to the curb as the patrolman, James Sims, pulled up behind them and got out of his black-and-white. Sims was about five-nine in his stocking feet and built like a small bull. He had been on the force for seven years and had made many a routine traffic stop. He didn't know that this stop would be anything but routine.

He walked slowly toward the driver's side, pulling out his citation booklet in preparation for writing Charlie a ticket.

"If you scream, I'll slice your throat." Burnson whispered in a vicious snakelike hiss. In his hand was a wickedly curved fillet knife.

"May I see your driver's license, please," Sims said, leaning into the window.

"Certainly," Charlie said as he dug into his back pocket for his wallet.

Sue's mind raced as she tried to figure out if she could get away by quickly opening the door and jumping out. She could get cut before she got out, but she felt sure this man wasn't going to let her live anyway. She decided to try and reached slowly for the door handle. Her heart sank as she noticed the passenger side door didn't have a handle. It was gone.

"Is there a problem, Officer?" Burnson had said, his voice oozing charm as he handed the cop his license.

"You were going a little fast, 65 in a 30-mile zone. I'm afraid I'm going to have to give you a citation."

Sue wanted to scream out, to yell for help, but the thought of being cut open with the knife kept her silent. She trembled violently.

The officer noticed her distress.

"Is there something wrong, Miss?" he asked Sue.

Charlie had looked at her with murder in his eyes.

"No, I'm okay," she said weakly. The tremor in her voice did not make it sound as though she were okay.

Patrolman Sims noticed the red welt on the side of her face.

"Can I ask you to get out of the car, sir?" Sims said, pulling the strap from his pistol.

"Why, certainly, Officer," Burnson crooned as he took the keys out of the ignition and put them in his pocket.

Patrolman Sims stepped back as Charlie climbed out onto the curb. Now was Sue's chance.

"Help me!" she screamed. "He's trying to kidnap me."

Officer Sims reached for his gun, but it was too late. Charlie drove the blade of the knife deep into the patrolman's gut and pulled it across. A crimson line sprayed out from the slash.

The cop pulled his gun and tried to aim it at Burnson. Charlie slashed again, laying open the patrolman's forearm like he was carving roast beef. Blood spouted from the gash and splattered Burnson's face. Charlie greedily licked the red, sticky fluid from his lips. The gun dropped from Sims's hand, his tendons useless from the knife blow, but still the valiant cop fought on. Using his left hand, Sims grabbed his nightstick and landed a shot to the temple of Charlie Burnson. Stars flashed before Charlie's eyes as he rocked back from the blow, but he wasn't knocked unconscious.

Before Sims could swing again, Charlie slashed him with the blade, slicing the patrolman's cheek in half, exposing his white teeth through a flap of flesh. Sims continued to try to fight, but he had already lost too much blood. He swung feebly with the stick. It glanced softly off the madman's shoulder.

Charlie grabbed the knife with both hands and jammed the blade through the officer's eye. A thick aqueous humor jetted out as the blade made its way into the cop's brain, killing him instantly.

Sue froze in terror as she witnessed her second gruesome murder of the night. She was locked in a never-ending nightmare. She watched as Charlie dragged the body of the dead cop out of the road. He pulled Sims out of sight and then jumped in the car and started it. The tires screamed as the car took off. Sue screamed too, but a hard right to her temple jarred her brain in its fluid and knocked her unconscious. When she awoke she was staring into the eyes of death.

161

As Chris concentrated with all his might, the image of the warehouse focused to crystal clarity. He could see the inside of the musty old building as if he was standing inside it. There were crates of old boxes scattered across the dusty floor. A few old wooden stools stood in disarray. An old case of empty Coke bottles sat beside a broken-down soda dispenser. The clear plastic Coke sign on the front of the machine was clouded over like a cataract. Then he saw a door open. And then he saw her. It was Sue! She was with a man. The sign above the door said Harrimans. He knew that the vampire was there waiting for her.

"Oh my God," Chris said, "he's at Harriman's department store."

"The old closed-down Harriman's?"

"Yes!" he shouted, "and he's got Sue!"

"Son-of-a-bitch!" Reggie said as he gunned the engine and raced toward the deserted store. "Are you sure it was Sue?"

"Not positive," Chris said aloud, hoping that somehow the sound of his own voice would make it true, but he knew that the other vampire had her.

"Let's hope you're right."

"Hurry up, Reggie. We've got to get there before it's too late."

Reggie nodded grimly and put the pedal to the metal. "We're almost there. It's just another couple of blocks."

On the police radio they heard a report of an officer being down after a routine traffic stop. They didn't think anything about it at the time. They were unaware that the officer, James Sims, might have been Sue's last chance to live.

24

She was beautiful, he thought as he stared deeply into the green eyes flecked with yellow. What a lovely bride she would be. Worthy of spending eternity with him.

"Did I do well, Master?" Charlie groveled.

"Excellent," Rakz said as he tossed a reward to Charlie, who opened the cap on his rat soda with his teeth and drank deeply.

She hadn't even noticed the grisly display as she was entranced in the deep, fathomless eyes of Yosekaat Rakz. Soon she would be on her way to becoming his bride.

25

Reggie slammed on the brakes as the little old lady stepped out into the street. Hot rubber squealed. The squad car stopped about a foot from hitting her. The old woman was oblivious to the fact that she had almost been run over. She shuffled along one little step at a time.

"C'mon, lady!" Reggie shouted and beeped the horn. "Move it!"

No response.

"Come on! Come on!"

Shuffle. Shuffle. Shuffle.

Reggie laid on the horn again. The woman stopped and looked. Reggie motioned for her to get out of the way. She waved back to him as though Reggie was an old friend.

"Damn!" an exasperated Reggie cried.

Chris was beside himself.

The old woman looked at him and smiled. Chris growled and exposed his fangs.

The road was clear in two seconds. They sped on.

Reggie pointed ahead. "There it is!" Carver shouted as he saw their destination.

Harriman's had once been one of the most popular department stores in the city. Everyone shopped there. But the coming of the megastores, the marts, had put an end to the family-owned single store. The old place hadn't been used in ages. The windows were boarded up. Padlocks sealed the doors. Everything was quiet. The building looked dead.

Reggie pulled the car up to the curb and parked.

"Are you sure he's in there?" Reggie asked Chris, almost wishing that he wasn't.

163

Blaze could feel the other vampire's power vibrating through his body.

"Oh, yeah, he's here," Chris said with the certainty of death.

They got out of the car. Reggie pulled his pistol from his shoulder holster. The two detectives walked slowly toward the front of the old building and Chris tried the door. It was locked. Quickly they moved to the side door. The padlock had been twisted off by a powerful force.

Chris looked at Reggie. The black man swallowed hard and motioned for Chris to go ahead. Chris took the handle of the door and turned it slowly. Surprisingly, there was no creaking when he pushed the door open.

As they stepped inside, an aura of perverse evil hung in the air like a thick, choking fog of decadence and decay. It smelled like rotten meat. Chris led the way as his vampire powers allowed him to see perfectly in the darkness. It was at least thirty degrees colder in the building, even though there was no air conditioning.

Reggie's heart slammed against his rib cage. The gun felt slippery in his hand. He peered into the darkness, not knowing what to expect. The warehouse was pitch black. He gripped the gun tighter. Its cold steel was a comfort to him. Reggie thought to himself that if that vampire showed his face, he would empty his revolver into the son-of-a-bitch's undead body. Undead body? Oh my God! If what Chris told him was true, then his gun would be useless. How could he have been so stupid? Now he had nothing to protect . . . the cross! In the car!

"Chris," Reggie whispered urgently to his partner, trying to maintain his cool.

"What?"

"The cross, man. I left it in the car! I'm going back to get it!"

"Okay, but hurry up. He's close by, I can feel it."

"I'll be back in two shakes of a lamb's ass."

Reggie turned and hurried back through the darkened corridor.

Chris continued onward. The sense of omnipresent evil was stifling. As he drew closer to his destination, the air grew more foul. The temperature dropped another ten degrees. He knew at any moment he would meet the other vampire.

Quickly he moved through the warehouse, knowing that the vampire had Sue in his grasp and was going to kill her. His vision was as clear as if ten thousand watts of light illuminated the room. As he turned the corner, he saw them. His heart jumped as Rakz pulled Sue close and was opening his mouth to bite.

26

Reggie made it to the car and was fumbling in his pockets for the keys. Out of habit, the two cops had locked the doors. Sweat poured from Reggie's brow as he desperately tried to pry the keys from his pants. Carver liked to wear his pants tight so the ladies could check out his goods before they sampled them.

"C'mon, you shitbird!" Reggie bitched. "Come out of there."

His fingers barely grabbed the key ring. He pulled. The keys popped out of his pocket with a friendly jingle. He jammed them into the keyhole and popped open the lock. Reaching in quickly across the seat, Reggie grabbed the bag containing the crosses and pulled out the large heavy silver one. He kissed it for luck and backed out of the front seat. He stood up, slammed the door shut, and turned. He didn't see Burnson until the blade was already on its way down.

27

"Stop!" Chris shouted, his voice echoing in the deserted warehouse. "Leave her alone!"

An unperturbed Rakz looked up and smiled. "Ah, brother, I was wondering when we would finally meet."

"Let the girl go!" Chris commanded.

The vampire continued smiling. "Allow me to introduce myself. My name is Yosekaat Rakz."

"You're under arrest for murder, Mr. Rakz."

The vampire laughed, a deep laugh that burst through the dusty cold air of warehouse like an erupting boil. "But, dear brother," he said, "I thirst. You of all people should understand that."

"I drink only to exist. You enjoy it. I can sense that in you."

"You are most perceptive for one so young," Rakz smiled. "You see, I am over three centuries old."

Chris was unimpressed.

"Put the girl down and back away," he said.

"Join me." Rakz said. "I will share her with you. I intend to make her my bride, but I have no qualms about bigamy."

Chris decided there was no point in arguing with Rakz. The vampire intended to have Sue no matter what Chris said. He would have to do something to stop it.

"What if I were to join you?" Chris asked, moving closer to Rakz. "What would I get out of it?"

"We could rule this city at night. Go as we please, feast as we please."

"I don't want to kill anyone."

He moved a step closer.

"But you have never known the joy of totally draining a human being of his life force."

"How do you know I haven't?" Chris asked.

A step closer.

"I know quite a bit about you, Christopher," Rakz said, the mesmerized Sue hanging limp in the crook of his left arm.

"How?"

Another step. He was less than three feet away.

"As you know, we vampires can sense each other. I could feel your clumsy probing earlier, and I must say it gave me quite a headache."

Chris took a step closer.

166

"So you knew I was coming?"

"But of course. I allowed you to find me. Now if you will excuse me."

Rakz pulled Sue close again.

28

The wickedly curved blade of the knife sliced its way downward. Pain jutted through Carver's arm as the knife slashed open his shoulder. Burnson raised the blade again to strike at Reggie's exposed throat. It sliced down again, but this time it collided with the hard metal of the car. Reggie had moved out of the way a split second ahead of the death strike. The force of the blow was stopped by the steel of the car, but the momentum drove Charlie's hand down across the blade. It cut deeply into his palm.

Reggie slammed Burnson in the face with an elbow and the madman fell to his knees. The blood streamed down Carver's shoulder as he tried to pull his gun. He had it in his hand when a crisp punch struck him squarely in the testicles. A sickening sharp pain drew the breath out of his body. His stomach did flipflops. Weak knees tried to support rubber legs. The gun dropped to the pavement.

"You fucking bastard!" Burnson cried in a voice that was an inhuman howl. He picked up his knife and rose up. "Now I'm gonna cut your fucking head off!"

The slippery blood from the gash in his palm caused the knife to slip out of his grasp. It fell to the ground with a ping.

Reggie tried to get his gun, but his stomach was threatening to revolt and pain immobilized him.

Burnson bent over and picked up the knife with his other hand. "I've waited a long time to kill you, nigger," Burnson growled.

Through the pain that clouded his mind, Reggie knew he had to do something or this crazy bastard was going to send him downtown in a body bag. Summoning all his will, he forced himself to stand, his stomach churning like a steam engine.

Burnson drew back the knife and was preparing to drive it deep into Reggie's guts when the explosion occurred.

Chris made his play.

The powerful blow had knocked the vampire down. He hadn't expected it.

Rakz laughed as Chris got up. "Did you think you could fool me?" the elderly vampire chortled.

Chris charged him, knocking Sue out of his grasp. She collapsed to the floor.

"That was a foolish mistake, my friend," Rakz said, still smiling.

Chris swung the handcuffs and they slapped shut on one of the vampire's wrists. "You're under arrest."

The vampire sighed. "Very well, if you insist." He extended his other wrist and Blaze clicked the other cuff tight onto it.

"You have the right to remain silent," Blaze said. "Anything you say can and will be used against you in a court of law."

All of a sudden this had become too easy, Blaze thought.

"You have the right to an attorney . . ."

Rakz had given up too easily.

When he finished reading Rakz his rights, the vampire asked nonchalantly, "Finished?"

Chris nodded.

"Good." Rakz thrust his arms out and apart, breaking the handcuffs as though they were made of rotten twine. The vampire stuck one long finger under the right cuff and snapped it open. He did the same with the second cuff. Chris knew that he himself was strong, but he didn't think he could break tempered steel handcuffs with one finger.

"You see, as a vampire grows older he grows more powerful. If he chooses the dark side, he can attain even more strength." Rakz spoke to Chris the way Robert Young did to

Bud after the boy had not done his homework. "I could crush you like a grape and yet I offer you partnership."

"I don't want anything to do with the path you have chosen."

"Ah," Rakz shrugged. "Very well, then." He picked up an old wooden stool and snapped off a leg—a jagged, pointed leg. "I shall have to end your short life as a vampire," he said nonchalantly, as though it were a forgone conclusion.

30

The stream of vomit hit Burnson right in the face, blinding him. He swung the knife wildly, slashing great amounts of air and nothing else.

As he tried to avoid the blade, Reggie fell back onto the pavement, the jarring thud sending his shoulder into another dimension of pain. As agony coursed through his arm like an electric needle, the detective backpedaled on his good arm, trying to get away. His stomach was still queasy from the blow to his privates, a blow that had probably saved his life.

Burnson wiped the digested burrito Reggie had eaten for dinner out of his eyes, cursing horribly.

As Burnson tried to clear his vision, Reggie tried to clear his mind. The pain was clouding his thoughts. *Your gun!* his mind roared. *Get your gun!*

"My gun," he said aloud, as though he had just discovered the cure for the common cold. Reggie dived for his .38. He grabbed it and fired. The slug split the middle of the "b" in the "curb your dog" sign beside Burnson's head.

A startled Burnson turned and ran. He was crazy, but he wasn't a fool. He knew that a knife was no match for a pistol.

Reggie popped off a couple of shots at the fleeing target, but both missed.

As Burnson vanished, Reggie lay back on the pavement. His balls ached dully. His shoulder had gone numb, and the bitter grapefruit taste of the vomit attacked his tastebuds. He was in bad shape. He didn't know that his partner was in worse shape, much worse.

The makeshift stake Rakz held in his hand was soon to make a place for itself in the heart of one Christopher Blaze. Chris knew he was no match for the vampire's strength or cunning, but he had to fight back for Sue's sake. He glanced over and saw her inert form lying helpless on the floor. He loved her and was determined not to let the vile creature advancing toward him have her. He moved backward in an attempt to lure Rakz away from Sue should she wake up from her trance. If she did, she might have a chance to get away.

Rakz no longer had the ever-present grin on his face. His countenance was now twisted in a black rage. He moved with lightning speed and grabbed Chris by the shirt. He launched him thirty feet across the warehouse, where the detective landed with a crash on a stack of empty crates. A moment later, Chris was flying through the air again. He fell in a heap on top of some boxes. Rakz was on him again, moving so fast it was as though there were two of him and they were playing catch. He picked Chris up once more and slung him into the wall. The detective hit it like a bug on a car windshield. He slid down into the waiting talons of the evil bloodsucker.

"Isn't this fun?" Rakz asked, as though they were playing a game of volleyball on the beach.

Chris threw a punch and caught Rakz a glancing blow off the chin.

The vampire bellowed with rage. "That is the second and last time you will ever strike me! Now I shall end this farce!"

"Not yet, blood breath," Reggie shouted as he thrust the cross into the face of the shocked Rakz.

The undead creature screamed in pain at the sight of the crucifix. "Take it away!"

"Not too fucking likely!" Reggie said, holding the cross in front of him.

Chris tried to see what was happening, but couldn't look at Reggie because of the cross.

The hatred that Rakz exuded at that moment was a living,

breathing entity. It filled the room with its presence and lashed out at the black cop. As the force of that hatred hit him, Reggie dropped the cross. It clattered to the floor.

Carver was vulnerable.

Rakz moved to attack the black police officer, but the effects of the cross had weakened him just enough to let Reggie reach down and pick up the cross before Rakz could crush his skull. He thrust the crucifix into the vampire's face. The image of the silver cross seemed to wither Rakz.

Chris got up and went to Sue's side as Reggie held the vampire at bay.

"Very well," Rakz said, backing away toward the boarded bay window behind him. "Tonight the lines were drawn. You have chosen your destiny, Blaze."

He looked at Reggie with contempt. "And you too, my black friend," he hissed. "You will both suffer in ways you cannot imagine."

He turned and crashed through the boarded-up window, sending glass and wood flying. He landed outside. As he pulled a shard of glass bloodlessly out of his cheek, he added one more chilling note. "Oh, by the way, I will have that girl."

He laughed and disappeared into the shroud of night.

32

They were a fine trio.

Reggie Carver's left arm was covered in rapidly coagulating blood. The front of his shirt speckled with blood and puke. His entire body was one big ache.

Sue Catledge was dazed and disoriented. The whole night had been like the proverbial bad dream. Jonathan's death. The stranger who had gone from kindness to madness. The murder of the policeman. The strange eyes. And now she was with Chris.

And what about Christopher Blaze, the defeated vampire? He had tried for so long to try and retain his humanity. But the creature that had confronted him tonight had taken his humanity, chewed it up, and spit it in his face. He had totally outmatched Chris in every way—cunning, strength, speed. It was like a man with no arms trying to fight the heavyweight champion of the world. He felt helpless. If his partner hadn't arrived when he had, Chris would now be dead and Sue would be dead or even worse, a vampire under Rakz's power.

When they did get the upper hand, Chris couldn't even help Reggie because the power of the cross was as powerful a charm against him as it was against Rakz. He wondered how in God's name he was going to defeat Rakz, or whether he could defeat him at all.

Reggie wobbled and stumbled a bit as he walked toward Chris and Sue.

"You okay?" Chris asked the black man.

"Yeah, I'm fine, I just feel kinda wea . . ." He collapsed.

"Reggie," Sue said, snapping out of her funk. Her doctor's instincts took over as she pulled back Reggie's shirt and looked at the wound. It was fairly clean and not as deep as all the blood made it look. By the looks of it, Reggie had lost a lot of blood and had fainted because of the loss.

"Chris," Sue said, "help me get him into the car."

Chris bent over and lifted his partner as easily as if he were an infant and carried him down the corridor and out of the building. Sue followed.

The detective put Reggie into the back seat. "Let's go, Sue."

They got into the vehicle and drove toward the hospital. Chris radioed ahead as Sue checked the black man's vital signs to be sure he was okay. They checked out fine and she settled back into the front seat.

"Jonathan's dead," she said as the thought popped into her mind.

"Oh, my God . . . what happened?"

"We had an argument after I told him I wanted to end the engagement. We were at the 2001 Club and I tried to leave. Jonathan got upset and became very cruel—calling me names. I lost my temper and slapped him, and then he tried to punch me, but this man stopped him, and Jonathan . . ." She began to lose her composure. "And Jonathan tried to fight him. The man he . . . he . . . killed him."

She broke down, crying.

Chris pulled her close. "I'm sorry, babe," he said. "God, I'm so sorry."

"And then in the hospital," she said in a hitching sob. "This man was being so nice and he offered to give me a ride and so I went and he . . . he hit me and a policeman pulled us over and the man killed him." She began to sob even louder. "He took me to that place, and the other man was there . . . the one who killed Jonathan. And I . . . I just can't remember!"

Chris felt more helpless now than he had in the warehouse as he listened to the love of his life crying. He could do nothing to relieve the horror she would probably have to live with for the rest of her life. And wasn't he responsible? If it weren't for him, Rakz might never have seen her. She wouldn't have gone to the 2001 Club if she hadn't met him. He was racked by guilt as he thought of how much he loved Sue and how he knew he was helpless to protect her.

She snuggled closer to him, burying her face in his chest. Her love gave him courage. *No!* His mind screamed. He wasn't helpless. He could fight back. *Stop feeling sorry for yourself, Blaze! You can figure out a way to win.*

"Hey, are we there yet?" Reggie said from the back seat.

"Not yet, partner. A couple more minutes."

"How are you feeling?" Sue said, sniffling, trying to sound brave.

"Okay. Just a little woozy."

"We'll be there very soon," Chris said.

They turned the corner and there was the hospital. Chris pulled into the emergency room parking lot and parked the car. He jumped out and opened the back door. Gingerly he slipped his arms under Reggie and lifted him out.

"Gee, Daddy," Reggie said, "are we gonna go beddy-bye?"

Even in pain, Reggie was a joker.

Chris smiled.

173

"No, son," he said, "your mother and I have decided we're going to get you bleached so that there's more of a family resemblance."

Reggie laughed, wincing. "Ooh, shit, that hurts."

"Don't worry, Reggie," Sue said, "in a few minutes I'll get you some pain pills and you'll feel much better."

The trio hurried through the doorway and Sue took over, shouting orders left and right to nurses and orderlies. A couple of guys came out with a stretcher, and Chris put Reggie on it. As he was being wheeled away, Carver saw the strange turbaned man he had seen on the night of his fight with Burnson. The man smiled and waved. As Reggie went through the doors with Sue and Chris following, he thought he heard the fellow express himself again. It sounded like someone had stepped on a frog.

As Chris walked down the hospital corridor, he felt that strange tingling sensation that meant . . . oh no! He looked up in horror at the clock. It was 5:55! In ten minutes the sun would be rising. He had to get out of there and into the safety of his darkened apartment.

They turned into the hospital room and Sue began to set up to give Reggie a transfusion.

"Sue, I have to go!"

"But, Chris, I wanted to . . ."

"My allergy, the sun . . . I have to leave now."

"But you can stay in the hospital. There's no need to go out . . ."

"I have to go *now!*"

"But, Chris . . ."

"Please—I don't want to take the chance of exposure."

"Okay," she said reluctantly, wondering if Chris was developing a photophobia. "Can I come over to your apartment today and . . . ?"

"No!"

He regretted the intensity of his answer; it had just slipped out. He pulled her close. "Sue, I *have* to get some sleep. You do, too. I'll call you tonight at about 6:45. It's best that you take off work for a little while until we catch Jonathan's killer. He may still be after you. I'm going to get someone to protect you."

"But why? What have I done to him?"

"Nothing. I'm afraid he's doing it to hurt me."

"But why?" she repeated, her voice rising in a high-pitched panic.

The sun would rise in five minutes.

"Sue, I'll explain it all tonight."

He kissed her and started to hurry away.

"Chris!" she said.

He turned to her.

"What if he tries to get me during the day?" she said.

"Don't worry, he won't."

Chris ran off, leaving Sue to wonder exactly how he knew she'd be safe during the day. Her attention shifted to Reggie as the nurse came in with two pints of blood. She began to hook Reggie up for a transfusion. It would be a couple of hours before Reggie would awaken and Sue would learn more about Yosekaat Rakz.

33

The sun was almost up when the vampire Rakz opened the lid of his casket where he spent his daylight hours. He could sleep in a darkened room, but he preferred the old world charm of his coffin. Besides, he had to sleep on a bed of soil from his birthplace, and it was much easier to transport in a coffin than if it were spread all over the floor of an apartment. Rakz had many coffins throughout the city and changed locations frequently to keep from being discovered.

He spoke to his servant. "Charles, I think we will take a trip to the country for a few days to collect our thoughts and make plans."

"Yes, sir."

"I'll need you to take one of my boxes to the abandoned carnival outside of town and place it in the old House of Horrors exhibit. That will be our home for a short while. I want Blaze and his friend to think about the little surprise I left for them."

Rakz glided into the coffin and lay down.

"I think a week of waiting for me to strike will be enough time for their fear to weaken their resolve, then I will come back and kill them."

Charlie smiled. He couldn't wait.

34

Patrolman Matt Stone thought the girl was asleep on the park bench. A newspaper covered her face. He didn't want to wake her, but he had to do it . . . it was his job. He walked over to the woman and tapped her foot gently with his nightstick.

"Hey, lady, you can't sleep there."

She didn't move.

He tapped her a little harder.

"C'mon, ma'am. You need to get up," he said.

Still no movement.

"Look." He grabbed her arm and pulled. Something tumbled out from under the paper.

Stone gasped in shock as he saw the girl's head fall with a dull thump to the pavement. It had been twisted off her shoulders. A note was pinned to her dress. The cop snatched it off and read it. He couldn't make sense of it. He went to the police phone to call in that there was a DB in the park. It was the start of a lousy morning.

35

Chris made it home just before the sun rose. The night had been a tough one. He fell into the bed and the death sleep took him. His last thoughts were of Sue, his beautiful angel. They were together in the woods, locked in a warm embrace. Chris looked at her and Sue smiled lovingly. Her teeth were pointed and sharp. Her green eyes burned like fire.

Chapter 4

1

Reggie woke up and moved his arm up and down to gauge the damage from the knife wound he had received. It hurt like hell, but it wasn't too stiff. Sue was in the chair next to his bed. She was sleeping soundly. It had been a long night for both of them.

Reggie lowered his injured arm and accidentally hit the steel tray next to the bed. It clattered loudly.

Sue awakened with a gasp of fright, her eyes wide with terror.

"Hey," Reggie cried, "take it easy, Doc, it's only me and my clumsy-assed self."

"Oh," she said, gaining her composure. "I'm sorry, Reggie, my nerves are on edge. The whole night was very upsetting."

Reggie nodded. "Very upsetting is an understatement. You okay?"

"I'm a little shaky, but I think I'll be all right. How are you feeling?"

"Woozy, and my arms hurt, but I feel okay. What's the doctor's opinion?"

"You're fine. You just lost a lot of blood, but the cut isn't too deep. It should be fine in a week or so."

"What time is it?"

"Nine o'clock in the morning."

Reggie's face grew alarmed. "Chris! Is he okay? Did he leave before the sun came up?"

"Yes, he's fine."

"Good. That, uh, allergy thing is really bad news if he gets in the sun."

Sue wondered if there was more to Chris's allergy than he had told her. Both Chris and Reggie had seemed unduly alarmed. From what she had read about PMLE, sunscreens and protective clothing were an acceptable means of prevention, along with medication such as antimalarial drugs, beta carotene and psolaren, and UVA of photoallergic reactions. She was about to ask Reggie if he knew something Chris wasn't telling her when she was interrupted by a loud groan. She saw Reggie reaching over to pick up the pitcher of water beside his bed.

"Ooh," he moaned again, "man, that hurts."

"Here. Let me do that," Sue said as she took the pitcher out of Reggie's hand and poured him a drink. She handed him the water.

"Thank you." Reggie gingerly touched his shoulder. "Damn, what a trip! Those two dudes are bad news. We'd better be on our toes tonight."

"Tonight, you said tonight!" She exclaimed. "Chris said it, too. He said that this man, this Rakz, couldn't get me during the day—only at night. You know what he meant by that, don't you?"

Reggie took a long drink of water. He wasn't sure whether he should tell her the truth.

"Do you know?" she asked again.

He decided she had a right to know.

"Yeah, I know," he said, "but you're not going to believe it."

"Try me."

"Okay, but you really aren't going to believe it."

Reggie began to explain the story.

Captain Tom Draper had been called in on this one. It was a horrible affair. A young girl had been killed, her head torn off from her shoulders. There were deep purple bruises on her cheeks from where the murderer's powerful fingers had gripped her face.

This guy was some kind of strong, Draper thought, but then, so was the man who had killed Dan McIrney and the girl in the alley. The reports said the girl had strange marks on her throat and a shaft of wood through her chest, just like the unsolved case a couple of months before. They all had to be related somehow.

Draper shuddered at the thought of a super-strong maniac running around loose who had already in all probability killed four people. He would probably kill again. Draper held the note that had been pinned to the girl's body. If they could only figure out its meaning, they might have a chance to get a lead on the murderer. The note had been written in what appeared to be brown ink. Upon analysis at the lab, it in fact turned out to be dried blood.

Draper knew he needed someone to work full time on this case. If his suspicions were correct, the city of Miami had a serial killer on its hands. He decided to assign the team of Blaze and Carver to work it full time. They were the best detectives he had, and they had already done some preliminary work on the murders. Maybe they could make some sense out of the note.

As Draper read it again, he still couldn't figure out what it meant. But even though he didn't understand the true meaning of the message, he knew what the underlying theme was. Someone else was going to die.

3

"I don't believe it!" Sue cried. "A vampire?"
Reggie nodded solemnly. He had told her the truth.
She continued. "This guy really thinks he's a vampire?"

Almost the truth. Sue was frightened enough without having to learn that vampires really existed . . . especially in light of the fact that she was in love with one of them.

"Yeah," he said. "This guy thinks he's a regular Count Dracula."

"Who was that other man? That Charlie . . ."

"He's an ex-cop named Charlie Burnson. I used to work with him down at the station house. We had a few run-ins. He got shitcanned, I mean, fired, after he kept missing work and messing up assignments. He was the one who stabbed me."

"He also killed a policeman. I saw him. It was horrible." She covered her face with her hands.

"That must have been the call we heard last night. Jesus Christ, Burnson's really gone over the edge."

"Shouldn't we call the police?"

"I *am* the police," Reggie reminded her.

"Don't you need a statement from me?"

"Sure, but that can wait until after I wake up a little," he said.

"Right now, I'm still feeling a little funky."

"We both need to get some more rest."

"Don't worry, Sue. When I get to the station I'll swear out warrants for their arrests."

She didn't know Reggie was lying to her. He had no intention of doing any such thing. If he told anyone at the precinct that a vampire was responsible for the killings in the city and that Charlie Burnson was in league with him, they would never believe him and would proceed as though they were on a regular murder case. A lot of cops would get killed if they ran up against the undead monster. Reggie had caught just a glimpse of the one-sided fight between Chris and the evil Rakz. It was enough to convince him that the vampire was unbelievably strong and that a great many of his friends would be killed if they confronted Rakz. Besides, Rakz wanted Blaze and him to suffer, now that they had interfered in his affairs. The thought made Reggie's stomach crawl with terror, but at least Chris and he knew what they were up against. The others would not.

And what *were* they up against? Reggie rolled the thought in his mind for a few minutes. A vampire was the answer, that's what they were up against. A vampire. The recognition of their foe gave Reggie an idea. After he rested up for a little while, he would go to the library that afternoon. He had a little research to do.

4

The big cop dropped into his favorite chair and sighed. It had been a long night, and the gruesome murder in the morning had made it even longer.

As he kicked off his shoes, his little seven-year-old daughter, Mary, came skipping down the stairs of their townhouse and plopped into his lap. She gave him a big kiss and a hug, then caught him off guard with a very simple question.

"Daddy," she said in her cute tiny voice. "When are you gonna retire?"

He looked at her in wonder. *Out of the mouths of babes,* he thought.

"What makes you ask that, honey?"

"You look tired alla time. Don't you getta take a nap at work?"

Draper laughed. "No, we have to work. I don't have time for a nap."

She shrugged. "That must be a yucky job, then."

"Yeah, it can be a yucky job."

Especially when a young girl has her head torn off her body, Draper thought to himself.

"So, Daddy, when you gonna stop bein' a policeman?"

"I have about three more years to go, and then I'm going to retire and take it easy."

"Gosh, that'll be cool, havin' you home alla time."

"Yeah," he said as he pulled his little daughter close to him and hugged her. "It'll be really great."

She smiled broadly in a gap-toothed grin. She had just lost her front teeth.

He kissed her cheek.

"Now, don't you have to get off to your ballet class?" he said.

"Yeah," she said, then shouted toward the kitchen. "Mom! I gotta go!"

Connie Draper came out of the kitchen. She was an attractive brunette about forty years old. She still had a good figure, even though she thought her butt could stand to lose a couple inches here and there . . . still, all in all, a good figure. Her smile was her most captivating feature. It could be best described as radiant and was one of the things Tom loved most about his wife. Her smile could make him feel good even on the worst of days. It was a warm smile, the kind that makes you feel like everything is going to be just fine.

As she walked into the living room, Tom thought about how much he loved her.

"You ready?" Connie said to her daughter.

"Yeah, let's go."

"Give your daddy a kiss," Connie said.

"Okay."

The little girl ran over and kissed her father.

"Bye, hon," Tom said, then looked at his wife. "How about a kiss from you?"

His wife smiled and walked over to his chair. As she bent down to give him a little peck, he pulled her close and gave her a warm, wet kiss full on the lips.

"What was that for?" she asked, pleasantly surprised.

"Just because I love you."

"I love you, too," she replied, kissing him on top of the head. "We'll continue this later," she whispered huskily in his ear.

Tom smiled.

"'Bye," he said, "have a good time."

"Where are they going?" a voice called out from behind the police captain.

Draper turned and saw his very pretty daughter, Chrissy, standing in the doorway to the Florida room.

"To ballet class," he said, "and how are you doing this morning?"

She walked over to her dad and kissed him.

"I'm fine, but you look awful."

Draper wearily ran his fingers through his hair. "Gee, thanks."

"I'm sorry, you just look so beat."

"I am, baby," he sighed then added. "Y'know, my job really sucks sometimes."

She took his hand. "Bad night?"

"The worst. But I'll get over it. Where's the Toddster?"

"He's over at Bobby McCutcheon's house. They were going to play Masters of the Universe."

Draper wished his son, Todd, was there, but he understood the importance of saving the world from the evils of Skeltor.

"I need to get some sleep," Draper said, taking off his glasses and rubbing his bloodshot eyes. He set the glasses on the table next to the chair and kicked back in the easy chair.

Chrissy began to massage his temples. "Feel good?" she asked.

Her father groaned with pleasure.

She continued to massage his temples for about a minute, gently soothing him and taking the tension away.

"Well, Daddy," she said, "I have to be getting ready for work."

He didn't respond.

"Dad?" she asked quietly.

Chrissy looked at her father and smiled. He was fast asleep.

5

"Shh," the old librarian said, issuing the classic warning to two teenagers who were giggling over in the medical section. The boys were checking out the book *The Ins and Outs of Sexual Reproduction*. They had just gotten to the section that described that strange, unknown creature known as the vagina.

Reggie glanced over at the boys and grinned to himself.

He remembered when he and his buddies used to do the same thing with *The Joy of Sex.*

Carver was across the aisle from the boys in a different section of the library, the section that covered myths and legends. He started pulling out all the books he could find on the subject of vampirism. When he had all the books he could carry, he made his way to the checkout counter and plopped the books down with a grunt. The old librarian took his card and ran it through the computer. As she ran the scanner over the books to log them into the computer, she glanced over to see what the two boys were doing now. She saw that they had tired of the book and were playing paper football across one of the tables. She frowned and finished checking out Reggie's books.

As she handed him back his card, she said, "So are you going vampire hunting?"

"Excuse me?" Reggie replied, not believing his ears.

"Vampire hunting . . . is that why you need all the books? Is there a vampire loose in the city?" she asked in all seriousness.

Carver couldn't believe it. How did this woman know? Had she met a vampire before? Was she under Rakz's spell, like Burnson?

"Uh, no, ma'am. I'm doing some research for a book."

"You never know when a vampire is going to strike," she said. "Yes, they're a big problem in the city."

She smiled, and Reggie realized that she had been putting him on. He had been so uptight about the situation in which he was involved that he hadn't picked up on the fact that the old lady was just having a bit of fun. He scooped up the books.

"Thanks," he said and started for the door.

"Good luck, I hope you get your vampire."

She giggled.

"So do I," Reggie said to himself. "So do I."

Chapter 5

1

Night had fallen. Sue was alone and walking home. She knew she should have left the hospital earlier, but an emergency case had come in and she had had to help out. She hurried along. The click-clack of her shoes on the pavement echoed off the walls. The streets were totally empty. No one was anywhere to be seen. It was as if a plague had swept through and left the neighborhood for dead.

Click . . . clack . . . click . . . clack . . .

Her shoes sounded on the pavement. She was totally alone—or so she thought, until she saw a car come around the corner. For some reason the lone vehicle struck a chord of terror in her heart. It moved slowly up the street, making its way toward her like a panther stalking a deer. Its headlights seemed to leer at her like a malevolent specter. She picked up the pace.

Click . . . clack . . . click . . . clack . . . click . . . clack . . .

The car stopped about twenty feet in front of her and idled. The driver flashed his brights, blinding her momentarily. Somehow the car seemed familiar, and Sue was hit with the growing realization that she was in grave danger. She wanted desperately to run, but something compelled her to keep going toward the car. She tried to stem the tide of fear that was welling up inside her, causing her heart to beat like a jackhammer.

She began to walk even faster, hoping she would pass by the car quickly and confirm that her fear was just in her imagination.

Click . . . clack . . . click . . . clack . . . click . . . clack . . . click . . .

As she went by the car, its lights went out and the engine stopped running. She turned and looked back. Fear grabbed her by the throat. It was the car, the green sedan, the same one which had taken her on her nightmare journey the night before!

She turned to flee and ran straight into the drooling Charlie Burnson. He tried to grab her, but she lashed out and kicked him in the shin.

Burnson howled in pain as Sue ran away from him.

She felt strange, her legs didn't seem to be working properly. Her muscles felt exhausted as though she had just gotten done with two hours of aerobics. She kept stumbling.

Click.clack. cla . . . click . . . clack . . . click. clack . . . click . . . clack . . .

It was as though she was trying to slog through mud that was up to her shins—thick, clinging mud that sapped the life out of her legs. Behind her she could hear the raspy breathing of her pursuer.

"Come on, baby, the master is waiting. He wants to hold you," he wheezed. "He wants to kiss you. He wants to drink all your blood!"

Where is everyone, where are all the people? her mind screamed.

But it was just her and the madman.

She turned quickly to see how far behind he was and didn't see the trashcan ahead of her. She hit it full speed and tumbled hard to the pavement, striking her head. As she opened her eyes, the world around her was vague and cloudy. A misty fog blurred her vision. She could only make out impressions of objects moving about her. *Oh, my God, not now! Please, not now!* She tried to clear her sight, but it was no use. The harder she tried to see, the thicker the mist became. A flash of movement to her left . . . a shape to her right. She tried to concentrate all her efforts to see. At any moment she expected to feel the sweaty, greasy hands of the maniac around her throat, or the cold steel blade, slicing her open like a ripe melon.

But she didn't. Nothing happened.

Suddenly it had become as quiet as a tomb. She couldn't hear anything except for the blood pounding in her ears.

As she backed up on her hands and feet, trying to get up and escape, she cut her hand on the jagged edge of a broken bottle. She grabbed the neck of the bottle and prepared to use the sharp, pointed end on her attacker if he touched her.

She closed her eyes and opened them, hoping to clear the fog. Her vision snapped to crystal clarity.

"He wants you!"

Her heart jumped. Burnson was right in her face!

She thrust out the makeshift weapon. It collided with the throat of Charlie Burnson and buried itself in the soft flesh. Blood began to pour out of the bottle. The sharp edge had sliced open his jugular vein.

Burnson gurgled and fell to his knees, his life's blood pouring out of him, covering the ground and Sue.

As she got up to flee, he reached out and grabbed her, trying to pull her toward him. She kicked out and her foot connected with the end of the bottle, driving it deeper into his throat. The blade severed the tendons in the right side of his neck. His head hung limply to one side.

She tried to get up again, slipping in the growing puddle of gore that was pouring out of the gruesome specter.

A hand lashed out again and grabbed her ankle. She tried to kick free, but the hand held firm.

"Die, you bastard!" she screamed and kicked again.

The grip slackened and she pulled free. She scrambled to her feet. As she got up, she looked to see if Burnson had died and her fear escalated to a higher pitch. Not only was Charlie Burnson not dead, he was smiling, his brown teeth streaked with blood . . .

And he was getting up!

She turned to run, and this time, Yosekaat Rakz was there. He grabbed her and drew her toward him.

She knew she was dead.

As his fangs pierced her throat and he began to suck the life out of her, she screamed. Before she could die, she woke up.

She was in her own bed. The sun had just gone down.

2

Chris felt the energy course through his body, signaling that the sun had set and another night was beginning.

He got up and went to the kitchen. He opened the fridge and pulled out one of the bottles of plasma he kept there. He drank down the thick fluid, quenching his awful thirst for a moment. Chris never fully satiated himself because he didn't relish the thought of having to steal more blood from the hospital than he had to steal. But even more than that, he didn't do it because he feared that by giving in to his vampiric urges, he would set the course to become another Rakz, a taker of life, a leech who preyed on others to sustain his unholy existence. It was for that reason that he lived with the constant gnawing pain, the hunger that always cried out for more, never to be completely fulfilled. Chris thought it was a small price to pay for his humanity.

The phone rang in the other room, and Chris hustled in to answer it before the answering machine kicked in. He switched off the machine and picked up the telephone. It was Sue, and she sounded upset.

"Chris, I just had the most awful dream. I'm shaking like a leaf. Could you come over? I really need you."

"I'll be there in twenty minutes," Chris said.

"I love you, Chris. Please hurry."

"I will. I love you, too."

He hung up the phone and hurried to get dressed.

He was about to leave when the phone rang again. He rushed over to answer it.

"Hello?"

"Hey, Vampocop."

It was Reggie.

"Listen, Reg, I'm in a hurry. Sue is really shaken up by a dream she had. This whole mess has got her very upset."

"I can relate to that. I went to the library today and got some books on vampirism. I figure we can test what works and what doesn't."

"On me, I take it?"

"Well, as the resident vampire, I thought you might be a good choice."

"I don't know."

"Listen, I'm not talking about ways to kill a vampire. We just want to find out how we can prevent him from getting us. We need something to stop Rakz. I mean, no offense, but you didn't exactly overwhelm him last night."

Chris remembered how easily Rakz had dispatched him.

"None taken. I'll do it," he said. "Come by Sue's at 102 North Palm. Do you know where that is?"

"Sure, I'll be there about eight."

"Okay. Be sure to bring some crosses and maybe some garlic. I hope Sue doesn't ask too many questions . . ."

Reggie interrupted.

"Don't worry. I told her Rakz was a psycho who thinks he's a vampire. She should expect this stuff to ward him off."

"Good. I'm going to hire Burley Fayer to stay with Sue, just in case Burnson tries anything."

"He's a good man," Reggie said, then a thought came to him. "You should tell Sue that Burley's a cop so she thinks the police department is backing us up. I told her we were going to make out a report and tell the department, but you and I know they won't believe us."

"Yeah, that's a good idea. I'll be sure to tell him. After he gets there we'll leave and go over to your place to do the tests."

"Okay. See you at eight."

Chris hung up the phone and left. As the door closed behind him, the phone rang for the third time, but this time he didn't hear it. The party on the other end was pissed. It was Captain Draper. He'd been trying to reach Chris all day but had kept getting the answering machine.

"Damn it, I need those guys here."

He hung up and dialed Carver's number. The phone rang and rang.

Unfortunately for the captain, Reggie had just left too. He would have to wait until ten, when they came on duty, to see if they could make anything out of the note.

3

Sue was just putting the finishing touches on the steak dinner she had prepared to surprise Chris. She had busied herself with the meal to take her mind off the frightening dream.

The doorbell rang.

"Perfect timing," she said to herself as she set the sizzling platter of meat down on the table.

Sue walked over to the front door, peered out through the peephole's fisheye lens, and saw the face of her lover. She unlocked the deadbolt and opened the door.

"Hi," she said. "Come on in."

Chris stepped in and gave her a kiss.

"Hey, babe, how are you holding up?"

"Pretty well, I guess. It still seems so unreal."

"I'm sorry I got you involved," Chris apologized.

Sue took his hand.

"Listen you, I love you more than I thought I could ever love another human being."

Inwardly, Chris cringed at the words "human being."

Sue continued. "To tell you the truth, I'm sorry I'm involved, I'm sorry you're involved, I'm sorry Reggie is involved, but the point is that we're all in this together, and we need to do the best we can to protect each other."

This was one special lady, Chris thought to himself, and at that moment he loved her even more, if that was possible. But still he wondered if she was placing her faith in the wrong person. He had creeping doubts that he could defeat Rakz but swept them back into a dark corner of his mind. He had to think positively.

"Listen, Sue, Reggie is coming by about eight. He has something to give you. Also, I've got a cop from the witness protection agency to come over and protect you."

"Great. I feel better already." She smiled, but her eyes still registered fear.

"Did someone tell Jonathan's parents?" she asked.

"Yes, they were notified."

"God, he didn't deserve to die that way."

"We're going to catch his killer," Chris said. "I guarantee you that."

He tried to sound confident, but in his heart he wasn't so sure.

As Sue thought about the brutal slaying of Jonathan, the horror of it threatened to overwhelm her. She changed the subject.

"I made us dinner. I hope you like steak."

Chris smelled as he remembered Reggie's comments about steaks the night before. "I'm not really hungry, I had something before I came over. I'm sorry."

"You sure? It's New York strip."

"Yes, I'm positive," Chris demurred. "I really appreciate the thought, though."

"Okay. Maybe Reggie will want some when he gets here."

"If I know Reggie, you won't have any leftovers."

"Good. Well, if you don't mind, I'm going to go ahead and eat before it gets cold," Sue said as she walked toward the dining room table.

"Enjoy," Chris said. "I've got to make a phone call."

Chris took out his little address book, looked up the number for Burley Fayer, found it, and dialed. He hoped the big Georgian would be able to help him out.

4

Yosekaat Rakz arose renewed. He always did enjoy a good fight. His new foes were not on par with the great general Karlokia or even his second-in-command, Captain Dimitri Macheras, but nevertheless they were a challenge.

The old House of Horrors where he was now staying temporarily was in a state of disrepair. The air in there smelled vaguely of musty wet dirt, and the place had the dank, cloying feel of a cave. The decorative spiderwebs that clung to the walls, which had once been sprayed out of a bottle, had now been replaced by the genuine article. The aged mannequins of the various horror characters from the heyday of Universal Pictures all looked as though they had an advanced case of leprosy. Their wax skin was cracked and riddled with pockmarks. The mummy was half unwrapped. The sockets that had once held the haunting eyes of Dracula were now empty, the summer residence of a family of cockroaches. The Wolfman looked as though it was only a half moon out. Frankenstein's monster, the Hunchback, the Creature from the Black Lagoon, they were all there.

Rakz felt a certain kinship with these creatures. In times gone by, he had known many strange beings, good people and bad people who had been claimed by the dark side and become the creatures of legend.

When he was a boy, Rakz had known of a man named Janos Kruk who suffered from lycanthropy, the curse of the werewolf. Kruk had viciously murdered ten villagers in the small town of Vasaria and would have kept on killing if his father, Valdemir Kruk, hadn't beaten him to death with a silver candlestick. After the deed was done, the old man cut his own throat, unable to cope with the grief and guilt of having had to kill his own flesh and blood in order to save the lives of the innocent.

Much later, a century and a decade, to be precise, Rakz had met another man who suffered from the mark of the beast. The vampire had been on the prowl for victims and had seen the werewolf kill a farmer who had stayed out in his fields too long. Rakz followed the wolfman to a cabin that Rakz believed to be his lair. The next night Rakz had come back and fired a silver bullet into the heart of the werewolf. He didn't need the competition. One creature of the night was enough for any small town.

As Rakz looked at the decaying form of Count Dracula, he remembered how he himself had been tainted by the bite of the vampire, Armand Dracul, those many years ago.

"Master," Burnson said, breaking Rakz's chain of thought. "Are we going to hunt tonight?" His voice was filled with the anticipation of a child getting ready to hunt eggs on Easter.

"I am, but you will stay here. I travel faster alone."

"But I want to go."

"Silence!" Rakz's voice was like thunder. "I have told you once, that is enough!"

His eyes were death.

Burnson closed up tighter than the lid of a coffin. He had no wish to suffer the consequences of his master's wrath.

"Now I shall go," Rakz said as his body began to change. It shimmered and shrank. His arms stretched out, becoming thin and bonelike appendages. The skin from his sides stretched and attached to his bony arms. His legs shriveled, his toes curling into powerful claws. Rakz' face shrank into a horrible pug-nosed creature. His ears stretched into points and shifted on top of his head.

When the transformation was complete, he squealed and flapped his wings. The great vampire bat took off and flew out of one of the shattered windows of the House of Horrors.

As his master flew out of sight, Charlie began to search for some small creature to feast on.

Yosekaat Rakz went to search for bigger prey.

5

Reggie arrived at Sue's place at the same time as the big private detective, Burley Fayer. He was glad that the former beat cop turned private eye was going to help.

"Hey, Big Burl, what's happening?"

"You, Reggie," the big man from Stone Mountain, Georgia, said as he shook the black man's hand.

"You're looking as massive as ever," Carver said, patting Burley on the shoulder. It was solid muscle. Reggie admired the sheer size of the man: six-four, about three hundred pounds. In his heyday as a no-nonsense flatfoot on a beat,

Burley Fayer had been the biggest cop on the force. He had used his size to help keep the streets clean from crime. He didn't tolerate pimps or pushers on his beat and made sure when he busted them that they understood that fact, usually with a swift kick in the ass or a nightstick upside the head. Although he was known to be tough on his enemies, Burley was a big softie around his friends and the people that he protected. They loved the big man. Burley was always willing to do somebody a favor or loan them some money if they were down on their luck. Whenever anyone thanked him for doing them a good turn, Burley would get a goofy embarrassed half smile that everybody called his "aw shucks" look. But with Burley it was the genuine article. He really was embarrassed by the attention. He would rather just stay in the background, not an easy feat for a man as big as a bear, and let his good deeds speak for themselves.

A lot of cops were disappointed when he decided to call it a day to retire and open his own detective agency, but it was a good move for the big guy, so everyone felt good about his decision.

"I'm glad to see you decided to help us out," Reggie said.

The "aw shucks" look spread across Burley's face.

"Shoot, I know Chris or you would do the same for me."

Reggie nodded.

Burley scratched his head, which sounded like sandpaper because of his burr haircut.

"So ol' Charlie went apeshit, huh?"

"Madder than a fucking hatter," Reggie said, ringing the doorbell.

"Never did like that ass-faced bastard. I hope he does try somethin'. I'll shove ol' Ruthie up his butt."

He patted the big gun in his shoulder holster as if it were a trusted friend.

"Who is it?" a muffled voice called out from inside the house.

"The cavalry," Reggie shouted.

Sue recognized her friend's voice and opened the door. As she saw Reggie and the huge man who was with him, she began to feel safer already.

The wind cut through Beth Stern's flimsy dress as she tried to thumb a ride on the deserted interstate beside the Homestead exit. The elderly man who had given her a lift from Palm Beach had just dropped her off and was on his way home. The threat of rain loomed overhead as ominous clouds covered the stars in the sky. Lightning flashed in the distance, followed by the rumble of thunder a few seconds later. She would need a ride soon, or she'd probably be caught in the middle of a downpour. Her spirits soared when she saw a set of headlights coming up the road. She knew she'd have little trouble getting a ride if there was a man behind the wheel of the oncoming car. She was a good-looking girl with a long mane of blonde hair and a figure that could jumpstart an eighty-year-old's sex drive. The short skirt she wore exposed just enough of her to ensure that her wait on the highway would be a short one.

She stuck out her thumb, and the car her hopes were riding on passed by. She turned to see if it was stopping, but the red taillights disappeared into the night. Beth thought that maybe she should forget trying to catch a ride and head for town and try to find a place to crash for the night.

Thunder rolled and the air began to smell like rain. Still she decided to wait for one more car and try to hitch a ride.

7

He had seen the young hitchhiker by the side of the road and a perverse glee struck him. *How fortuitous!* Rakz thought. He had been on his way to town to stalk his prey, a move that always put him at risk. Now he didn't have to worry. This girl was an easy target. He swooped down and decided to have a little fun before he dined.

Beth screamed as the large furry creature buzzed by her face, its bristly hair brushing her cheek. As the bat flew by her again, she waved her hand in front of her as though she was shooing away a pesky fly. The bat changed direction and dived at her again.

Although the bat was unusually large, Beth wasn't really afraid. At first she had been startled by the creature's sudden appearance, but now she was more annoyed than frightened.

Beth had been a tomboy as a young girl. She and her brother would go bat hunting at dusk in their neighborhood. They would walk down the street until they saw a bat flying overhead. They'd toss a rock at the flying creature in an attempt to confuse its radar. Invariably the bat would be fooled into thinking the stone was an insect and would come diving down after it. The bat would swoop right above their heads, and when it got too close, they would run away, screaming in fear and delight. Once they had even caught one of the furry creatures in a fishnet, but their mom made them let it go. She also told them never to go bat hunting again, because bats carried rabies and might bite them. When their mother described rabies and the treatment you had to get if you were bitten—the thirteen shots in the stomach—they decided that bat hunting wasn't so much fun after all.

The big bat buzzed her again. She thought its radar must really be screwed up. It was only when Beth saw the face of the creature that her body went numb with terror. It was the visage of a bat, with a pug nose and a mouthful of sharp, needlelike fangs, but the eyes . . . the eyes were human.

Human eyes in a horrible bat's head.

Just then, headlights appeared on the horizon and Beth ran quickly toward them, screaming for help.

The bat dived at her again, but this time it slammed into her back, knocking her to the hard asphalt. The shells in the road tore into her knees like rough sandpaper. The bat rose into the night and disappeared.

The terrified girl got up. Her hands and knees burned where her flesh had met the unyielding pavement. As the car approached, Beth waved her hands frantically, trying to signal the driver to stop.

"Stop! Please, stop!" she yelled her voice tearing into the stillness of the night. The car passed her and her heart sank. She turned to see if they were stopping and was uplifted as she saw the Camaro pull over about 25 yards down the road.

She was saved.

8

"Hot damn," Ricky Ronat said.

He couldn't believe his good fortune. There, in front of him by the side of the road, was a good-looking woman looking for a ride. It was a long way down to the Keys. It sure would be nice to have a lady to talk with on his trip. Even nicer if he played his cards right and got her to spend the night in a hotel with him. He pulled out his breath deodorant spray and blasted away the last trace of the onion that he had eaten on his burger earlier. Ricky looked in the mirror and pushed down the unruly hairs that shot out of the top of his head like corn stalks. He wanted to make a good first impression. He pulled over to the emergency lane and waited for the girl to get in.

He waited about thirty seconds, and then the door opened . . . the driver's-side door!

"Hey, baby, you need to get in on the other side," he said.

They weren't the kind of famous last words that made it into *Bartlett's Quotations,* but then, Ricky Ronat had never intended them to be the last words he would ever speak.

9

Beth was about ten yards away from the safety of the car when she saw a sight that she would remember for the rest of her life.

All five minutes of it.

A nicely dressed man in black evening clothes had come out of nowhere and grabbed the driver of the car. He pulled the screaming man out of his vehicle and picked the driver up. The man in black slammed him to the ground as if he was a little boy trying to see how far he could get his superball to bounce. But this ball didn't bounce. It landed with a sicken-

197

ing thud and a loud crack that was the driver's neck snapping.

The man picked up the limp body and put him back into the car. In an unbelievable feat of strength, he grabbed the side of the automobile and flipped it over. The Camaro tumbled into the ditch.

The man turned toward her. She had nowhere to go. As he approached her, the first thing she saw was his eyes. They drew her in and she began to feel calm and relaxed. Her fears subsided. It wasn't unlike the feeling she got when she did a little smack—that peaceful, dreamlike feeling. She didn't even feel the razor-sharp fangs bury into her jugular vein or the vampire sucking the life out of her. She was at peace, and she died that way.

Rakz drove the stake through her heart and then tossed her body onto the wrecked Camaro. He searched through the girl's purse and found a lighter. He lit the cloth purse on fire and tossed it onto the trail of gasoline that had leaked out of the gas tank when he had overturned the vehicle.

The flames licked at the trail and then ignited it with a *whoosh*. The car's nearly full tank exploded in a ball of flame.

The satiated vampire changed back into a bat and flew off. He had plans to make, evil plans.

10

"Sue, this is Burley Fayer, he's going to be your shadow for a little while," Chris said.

"How do you do, Mr. Fayer?" Sue smiled and extended her hand.

The big private eye took it and pumped it three times.

"Burley, ma'am, if you don't mind," he said in a deep southern accent.

"Okay, Burley it is," she replied.

"We've got to get going now," Chris said as he kissed Sue. "You take care of this lady, Burley."

198

"That's what they pay me for, partner," the big Georgian drawled.

Chris left first and then gave Reggie the high sign. The black detective nodded, went back into the house, and handed Sue a big cross and a string of garlic cloves. He also gave a cross to the big private eye.

"What in hell's this for?" Burley asked, incredulous.

Reggie was about to answer when Sue beat him to the punch.

"This man Rakz is a psychotic who believes he is a vampire. Psychologically, these things will have an effect on him because he believes that they are supposed to harm him."

"All right. I guess I could use the thing. But I still trust my gun better."

"Just make sure you keep the cross handy," Reggie warned.

"Whatever you say, Reggie."

Sue nodded.

"Gotta go," Reggie said as he turned and walked out the door.

"Take care, Reg," Sue said.

"Always, Doc, always."

Reggie hustled over to the waiting sedan. Chris reached over and unlocked the passenger door, and the detective got in.

"We still going to your place?" Chris asked.

"Yeah, I've got it all ready."

Chris did a U-turn and headed in the direction of Reggie's apartment.

"Did you give Sue the cross and the garlic?"

"Yeah."

"And Burley?"

"Yeah, him too."

"Any trouble?"

"Nope, Sue explained the whole thing to him."

Chris raised his eyebrows. "Sue explained it to him?"

"I kid you not. She really believes that Rakz thinks he is a vampire and said that we should proceed as if he were the real thing."

"That's great. Now she won't think it's stupid to use the cross or anything else against him. It's like she knows enough of the truth to save her."

Reggie shook his head. "Man, if she only knew the whole truth."

"Yeah, well, someday I'm gonna have to tell her," Chris said solemnly as he turned the corner. "Because I plan on marrying that woman when this is over."

11

Rakz arrived back at the House of Horror exhibit and landed gingerly on the outstretched arm of the Frankenstein monster. The ancient vampire studied Charles for a moment.

His insane slave had somehow gotten ahold of a kitten and was stroking it gently.

"Nice kitty," he crooned to the little white bundle of fur. "You and I are going to be great friends. Blood brothers."

Rakz continued to watch, his curiosity piqued.

"Yes, we are going to be blood brothers."

Burnson kissed the kitty on its little button nose and then snapped its back like a dried twig. He bit deeply into the still-alive kitten. It mewed pathetically, then screeched as Charlie tore away a chunk of flesh and hair. The blood flowed freely from the open gash, and Burnson was only too glad to drink it up. As the flow began to slacken, Burnson placed his lips around the ghastly wound and sucked greedily, trying to drain the last drop of blood from the kitten.

Rakz flitted down to the floor and changed back into his human form.

"I see you were as successful on your hunt as I was."

Burnson looked up and grinned like a shark, his lips smeared with the sticky red blood. "Yes, I found it outside. There are others, too."

"Very good. Perhaps one day I will give you the pleasure

of enjoying a small child."

"That would be a joy, Master."

Rakz smiled. "One you can only imagine."

"Master, when are we going to make the nigger and Blaze pay?"

"Soon, very soon. But for now we must go to the penthouse in the city. We have much to do."

12

"Okay, Count Blaze. Are you ready?"

Chris nodded. "As ready as I'll ever be."

"Here goes nothing. Okay, first the cross."

He picked it up and put it down.

"We already know that works. Same thing with garlic. Okay, here's something different—wolfbane."

"Wolfbane? Where the hell did you get that?"

"Over on 33rd at Rasta's House of the Occult and Haitian Deli. This weird old guy Rasta deals in the occult."

"Okay," Chris said, "let's see what it does."

Reggie thrust the leafy dried plant into Chris's face. He moved back, then realized it had no effect on him.

"Nothing," he said.

"Okay, wolfbane. No effect."

Reggie marked a check in his notebook.

"Stick out your hand," he said.

Chris did what Reggie asked. The black cop took out an eyedropper filled with water. He squeezed out a drop onto Chris' hand. It sizzled the flesh and a blister arose.

"Shit," Chris hissed, "that burns like fire."

"Holy water, check."

He made another mark in his book. Reggie and Chris continued to go through the list Reggie had compiled.

"Hawthorn branch?"

"No."

"Jewish Star?"

Chris recoiled.

"Star, check," Reggie said as he marked it in his book.

"I'm glad to see that there's no anti-Semitism in the vampire world."

Chris smiled. "I guess not."

They finished up at about 9:30 and got ready to go to the precinct at ten. Reggie asked a few more questions.

"Chris, can you change your shape? It says in almost every book that a vampire can turn itself into a bat or a wolf, even mist."

"I don't know. I've never tried that and I'm not going to try."

Reggie knew by the sound of Chris's voice that he shouldn't pursue it.

"Okay. Here's some other stuff I wrote down."

Reggie read from his pad. *A vampire has to be in before sunup*. We know that. *Casts no reflection*. Knew that. *A vampire cannot enter a home without the owner inviting them in.* Didn't know that."

Chris interrupted. "Reggie, it's time to get down to the precinct. We're still employed by the City of Miami, you know."

"Yeah."

The black man put away the pad.

"Well, I think we've learned some things tonight, don't you?"

"Yeah, trouble is, I can't use any of them."

"Don't worry, Buddy. I can." Reggie put his hand on Chris's shoulder. "I'll make a deal with you. You keep Charlie Burnson off my ass and I'll keep Rakz off you. Deal?"

"Deal," he said, and gave Reggie five.

"Now let's get to the station."

Draper was waiting for them when they got in. He had to tell them about the girl and the note.

13

"So you and Blaze got somethin' goin', Doc?" Burley Fayer asked Sue as he crunched a potato chip.

"Yes, we've been seeing each other."

"Good guy, Chris is. Damn good cop, too. I used to work with him when he was a rookie." The huge detective grabbed another handful of chips and spread them across his ample waist. He picked up a couple and crunched them between his white teeth. "You got yourself a nice place here. I like it." He put his feet up on the ottoman in front of his padded chair.

Sue liked the private eye. She reminded him of a big farm boy who was as honest as he was strong. Sue stood up and went into the kitchen.

"You want something more to drink?"

"Naw, I'm fine. Haven't finished my tea yet. Appreciate the offer, though."

Sue poured herself a glass of water.

"How long were you on the police force, Burley?"

"Put in my twenty and then went into business for myself."

"I thought Chris said you were in the witness protection program."

"Oh, yeah . . . well, I, uh, do still work for them when they have an important case. And you little lady are an important case."

"Oh, so what's your business?"

"I have an investigations business. Do mostly divorce investigation and an occasional bodyguard duty. One time I got to guard Willie Nelson at a concert. Biggest thrill of my life. Always did like Willie."

A big grin stretched broadly across the vast expanse of his face. He popped a couple more potato chips into his mouth.

14

As soon as he saw the team of B and C, Captain Draper called them into his office.

"Sit down, guys," he said, motioning to the two chairs in front of his mahogany desk.

The two detectives sat down. They noticed that Draper looked like a man who didn't know the meaning of the word "sleep."

Wearily the big man pulled off his glasses and rubbed his eyes. "Last night another girl was killed. Her head was ripped off. The son of a bitch that did it had to be one helluva strong bastard. We think it's the same guy who did McIrney and the two girls. Here."

He handed them the gruesome photos. As they looked them over, Reggie gave Chris a knowing look.

Draper continued. "There was a note this time. Our man seems to be getting a little bolder."

"What did it say?" Reggie asked, almost afraid of the answer.

Draper looked down at the bloodstained note. "It says 'In ways you cannot imagine.' That's all. Mean anything to either of you?"

Reggie's mouth went dry.

Chris stared at the photo, sickened by the brutality.

"Well?" Draper asked impatiently.

"No. No idea, Captain." Chris said wishing he could tell Draper the truth. He knew he couldn't.

"How about you, Carver?"

"Uh, no, I don't have a clue, Captain."

"Well, you two are going to find out. I'm assigning you to this case full time."

"Great!" Chris said almost too exuberantly.

"Don't be too depressed, Blaze," Draper said sarcastically.

"Sorry, Captain, but I really want to nail this guy."

Chris hadn't meant to get so excited, but it was a good break. Now they could concentrate on Rakz and there would be a much better chance that no other officers would get involved.

Reggie put his hand on Draper's shoulder. "Captain, this sounds like the kind of case that could get me assigned back to regular duty. I mean, now that Burnson's gone."

"Listen, Carver, if you crack this case you can have your old duties back, okay?"

"Consider this puppy closed," Reggie said confidently.

Chris wished he felt as confident as he glanced down at the picture of the horribly mutilated girl.

"Let's go, Chris," Reggie said.

"Right."

"Oh, by the way, Blaze," Draper said, "how's your allergy?"

"Huh?"

"Your allergy to the sun. Remember?"

"Oh yeah, right. It's still the same, I'm afraid."

"You know, Chris, with all this vampire talk and you not being able to go out into the sun, somebody might think you're a vampire."

"Me, a vampire?" Chris said, laughing. "That would be something, wouldn't it, Reg? A vampire cop in Miami."

"Yeah," Reggie said. "That'd be something all right. Heh heh heh." His laughter was as false as a television evangelist's smile.

"We'd better get going," Chris said, getting up.

He started for the door and Reggie followed.

"Hey, Chris," Draper called out, not letting the joke go.

"If we go on a grave-robbing sting, maybe we can use you as a corpse."

Chris pointed at the captain, waving his finger.

"Very funny, Captain," Chris said.

He and Carver kept walking. The captain came out to his office doorway.

"Seriously, though, you guys be careful out there. I want you to come back in one piece."

Reggie shivered as he thought of the headless girl and the unintentional play on words by the captain.

Chris looked over at his partner grimly.

None of them knew at the time that the captain's warning was prophetic.

A prophecy of things to come.

A prophecy of death.

15

The night passed uneventfully for Sue and Burley. They played a couple of games of cards, watched television, and generally got to know each other a little better. Chris called around midnight to check in. He talked to Sue for a little while and then had to leave to get something to eat. Sue went to bed a couple of hours later but was only able to doze slightly. The thought of having another awful dream always kept popping in and out of her mind.

Burley kept awake by cleaning his gun and watching a late-night horror flick, *The Curse of the Undead,* a curious tale of a vampire gunslinger who terrorized the old west only to be gunned down by the sheriff with a bullet made from a cross. The flick had been fairly interesting but had one flaw that really irritated the gentle giant. The vampire, Don Drago, walked around in broad daylight. Burley was a traditionalist, and that kind of crap made him mad. He knew there were no such thing as vampires, but hell, in the movies they oughta at least get the facts straight.

16

It was 12:30 when they got the call. Chris had been trying to get a psychic fix on Rakz's whereabouts but he'd had no luck. They'd driven around the perimeter of the city, but Chris didn't get any psychic images of the elder vampire. Perhaps there was a limit as to how far away they could be to contact each other. He might have left the city's limits and could now be out of that range. Even if Rakz was out of the city, Chris knew he'd be back. The thought chilled his bones.

They were just about to take a break so Chris could satisfy his hunger when Dispatch called about a family disturbance in progress. All other available units were involved in a major gang fight that had broken out in Freedomtown. Chris and Reggie had to respond to the call.

As they pulled up into the driveway of the home where the disturbance had been reported, the two cops heard the loud voices of a man and a woman in heated dispute.

"Man, I hate this shit!" Reggie complained. "An FD is the worst kind of a damn call."

"I know. Let's just get it over with," Chris said, getting out of the car.

"Goddamn family bullshit," Carver grumbled. "Probably some big fat bitch and her gross husband fighting it out over what they're gonna watch on the tube."

"Yeah."

Chris rapped on the door.

"Police," he called out.

Through the door they could hear voices.

"Bert, I'm gonna shove this knife right up your ass."

"C'mon, ya bitch. I'll punch your lights out."

"Police, open up." Chris shouted, rapping on the door.

"You're dead, you hear me, Bert? I'm gonna kill you," the woman shouted.

"This shit can't wait," Reggie said as he kicked open the front door. "Let's boogie."

He bolted into the living room. It was just as he'd imagined: a fat woman in a faded print dress had a large butcher knife in her hand and was circling the kitchen table. On the other side of the table was an equally fat tattooed man in a grease-stained t-shirt. He had a five o'clock shadow that had struck midnight long ago.

"All right, freeze, both of you! I'm a police . . ."

A vase flew and crashed beside Reggie.

"Who the hell are you?" the fat Rosie screamed. "And what are you doin' buttin' into our business?"

"We're police officers."

"What's this 'we' shit, ya gotta mouse in your pocket?" the man shouted.

Reggie looked around. Blaze wasn't at his side.

"Chris?"

He looked out into the doorway and saw Blaze. He was trying to enter, but was struggling, as if there was a never-ending wall of glass blocking his path.

The big man howled, "I'm gonna kick your black ass."

The enraged giant headed toward Reggie, his fists opening and closing like the claws of a lobster. His wife joined him.

Reggie shouted to his partner, "Chris! I need you, man."

"I—I can't come in," Chris shouted back. "I don't know what's wrong."

"Well, you'd better figure it out soon."

Bert, the husband, moved with surprising speed. He grabbed Reggie by the front of his jacket and tossed him. Reggie sprawled over the couch and landed with a thud. He got up and backed away.

"Chris!" he shouted.

Chris realized what was wrong. "Reggie, I haven't been invited in. The book, remember?"

"Oh shit, that's right."

A portrait of the loving couple, Bert and Rosie, whistled past Reggie's ear and shattered against the wall.

"Come on in, Chris," Reggie shouted.

"You're not the owner, Reggie. You can't invite me in."

Reggie tried to pull his gun, but Bert grabbed him again and tossed him. This time he landed on a card table, smashing it.

The woman ran over and kicked him right in the tailbone. Pain shot up his spine.

"Stop!" Chris roared, "you're under arrest!"

The big man looked over at him and sneered. "Another damn cop."

"You're under arrest, sir."

"Sir, my ass . . . why don't you come on in and get some of what your black buddy got."

"I thought you'd never ask."

Chris heard the magic words and stepped through the doorway. Bert charged him and fired a punch at his head. The vampire cop stopped it with one hand and launched Bert backward. He literally flew through the air into a cabinet and collapsed unconscious.

His wife stopped in her tracks. The sight of her husband soaring through the air like a fat parakeet had taken the wind out of her sails. She said meekly to Blaze, "You wouldn't hit a lady, would you?"

Chris shook his head no.

"But I would," Reggie shouted as he caught her flush on the jaw with a right cross. She dropped like a lead weight.

"In your face, fat mama," Carver added.

He rubbed his butt where the woman had kicked him.

"Y'know, Blaze, you and your illness can be a real pain in the ass sometimes."

"Very funny." Chris said, then hesitantly added, "Reggie, I need to drink."

"What? You mean blood?"

"Yeah."

"Well, don't look at me."

"No, I meant her." Chris pointed to the fat woman.

Reggie gulped. "You're not going to drain her?"

"Of course not. I'm just going to take enough to satisfy the hunger."

"Well, I guess a vampire's got to do what a vampire's got to do."

Chris nodded.

"Just watch your cholesterol level on that fat pig," Reggie said.

Chris bent down and exposed the fat lady's throat. He opened his jaws and bit deep, slaking the great thirst that gnawed at him.

"Jeez," Reggie said, wincing as he rubbed his neck, "that shit must hurt. Remind me never to have you over for dinner."

Chris finished drinking and got up. "Let's take them down and book 'em."

"Whatever you say, Chris."

Reggie bent over and slapped the cuffs on big Bert. He hoisted him up. "C'mon brother, you're gonna be spending the night in the county jail."

The subdued Bert rose groggily to his feet and stumbled out the door. Reggie had a firm grip on the handcuffs.

Chris put his cuffs on the wife and picked her up. He carried her to the car and put her in the back with her husband. He got in the front and the two proceeded to the station house.

Reggie and Chris deposited the loving couple at the station and were filling out the paperwork on the case. Reggie did most of the work as Chris concentrated on trying to locate the vampire. Blaze tried to get a fix on the undead creature's whereabouts, but he couldn't get any images at all.

209

He figured it was probably because Rakz was out of range and their telepathy just couldn't make the connection. Chris didn't know that Rakz was in the city and that he was planning Chris's death.

<h1 style="text-align:center">17</h1>

Ravenswood was an exclusive resort condominium complex that catered to a rich clientele with a craving for privacy. The complex had security both inside and out. A ten-foot-high electrified gate surrounded the entire area. There was only one access point for getting through the gates, and that was manned twenty-four hours by armed guards. A doorman greeted all guests. Most of the residents at Ravenswood were celebrities, high-powered executives and professionals who wanted to have a place where they could find sanctuary from the outside world. There were singers, actors, doctors, lawyers, *Fortune* 500 CEOs, and . . . a vampire.

Yosekaat Rakz had amassed quite a fortune in the three centuries in which he had lived. He could well afford to pay the exorbitant rent of the penthouse in which he sometimes lived. The vampire had chosen the Ravenswood Complex because he, too, needed sanctuary from the outside world, a safe haven in which to spend the daylight hours.

He and Charles had arrived there earlier in the evening and had just finished making plans for the torment and destruction of Christopher Blaze and his friends.

Rakz had just explained to Charles what his part in the plans was to be when the vampire felt a strange tingling in his head.

"This Christopher Blaze is a fast learner," he said to his servant. "I can feel him trying to probe into my mind."

"Can you stop him?" Burnson asked.

"As easily as I could rip your heart out, if you ask another stupid question like that."

Charlie clammed up.

Rakz rubbed his chin with a long clawed finger. "He has

picked up on our powers of communication rather well. I can block him out easily enough, but it takes a little more power than I thought it would. It's such a shame that he's chosen the wrong path to follow. That path will only lead him to his death."

The sun was rising.

Rakz climbed into his coffin and closed the cover as he had a hundred thousand times before. He smiled, content with the awful pain that he had in store for the young upstart Blaze and all his friends. The next evening he would begin with the first phase of his plan, a phase that would cost one of his enemies their life.

PART 3

Chapter 1

1

The cleaning lady, Ethel Grummawicz, was running late on her daily rounds of the big condominium complex. She had run into some bad luck at the Johnson place when the plastic garbage bag she was carrying had burst open. It had taken her fifteen minutes to clean up the mess. She was glad the penthouse apartment was the last one she had to take care of that day. She was ready to go out and have a little nip of whiskey.

Ethel could best be described as knobby. The old woman's elbows and knees looked like they had golfballs hidden under the skin. Her nose was shaped like a doorknob, except that this doorknob bloomed with gin blossoms. Ethel liked her booze, and the veins in her face showed it. In fact, Ethel Grummawicz liked most everything and most everybody. But for some reason, she didn't like the owner of the penthouse. The old lady couldn't put her finger on it, but Mr. Rakz gave her the creeps. It was nothing he'd ever said or done. In fact, he was one of the most polite men she had ever met. But his presence, an intangible aura that he exuded, was one of malevolence. It was as though the polite facade was a deodorant that covered up something foul underneath. On the surface everything smelled fine, but occasionally you would get a whiff of the bad smell that was lurking underneath. Ethel had only met him on a couple of occasions.

215

Each time she was running late, and tonight she was far behind schedule.

She knocked and opened the door.

"Anyone home?"

She flicked on the one light in the entire place. The sun still poured through the window, but it would not last long. She would have to hurry.

The condo looked as if it had been furnished by an ascetic monk with a taste for fine art. There was one couch. One end table. No plants. No chairs. Just the one couch and the one end table. But on the walls hung exquisite paintings by the masters: Van Gogh, Picasso, Renoir, all originals Rakz had collected over the years. The vampire was a connoisseur of the arts and was very proud of his collection.

The only impressionist Ethel had ever heard of was Rich Little, and the only thing she knew about Rakz's art collection was that occasionally she had to dust the top of the frames. She didn't know why she had to bother cleaning up in the first place. The apartment was never dirty, and there was nothing to clean. If she didn't have the contract with Ravenswood's management to clean all the condos, she would just as well forget about Mr. Rakz and his penthouse of gloom.

As she dusted, Ethel worked up a powerful thirst. She rubbed the back of her hand across her parched lips. A nice cold beer or a whiskey on the rocks would be mighty quenching, but she knew she wouldn't get any at this apartment. This guy never kept any beer in the refrigerator and didn't even have a liquor cabinet. She couldn't believe that someone wouldn't have a nip or two of the good stuff lying around somewhere. There had to be something to drink.

She glanced over to the room she was forbidden to clean. He had told her never to go into that room for any reason. *That's probably where this cheapskate keeps his booze,* she thought.

She continued to dust, occasionally looking over at the closed door. She could almost taste the whiskey that surely waited for her behind that door. She licked her withered lips.

She finished dusting and started to vacuum in the ever-darkening room.

The door seemed to call to her.

"Come on in, Ethel. You've only seen him twice before. The chances of him being around are pretty slim. Come on. Have a drink."

She was awful thirsty, and a belt of Kentucky Gentleman would go down good. What was she thinking? In a fancy place like this, the bourbon would have to be Makers Mark or Jack Daniels.

The door whispered to her.

"Jack Black sold here. First drink is free. Last drink, too."

She looked at the door and as if by magic the vacuum cleaner began to make its way toward it.

Back and forth, she inched her way toward the waiting door.

The sun had just gone down.

Back and forth.

Back and forth.

Closer and closer.

The vacuum cleaner whirred to a stop. Its plug lay dead twenty five feet away. She was only three feet from the door.

"Better get that cord and plug it in. Gotta finish up before it gets too dark to see," she said to herself.

The door beckoned her.

"You know you're thirsty. Behind me is lots and lots of bourbon and ice. Cool refreshing bourbon on the rocks."

"I guess it could wait a minute."

Miss Grummawicz reached out for the doorknob, then drew her hand back as the last vestiges of her conscience tried valiantly to persuade her to change her mind.

It failed.

She reached out and turned the knob.

Suddenly the door flew open, and before her stood Yosekaat Rakz, his eyes blazing like red-hot coals.

Captain Tom Draper was in the bathroom shaving, getting ready for another night on graveyard shift. As he pulled the blade across his face, scraping off the stubble, he hoped that Commander Brown would be back soon so he could get back onto his regular schedule. This night-shift crap just wasn't where he wanted to be at this stage of his police career.

As he continued shaving, Draper felt a tug on his robe. He looked down and saw his little son, Todd. "Hey, Toddster, what can I do for you?"

"Doan go to wook tonight, Daddy. I'm afwaid."

The earnest look on the little boy's face sent a shudder through Draper's muscular frame. The boy's speech impediment made him sound even more vulnerable. Draper picked his son up. "Why? What are you afraid of, son?"

"I hadda dweam a bad man was gonna getcha. I doan wanna bad man to getcha, Daddy."

Tom hugged him close. "What's gotten into you? Nothing bad's going to happen to your dad."

"But, in the dweam, the bad man had shawp teef anna . . ."

Tom put his finger to the boy's lips.

"Hush now. It was just a dream, Todd. And there is nothing in a dream that you should be afraid of. Dreams aren't real."

His father gently patted the boy on the head.

"I doan care. I still doan wan you to go."

"Todd, honey, it's my job. I have to go, okay?"

Todd fiercely hugged his father's neck. "No, no, hew get you. I know hew get you."

"What's wrong, Tom?" Connie Draper said as she entered the bathroom. She had heard Todd's crying plea from the bedroom.

"Todd had a bad dream, and he doesn't want me to leave for work."

"C'mere, sweetheart," Connie said lovingly as she reached

out for her youngest child. "Now, you know daddy has to go to work, don't you?"

"Yeah, but the dweam."

"Dreams aren't true. They're just imaginary. Like a movie on television. It's just make-believe."

Connie looked at her husband over her little son's shoulder. She shrugged. He raised his eyebrows. He didn't have an explanation either.

"Come on, honey," she said, "let's get you back into bed."

"But . . ."

"No buts, you have to get some sleep. Now let's go."

She kissed Tom on his shaved cheek.

"Have a good night at work. I'll stay with Todd until he falls asleep."

Tom nodded and stroked his son's fine blond hair.

"Goodnight, Toddster. I love you, son."

"I wuv you too, Dad. Watch out fow the bad man, okay? Pwomise?"

Tom helped up three fingers in true Boy Scout fashion. "I promise."

The little boy smiled.

"G'night, Tom," Connie said as she kissed him again, then left with her son.

Tom continued to shave, thinking about his son's dream.

3

"Mr. Rakz, sir. You gave me a death of a start," Ethel said, terrified.

"Where were you going, Miss Grammawicz?" Rakz asked in the overly courteous tone he used when talking to those he thought were beneath him.

"Going? No, sir, I wasn't going anywhere. I was, uh, just polishing the doorknob."

Rakz shook his head. "Now, now, Miss Grammawicz, lying doesn't become you. You wanted to see what was in here, didn't you?"

219

His eyes burned into hers, searing the truth from her.

"Yes, sir."

"Well, then, let us satisfy your curiosity. Come in."

"No, I couldn't."

"But I insist," Rakz hissed in a tone of voice that ended any chance of argument.

It took Ethel three steps into the room before she began screaming at the sight of the polished ebony coffin in the middle of the room.

"Who . . . what are you?" She cried.

Rakz opened his mouth, exposing his fangs.

"For you, my dear, I am the angel of death."

4

Chris had stopped over at Sue's before meeting Reggie at the station. He wanted to be with her for a couple of hours before Burley showed up.

They sat together on the couch. Neither spoke. They just wanted to be together and enjoy each other in the short time they had before Chris had to go to work.

Chris looked deeply into Sue's eyes, the beautiful eyes that had been the first thing he'd seen after the car accident. He took pleasure in their beauty.

He loved this woman.

Gently he pulled her toward him and they kissed, tongues entwined, their lips melding together as one.

Their passion, their fear of the future and what it might hold, their love, all blended together in that one kiss.

Chris reached over and cupped her breast in his hand, sliding his hand under her bra, stroking her nipple. The flesh erected under his touch.

Sue shuddered with delight.

Chris pulled the sweatshirt she was wearing slowly over her head. He dropped it onto the carpet.

She reached behind her back and unsnapped the bra. It fell to the floor. Her breasts were firm and round. Perfect.

Chris bent over and gently sucked on her erect nipples as she moaned with pleasure. His hand slid between her legs and lightly rubbed her sex through the cotton sweatpants. Sue lay back and enjoyed his loving touch.

Chris slid her pants and panties off at the same time.

Her brown pubic hairs framed the loveliness of her mound.

He kissed her nipples.

Then her soft stomach.

Then her thighs.

The aroma of her femininity made his heart pound. He kissed the soft lips of her sex, then slid his tongue between them and slowly encircled her stiff clitoris.

She moaned loudly. It had been so long since anyone had made love to her the way Chris was doing now. She began to feel the warm, tingling sensation that signaled the coming of an orgasm.

He continued his exquisite kiss until her whole body was racked by a pulsating climax.

She wanted him inside her more than anything in the world.

"Take off your pants," she said huskily. "I want you."

Chris stood up, unbuckling his belt. He unzipped his pants and let his jeans drop to the floor. His member stood erect, flooded with passion. She kissed it softly and then guided it into her moist sex.

Chris shuddered as he thrust his manhood deeply into her. It had been a long time for him, too.

They moved together in perfect unison, two people joined in the ultimate act of physical love.

Sue had never known it could be like this. She felt as though she was going to pass out. Her whole body was flush with feverish passion as Chris thrust in and out of her.

"Do it, baby, make love to me," she whispered.

Her warm breath in his ear gave Chris a rush and he felt his manhood tremble with pleasure. He thrust deeper inside her.

"Oh, Chris, give it to me. I'm gonna come."

He moved his hips faster, driving it into her.

"Yes, yes."

Tears of joy were in her eyes.

He could hold back no longer.

They climaxed together in one powerful orgasm.

Chris arched his back and came hard, the release so strong that it curled his toes. He slumped on top of her, laughing with delight at the strength of his orgasm.

They kissed again.

No words needed to be spoken.

They both knew it had been the best time for both of them.

Sue got up and turned on the shower. In moments the bathroom was steamy. "You coming?" she shouted from the shower.

"No, thanks, I just did."

Sue smiled sexily. "Could try again."

Chris got up and made his way into the shower.

He got in and they kissed while the warm water soothed. "I love you, Susan Catledge, M.D."

"I love you too, Christopher Blaze, P.D.," she whispered.

As the water rained down on them they made love again. It was just as wonderful as the first time.

Sue got out of the shower and toweled off. Chris waited until she was out of the bathroom before he got out. He didn't want to take a chance that she might see that he cast no reflection in the mirror of the medicine cabinet.

Chris dried off and dressed quickly.

As he buttoned his shirt, the doorbell rang. He went to the door. It was the big Georgian, Burley. Chris opened the door.

"Hey, Burley, come on in," he said as he ran a comb through his wet hair.

"Evening, Chris."

Sue came out of the bedroom. Her hair was still wet, too. Her bra lay on the floor by the couch.

It didn't take twenty years of investigative experience for Burley to figure out what had happened. He waved to the doctor. "Hi, Susie."

"Hi, Burley," she called back.

Chris put his hand on Fayer's shoulder. "Listen, Burl, and you especially, Sue—if anyone you don't know comes to that door, do not invite them in. Don't ask me why, just trust me. Okay?"

Burley grinned. "Sure, Chris. I trust you."

Sue nodded.

"Well, Reggie's waiting for me. I've got to go," Chris said. "Remember what I said. Under no circumstances do you invite anyone in."

"I got you, don't worry. No one's coming through that door tonight."

5

As Captain Tom Draper drove to work, he couldn't get his son's voice out of his mind.

"Doan go, Daddy. The bad man's gonna getcha."

The boy had been so frightened. Draper wondered what had triggered the boy's dreams about the bad man. Perhaps he had overheard Tom telling his wife about the gruesome slayings and for her to stay home at night until this guy was caught. Or it could have been one of the scary movies that his older sister, Chrissy, watched with her boyfriend, Larry. Draper had laid down the law about letting Todd and Mary watch those horror shows, but sometimes the youngsters snuck in and watched anyway. Somehow it wasn't so scary for them when they saw a monster picture with other people in the room. The creatures couldn't get them with grownups in the room. But afterwards when they have to go to bed alone in their rooms with the lights turned out, the images of the monsters they had seen on the television began to form in the shadows and shapes of the room. A dirty pile of clothes becomes an alien that eats kids. A picture of Pee Wee Herman changes into a hairy demon. The closet is filled with giant bugs. Those were the nights Draper could expect little sleep because he and his wife would have two children squeezed in between them in their bed. He made a mental note to have a talk with Chrissy, to see if she and Larry had rented a horror movie recently and if Todd had somehow accidentally seen it.

The whole incident had left Draper feeling tense and apprehensive. He needed to relax. He flicked on the radio and turned the dial to the "beautiful music" station. The captain hummed along with an instrumental version of the Beatles song "Let It Be" and settled back into his seat.

6

Chris and Reggie began their rounds by driving around the perimeter of the city again, trying to track down Rakz through the vampires' innate sense of each other. Chris kept getting flashes of Rakz on and off.

"He's in the city," he said solemnly.

"Whoah, shit," Reggie said. "Are you sure?"

"Not one hundred percent, but I am getting some images."

"Can you figure out where he is?"

"No. Like I said, I'm only getting flashes."

"Can't you kinda zoom in on them?"

"I'm trying, but it's almost as if he's blocking me out."

"Damn, can he do that?"

"I don't know. It sure seems like that's what he's doing."

"Do you think maybe it could just be that he is far enough out of range that you can only get brief images? Y'know, sort of like a radio station that's too far away and doesn't have enough wattage for you to get the signal."

"That's probably right," Chris said, hoping that saying it would make it true. He didn't know.

"I'll keep trying," he said. "We'll catch up to him."

Reggie nodded. "Just tell me which way to go."

Chris closed his eyes and concentrated. "Head west, young man, we'll see if our friend Rakz is there."

Burley Fayer had just finished preparing a peanut butter and banana sandwich, his favorite, when he heard a strange scratching sound on the big glass doors that led to the patio of Sue's house. He pulled his gun and motioned for Sue to remain where she was and to be quiet. She reached for the cross on the table and crouched behind the couch.

Burley walked slowly over to the windows. Their curtains were closed. The big man's heart began to beat harder. The familiar rush of adrenaline shot through him, honing his senses to a fine edge. Burley had seen a lot of action in his day and could handle himself in just about any dangerous situation. This definitely qualified.

Slowly he moved toward the window. As he drew nearer, the scratching became louder, more frantic. It sounded like the skittering of a huge cockroach in a paper trash bag.

Sue wished Chris was there to hold her and make sure she was safe. Sweat poured down her forehead and dripped into her eyes, burning them. She wiped it away with her forearm and watched as Burley made his way to the cord of the glass door's curtains.

The private eye reached out slowly and grabbed the cord in his huge hand. He would pull the curtains open and find out who or what was making that noise. As he was about to pull them open, the frantic scratching stopped. Fayer wondered if whatever it was had heard him and fled. He relaxed his grip on the cord. Part of him didn't want to know what was out there. The other part had to know. As he prepared to open the curtains, the scratching returned louder and more frantic than before. Burley looked over at Sue and mouthed the words "get ready."

Sue acknowledged him and crouched down.

Fayer gave the cord a solid yank and the curtains flew open.

Draper heard the call about a possible hit-and-run across the street from the swanky Ravenswood Condos. He was on Orange Avenue, which wasn't too far from the expensive residence. He turned the car around and started heading for the scene. He stuck the portable blue light onto the roof of the car and switched it on. Draper radioed in that he was going to investigate and pressed his foot down on the accelerator.

Hit-and-run, he thought to himself. A crime of panic, usually. In most cases, hit-and-run drivers just freaked out and fled the scene of an accident, leaving the victim for dead. Sometimes it was not even their fault, but they figured no one would believe them, so they'd just decide to make a run for it. They didn't stop to consider the consequences of their actions: that they risked a prolonged jail sentence, that the person they'd hit might be in need of medical attention, that the person could die before someone else found them. Most hit-and-run drivers just didn't think. . . .

Thump!

Draper jumped as he heard the loud thud on top of his car. The bad man had arrived.

9

"Jesus Christ, this is frustrating," Chris cried. "I keep getting images, but they disappear too fast. I keep seeing an apartment house or something."

The radio blared. "2/25 signal three across from Ravenswood Condominiums."

"Holy shit, not an apartment house, a condo," Chris gasped.

He grabbed the radio's microphone. "Unit 2 responding to signal three. We are enroute to Ravenswood Condominiums."

"Roger, Unit 2."

"What the hell are you doing?" a confused Reggie said. "We don't have time to be jacking around with some hit-and-run. We've got to find those two maniacs."

"Reggie, the name of the place that I keep seeing in the vision is Ravenswood. That's where Rakz is staying. We found it. Now let's go find Rakz."

10

As the curtains flew back, Burley pointed his pistol at whatever was making the noise. He grinned when he saw the source of the frantic scratching: it was a little calico tabby at the bottom of the door, clawing at the window to get in. The big ex-cop lowered his weapon and bent down to shoo the cat away.

Because it was dark on the patio, it wasn't until Burley got close to the animal that he realized something was very wrong.

The glass was being splattered with blood as the cat tried to scratch its way through the doors. He stared in horror when he saw the little creature's throat slit open, its heart systematically pumping its life away. Fayer didn't see the hand holding the cat up to the window until it was too late.

Burley Fayer rocked back as the first bullet from Charlie Burnson's silenced .38 ripped into his chest. He fell to the ground, spun into a shooter's position, and fired two shots at the shadowy figure outside the glass doors. The door exploded and a rain of glass showered down.

"Get down, Sue!" Burley winced. "And stay down."

"Surprise!" Charlie shouted and he tossed the dead cat into the living room. It landed with a sickening thud in the middle of the floor.

Sue wanted to scream but held it in. The sight of the pathetic creature filled her heart with rage for the sick monster who had killed it. She looked over at Burley to see how he was doing. The big detective was bleeding badly from the bullet that had pierced his chest and punctured his right lung. He wheezed as he tried to suck in enough air to stay alert and alive. Fayer crawled over to her, leaving a gruesome trail of blood.

"Susie," he gasped in a tortured voice. "I'm hit bad. I don't know how long I can stay conscious. I want you to take this." He pulled a gun from his ankle holster. "And use it if you have to."

"Let me see your chest, Burley," Sue said as Burnson's gun hissed and the vase beside her head exploded.

"Get down, damn it!" the injured Burley shouted. He rose up and returned fire. "Listen, Susie, I ain't gonna make it. We've got to try something before I get too weak. Now I'm gonna rush the bastard, and when I do, I want you to get out that front door and get into your car and haul ass outta here. It'll take him a little while to realize what's happening. It's a long run from the backyard to the front."

Hiss!

Ping!

A bullet ricocheted off the heavy steel vase that Sue kept her silk flowers in.

"But Burley, I can help you, I'm a doctor."

"Look, we haven't got time. If I don't do this now, I'm going to pass out from losing all this blood and then it'll be you against him. I don't like that match-up."

Sue had to agree. "Okay, I guess it's the best plan," she said.

"The only plan," Burley corrected her. "At least this way you have a fighting chance. Besides, I might get lucky and kill the sumbitch."

She nodded.

"Now, first, I'm gonna make it as hard as I can for the bastard."

Burley aimed and shot out the lamp. He fired again and the kitchen light went out. The house was dark except for a slight glow from the bathroom light. He loaded a full clip into his .45 and got ready.

"Okay," he said, "on three. One . . ."

Hiss!

228

Ping.
"Two . . .
Hiss!
Crash.
"Three!"
Sue took off for the front door as Burley stood up and charged the shattered door like a mad bull, firing his big gun and screaming in a bloodthirsty death cry.

11

"What the hell was that?" Draper said. It sounded like someone had thrown something on top of his car. Draper pulled the car over to the curb and shut the engine off. He opened the door and helped push his muscular frame out the door with the steering wheel. He got out, stood up and adjusted his shoulder holster. In the glow of the street light, Draper examined the roof of the car to see the extent of the damage. It was dented in as though some heavy object had landed on it.

"Son-of-a-bitch," Draper said as he surveyed the dent. He wanted to find out what it was that had hit the roof. He reached into the car and got out the heavy flashlight. He switched it on and pointed the beam down the road. It cut through the darkness but revealed nothing. He started walking down the road, backtracking his car's path. He wanted to find out what it was that had damaged city property and if possible who was responsible.

Draper swept the area with the powerful light for a clue. There was nothing there. "Goddamn kids, must have been throwing rocks," he said to himself.

He gave up and switched off the flashlight. He whistled softly as he walked back to the car. Standing beside the front door was a tall man dressed in black. Draper couldn't see his face. Maybe he had seen who had dented the car and wanted to report it.

He flicked the light back on and pointed it at the potential witness. Draper approached the man beside his car. "Excuse me, sir, but I was wondering . . ."

Rakz reached out and grabbed him by the throat. The detective instinctively swung the flashlight and caught him in the forehead. The skin split, but no blood appeared. The vampire bellowed with rage and picked Draper up high above his head.

The police captain gasped as he frantically tried to pry the long talons from around his throat. The fingers were like steel bands.

He had one chance.

With his right hand, he reached under his windbreaker and pulled out his weapon. He jammed it into the man's ribs and fired.

The fingers remained locked around his neck.

He fired again and again. The bullets had no effect.

Draper wondered if somehow someone had loaded his gun with blanks. But as the man held him out away from his body, the policeman could see the three bullet holes that he had made in the man's chest. Three bloodless holes. It didn't make sense.

As he struggled to remain conscious, it felt as though he was being lifted high into the sky. Cool air rushed passed him as did thoughts of the wife and family that he would never see again. So this was death, his mind wondered in the split seconds between him and eternity. Through the haze that clouded his vision, he thought he saw black wings protruding from the back of his assailant. Large, leathery wings flapping in the calm dead air of the night.

Captain Tom Draper's last thought before he died was that his little son, Todd, had been right. The bad man did get him. He most certainly did.

12

Reggie and Chris pulled up to the scene of the hit-and-run across the street from Ravenswood. The victim was a woman of about fifty. She was crumpled in a heap. Her head was twisted around in a gruesome way. It looked as though someone had put her clothes on backward as a joke. But this was no joke, this was murder. The woman's eyes were glazed over in an expression of sheer terror. A uniformed officer approached the two detectives.

Reggie recognized him as George Stephens, a five-year man with a penchant for bowling.

"What happened, George?" he asked the patrolman.

"That guy found her lying here all twisted up like that," Officer Stephens said, knitting his thick eyebrows. "Looks like a hit-and-run."

"Yeah, it does. Did you find any ID?"

"No, but the guard over at Ravenswood says her name is Ethel Grummawicz. She was a cleaning lady who worked over there. Must have been leaving work when somebody clipped her and took off. Funny thing though," he added as he scratched his cleft chin. "There's no evidence of the vehicle. No paint on the body. No skid marks. No glass. Nothing. Pretty strange, don't you think?"

"Yeah," Reggie replied.

He glanced over at Chris, who was staring glassy-eyed off into the distance.

"Real strange. Look, Stephens. The wagon should be here any minute. I want you to take the guard's statement and write up your report, okay?"

"Sure, Carver," Stephens said wearily, then trudged off to finish interviewing the doorman.

Carver went over to his partner, who was staring across the street at the top of the high-rise. Carver tapped him on the shoulder. "What's up, buddy?"

"She wasn't killed by a car. She was killed up there," he said, pointing to the top of Ravenswood Condominiums.

"But how did she get way over here? The guard would have seen someone carry her out of there."

"Unless somebody threw her from the roof, somebody with enormous strength."

"Oh, shit. Rakz."

"Yeah, he lives there. I can feel it," Chris said.

"Well, what are we going to do?"

"We're going to go up there and kill the bastard if he's there and if he isn't, we are going to ruin his resting place."

"I was afraid you were going to say that."

Chris looked determined. "Let's go," he said.

"Just a minute," Reggie said as he ran to the car. He grabbed the black Adidas bag and hustled back to Chris. "My vampire kit. I never leave home without it."

Chris smiled at his friend who was using his sense of humor to try and cover up the terror they were both feeling.

Reggie started to walk toward the apartment complex. "Okay, I'm ready. Watch out, blood breath, here we come."

13

Sue ran out the front door just as Burley reached the shattered glass door. She didn't see the four shots from Burnson's gun hit him, one in the arm, one in the thigh, and two more in the chest.

The big detective hadn't wasted all his ammunition. A slug from his weapon had slammed into Burnson's leg.

Burley's momentum sent his body through the remaining glass and crashing solidly into the stunned Burnson. The huge detective was still fighting for Sue even though his life's blood was pouring out of his body. He had emptied his pistol and was now brandishing it like a club. He brought it down hard trying to brain the maniac that had just shot him. It was a fierce blow that would have crushed Burnson's skull like an egg if the wily murderer had not dodged it. The gun sank harmlessly into the grass. Burley raised it again and swang. This time he partially connected with the side of Charlie's head. Burnson saw stars from the blow.

"You motherfucking son of a whore," Burley roared as he raised the gun for the third time, hoping to land the blow that would finish Burnson off for good.

As Fayer prepared to swing, the stunned Burnson raised

his gun up under Burley's chin and fired, sending the back of the private eye's head flying into space. The big three-hundred-pounder collapsed onto the squirming Charlie, dead before he hit the ground.

Burnson struggled to free himself from the dead weight that lay on top of him. His leg burned from the chunk of metal that was lodged in his thigh muscle.

As he pushed Burley's dead body off of him, he got up and hobbled toward the back gate. He had seen the girl leave. He had to get her. The master was depending on his success. Failure would mean a slow and agonizing death.

14

Sue hopped into her 1988 Honda Prelude and cranked the engine. No sound came out from under the hood. The engine was totally dead. She slammed her hands on the steering wheel in frustration. She didn't know Burnson had ripped out the battery.

Grabbing the pistol Burley had given her, she got out of the car and took off running. If she could make it to the woods a block away, she might have a chance.

Sue hadn't had time to put on her shoes before she fled the house, so she was going to have to run barefoot across the pebbled dirt road and into the woods. As she started to run across the road, she saw Charlie Burnson come around from the backyard. In her heart she knew that the big teddy bear was dead. He had given his life so that she could have time to get away, and Sue wanted to be damned sure he had not sacrificed it in vain.

She ran as fast as she could across the street. The pebbles ripping at the bottoms of her feet like miniature talons.

"Come back, you little slut!" Charlie shouted as he chased after her. Blood streamed down his leg from the wound that Fayer had inflicted on him.

She turned and fired the gun. It was the first time she had ever shot a gun. She hadn't expected the kick to be so strong.

Burnson kept coming.

She aimed again, desperately trying to get the hobbling murderer in the gun's sights. She pulled the trigger.

The gun's report shredded the still of the night.

Burnson went down.

Sue's heart soared. "I did it. I nailed the bastard."

She held the gun out in front of her as she walked slowly back across the road toward the fallen man.

"Don't move," she said in her best Cagney and Lacey voice. "Don't move, or I'll blow your head off!"

Burnson lay perfectly still as she moved closer to his prone body. She wanted badly to fire another shot into him to be sure he was dead, but couldn't do it. She was no killer. She was a healer. A doctor for God's sake. She couldn't just shoot a man in cold blood.

Burnson started to convulse. He was lying face down and his back was shaking up and down.

She lowered her gun.

Charlie rolled over and continued to convulse.

The dead silence was broken as the peals of laughter ripped out of Burnson's foul mouth. He was convulsing . . . with laughter.

He started to get up.

Sue aimed the gun and was about to fire when a hand reached out and plucked the gun from her grasp.

Yosekaat Rakz had come to claim his bride.

15

Reggie and Chris walked past the security guards at the gate flashing their badges as they went by them. The guards waved them on. The two detectives went into the lobby of the exclusive condominiums and went to the directory to see if Rakz was listed as a tenant. They read through the names, hoping to verify what Chris knew was true.

About halfway through the list, Reggie saw it. "You were right, Chris. Check it out."

Chris looked at the name Reggie pointed at but didn't understand the connection. "Number 1P is owned by a Baron Meinster. So?" he said.

"So, Baron Meinster was the name of the vampire in the movie *Brides of Dracula*. It seems our friend has a sense of humor."

"Yeah, and my guess is that 1P is a penthouse condo."

"Makes sense."

Chris looked at his partner. "You ready to do this thing?"

"Yeah. But first," Reggie said earnestly. "I have got to take a pee."

Chris waited as Reggie went to the men's room to relieve himself.

A few minutes later, Carver came out. "Well, let's go get this over with," he said.

Chris and Reggie slowly rode up the elevator to the top floor. Carver held the gym bag tightly in his grip. "Hey, Chris, what do we do if he's there?"

"You hold him off with the cross and I'll try to drive the stake through his heart," Chris said, then added, "You did bring everything?"

"Yep, it's all in here," Reggie said, patting the bag he held, then asked, "But how can you get him with the stake without the cross affecting you?"

"When I tell you to, drop the cross. I'll charge him and hope that my aim is good."

"And if it's not so good?"

"Then you just bring the cross up again."

Reggie smiled as he realized the plan just might work. "And then we can try again."

"Right," Chris said. "And if he's not there, then we'll make his resting place useless to him. Maybe if he stays out too late and doesn't have another place to stay, the sun will do our job for us."

"There's one thing we're forgetting. What about Assface Charlie?"

"Burnson's still human as far as we know. If we can we'll arrest him."

235

"And if we can't?"

"If we can't, we'll have to kill him."

The elevator stopped and Chris and Reggie got off. Reggie reached into his bag and took out the cross. Chris recoiled from the sight.

"Sorry," Reggie apologized.

"Just try to keep it out of my sight until we need it, please."

"Okay, Chris."

They walked slowly down the hallway toward the second penthouse. A black policeman with a penchant for practical jokes and a vampire who just wanted to be human. The team of Carver and Blaze were ready as they approached the front door.

"Look, this has got to be it," Reggie whispered.

A small note on the door read, *Enter freely and of your own will.*

"That's from another vampire movie," Reggie whispered.

"That Rakz is a real comedian," Chris said with no humor in his voice. "Come on."

The door was unlocked as if they were expected. Chris opened the door to the pitch-dark apartment and slipped in. Reggie followed closely behind.

"Can you feel anything?" Reggie asked Chris.

"Yes, this is his home all right. But he's not here. Let's look around. You check the den and I'll go in here."

Reggie smiled wanly and headed for the room that was forbidden to cleaning ladies.

Chris went toward the door to Rakz's den. As he entered the den, Chris looked around. Trophies hung on the walls, their dead eyes staring at him. A tiger roared in silence. A black leopard glared at him. All the trophies were predators.

Carnivores.

Hunters.

The smell of blood.

Chris didn't even see the fresh trophy that hung in the dark shadows on the wall behind him.

In the other room, Reggie stood, eyes wide with terror. He was staring at the ebony coffin in the middle of the room as

236

the first pair of red beady eyes rose up out of the coffin and glared at him in the darkness.

Then another pair.

And another.

They were rats.

Hundreds of hungry rats.

16

Sue knew that she would be killed. She would never see Chris again. Even with all their precautions, she had fallen into the clutches of their enemies.

The temperature around her fell drastically, dropping thirty degrees within a few seconds. Sue began to shiver, her whole body shaking with the chills.

"Why are you doing this to me?" she cried.

"Because that is what I choose to do," Rakz crooned.

"You need help, Mr. Rakz. I can help you with your problem. I'm a doctor."

"In what way?"

"You only think you are a vampire . . ."

"No," he interrupted her. "I don't think I'm a vampire. I am. And I intend to make you my bride."

"Just like in them movies," Charlie cackled.

Sue's face flushed with fear. "You need psychiatric help, Mr. Rakz."

"And you need proof."

Rakz's body rippled and huge wings sprouted out of his back. He flapped them and flew ten feet up into the freezing air.

Terror seized Sue as she realized that Rakz was indeed telling the truth.

"Now that I have shown you some of our powers, don't you want to be one of us?"

"There are more of you?"

Rakz laughed loudly. "Of course. Why, your dear Christopher is one of us."

237

Sue put her hand to her mouth.

"You lie," she whispered.

"Have you ever seen him out in the sun? Or even during the daylight hours?"

"He has an allergy to the sun," Sue said, trying to sound as if she believed it. She had a creeping sensation that something was wrong.

Rakz laughed again. "Allergy to the sun . . . I must remember that."

He put his finger to his temple. "Think back to the first night we met. The old department store. Remember when the black man took out the cross and held it before me?"

Sue tried to think, but the memory of the store was vague. She couldn't remember anything about that night.

"I can't remember."

"Try again," Rakz said as he prepared to control her thoughts.

Sue closed her eyes and suddenly her mind was filled with images. It was as if someone had connected a VCR to her brain and plugged in a video-cassette recording of the night at Harriman's. She could see Chris and Rakz fighting. Then she saw Reggie holding the cross and Rakz shunning it and . . . Chris doing the same thing. She could hear him tell Reggie to put the cross away after Rakz left. At that moment she knew Rakz was telling the truth.

"Now, I grow weary of this game. It's time to begin the engagement."

He fixed his gaze on Sue. "Look at me," he commanded.

Sue tried not to look.

"Look at me!"

She couldn't help herself. She looked up into the face of Yosekaat Rakz.

His eyes drew her in, pulling her toward the darkness within them. Her body seemed to float unencumbered by the forces of gravity. She was no longer cold. She felt warm and safe. Her fear dissipated as she was swept into the whirlpool of those eyes. As she fell deeper and deeper under Rakz's spell, she was totally relaxed. She didn't even feel the sharp fangs of the vampire as they pierced her soft throat.

The engagement was on.

17

The beady eyes of the rats stared at Reggie as if he was a piece of fine cheddar. They were climbing out of the black coffin in a wave of undulating flesh, a squeaking mass of little eating machines, their teeth clicking together as they advanced towards the paralyzed black detective.

"Chris . . ." Reggie said quietly for fear that a loud noise would signal the rats that dinner was served. "Chris, come here, man. I need you."

In the semidarkness, the rats looked like one singular creature. A huge, furry eating machine with a hundred eyes and a hundred mouths, each one wanting to take a bite out of Reggie Carver.

Reggie was afraid to move, afraid to cry out because it might trigger the rats into a feeding frenzy. He took one step back and froze. Behind him he heard a low growl. The hair on the back of his neck stood up, and gooseflesh rippled across his arms in an epidermal wave.

Slowly he turned toward the source of the growling. Reggie's head spun as the overwhelming terror of his situation dawned on him.

In front of him, a few feet away, were hundreds of hungry rats. Behind him stood a full-fledged, honest-to-God, genuine wolf.

As he tried to decide between a hundred little bites or one big one, his decision was made for him.

With a vicious snarl, the wolf leapt and began to tear flesh.

18

Charlie Burnson watched in envy as Yosekaat Rakz drank deeply from the woman. The bloodlust he felt was so strong that he didn't even feel the wound in his leg inflicted on him by the late Burley Fayer. He watched the feasting with envy. Sure, he thought, it had felt good when he had killed the big detective, but that was nothing compared to the feeling of taking a life and giving it to yourself. He wondered if his master would ever make him one of the undead. He had done well so far in all the tasks his master had assigned him. Perhaps he would someday enjoy the feeling of rejuvenation that he knew a vampire received when they took the life force out of one person and gave it to themselves. That was the ultimate sensation. That's why Charlie was confused when the master stopped his blood feast of the doctor before she was drained.

The girl was still alive.

"Master, why are you stopping? Aren't you going to finish her?"

"You've so much to learn, Charles," the elegant vampire said, patting a dab of blood from the corner of his mouth with his handkerchief. "In order for her to become my bride and a part of me, I must first drink from her three nights and on the third night I must drain her of all her blood. Afterward she will rise and become the flesh of my flesh, blood of my blood for eternity."

He looked lovingly at his bride-to-be. "But first, our little reception at the apartment should be almost over. I think it's time to liven up the party a little bit."

19

The wolf flew over the frozen Reggie Carver and began ripping into the rats, snapping and tearing them to pieces. A head flew here, a leg there, as the large canine slashed into the horde of rodents.

A tail landed on Reggie's shoe.

An eye hit him on the forehead and stuck there.

Rats flew in all directions.

The squealing of the creatures as they were torn apart was

awful, like a hundred fingernails scraping across a black-board.

As the wolf killed three rats with one vicious bite, the remaining twenty-five or so scattered.

With no more prey, the wolf turned and began padding his way toward Reggie. It bared its teeth at Reggie as the frightened detective backed away.

"Nice wolfie," Reggie said, "good wolf." He pulled one of the wooden stakes out of his bag. "Wanna play fetch?"

The wolf stopped and almost seemed to smile. The big animal reared up on its hind legs. Its spine cracked as its body began to elongate and thicken. A strange, rippling shimmer sparkled across its form. The snout shortened and the hair began to withdraw, as if someone were pulling it from the inside.

As the transformation was completed, Reggie stood in amazement. What had been a snarling, ferocious wolf moments ago was now his partner, Chris Blaze. "Son of a bitch!" he shouted. "Chris!"

"Yeah," Chris said as he pulled a rat's tail out of his mouth. *"Blech."*

"How the hell did you do that?" Reggie asked.

"I really don't know. I saw you in trouble and I just sort of concentrated and it happened."

Reggie stuck the stake back in the bag.

"Well, next time, bark or howl or some shit so I know it's you. I keep getting scared like that, and I'm gonna have to start wearing some of those adult diapers."

"Sorry, I didn't—" Chris stopped in the middle of his sentence. He stared at the wall behind Reggie.

Reggie saw the look of fear on Chris's face.

"What? What is it?"

Chris pointed to the wall.

It had begun to bleed. Red splotches had begun to form on the white paint of the walls of the condo. The blood puddled up and began to drip down the wall and form into patterns. The patterns started to take shape. They were letters, letters that formed a message.

It read, *The engagement is on.*

Chris's heart sank. "Oh, no, he's got Sue. He must have planned this whole thing to get us away from her. I've got to go and find her!"

Reggie put his hand on his partner's shoulder. "You do that, and I'll make sure that fucker can't use this coffin and . . . look out!"

Reggie screamed as the animated corpse of Captain Tom Draper grabbed Chris from behind.

20

"I have an errand to run, Charles," Rakz said, holding Sue in his arms. "I'll be staying at the house of horrors. You may join me there after you've gone back and disposed of the private detective."

He smiled at his servant. "You've served me well, Charles. Tomorrow evening I will reward you."

"Thank you, Master." Burnson crowed. "May I ask what the reward will be?"

"Certainly. I will even give you a choice. Remember, you don't have to decide right now. I will either bring you a young child to feast on, or you may have the privilege of killing our dear friend Mr. Carver."

He paused for effect.

"*If,*" Rakz emphasized the word, "he survives the night." He turned a palm up toward the ex-policeman. "The choice is yours."

As Burnson contemplated his decision, his master took off into the darkness with Sue in his arms.

21

Chris struggled in the powerful grasp of his dead friend. As he tried to break free, the corpse squeezed tighter. Chris was trapped. The image of his father as the spider in the

242

game of spider and moth of his youth flashed in his mind. Only this spider was a creature animated by the evil force of an ancient vampire, and it was trying to kill him.

As the vampire and the zombie fought, Reggie stood in shock. He was unable to move, unable to help his partner because fear had frozen him.

Chris struggled to break free.

Draper held fast.

But Chris would not be held, not with Sue's life at stake. "No!" he shouted in an inhuman howl. "I will be free!"

With all his strength, he threw his arms out and broke the grasp of the zombie.

The creature stumbled back and then resumed its attack.

Chris swung his arm with all his supernatural power and caught Draper coming in. The sheer force of the blow slammed into the side of the man's head. Tendons and bones snapped. Blood flew across the room as Draper's head was ripped from his shoulders. It tumbled to the floor as his body slumped and fell.

The threat was over.

Reggie looked at the dead man and felt a deep sense of loss. "Dear God, the poor captain . . . Rakz must have caught him and done that . . ." he pointed to the corpse ". . . to him."

"That fucking son-of-a-bitch has caused too many deaths," Chris said in a voice that seethed with murderous rage. "I'm going to kill that bastard if it's the last thing I ever do."

"Look, Chris, I'm going to make this place taboo to Rakz, there isn't anything we can do for Draper, but we can still help Sue."

"Right, I'm outta here. I only hope I can find her. If I don't, I'll meet you at Fourth and 33rd."

Chris knew he could cover more ground from the air and decided to try something. He closed his eyes and concentrated. He began to feel a change start to come over him. As he shimmered, he felt his legs shrivel and his body become lighter. His skin stretched and popped.

Reggie stared at the transformation in amazement. First a wolf. Then a bat. Carver wondered in what other ways vampires could change their shape.

Chris in batform flew into the window, shattering it, and flitted off into the night in search of his beloved.

Reggie pulled out his cross and a couple of wafers of the sacrament. He broke the wafers and placed them in the outline of a cross in the soft soil that lined the coffin's bottom. He placed the cross in the center of the casket and mouthed a silent prayer. Carver closed the lid shut as the headless corpse of Tom Draper sat up behind him.

22

Sue felt completely drained, weak.

As she barely opened her eyes, she saw a spectrum of lights that smeared together in a rainbow blur of color. She was moving very fast. The wind rushed through her hair as though she was sticking her head out of the window of a fast-moving car. She tried to open her eyes further so she could see where she was going, but the wind caused them to tear, and the images became even more blurred. She tried to raise her head, but the effort was too difficult. For a moment her vision cleared and she saw a familiar building. She didn't know why Rakz was taking her here, of all places, and she didn't have a chance to figure it out.

The world grew dark as she passed out again.

23

"This is the biggest mess I have ever been in," Reggie said to himself as the corpse behind him rose to its feet.

"I almost became a plate of Reggie's rat chow, I've got a partner who can change into animals, a three-hundred-year-old vampire is out to kill my ass, and to top it all off, I'm missing The Honeymoonurghs . . ." Reggie gasped as the big forearm of the late Tom Draper wrapped across his throat. He shifted his weight and flipped the headless body over his shoulder. It landed with a thud.

"Sweet Jesus, let him stay down," Reggie cried.

But the gruesome monster got up unsteadily, like a puppet with its strings tangled. Clumsily it advanced toward the freaked-out detective.

Thinking fast, Reggie went over to the coffin and pulled out the cross. He thrust it in front of him and in his best Van Helsing imitation shouted, "Stop!"

The zombie hesitated and then kept on coming toward Carver.

"Oh, shit," Reggie mumbled to himself. "I guess I've got to go conventional."

He pulled out his pistol and aimed. He fired four shots grouped right in the kill zone. The impact of the bullets drove the zombie back but didn't stop its slow, inexorable march of death toward Carver.

"Well," Reggie said to himself, "there's only one thing left to do. *Ruuuun!*"

He took off, tossing the cross back into the casket. He faked once and zoomed past the headless creature, heading for the door.

The zombie tried to grab him as he went by but was too slow.

As Reggie left the penthouse, the corpse of Captain Draper fell to the floor in a lifeless heap, its mission unfulfilled.

Reggie got down to the car and realized that in his haste to get away from the headless monster he had forgotten the bag with all his charms up in the penthouse.

"Shit," he cursed himself.

He started to go back up when he remembered that the zombie was still up there. He decided to forget about the bag. He didn't relish the thought of going back up to the penthouse and finding out what else Rakz had in store for him up there. He got in the car and started it, gunned the engine, and pulled away.

He would meet Chris as they'd planned. Reggie hoped with all his heart that Sue would be with him.

24

Chris had been flying over the city for two hours, but had had no luck finding Rakz or Sue, although the images from Rakz were getting stronger.

As he continued to fly, he began to feel strange, as though his body wanted to change back into human form. Chris wondered what was wrong. He had never felt this way before, but then again, he had never used his vampiric abilities for so long, either. Maybe a vampire's powers weakened after they used them for long periods of time. That would explain the strange feeling he was experiencing and also explain why now, later in the evening, the images from Rakz were stronger. Perhaps the ancient vampire was getting weaker and less able to keep blocking Chris out. But if that were true, then Chris couldn't continue his search for Rakz in batform because even if he did locate the bloodsucker, he would be too weak to fight him. The vampire cop decided to land and conserve his strength. He swooped down toward the corner where he was to meet his partner. He would rest there for a little while. He would need all the strength he had if he was going to stop Rakz.

25

Charlie heaved the heavy body of Burley Fayer over his shoulder and carried the dead private eye to the trunk of his car. He flopped the corpse into the trunk and shut it. Some blood from the dead man dripped onto Charlie's hand. He licked it off and headed back into the house.

Burnson straightened up the living room in case someone came to the house and noticed something was wrong. He broke out the remaining glass of the sliding doors so that no one could tell that it was gone unless they were up close to it. Burnson wiped up the blood of the detective as best he could, pausing every so often to sample the coagulating fluid.

Fifteen minutes later, he was almost done.

He hummed a happy tune as he finished his housekeeping chores and headed for his car to go and dispose of the body of the detective.

Burnson dumped the body of Burley Fayer into a shallow grave that the lamia had dug in the woods outside Sue's house.

After he was finished covering the dead private eye, Burnson headed for the condo to dispose of Draper's body and make the coffin available to his master for another day.

As he drove, Charlie marveled at his master's ability to control the others. Rakz had planned the whole evening, knowing exactly what the others would do, planting the proper thoughts in their minds. He had orchestrated it all.

And tomorrow night his master would make new plans, plans that would give Charlie Burnson the opportunity to kill Reggie Carver. He would make sure he didn't waste it.

26

Reggie pulled up to the curb and waited. It was almost time for his rendezvous with Chris. The black man jumped out of his skin as the door to the passenger side flew open.

It was Chris.

"Damn, you scared the pee out of me," Reggie said.

"I couldn't find her," Chris said as he got into the car.

"You tried the sense thing?"

Chris nodded grimly. "Yes, but I'm sure Rakz has the power to block me out."

Reggie slammed his hand on the dashboard in frustration. "Damn, we're really up against it with this son-of-a-bitch!"

"I also found out that as we use our powers we get weaker."

A tiny ray of hope cut through the gloom in Reggie's heart.

"If that's true, then Rakz has got to be weaker, now that he's been blocking you out all night," Reggie said, then added, "And he had to use some power to control the rats and Draper. It makes sense."

Chris said, "None of this makes sense, but I guess in the scheme of things it's logical."

"Then why don't you try again? Maybe he's weak enough so you can get a fix on him."

"Okay, I'll give it one more shot."

Chris closed his eyes and began to concentrate. He focused his mind on one thought, one feeling, the whereabouts of Yosekaat Rakz. He strained to break through the barrier the vampire was throwing up. His mind worked feverishly to get through. To get that one image that would tell him where to find the evil creature. Then, suddenly, with the clarity of a bolt of lightning in the black of night, he saw where Rakz was.

"He's here! He's right here!"

A taloned claw crashed through the window and grabbed Reggie by the front of his jacket. The glass broke into little cubes and fell to the asphalt. Rakz pulled the struggling black cop out of the window in one motion.

At the same time Chris bolted out the door and launched himself over the top of the vehicle. His feet landed squarely in the middle of Rakz's chest, driving the vampire back.

The creature's grip slackened, and Carver fell to the ground.

"Where's Sue, you fucking slime?" Chris roared, his eyes ablaze.

Rakz answered in his usual calm and calculating tone of voice. "She's fine for now, and I assure you, quite alive. As I told you, I want to take her as my bride."

"You'll never have her!" Chris hissed.

"But it's been so easy, Christopher. Child's play. You tried to protect her with your best-laid plans. Now your valiant detective friend is quite dead, as is your captain, and I was

248

able to get the girl." Rakz's voice changed to a menacing tone. "As I said earlier, you two will suffer in ways you cannot imagine."

Chris charged Rakz and crashed into him with the force of a freight train. The vampires slammed into the wall, leaving a vague imprint of Rakz's back in the cement block.

Rakz pushed Chris off with a mighty shove that sent the vampire cop flying through the air. He landed on the windshield of a car, shattering it.

"You must learn never to touch me," Rakz warned, still with that friendly tone of voice.

Kabloom!!

The shotgun erupted, its deadly payload exploding into the smiling vampire's chest. Fabric flew into the air. Small chunks of flesh.

Reggie pumped another shell into the chamber and fired. The pellets plowed harmlessly into the wall. The vampire was no longer there; he was at Reggie's side.

Rakz grabbed the shotgun and very deliberately began to bend it. "You, my black friend," he said, "are a walking dead man."

"That makes two of us, asshole!"

Rakz bent the gun all the way around until the barrel touched the stock. He tossed it away. His face began to change into a hideous mask of rage. His fingers lengthened into wicked, curved claws. "Now," he hissed, "I am going to hurt you very badly."

The vampire advanced on Reggie.

The black man backed away, knowing for certain that he was going to die.

As the undead creature was about to attack, Chris shouted to him. "The sun, Rakz. It's coming up."

The vampire stopped in his tracks and peered toward the horizon. He could sense the coming of the sun. "So it is. This will have to wait."

He pointed to Reggie. "You have one more day to live on this earth. Enjoy it!"

Then he pointed the horrible hooked finger at Chris. "And

I have a surprise waiting for you at your apartment. You enjoy that."

He shimmered, transformed into a huge bat, and flew off into the lightening sky.

"Reggie, we've got to hurry to my place."

"Right."

They ran and got into the car and drove off in the direction of Chris's house.

As they sped toward his place, the vampire detective wondered just what was in store for him at his apartment.

The car squealed to a stop as they arrived at the Carfax Apartments. Chris bolted out of the car and ran toward his apartment. Reggie followed close behind.

The door flew open as Chris entered his place. Reggie came in and closed the door behind him. The two detectives looked around the dark apartment. They didn't see anything out of the ordinary.

As Reggie was about to speak, he heard a faint whisper outside of Chris's window.

"Chris," the thin voice cried, "Chris."

"Sue!" Chris shouted and ran toward the window. He threw open the curtains and opened the window. He hadn't even considered that the sun might be up peeking out just enough to reduce him into a pile of ashes.

It wasn't.

Chris tore out the screen and pulled his lady in from the window ledge.

Reggie gasped as he saw the twin puncture marks on her throat. She was as pale as a ghost. A note was pinned to her body. It was written in blood.

Chris plucked it from her and read it aloud. *"I assume you have destroyed my penthouse resting place. Not to worry, I have many more. Oh, by the way, the girl will be mine."*

Chris violently crumpled the note. "No, you're mine!"

"What are we going to do about Sue?" Reggie asked. "The sun will be up in a couple of minutes."

"I'm going to put her to sleep. You get to a hotel and get some rest. I don't want Charlie Burnson sneaking up on you in the middle of the day."

"Right, I'll check in at the Yates Motel and meet you guys at my place after the sun goes down."

"Wouldn't it be safer to meet at the hotel?" Chris asked.

Reggie shook his head. "I don't think so. Since Rakz has bitten Sue, he's probably linked to her in some way. He'll know where she is."

Chris nodded as Reggie continued.

"He can probably get into a hotel, but we know he can't come into my house unless I invite him in. Besides, I know the layout of my place, and I've got all my vampire fighting gear there."

"Good thinking, partner."

Reggie saluted a farewell. "I'm outta here."

The black man walked towards the door. He turned back to Chris, his face as solemn as a judge about to pass the death sentence. "Chris," he said, "How the hell are we gonna beat this guy?"

"I don't know, Reggie. I just don't know."

Chapter 2

1

Night fell over the city.

Sue awakened at the same time as Chris. She immediately sat up and pulled away from him.

"What's wrong?" he asked, concerned about her reaction.

"Why? Why didn't you tell me?" she said. Her voice was tinged with anger and disappointment.

His beloved Sue knew his secret. He looked at her, mouth open, searching for the words.

"I'm sorry," he finally said. "I didn't know how to tell you. I thought about it, but I didn't want you to leave me. I couldn't . . ."

His voice cracked, and tears welled up in his eyes. "I'm still a human being. I still feel. I still love. It's just that I have this affliction."

She was confused by her love for this man and her fear of the terrible secret he had kept from her.

"Sue, I never kill people. I drink only to exist. I get it from the hospitals. I swear I never hurt anyone." His voice was on the edge of panic. "You're the one thing in my life I couldn't live without."

As she listened to his plea, Sue felt her heart go out to him. She still loved him. He was still the same man she'd fallen in love with before she knew about his . . . sickness, the same man who had saved her from Rakz at the old department store, the same man with whom she'd shared the most exciting, intimate moment of her life.

Slowly, she reached out and took his hand. "How did it happen?"

Chris smiled tenderly at her and started to tell her the story of Legendre and the curse. He hoped that when he had finished, she would still feel the same about him.

2

The alarm rang.

Reggie stuck his arm out from under the blanket and picked up the phone. He pulled the receiver under the blanket.

"Hello," he said groggily.

There was no answer.

The bell kept ringing.

Realizing his mistake, Reggie reached over and slammed his hand down on the alarm's snooze button. It shut off. He put the phone back on the hook, fell back into bed, and shut his eyes.

The bell rang again. He reached over and popped down the snooze button again. It stopped only to ring again a moment later.

Confused, Carver pushed the button down again. It stopped only to start up again in a few seconds. He realized his mistake.

"The phone," Reggie said groggily to himself as he picked up the receiver again.

"Hello?"

"Wake up call, sir," said the cheerful voice on the other end of the line.

Reggie yawned and rubbed his eyes. "Okay, thank you."

"You're welcome, sir," the girl said in the same irritatingly cheery tone. "Have a nice evening." She hung up.

"No problem," Reggie said sarcastically as he lay back

down and thought of the horrible apparition that Rakz had turned into last night. "Yeah, I'm gonna have a real nice evening."

Reggie shut his eyes to get rid of that last bit of sleep when the alarm went off, startling him. He picked the old alarm up and threatened to toss it up against the wall, but then remembered it had been a gift from his mom. He turned it off and set it down. "Damn, that thing could wake the dead."

3

The spiderlike hand skittered along the edge of the coffin lid and pushed it back. The heavy lid fell to the floor of the House of Horrors and Yosekaat Rakz rose from the dead once again.

He stood up and stretched. He looked forward to the evening's events and the challenge of the competition between himself and the young vampire. So far it had been almost too easy, but it was pleasant diversion from the otherwise mundane existence that he had been living for the past few years. The last good fight that he had engaged in was against Willem Litke, an immigrant from Germany who in 1909 had discovered Rakz feasting on his daughter. The enraged father had sworn vengeance. Litke was a superstitious man, and that no doubt aided him in his battles against the vampire. He armed himself with crosses, garlic, and stakes, and set out to destroy Yosekatt Rakz. After much searching and a series of confrontations with the vampire, Litke finally found Rakz's hiding place and was set to drive the stake through the vampire's heart when the police arrived and arrested him for desecrating a tomb. When Litke explained to them that Rakz was a vampire, he was put into a sanitarium. Willem Litke hanged himself a year later, or so they thought. No one knew that Rakz had snuck in one night and done the job.

But that was long ago, and he had much to do in the night that lay ahead. He had to complete the second night of the ritual. But first, he was going to need a little refreshment.

Chris had just finished telling Sue about the circumstances of his vampirism.

She sat back and shook her head.

"My God, Chris," she said, "the whole thing is so unbelievable. And Reggie knows everything?"

Chris nodded. "I didn't want either of you involved, but Rakz has made that impossible."

"Poor Burley, he fought so hard with that Burnson, but . . ." She broke down crying. "When is this going to stop? So many people have been killed or hurt."

Chris pulled her close. "I don't know, baby. Soon, I hope." She hugged him tight.

Chris breathed a sigh of relief, as he knew that she had accepted the bizarre circumstances of their relationship.

"I've got to go out tonight and look for Rakz. You'll stay with Reggie in case Burnson or Rakz comes after you again. It will probably be Burnson, because Rakz can't come in unless he's been invited in. As long as you don't invite in any strangers, you'll be safe."

"Why can't you stay with us?"

"I'm the only one who can track him."

Sue looked at him with concern. "But didn't you say that that didn't always work?"

"Yes, but now I know that he can't block me out all night. He knows I'm after him, so he'll be trying to stop me. At some point in time, I'll probably be able to find out where he is."

As Chris said this, he wondered if he was just blowing happy smoke. He didn't know if he was positively right about Rakz weakening. It made sense, but Chris didn't know enough about the undead to be sure. He was a vampire, and he had weakened from using his powers for too long, but maybe that was because he was not as old as Rakz. He remembered Rakz telling him that as a vampire grew older he grew more powerful. Chris could only make educated guesses about the ancient vampire and his abilities, and so far his grades were failing. In fact, he hadn't guessed right yet about anything regarding the vampire. So far, Rakz had beaten Chris at every turn.

But there had to be a weakness, some way to get close to the vampire, close enough to drive a stake deep into his heart and end his unholy existence. There had to be a way.

5

Reggie had gotten home about twenty minutes earlier and was in the kitchen, heating up his favorite gourmet treat, a can of Beefaroni, when he heard the phone ring. He hustled into the living room, licking the spoon with which he had just stirred the pan. He picked up the phone.

"Hello?"

"It's me."

"Hey, Chris, how's Sue?"

"She's a little weak, but other than that, she's fine. Listen—I'm going to bring her over to your place now, and you can stay with her tonight."

"Sounds cool. You going to find our pal Rakz?"

"Yeah, I'm going to try," Chris said. "You have to watch out for Burnson. He's the one who killed Burley and got Sue out of the house so that Rakz could get at her."

"How could he enter the house without her permission?"

"He's not a vampire. He's a lamia."

Reggie raised his voice. "A *what?*"

"Lamia," Chris replied. "Remember in the book? A lamia is a human being who is a servant of a vampire—their contact with the outside world during the daylight hours."

"That would explain a lot. He must be doing the legwork during the day and then Rakz does the dirty work at night."

"Charlie does his share of the killing. If I'd thought of that last night, Burley might be alive."

"We told him about Charlie, Chris. You can't blame yourself."

"I guess not." Chris clenched his fist. "I just feel so damned helpless. I mean, Rakz has won every fight. In every encounter, he's had the upper hand. The only thing keeping us alive is luck and the fact that Rakz sees this as some kind of competition. I'm sure he could kill us anytime he wanted to."

Reggie kidded Chris. "Hey, we're just trying to let him get overconfident. Shit, I'd have whipped his ass last night if the sun hadn't come up."

Chris laughed at his partner's braggadoccio. "Well, I hope he does get overconfident. Then he might make a mistake and we can nail him."

"Yeah, I hope so, too." Reggie said. "So when will you be here?"

"Twenty minutes."

"I'll be waiting," Reggie said as he hung up the phone.

"Oh, no!" he cried suddenly, remembering his can of Beefaroni on the stove.

He ran into the kitchen muttering to himself.

"Damn, you can't overcook that stuff. It'll taste like dog food."

6

The big Rotweiler pulled Monica Sinclair along in his search for the right spot in which to do his business. It was a perfect example of the dog walking his master. The dog, Manfred, was a solid 130 pounds of eating machine. Monica had gotten him for protection after she'd been mugged one night on her way home from work. He was a trained attack dog, but usually just one look at the huge animal was enough to scare off even the most brazen of criminals.

As they walked, Monica could sense the presence of someone else. She looked around but saw no one. She chalked up the creepy feeling to the sense of paranoia she had developed since the mugging incident.

The Rotweiler stopped and urinated on a bush. After he finished, he scratched the ground in the strange way dogs did sometimes. Suddenly he growled in a low, menacing snarl.

The hair of Monica's neck stood up straight and goose-flesh spread across her body. "What is it, Manny?" she said, peering into the darkness, suddenly very afraid. Maybe her paranoia was well founded.

The dog continued to growl menacingly.

She called out into the night, "Who's there?"

No answer.

"I have an attack dog."

Still no answer.

"He's trained to kill."

She hoped the threat would chase off the thing hiding in the shadows.

"If there's someone there, you'd better answer, or I'm going to let the dog go."

Manfred strained at the leash, snarling, ready to sink his teeth into whatever it was that was out there.

"I'm warning you," Monica said.

She saw a shape pass by quickly under the dim street lamp. She shouted the command to attack. *"Blitzkrieg,* Manfred."

The Rotweiler barked viciously and ran into the darkness.

Monica could hear his fierce snapping jaws as he attacked whatever was there in the shadows. The dog was snarling and snapping when Monica heard a loud pop.

Total silence.

A huge shape flew toward her and landed at her feet.

She cried out in terror.

It was her dog, his neck twisted horribly, dead.

Then she heard footsteps coming toward her.

7

Chris and Sue arrived at Reggie's place. The black detective was scraping the charred beefaroni from the bottom of the saucepan when the doorbell rang.

"Just a minute," Reggie shouted, putting the pan down in the sink.

He walked across the living room and opened the door a little bit, keeping the chain on. He saw his friends, unlatched the chain, and let them in.

"Hi, Reg," Sue said.

Chris patted him on the shoulder and started walking into the living room. Reggie hustled over to stop him. "Uh, Chris, you don't want to go in there. There's, ah, well . . ."

Sue finished his sentence for him. "Charms against vampires?"

"Yeah, charms against . . . hey, you know!" A surprised Reggie cried out.

"Yes," Chris said, "Rakz told her last night, and I filled her in on the details a little while ago."

Reggie looked over at the doctor. "Some kinda funky stuff, eh, Doc?"

"You could say that."

Chris interrupted. "I have to go and start looking for his hideout. I don't think I can beat him in a fight, but if I can find out where he sleeps you could drive a stake through his heart during the day."

"It would be a pleasure," Reggie said, thinking of his good friends Burley and Tom.

"Good luck, Chris," Sue said as she kissed him. "Remember, I love you."

"I love you, too, babe."

He kissed her on the forehead.

"For luck," he said.

She kissed his forehead.

"For luck."

"Now remember," Chris said, "Rakz can't come in unless you invite him in. Burnson can, so watch out for him."

"I will," Reggie said. "Now you go out and find where that bastard lives and I'll end this thing tomorrow."

Chris nodded and left.

Reggie went over to Sue and hugged her, hanging a cross around her neck.

"What's that for?" she asked.

"For luck."

She hugged him back.

"For luck."

They would need all the luck they could get before the night was over.

8

The footsteps grew louder and the terrified Monica could see the silhouette of a man coming towards her. She took off running. As she did, she heard an eerie sound coming from behind her. It was only a moment later that she recognized the sound as laughter, evil, rancorous laughter. Monica ran as hard as she could away from the dreadful sound, her legs churning like pistons.

The laughter grew louder, a hideous chuckling straight from hell.

Monica's heart pounded against her ribs, threatening to explode from the exertion of her escape efforts and the unbearable fear that engulfed her. Still she ran, ran for her life, her tennis shoes slapping hard and fast on the pavement. She ran and ran and kept running, even though her feet had suddenly lost contact with the pavement. Her legs became a tragic parody of running as they kicked frantically while the man held her above the ground by the hair.

As she dangled in his grasp, Rakz whipped her up in the air and snapped her like a bullwhip. He held her up like a dead chicken in a butcher shop and pulled her close. Quickly he drained her and drove the stake into her heart. He had wanted to toy with her a little longer, but alas, he had to attend to more important things. He flew off to dispose of her body.

9

"What's up with you and Chris?" Reggie said, munching on a cheese puff. "I mean, how is his, uh, condition gonna effect your relationship?"

"I really don't know, Reggie," Sue answered. "I guess I'm going to learn to deal with it. I mean, I love the guy."

"Yeah, me too." Reggie smiled. "Besides, I'd be the last one to stop caring about somebody because of prejudice. I know how it feels, and I'm no bigot . . . even against vampires."

Sue laughed gently. "I guess it really doesn't matter what he is. It's what's in his heart that counts."

"Hell, the only difference between him and me is that he can change into animals and has strange eating habits."

"I agree with the first part, but I have seen what you have in your cupboard."

"Hey, that stuff's not weird. That's fine cuisine."

Sue rolled her eyes. "Right—Beefaroni, Twinkies, Captain Crunch, a whole chicken in a can. That junk is a one-way ticket to bad health."

"All aboard on the bad health express," Reggie laughed as he chomped on another cheese puff.

Sue shook her head and sat down on the sofa. She picked up a magazine and started to read. She couldn't get into it. Her mind was preoccupied.

"Reggie," she said, "do you think we're really gonna win this thing against Rakz?"

Reggie nodded. "Sure, the good guys always win. We wear the white hats, and we always shoot the straightest."

10

Donald Twitty, the building superintendent, was sitting in his usual position in front of the television set, beer in hand, ballgame blaring. Sometimes his wife, Joan, believed that she was married to the stereotypical American male. She would scream and shout at him to get up and attend to their tenants' needs, but he would always put her off with one of his patented lines:

There's only a minute to go.

After the game's over, dear.

It's the last quarter. Shut up.

Those types of wonderful reasons. She could take care of most of the little problems, but for the big things, the air conditioners, the backed-up sinks, the broken heaters, she needed him. The Twittys had been the supers at Reggie's building for only about a year, but they had already earned the animosity of most of the tenants.

Joan was about to begin another tirade about the condition of Mrs. Kowalski's bathtub when the doorbell rang.

"Could you get that, Don?" she shouted.

"The Heat's behind by only two points with ten seconds left."

Typical. She threw up her hand in disgust and went to the door. Joan Twitty looked through the peephole and saw a man standing there whom she didn't recognize. He was probably some kind of salesman, and an ugly one, to boot. He had a big nose, a crummy little beard, and strange green eyes. She opened the door.

"What do you want?" she asked.

The man smiled and raised a gun. The silenced .38 hissed and a bullet tore into the throat of the stunned Mrs. Twitty.

Another hiss. A brain shot and the overweight woman fell over dead.

The ugly man stepped over her and moved toward the living room.

"Honey, who is it?" Donald yelled from his chair. "If it's some salesman or a charity case, tell them we don't want any."

He went back to watching the game.

Charlie Burnson entered the living room.

"Who was it, dear?" the fat man said, turning in his chair to face his wife.

"The boogeyman, dear." Charlie laughed. He pumped three shots into Twitty, who was a corpse after the first shot hit him right between the eyes.

The big man fell back into his chair, still gripping his ever-present can of beer. His eyes stared blankly at the TV screen as Rory Sparrow made the winning basket for the Miami Heat. His wife, God rest her soul, would not have noticed anything different about him except for the three bloody holes that now pocked his body.

Burnson started tearing the apartment apart as he searched for the object that he had just murdered two people to get. He ripped open drawers and flung their contents onto the floor. He went from room to room, ransacking the place until he finally found what he was looking for.

The master keys were in the kitchen drawer. Burnson picked them up and jingled them happily as he put them in his pocket.

Now the fun would really begin.

11

Chris flew over the city in his search for a clue to Rakz's hideout. He had changed into a bat for a little while so that he could cover more ground.

As he concentrated on Rakz, he began receiving images. Strange images. A black dog. A woman. A partially hairy werewolf. He smelled a musty smell. *What did they all mean?* Chris wondered. *How did all these things tie together?*

As Chris was trying to put the pieces of the strange puzzle together, a small object glanced off his wing.

Then another. But this one was accompanied by a sharp pain.

Chris's radar sensed a hundred such objects behind him. He turned to see what it was that was following him.

When he saw them he knew Rakz was behind it all.

12

"You want something from the kitchen, Sue?" Reggie shouted as he threw away the empty bag of cheese puffs and grabbed a box of Little Debbie snack cakes.

"Maybe something to drink," Sue said.

Carver opened the refrigerator. "I've got Mr. Pibb, Fresca, Yoo Hoo, and water."

"Well," Sue said sarcastically, "at least your drinks are nutritional."

"Only the best for the kid," Reggie replied. "Now what'll it be?"

"I think I'll just stick with good old water."

"Sure thing."

Reggie took out the pitcher of ice-cold water from the fridge, poured Sue a glass, and took it in to her.

"You want to watch some TV?" Reggie asked.

"No, I'm fine," Sue replied. "I'm just going to read my book for a little while."

"What are you reading?"

"A journal on diseases of the lymphatic glands."

It was Reggie's turn to be sarcastic. "That must be real interesting," he said.

Sue smiled and went back to her book.

"Mind if I watch some?"

"No, go ahead."

Reggie pressed the power button on the remote and the television switched on. He clicked through the stations until he came to his favorite channel. He turned it on just in time to hear the familiar voice he had loved since he was a kid.

"Geee, Wilburrr."

It was time to talk with Mister Ed.

Reggie settled back into his chair and prepared for a half hour of nostalgia and fun.

13

Bats!

Hundreds of bats clouded the air behind Chris. The vampire veered downward as the furry creatures started to attack him. He flapped his leathery wings furiously in an attempt to outrun the horde.

A speedy bat caught up to Chris and latched onto his leg. Chris shook it off as another buzzed his head, nipping his ear as it went by him. Another attacker flew too close, and Chris snapped it in two with his powerful jaws.

As some of the speedier bats flew at him, he lashed out and killed several of them.

But there were too many. They began to close in on him. Chris had to find a way to escape the trap that Rakz had set for him.

As he looked down, he saw the answer.

He dived towards the bright lights below him.

14

Rakz had dumped the body of the girl in the river where no one would find her. Now he sat on a rooftop, concentrating furiously to control the creatures he had sent to attack Chris. He wanted to be sure the young upstart was busy as Charles did his dirty work and got the girl for him. He wished he could get her himself, but he couldn't unless the black man invited him in, and that was very unlikely. Unless . . . an idea began to germinate in the malevolent bloodsucker's mind, but the thought never reached fruition as it was interrupted by the sudden, violent disruption of the psychic link between him and the bats.

15

Chris hurtled toward the power plant that glowed below him. He would have to time it just right, or he could injure himself. He knew he couldn't be killed, but the hot power lines could burn him badly. He didn't relish the thought of going through eternity looking like Freddie Krueger.

Faster and faster he dived, the bats in hot pursuit. One of them caught up to him, buried its fangs into his leg, and held on. Chris ignored the pain as he plummeted downward.

Faster and faster.

The bats getting closer and closer.

They were less than ten feet from him as he approached the crackling transformers below. He would try to pull up in the last moment unexpectedly and hope the bats would not be aware of the power lines until it was too late.

Faster.

Faster.

Closer.

Closer.

The bats were right on his tail.

Now!

He arched his back and caught the wind beneath his wings. He swooped upward a foot away from the thousands of volts that sizzled through the lines.

The bats weren't so lucky. They hit the power plant in one collective bunch and the station erupted in a fury of sparks and burnt flesh. The bats squealed and scattered as the majority of them sizzled in the shower of electricity. A few of the luckier ones escaped the blaze of death and fluttered away. Their unlucky companions fell to the ground in charred lumps.

The power went out for fifteen blocks around the plant.

Fortunately, Chris was unhurt.

Unfortunately, Reggie's apartment was only ten blocks away.

16

Mr. Ed was just about to explain to Wilbur why he had ordered the television set over the phone when the power shut down.

Sensing danger, Reggie immediately reacted. "Sue, get over here," he whispered.

In the darkness she groped her way to his side. "Do you think it's him?"

"I don't know. But if it is, I'm ready," he said solemnly, pulling the .38 special from his holster. "I've got some candles in the kitchen drawer."

Before he left for the kitchen, he reached under the sofa and pulled out a sawed-off shotgun.

"You take this," he said, "while I go get them."

"But I'm not a good shot," she cried.

"With that puppy, you just need to get close."

He heard the fear in her voice. "Don't worry, it's probably nothing. We'll be okay."

Reggie scooted his way toward the kitchen, bumping into the end table.

"Shit," he yelped.

"Reggie, are you okay?"

"Yeah, I'm fine. I just caught my shin on the damn table."

He continued toward the kitchen, trying to feel his way in the total darkness as a key slid into the lock of his front door.

As Reggie opened the drawer that held the candles, he heard the front door burst open, ripping the chain lock out of the doorjamb.

"Get down, Sue," he shouted.

Burnson's gun hissed like a snake and Reggie was covered in broken pieces of flatware. He could hear Burnson's footsteps as the lamia entered the living room.

"It's me, Carver," Burnson said in an excited voice. "I'm here to kill you and take the doctor to the master."

Reggie pointed the gun in the direction of the voice, but he was afraid to shoot for fear of hitting Sue. She could be in the line of fire.

Another hiss and a coffee cup exploded.

Carver could hear the soft footsteps of the madman as Burnson made his way across the carpet towards the kitchen.

Reggie wondered if Assface could see in the dark. His steps sounded so sure. He tried to remember if any of the vampire books he had read said that a lamia could see in the dark. He couldn't recall. The black man decided to take a chance and make a move that Burnson wouldn't expect. If Burnson could see in the dark, then in all probability he would shoot Reggie dead before he reached him. If not, then they had a chance.

Reggie crouched and readied himself.

He said a short prayer and then launched himself at the murderous servant of Yosekaat Rakz.

17

Rakz screamed in agony when the psychic link between him and his minions was broken by their abrupt electrocution. The telepathic energy of their life force was sent back to Rakz in one powerful burst. When it hit him, he felt as though his brain had suddenly been expanded beyond its bounds as it filled up with the incredible surge of energy.

It had ended as quickly as it had come, and Rakz collapsed. He lay quiet, resting from the sudden jolt. It would be some time before he would have the strength to block Chris out or make contact with Charles. He would be vulnerable for a short time.

He hoped Charles was having more luck than he was.

18

Reggie slammed into Burnson at full tilt, the silenced pistol flying out of the lamia's hand. The momentum of their collision carried them into the La-Z-Boy chair. They toppled over it and landed hard on the floor. Burnson was on top of the black man.

Reggie brought his pistol up to fire, but Burnson was quick. He grabbed a lamp and knocked the gun out of the detective's hand. He swung it again and caught Carver with a glancing blow to the shoulder.

The black man retaliated with a punch to Burnson's forehead that felt like it probably broke one of Reggie's knuckles. He threw another punch and connected with the top of Burnson's head. White-hot pain shot through his injured hand as it collided with the hard bone. Carver struggled to get out from under the lamia and fired a punch that struck Burnson on the forearm.

Burnson swung the lamp at Reggie again. It hit Carver in the same spot on his shoulder. The black cop howled in pain. He shot a left hand out and caught Burnson in the face.

He dropped the lamp.

Reggie grabbed him by the front of the shirt and twisted him to the ground. He jumped on top of Burnson and locked his hands around the murderer's throat. He started to squeeze with all his might, trying to choke the life out of the man who had murdered his friends.

Burnson gurgled as he tried to extricate himself from the death grip, but it was to no avail. He could feel the world around him getting louder, the sounds echoing off the walls. It was just like the feeling you get when you are on the verge of falling asleep during an afternoon nap, but this nap was permanent.

Reggie continued to squeeze with all his strength. The fingers on his right hand coursed with pain. His injured shoulder throbbed violently, but he held on. He had to end it now.

Squeezing.

Harder.

Harder.

A gasp.

The body of the ex-police lieutenant went limp.

Reggie kept his grip on Burnson long after the man had stopped struggling. He wanted to be sure that Assface was really dead before he quit.

After Burnson rattled one last time, Carver released his hold and got up.

It was over.

"Sue, are you all right?" Reggie asked the frightened doctor, who could see nothing of the struggle in the total darkness.

"Yes, I'm fine," the trembling voice cried out. "How about you?"

"Fair. I took a couple shots in the shoulder and I think I broke my knuckle. He's dead."

"Are you sure?" Sue asked with a twinge of doubt in her voice.

The lamp crashed against Reggie's skull and he crumpled to the floor.

"Yes," Charlie cackled. "He's dead."

The raspy voice of Burnson petrified Sue with fear. From the sound of it, Reggie had been knocked cold and Burnson was preparing to finish him off.

She had to do something.

She stood up and pointed the shotgun in the direction of Burnson's voice. She put her finger on the trigger and prepared to fire.

"I have a sawed-off shotgun pointed at you, Mr. Burnson," Sue said in an even voice. "I want you to back away from Reggie."

Burnson laughed. He was going to kill the little nigger and no one was going to stop him. He raised the lamp over his head and prepared to strike the blow that would end the black man's life.

19

Chris landed on the rooftop of the apartment building. He had to rest. He had used up a great deal of energy in his confrontation with the bats.

He had won his first victory against the vampire, but still he felt empty.

He hadn't found Rakz.

He hadn't found his lair.

He hadn't accomplished a damn thing.

He decided he would fly back to Reggie's apartment and check up on Sue and his partner. But first he would have to rest for a little while in order to regain some of his strength.

It was too bad that he had chosen that particular moment to do so as Rakz was across town totally unable to stop Chris from finding him.

It would be his only chance that night.

20

Sue aimed the gun in Burnson's direction. "I'm going to fire."

She just might, Charlie thought to himself, then said, "Go ahead. I have the nigger right in front of me. If you shoot, you'll kill him too."

"You're bluffing."

He was, but in the pitch-dark apartment she couldn't see that he was.

"If you think I'm bluffing, then go ahead and shoot."

Sue thought for a moment, then lowered the gun. She couldn't take the chance that he was telling the truth.

Burnson raised the heavy metal lamp over his head to crush Carver's skull like a honeydew melon. He was about to swing down with all his might when suddenly the lights flicked back on.

Sue saw Burnson standing over the unconscious Reggie. The lamp poised over his head, a shocked look on his face. She raised the gun and aimed it.

"Put the lamp down!" she commanded.

Burnson looked at her and his shocked expression slowly changed into a smile. *She didn't have the guts to kill me in cold blood,* he thought to himself. He turned his attention back to Carver.

Reggie had awakened and looked up through the red haze of blood that leaked into his eyes from the gash in his head. He saw the gleeful expression on Assface Charlie Burnson's face and knew that he was a dead man.

"Bye, bye, blackbird," Burnson chortled as he started to swing the lamp down.

"Bye, bye," Sue said evenly as she pulled the triggers on both barrels of the sawed-off shotgun.

Burnson's body exploded in a splash of gore. He careened

271

off the wall and spun into the glass cabinet that held all of Reggie's movie memorabilia. His torn body fell to the floor in a dead heap. A picture from Reggie's collection floated aimlessly downward and landed softly covering the stunned expression on Charlie's dead face.

It was a picture of Francis, the talking mule.

Sue dropped the gun and ran to Reggie's side. "Are you okay?"

"Not too good," he moaned as he tried to get up. His head throbbed like a Thunderbird hangover.

Sue gently pushed him back down to the floor. "You lie down for a minute and relax."

He looked up at the woman who had just saved his life. "You done good, Doc."

She smiled shakily. "I couldn't let him kill you."

He returned her smile. "Thanks."

As Sue went into the bathroom to get a cold towel for his head, Reggie smiled to himself. "One down and one to go."

An hour later, a sudden knocking on Reggie's front door froze the black man in his tracks. He was trying to drag the dead body of Charlie Burnson out of the living room and into the kitchen. Quickly, he pulled the dead lamia all the way into the kitchen and out of sight, and went to answer the door.

He opened it a crack, trying to hide the torn wood of the doorjamb with his hand, and saw Mrs. Kowalski, his neighbor, standing there, hands on hips, her face pursed in an angry expression.

"Hello, Mrs. K, what's up?" Reggie asked, trying to act nonchalant.

"I heard a loud bang come from inside your apartment," she said. "What are you doing in there?"

Reggie put on his best happy face. "I'm really sorry if I scared you. I was cleaning my gun and it accidentally went off."

"My word!" she exclaimed. "You should be more careful. A gun is not a toy."

She shook her finger at him. "You should know a thing

272

like that, being on the police force and all."

"Yes, ma'am, like I said, I'm real sorry."

"Well, you should be. I mean, you could scare a person to death."

Reggie hoped the little old lady would just shut up and go away, but she continued.

"If I didn't like you so much, I'd have half a mind to go down and complain to the super."

She had no idea her complaints would fall on dead ears.

"My husband always used to tell me, now . . ."

Reggie interrupted her before she could get started on one of her interminably long reminiscences about the good old days. "Listen, Mrs. K, I have to clean up in here. I'm expecting company in a little while, so I need to get back to it, okay?"

"Very well, but you be more careful in the future," she scolded him.

"Yes, ma'am. I will. G'night."

He closed the door as Mrs. Kowalski opened her mouth to get started again.

"Who was that?" Sue asked, alarmed.

"Just a harmless little old lady from next door, nothing to worry about," Reggie assured her.

"What are we going to do with him?" she said, pointing toward the kitchen. "Are you going to call the police?"

"And tell them what? That a former lieutenant in the Miami Police Department was the servant of a three-century-old vampire, and that he was here to kill me and take you to be the bloodsucker's wife?"

"But we could just bend the truth a bit."

Reggie shook his head. "They'd take us both down to the station for questioning and probably hold us in separate places. I'm sure Rakz would love that. It would make it easy for him to get you. If we stay here, we're safe, especially with Burnson dead."

Sue was forced to agree. "I guess you're right."

"I know I am. Besides, what are you going to tell them? They'd never believe the truth, and we'd both become suspects in a murder case. I mean, I've had enough fights with Burnson to make me a likely candidate to kill him."

Sue looked toward the kitchen and back at Reggie with shame in her eyes.

"I had to do it, Reggie."

Reggie put his arm around her. "I know, Doc. It was the only thing you could do. Charlie had gone way over the edge."

"It still makes me sick to my stomach that I had to kill him."

"You probably did him a favor," he said. "I never liked the guy, but no one deserves to become what he had."

She nodded solemnly.

They both stood silent for a moment, then Sue asked Reggie a question: "What are you going to do with the body?"

He hadn't really thought of that yet. He paused for a moment. As the answer dawned on him, a shadow of a smile crept across his face. Reggie would give Rakz a taste of his own medicine.

He went to his closet and grabbed the canvas cover that had once protected the old MG he used to drive. He'd loved that car, but it was a bitch to maintain. It cost him an arm and a leg to repair, which seemed to be required at least once a week. Still he had kept the cover in the hopes that one day he would be earning enough to afford to get another one. Now he would have to get a new cover if he ever did get another MG. Tonight, the old one would serve another purpose—a grisly one.

Reggie went into the kitchen and bundled the stiffening body of the dead Burnson into the canvas cover. He hoisted it over his shoulder and walked slowly to the front door.

"I've got to get rid of the body. I'll be back soon. Don't let anyone in."

"Okay."

Reggie carried the concealed body outside to his car as Sue went about the gruesome task of cleaning up the blood.

She felt like a criminal, trying to conceal their dirty deeds. But Reggie was right: if they told anyone down at the station the truth, they would have a lot of explaining to do. Chris would be drawn into the investigation, and they might discover his affliction. She and Chris would never be able to be together if that happened. Besides, it was all so fantastic that Reggie and she could very well become suspects. From what Reggie said, he and Burnson had had troubles in the past. The police just might believe that he had killed Burnson. After all, it made more sense than Burnson being the servant of a vampire.

After looking at all sides, Sue was sure that they were doing the right thing by not telling anyone. But where was Reggie going to hide the body?

21

Rakz had gained enough strength to try and contact Burnson, but when he tried he could sense nothing. Nothing at all. This concerned the vampire. *Where was he?* Rakz wondered. Could he have captured the girl and already taken her to their rendezvous point at the House of Horrors? It seemed unlikely, but Rakz decided it would be his best course of action to go there and see. He changed into a bat and flew toward the abandoned amusement park.

When he arrived, he went into the exhibit and searched for his servant. He found no one, and it didn't look as if anyone had been there, either.

"Damn!" he lashed out in anger, shattering the Creature from the Black Lagoon into a green pile of wax. "Where could he be?"

Rakz was frustrated by his lack of control over the situation. He paused to regain his composure and collect his thoughts.

Perhaps the disruption had disoriented Charles and he had taken Rakz's fiancée somewhere else. *But where?* Rakz wondered.

The penthouse!
Rakz flew back towards the city.

22

Chris arrived at Reggie's apartment to see how everything was. He knocked on the door.

"Who is it?"

"It's me, Sue."

She opened the door and let her boyfriend in. She threw her arms around him. "Oh, God, I'm so glad you're here."

"Where's Reggie?"

"I killed Burnson."

"What?"

"He came in during a power loss and attacked Reggie. It was pitch black and I couldn't see a thing. I had the gun. Reggie thought he'd killed Burnson, but that maniac wasn't dead. He got the upper hand on Reggie and was about to kill him when the lights came up. I aimed and . . . then it was over."

"So where's Carver?"

"He took the body someplace."

"Where?"

"I don't know. He said he wanted to give Rakz a taste of his own medicine."

"What the hell is that crazy man up to?"

23

Reggie had shown the security guards his badge and told them he had to deliver something to one of the residents. Police business, he said.

The doorman, Ollie Bayan, who remembered Reggie from the other night, even offered to help him carry his package up to the resident's door. Reggie politely refused his help, gave him a beer, and told him he'd keep an eye out while the doorman drank it in the men's room. Reggie had also remembered the doorman and brought him the brew to keep him occupied while he took Burnson up to the penthouse. He just hoped that he had guessed right and that Ollie didn't get his red nose from too much sun. He did, and the doorman was soon ducking into the men's room with the cold one in his hand. Reggie lucked out when he found the big laundry cart and quickly wheeled it out to the parking lot. He loaded the body in it and pushed it back inside.

He made his way up the elevator. When he got to the top floor, he steered the cart out of the elevator and wheeled it down towards the penthouse condominium. He was going to show Rakz that they were quite capable of striking back.

He jimmied the lock and crept inside the darkened room. The heavy cart rolled silently across the carpet as Carver pushed it toward the door to the coffin room. Suddenly a chilling thought struck him: what if Rakz was in there? He reached for the cross in his pants pocket.

It was gone.

Frantically he patted his pockets for the cross. The crucifix had vanished. *It must have fallen out of my pocket when I lifted Burnson into the car,* he thought. He couldn't worry about it now. He had to take care of business.

He pulled the canvas covered body of Charlie Burnson out of the cart and flopped it onto the floor. As Reggie dragged it into the room where Reggie and Chris had confronted the rats and the zombified Draper, he accidentally knocked over the one lamp in the entire apartment. It crashed loudly to the floor.

"Shit!" Carver hissed, and continued pulling the body toward the room. Once he had dragged Burnson into the coffin room, he began unrolling the canvas cover. Reggie was totally unaware that the owner of the penthouse was on his way home.

Black, leathery wings stroked the air powerfully as Rakz flew quickly toward the penthouse.

The night was growing short.

He would check the condo to see if Charles was there with the girl. If he was, Rakz would complete the second night's ritual with the girl and leave her with Charles while he flew back to the House of Horrors to rest.

He couldn't risk spending the day at the penthouse. Even though Charles had made it safe and would be there to watch over him, his enemies knew it was one of his resting places. They could come during the day, and if they made it past his lamia, they could destroy him.

If his servant wasn't there, Rakz would assume that Burnson had met with ill fortune. If that was the case, he would go back to the amusement park, sleep, and regroup the next evening. In any event, tomorrow night he would end the lives of Chris and Reggie. He had grown tired of the game.

As he flew, he could see the lights of Ravenswood far off in the distance. He would be there very soon.

25

Reggie was just finishing up with Charles when he heard a key rattle at the front door. His heart leapt into his throat. Rakz!

Reggie gathered up the canvas cover and slipped out of the coffin room, closing the door silently behind him.

He hid in one of the hallway closets and froze. If the vampire found him, he was a dead man. He could hear the door opening and the footsteps that he knew belonged to Yosekaat Rakz. The footsteps stopped in the middle of the room, as if the person were checking out the situation. Reggie gasped in horror. The canvas cover was sticking out of the closet door! He pulled gently on the cover, but it wouldn't budge. Rakz was sure to see it. He pulled a little harder. The MG cover still wouldn't move. It was firmly stuck there in the door. Reggie decided to give it one hard tug. He grabbed a handful of canvas and set himself. He gave himself a mental countdown.

One.

Two.

Three.

He pulled the canvas just as the door was jerked open from the outside.

He knew he was dead.

26

"Where the hell is Reggie?" Chris said. "He should have been back by now. I'm getting worried."

"Oh no, look!" Sue shouted, pointing toward the kitchen.

Chris turned and was repelled by what he saw.

A cross—Reggie's cross—lying on the kitchen floor.

"Oh, my God," Sue cried. "He's out there with no protection."

Chris held her close. "Don't worry, he probably has another one with him, Sue. Reggie wouldn't go outside without any protection against Rakz."

"I hope you're right," she said.

27

Reggie waited for the powerful talons of Rakz to pick him up and pull him out of the closet. He expected to hear the chilling voice from hell tell him that he had enjoyed the game, but now it was over.

"What in hell ya'll doin' in they-uh, buddy?"

It wasn't a voice from hell. This voice sounded like it was from Tennessee.

"Get yo' ass outta they-uh."

Reggie looked up and saw the man. He was a security

279

guard. The guard must have heard the lamp crash.

Calmly Reggie stood up. "Boy, am I glad to see you."

"I dunno why," Bobby Ray Mattson said, "I'm arrestin' ya'll fo' breakin' 'n enterin'."

Reggie smiled, then tossed the canvas cover on top of the guard's head and punched him.

The guard went down.

Carver dashed out the door and headed down the stairs. Eight flights.

By the time he got to the bottom, he was exhausted. As he exited the stairwell, he jumped back through the door before it shut.

Yosekaat Rakz had just entered the lobby.

Reggie watched as the vampire walked casually over to the elevator and got in. After the elevator started going up, Reggie hurried out the front door, waved to Ollie, and went to his car. He was safe. He drove off, flashing his police badge to the armed guards at the gate. They waved him on.

He was home free.

28

As he rode up the elevator, Rakz was sure he was right. The more he thought about it, the more he was convinced that Charles would be there waiting for him . . . and he was right.

The vampire went up to the penthouse and saw the security guard, Bobby Ray Mattson, coming out of his front door.

"What were you doing in there?" Rakz asked in a harsh voice that startled the guard.

"Uh, I thought I heard somebody in they-uh, so I'se checkin' it out when alla sudden . . ."

Rakz was uninterested in why the man was in his resting place and coldly interrupted him. "Never enter my dwelling again. Is that clear?" The ominous tone of Rakz's voice made his sentiment crystal clear.

"Yessuh, clear as a dove cooin' on a Sundeh mornin'."

"Get out of here."

Mattson was only too glad to get away from the strange man with the weird eyes. If the weirdo didn't want to hear how he chased off a burglar, that was fine with him. He scurried down the hallway and left.

Rakz cautiously entered the condo and surveyed the area. A strange pile of material lay in the middle of the room. The closet door was open. Puzzled, Rakz rubbed his chin. He could sense no trace of his servant.

He went into the trophy room. No one was there. He frowned and headed for the room that held his coffin.

As he entered, Rakz screamed with rage at what he saw. Reggie had propped the dead Burnson up in the coffin and positioned his hand as if the dead man was waving. He had scribbled a note and stuck it in the corpse's other hand.

Rakz angrily snatched the note away and read it.

Dear Rakz,
    Next time, if you want to get it done right, don't send in the second team. Come yourself. Or are you afraid?
                Love and kisses,
                Reggie.

Rakz crushed the note in his powerful hand. He would make sure the dark one suffered greatly before he died.

He took off and flew toward the House of Horrors.

The sun would rise soon.

29

"You took him where?" Chris said incredulously.

"To the penthouse. I figured Rakz would show up there sooner or later and have to get rid of the body himself."

"I doubt it. Rakz knows that we know about the penthouse. He'll never go there again," Chris said.

"But he did! Rakz showed up in the lobby just as I was

about to leave."

"Did he see you?" Sue asked joining the conversation.

"No, I ducked back into the stairwell. He went up the elevator."

"He must have thought Charlie was there," Chris added.

Reggie smiled mischievously. "Yeah, and won't he be glad when he finds out that he is."

"I'm just glad Rakz didn't show up while you were still up there."

Sue added, "That really was a dumb thing to do, Reggie."

Reggie grew angry. "Hey, I just wanted to show that fang-toothed fuckhead that we weren't afraid of him and that he could be beaten."

Chris looked at his partner with raised eyebrows. "Fang-toothed fuckhead?"

Reggie looked at him with angry eyes. "Yeah, fang-toothed fuckhead. That's what I said."

Chris broke out laughing at this colorful description of the ancient vampire. Reggie's angry expression melted as he realized how funny the phrase sounded, and he started laughing, too. Sue joined them, and soon they were all roaring hysterically.

"Did you know that you went to visit that fang-toothed fuckhead without a cross?" Chris eeked out between giggles.

Reggie laughed uproariously. "Yeah, good thing that neck-nibbling numnut wasn't there."

Gales of laughter swept the room.

Sue had tears streaming down her face as she said, "Yes, that neck-nibbling numnut could have killed you."

They all screamed with hilarity.

It was the laughter of three terrified people caught in a web of dread.

After a few minutes of nonstop giggles, snorts, chortles, and chuckles, their revelry was reduced to an occasional snicker. Finally they all regained their composure and realized that another day would soon begin.

"I have to go," Chris said, a final titter escaping from his lips.

"Right," Carver said, wiping away a tear, "and I've got a chain lock to fix."

"We'll meet back here tonight."

Sue kissed Chris. "Better get going, Chris."

Chris smiled, then his face grew grim. "Tonight we end this thing. Agreed?"

They all nodded and joined hands. "Agreed. Tonight it ends."

Chapter 3

1

Sue woke with a start. She thought she had heard something coming from the kitchen. She glanced over at the clock.

It was two o'clock in the afternoon.

Maybe Reggie was in the kitchen getting a snack. She heard the clatter again and decided to check it out. She got up out of bed and slipped on her robe. There was nothing to be afraid of, she told herself. It was the middle of the day and Rakz was at rest. Still she wanted to see what it was . . . just to be safe.

As she left the bedroom, she saw Reggie snoozing comfortably on the couch. He must have been in a deep sleep not to have heard the noise.

A sliver of fear pricked Sue's mind.

She hurried into the kitchen and looked around, but saw nothing out of the ordinary. Opened cans sat on the counter. Dirty dishes were in the sink. Nothing strange about that . . . it just meant that Reggie had been in the kitchen. Convinced there was nothing wrong, she left the kitchen and went into the living room. There was a crash in the bedroom. Maybe she had missed something.

She hurried over to the sleeping detective. "Reggie, wake up. There's something wrong," Sue whispered.

He didn't react.

"Reggie? Wake up."

She shook him harder.

Reggie's head lolled over, and Sue saw the deep red slash across his throat. The blanket under his chin was soaked in gore.

"Oh, my God! No! Reggie! No!"

She looked up and saw Charlie Burnson. His corpse was smiling at her. She could see his lung breathing through the gap where she had blasted him open with the shotgun. In his right hand was a wicked-looking butcher knife. She glanced toward the front door. It looked as though it was a hundred yards away. She would have to make a run . . .

No . . .

Reggie's gun.

It must be on his body.

As Burnson crept toward her, a horrible grin on his face, Sue searched Reggie's body for his gun. She found his shoulder holster and frantically reached for the .38. It wasn't there! She looked under the couch. Not there!

Burnson was getting closer.

Where was it?

"Looking for this?" a familiar voice said.

It was Reggie. He was holding up the gun. His almost severed head hung grotesquely to one side.

"Oh no! Not you!" Sue cried, the terror building in her like an avalanche.

"What'sa matter, Doc? You look scared," Carver said as he pointed the gun at her.

"This can't be happening. It's 2 o'clock. Rakz is asleep. It can't . . ."

The loud report of the .38 was the last sound Sue heard on earth. The bullet struck her squarely in the heart and she fell back. A small red hole was the only sign of violence.

Burnson roared at the black man. "That was my kill. You ruined it."

He swung the big knife and lopped off Reggie's head.

The disembodied detective kept talking. "You shouldn't

have done that, Assface," he chided the lamia.

"Shut up, you shit!" Burnson kicked the talkative head across the room.

It landed with a thud, and Reggie woke up in a cold sweat. His heart was pounding in his chest as if it were going to explode. His mouth felt like the summer residence of a boll weevil. He wiped the sweat from his brow with the corner of his sheet.

The nightmare was a signal. Bad dreams . . . bad karma. It was an omen of the night to come.

Reggie reached over to the dresser, picked up the gold chain necklace with the small cross, and put it around his neck. He wouldn't be without a cross again. He glanced over at the clock and discovered that it wasn't two o'clock, but six o'clock. Soon Chris would be over and another night of terror would begin.

2

Rakz's eyes burst open as the last rays of the sun disappeared. He rose from his coffin. His mood was as foul as the air in the musty exhibit. The night before, he had suffered two defeats—the electrocution of the bats and the death of his servant. Losing was something to which the formidable vampire was unaccustomed. Blaze and his friend had proved to be more worthy adversaries than he'd first given them credit. But what disturbed him more than the defeat was that he had missed the second night of the vampire's marriage ritual. He would have to wait another night before Sue would be his forever. He could no longer afford to be generous and toy with them. Tonight, he would kill Blaze and Carver and take the girl back to the exhibit, where he could complete the second night's ritual.

Tonight he would end it.

Once and for all.

Across the city, Chris Blaze was thinking the same thing.

Reggie was in the kitchen, preparing an omelet for Sue and him to eat for dinner when the good doctor walked in, yawning and rubbing her eyes.

"Whatcha cooking?" she asked.

"A special omelet à la Reggie. Six eggs, ham, swiss cheese, mushrooms, onions, and peppers, with a special seasoning that I invented."

"Sounds great, except I don't like eggs."

"You don't like eggs?"

She shook her head.

"Well, that figures. One of the only healthy things I know how to cook, and you don't like them."

"I'm sorry, ever since I was a little girl I couldn't stand them. I'll just have some cereal, if you've got it."

"Sure, I've got some Captain Crunch up there in the cabinet."

"Uh, no thanks. Do you have any fruit?"

"Bananas are on top of the fridge, and I've got some strawberries in the bottom of the fruit bin."

"You don't happen to have any apple juice?"

"I think I do, check in the freezer. I might have a can of frozen."

She opened the freezer section. Behind a box of Tater Tots was a can of frozen apple juice. Sue could make a banana-and-strawberry smoothie, if Reggie had a blender.

He did, and she began to mix the ingredients to the frozen health drink.

As she blended them together, Reggie put the final touches on his omelet.

They both sat down at the kitchen table. She sipped on her drink as Reggie sprinkled a little pepper on his eggs.

"Doc, I want to thank you again for saving me last night."

Sue smiled feebly. She had still not gotten over the fact that she had been forced to kill. "When is all this going to be over?"

"I wish to God I knew. But it should be easier with

Burnson gone."

"Why won't Rakz just get another person to help him?"

"He probably will. That's why we've got to be ready for anything."

Sue shook her head. "We can't live like this forever."

Reggie agreed. "I know Chris has got to find Rakz or his hiding place so we can deal with that monster. Rakz's probably gonna be pretty pissed about what I did to Burnson."

"Maybe you shouldn't have taunted him."

Reggie shrugged. "Maybe not. I just wanted him to know that we weren't going to lie down and roll over. Besides, he might slip up if he loses his cool."

Sue took another drink of her smoothie.

"He's got to," she said unconvincingly as the doorbell rang.

Reggie looked at Sue.

"Stay here. It's probably Chris."

He got up and picked up the cross. As he went to the door, he called out. "Who is it?"

"It's me, Chris." The familiar voice called out.

Reggie looked out the peephole. It was Chris. He opened the door. "Hey, blood."

Chris nodded. "Reggie."

Sue took off the cross Reggie had put around her neck so that she could approach her boyfriend. She set it on the table, out of sight. She went over to him. "Hi, Chris," she said, kissing him.

"Hello, baby. How are you doing?"

"Pretty good."

"I think I might have thought of a way to find out where Rakz is."

Reggie's ears perked up. "Lay it on me," he said.

"If Rakz continues with his same pattern, he will try and block me out all night. But it takes energy to do that, a lot of energy. By the end of the night he'll be weak, maybe too weak to keep his location a secret. So I'm not going to spend any energy looking for Rakz tonight. Not one bit—that is until an hour before sunrise. Then I'm going to focus every ounce of telepathy I have on him. Hopefully he'll be too weak to stop me and I'll find out where he is. If I do, I'll come get you and we'll try and kill him."

"Isn't that cutting it a little close to sunrise?"

"Yeah, but we've got to chance it. This thing has to be finished."

Sue held his hand. "So you're going to stay with us tonight?"

"Yes, but first I have to go out for a little while."

"What for?" Reggie asked.

"I need nourishment. My last supply of blood is at Feldman's market in a couple of thermos bottles. Old man Feldman lets me keep it in his cooler. He thinks it's V-8 juice. I'm going to drink every drop so that I'm at the peak of my power." Chris headed for the door. "I'll be back soon. Be careful. We may have won a battle or two last night, but the war isn't over yet."

Sue kissed him, and Chris left.

She turned to Reggie. "I think we're gonna win this thing, Reggie. I really think we're gonna win."

"I hope so. Chris's plan sounds good."

Sue walked over and began to clean the dishes off the table.

"Here let me do that," Reggie said.

"No, I'll do it."

"Okay."

Reggie hated doing dishes so he quickly relented.

The doorbell rang again.

Sue turned slowly toward Reggie. He looked tense.

"Reggie! Open up, it's me! I forgot to tell you something." It was Chris.

Reggie went to the door, unlocked it, and let Chris in.

"C'mon in." Reggie smiled. "Now, what was it you forgot to tell me?"

The hard slap caught Reggie solidly across the face. He flew across the room and crashed into the already broken memorabilia cabinet. His cheek stung. His vision was blurred from the blow. Stars danced in front of his eyes.

"That was for the dearly departed Charles," Chris hissed.

Reggie's mind whirled. Why did Chris hit him? Was he under Rakz's power?

Sue's blood ran cold as Chris began to shimmer.

His face contorting.

Changing.

Changing into . . . someone else.

It was Rakz, the malevolent bloodsucking vampire, and he was in their apartment!

Sue tried to make a grab for one of the crosses on the coffee table a few feet away.

"Stop!" Rakz commanded.

She froze in her tracks, as if he had shot her with a freeze ray. Sue was still under his control. The two scabbed-over wounds on her throat were testament to that.

Through the haze, Reggie tried to see what was happening. His heart stopped when he saw Rakz standing across the room.

"Oh, no," he whispered.

Everything was not going to be all right.

Reggie tried to get up as Rakz advanced toward him. He knew in his heart that they had lost. Chris wouldn't be back for at least a half an hour, and he wouldn't be trying to find Rakz with his telepathic powers.

It was over.

Rakz picked up Reggie by the right arm. His grip crushed the black man's muscle against his bone. The incredible pain cleared Carver's head. Rakz held him up. They were face to face. The rancid breath of the vampire turned Reggie's stomach.

"Now, my black friend, it's time to have a little fun." Rakz turned his wrist quickly, snapping Reggie's arm.

The black man screamed in agony.

Rakz smiled. "I want you to know, Mr. Carver, that I admire you. I really do." He snapped Reggie's right wrist again.

Unbearable pain coursed through the cop's body.

"No one since Karlokia has been much of a challenge, yet you and your friend Christopher have survived for quite some time." Rakz crushed Reggie's hand, grinding the bones together.

Reggie almost blacked out from the pain.

"But your part in the game is over, I'm afraid. Although I think you deserve to know how it is going to end."

Reggie gasped. "You bastard."

Rakz shook his head, then continued. "Tonight I'm going to complete the second step toward making the woman my bride. The happy event is going to take place at the old House of Horrors outside of town. Are you familiar with it?"

Reggie was about to pass out when Rakz kicked his shin, snapping his legs backward. He fell to the floor. The pain snapped him awake. Through the white flash of excruciating agony, Reggie remembered the cross, the one that he had on the gold chain around his neck.

Rakz continued. "I shall leave one of my notes on your dead body so Blaze will know where we will be, and when he comes, I will end his life. Much as I'm going to end yours now." Rakz grabbed Carver by the throat.

Reggie reached quickly with his left hand for the chain and pulled. The cross flew out from under his shirt and the sight of it drove Rakz backward.

He dropped Reggie and turned away.

Reggie held the small crucifix in front of him, struggling to retain consciousness.

Rakz was beside himself with rage, but he was powerless against the cross. He would have to take the girl with him and leave the black man alive.

"You continue to amaze me, Carver. You are most resourceful. Your cleverness will give you another night to live, but the girl will be mine, and Chris will be dead. Oh— and you can be sure that one day I'll kill you, too."

He grabbed Sue and headed for the door.

Reggie tried to stop him, but couldn't move. His arm was totally useless, his leg grotesquely bent. The bone pierced the skin.

Rakz disappeared out the door, and Reggie blacked out.

Chris knew something was wrong when he saw that the front door to Reggie's apartment was wide open. He rushed in and saw Reggie lying in a broken heap. Sue was gone. His heart sank. Rakz had been there, and now he had Sue.

"Reggie," Chris said tenderly, "where's Sue?"

Reggie opened his eyes painfully. "I'm sorry, Chris," he whispered. "You . . . he looked like you. . . . Sue . . . I'm sorry . . ."

He cradled Reggie's head in his hand. "It's okay, man. It's okay. Do you know where he took Sue?"

Reggie fought to remain conscious. "Yeah, he said the House of Horrors, outside town."

"The old Carnival Town?"

Reggie nodded. "Gonna marry . . . stop him . . . gotta . . . stop . . ."

The injured detective tried valiantly to get up, but his crippled limbs would not support him.

"Stay down, Reg, I'm gonna call an ambulance and then I'm gonna go get Sue."

As Chris ran to the phone to call the emergency line, Reggie kept whispering, "Sorry . . . so sorry . . ."

He was slipping fast.

Chris dialed the number. The phone rang and a woman's voice answered.

"911. How may I help you?"

"My name is Chris Blaze, I'm a police officer. I have a man down with multiple fractures at 1717 Hibiscus Avenue, apartment 3. I need an ambulance."

"We'll have someone there in fifteen minutes."

"Good."

Chris hung up the phone and went to his fallen partner's side. He bent down and touched Reggie's face. "I have to go now. An ambulance is on the way. You're gonna be okay."

Reggie nodded painfully.

As Chris got up to leave, he gasped, "Chris?"

Chris bent back down so that he could hear his partner's tortured whisper. "Yeah, partner?"

"Nail that fucker . . . right through his blackassed heart!"

Chris nodded with the determination of a man who had seen too many of his friends hurt or killed.

He left the apartment and started to head for the old Carnival Town. He knew in his heart that this would end tonight. One way or the other, it would end tonight.

5

When Sue awakened from her trance, she screamed. A werewolf was about to pounce on her. As her eyes adjusted to the darkness, she saw that the monster was frozen in mid-leap, its vicious snarl etched permanently on its face. As Sue looked around, she saw other creatures of the night in various acts of murder and mayhem. *What was this place,* she thought to herself. She screamed again as one of the wax figures moved. It was Yosekaat Rakz.

"I'm glad to see you're all right. It was a rather bumpy flight," he crooned.

He had carried her to the holding place in the form of the giant bat creature. It had been a taxing flight. He would have to rest for a little while. If he didn't and Blaze arrived, the young vampire might have a chance against him.

"Why are you doing this to me?" Sue asked helplessly.

"As I told you before, I find you unusually beautiful, and for the simple fact that I want to do it."

"Chris is going to kill you," she said in a determined voice.

"Susan," Rakz said, "you're mistaken. It is I who will do the killing, and as part of the wedding entertainment I am going to allow you to watch."

"I'll never be your bride, you bastard."

Rakz chuckled. "But you have no choice in the matter, and besides, once the wedding ritual is complete, you'll want to be mine totally of your own free will."

He laughed again, and chills ran up Sue's spine.

"Of course," he added, "your free will will be my free will."

"I'll kill myself before that can happen."

"Oh, I couldn't let you do that," Rakz said.

"She won't have to," a determined voice interrupted.

"Chris!" Sue cried out.

Rakz was unperturbed. "Ah, I was expecting you a little later, but no matter."

"Sue, get out of here!" Chris shouted.

Sue started to run.

"No!" Rakz's voice sounded like a cannon shot, stopping Sue dead in her tracks.

Moving with catlike speed, Chris ran at Rakz and struck him with a punch that would have killed an ordinary man. Rakz flew back into the wall and went partially through it. A dust cloud erupted from the collision and clung in the air like a vapor of poison gas.

"Sue, run!" Chris shouted again, hoping the blow had stunned Rakz enough for him to release his hold on Sue.

It had the desired effect as Sue looked over at Chris.

"Go!" he shouted.

She took off down the corridor of the creepy house and vanished.

As Rakz tried to extricate himself from the wall, Chris grabbed the stake that the waxen figure of Van Helsing had poised over the heart of the helpless Dracula and charged the real vampire.

He slammed into Rakz and drove the vampire backward into the Frankenstein monster. It collapsed into a pile of broken wax, horsehair, and old clothing.

Rakz grabbed Chris by the face and pushed him off, sending him hurtling through the air onto the wax Van Helsing. It crumpled into the same mixture as the monster. Rakz was on him in seconds, but Chris was ready. Using the vampire's own momentum, he spun Rakz on top of the waxen dummy of Dracula. He raised the stake above his head and sent it crashing down into the heart of the vampire.

The wax version.

The real bloodsucker moved out of the way easily.

"I grow tired of this game," he said in a voice that had lost most of its cool.

His face began to change into a creature that was the very essence of evil. His ears raised into points and transversed to the top of his head. His lips pulled back into a hideous grin, revealing fangs that came down about three inches. The handsome roman nose pushed back into his face until it was just two open holes. His eyes turned a bright red in black sockets.

Fear shot through Chris like a thousand hot pinpricks. The hair on his neck prickled, and goosebumps spread across his body. He knew at that moment that he didn't have a chance.

"Now," the horrid creature hissed, "I shall end this farce." His voice was as certain as death.

6

The ambulance arrived at Reggie's apartment, and the two attendants, Kevin Wakely and Manny Paxson, hustled the stretcher up to Reggie's room. A crowd had gathered outside the apartment.

"Clear the way, folks," the overweight Paxson said as he had a thousand times before. He wondered what it was about people that made them congregate around the scene of tragedy. Was it in their nature to get a vicarious thrill out of seeing the misfortune of others? An unconscious primal urge to enjoy the results of violence? He didn't know the answer, but now was not the time for armchair psychology; he and his partner had an injured cop who needed their help.

The two ETs pushed their way through the crowd and entered the apartment. Reggie was lying in the same place where Chris had left him. Although they had both seen plenty of bad injuries, they were still shocked at the condition of Reggie's arm and leg. The arm looked like a plastic straw that had been broken in several places and bent at odd angles. His leg was bleeding from the bone that protruded from under his skin. The two emergency techs bent over and gingerly placed him on the stretcher.

"Take it easy, buddy, you're gonna be okay," Manny said, trying to sound convincing. He wondered how in the hell the arm could have been broken in such a strange way, but part of him didn't want to know.

Reggie mumbled incoherently as the two technicians lifted the stretcher onto its wheels. "Looked like you . . . looked like . . . you . . ."

As they headed for the ambulance, Mrs. Kowalski crossed herself as she saw the brutalized condition Reggie was in.

Through the haze, Reggie could hear voices, sounds.

"Oh, my God, what happened to him?"

Sirens.

"Ooh, gross, look at his arm!"

The unmistakable sound of someone throwing up.

He smiled. He knew he must be quite a site, and yet he smiled. He was alive. He just hoped that his partner was, too.

7

Chris was stunned by the ghoulish countenance of Yose-kaat Rakz. The hellish apparition hissed and rushed for him. He tried to avoid the crush but was hit full force. Rakz clenched Chris's face in his fetid claws and pushed his head through the wall of the exhibit. He pulled him back out and slammed him through again and again.

Chris was dazed, stunned.

Rakz seemed to have gained strength from the transformation.

Chris felt powerless as Rakz continued to batter his head into the wall. He was beginning to lose consciousness when he saw the cross lying less than a foot away. The sight of it repulsed him. He couldn't look at it, but he had to do something. As the wicked bat-faced vampire prepared for another assault, Chris grabbed the cross. The sensation of pain that shot through his hand was like nothing he'd ever felt. Once, when he was a child, he had accidentally placed his hand on the stove and burned himself. This was the same feeling, only a thousandfold. Still he was able to slap Rakz in the face with it. The flesh on his face sizzled as the burnt vampire howled in pain and released Chris. He held his clawed hand to his face and wailed in an unearthly scream.

Chris dropped the cross. His hand was a charred mess. He slipped away and kicked Rakz in the ribs, knocking him down. The vampire screamed in a voice that transcended hell, a sound so awful that it literally fried the ions in the air. Chris readied for another kick when Rakz rose up. His face had changed. He had a hideous burn on the left side of his face where the cross had made contact. His fanged mouth was dripping with thick saliva. His eyes burned with the brilliance of the sun. The vampire's arms grew longer, the wicked claws on his hand curved and clicked together.

He was the essence of evil.

Rakz reached out, his hand a blur, and grabbed Chris by the throat. He carried the struggling cop over to the Dracula exhibit. Deftly he plucked the stake out of the waxen Dracula.

"Now," he hissed in an almost unrecognizable voice, "I have to go find the girl." He held Chris to the wall and drew the stake back. "Stick around," he said as he plunged the stake in between the hollow of Chris's throat just above his sternum. "I promised Susan she could witness your death, and I always keep my promises."

As Rakz disappeared into the shadows, Chris struggled to free himself from the stake. He felt like a bug in a science project stuck to a board with a pin. He grabbed the stake and yanked. No good. The stake was firmly embedded in him and the wall. If he didn't get loose soon, Rakz would be back and he would most definitely keep his promise to kill Chris.

8

Sue was huddled in the corner of the "graveyard" at the beginning of the funhouse ride. She had tried the doors, but they were all locked. She hid behind the tombstone of one Jeb Nutter, who's apparently died when he'd fallen in a tubful of butter. Moments before, she had heard the sounds of the pitched battle that was going on at the far end of the house. There was no sound now. The graveyard was silent. She could hear nothing. The fight had to have ended. She wanted badly to call out, to let Chris know where she was. But what if Chris was not the victor? What if Rakz had killed her beloved and was now stalking her in the House of Horrors? She had to remain quiet and hope that Chris had won.

She could hear footsteps far away.

Someone was coming.

9

Yosekaat Rakz rubbed the tender wound on his cheek as he searched the exhibit for his bride-to-be. He crept into the corridor and moved toward the sarcophagus of the mummy. It would make an excellent hiding place. He grabbed the heavy door and yanked it open. A body flew out at him. In one sweeping motion, he swatted the mummy of Kharis into a pile of wax chips and bandages.

He continued his search. Moving quickly through the pitch-black building, he looked behind every exhibit, in every darkened corner. He found no one.

Rakz knew that he had to find her soon or . . . he hit himself on the forehead. How could he be so stupid? All he had to do was to connect with her mentally and force Susan to come to him. In the excitement, he had almost forgotten that she was under his control. But before he called her to him, he would change back into human form. Once, many years ago, a girl he'd wanted as his bride had seen him in the gruesome bat form. She had died of a heart attack. He didn't want that to happen again—especially not to this woman he'd gone through so much trouble to get.

He was about to summon her telepathically when he caught a glimpse of her running into the torture chamber. Moving with uncanny speed, Rakz was in the room.

This section of the House of Horrors was an authentic torture chamber, complete with an iron maiden with a suitably perforated maiden. A man was stretched out to comic proportions on the rack. Whips and chains hung on the wall. A wax Torquemada was reaching for a particularly nasty cat-o'-nine tails. And over in the corner was the cowering Sue Catledge.

Rakz smiled. The battle was over. Now the marriage could begin.

"I'm so glad I ran into you, Susan. I was afraid you were getting cold feet," Rakz laughed. "Now let's proceed with the festivities. Come here."

Sue remained in the corner.

Rakz's eyes blazed. "Come here, now!"

Sue tried to resist but couldn't. She moved slowly toward the undead creature. Rakz grinned. Sue was unable to resist the powerful force of the vampire. She walked toward him, a blank expression on her face, totally unable to stop her slow march toward doom. Her hands hung limply at her sides.

"That's good, darling. Come to me. I want you to see me end your ex-lover's life."

Sue walked toward Rakz.

The vampire extended his arms to her and pulled her close. He brushed the hair back, exposing her neck. "But first, I must complete the second night's ritual." He kissed her throat softly, licking it with his pointed tongue. Then he opened his jaws and screamed.

"Noooo!!! This cannot be!" he howled, backing away from the blankly staring doctor. A stake firmly embedded in his chest.

"You cannot kill me, I . . . argh . . . I own you."

Sue stepped forward and drove the stake deeper into the creature's heart.

Rakz's face contorted with rage as he changed into the horrible bat monster. He clutched helplessly at the stake, bellowing with rage. The walls of the torture chamber shook from the force of his voice.

"I . . . am . . . immortal," Rakz shouted, his voice weakening. "I cannot die . . . cannot . . . d . . ."

He fell to the floor, writhing. His flesh began to shrivel and crack off his bones in chunks. His forehead crumbled and fell off his face, taking his nose with it. His lips blistered and melted off. He reached out for her but fell short, his body rapidly deteriorating.

As the vampire disintegrated into a skeleton, Sue came out from another room and saw herself standing over the remains of the vampire.

"Oh, my God," she cried.

Her twin turned toward her and smiled. Her double's face began to shimmer and change, the body filling out. Shoulders broadening. Breast shrinking, tightening. Long hair seeming to evaporate into short.

It was Chris.

"Oh, Chris, you're all right," Sue shouted happily as she ran into her lover's arms."

"It's over, baby. Everything's going to be okay." Chris held her tight. "It's all over."

They hugged each other.

Suddenly, a scream so indecent that it defiled the air shook Chris and Sue. It was Rakz, or rather, what was left of him. The skeleton was getting up and starting to walk toward them.

They were transfixed with horror.

Would this never be over?

The skeletal vampire took one shaky step and then, with an incredible bellow, collapsed into a pile of dust.

It really was over.

Chris kissed Sue and scooped her up. He kicked open the emergency exit and they made their way out the gruesome exhibit and into the cool night air with a brand new start on life.

Epilogue

Chris and Reggie sat in the living room of the Blazes' apartment. It had been three months since Chris had fooled Rakz and driven the stake through his heart. Reggie's leg had healed up fine, but his hand was no longer of any use to him. Still, he considered himself lucky to have survived the ordeal. Sue and Chris had married a month earlier. Reggie had been the best man. The Blazes had sold Sue's house, too many bad memories, and purchased another in a suburb outside the city. It had a special room where Chris could sleep during the day. She volunteered to work permanent night duty at the hospital. Unfortunately, Reggie had lost his ability to function as a police officer, but he received a generous disability check every month. Carver wasn't unemployed, though. He and Chris had opened a detective agency, "Carver, Blaze, and Fayer," in memory of their fallen comrade. Business had been slow so far, but things were picking up. All in all, everyone was happy.

Chris and Reggie were waiting for Sue to come home from shopping.

"So, Chris, how's the married life?"

"Great, couldn't be better."

"How does Sue like living with a vampire?"

Chris smiled. "We've had to make some minor adjustments," he said.

"Oh yeah, what kind of minor adjustments?"

Just then the door opened and Sue came in with two bags

of groceries. She walked over and set them on the kitchen counter.

"Hi, Reggie."

"What's up, Doc?"

She rolled her eyes.

"What are we having for dinner?" Chris asked.

Reggie looked at him strangely. *Dinner?* He thought to himself. Was Chris eating regular food now?

As she called out the menu, Sue pulled the items out of the grocery bags.

"Fettucine alfredo."

"Asparagus."

"Fresh salad."

"Vino."

"And for the discriminating vampire—"

She pulled out two bottles from a smaller bag.

"—from Mercy General Hospital, two bottles of Miami's finest O positive."

Reggie looked over at Chris, then back at Sue. He broke into a wide grin, then laughed.

They all burst out laughing.

"Mom always told me," Chris said, "to marry a doctor and I would never have to worry where my next meal was coming from."

Life as a vampire was strange.

But good.

COLD-BLOODED MURDER FROM
PINNACLE BOOKS

NURSES WHO KILL (449, $3.95)
Clifford L. Linedecker and William A. Burt
RICHARD ANGELO—convicted of killing four patients
by lethal injection in a New York hospital
GENENE JONES TURK—serving 99 years for maiming
and killing infants in a Texas pediatric clinic
DONALD HARVEY—convicted killer of terminally ill pa-
tients in Kentucky hospitals
INGER LEMONT—Florida homecare worker convicted of
hacking a shut-in woman to death in her home
ROBERT DIAZ—convicted killer of 12 elderly residents in
two California nursing homes

This is the grisly true crime account of such hospital
killers—men and women who abused their sacred role to
save lives in order to take them, hideously, coldly, without
remorse and often for pleasure.

SPREE KILLERS (461, $4.95)
Edited by Art Crockett

No one knows what triggers it! Maybe it's a look, maybe
a word. But the result is always the same: Innocent people
are wounded and killed.

They are mass murderers, spree killers. If they escape the
scene of their bloody crime, they may never kill again. Unlike serial murderers like Ted Bundy, these killers claim
lives indiscriminately, usually in one mad burst of violence.
There's no way to hide from their insane acts once the killing urge is triggered. (From the files of *TRUE DETEC-
TIVE* Magazine)

*Available wherever paperbacks are sold, or order direct from the
Publisher. Send cover price plus 50¢ per copy for mailing and
handling to Pinnacle Books, Dept. 521, 475 Park Avenue South,
New York, N.Y. 10016. Residents of New York, New Jersey and
Pennsylvania must include sales tax. DO NOT SEND CASH.*

ED MCBAIN'S MYSTERIES

JACK AND THE BEANSTALK (17-083, $3.95)
Jack's dead, stabbed fourteen times. And thirty-six thousand's missing in cash. Matthew's questions are turning up some long-buried pasts, a second dead body, and some beautiful suspects. Like Sunny, Jack's sister, a surfer boy's fantasy, a delicious girl with some unsavory secrets.

BEAUTY AND THE BEAST (17-134, $3.95)
She was spectacular—an unforgettable beauty with exquisite features. On Monday, the same woman appeared in Hope's law office to file a complaint. She had been badly beaten—a mass of purple bruises with one eye swollen completely shut. And she wanted her husband put away before something worse happened. Her body was discovered on Tuesday, bound with wire coat hangers and burned to a crisp. But her husband—big, and monstrously ugly—denies the charge.